Are We Lost Yet?

another WALLACE the BRAVE collection

Will Henry

Andrews McMeel
PUBLISHING®

to Porter

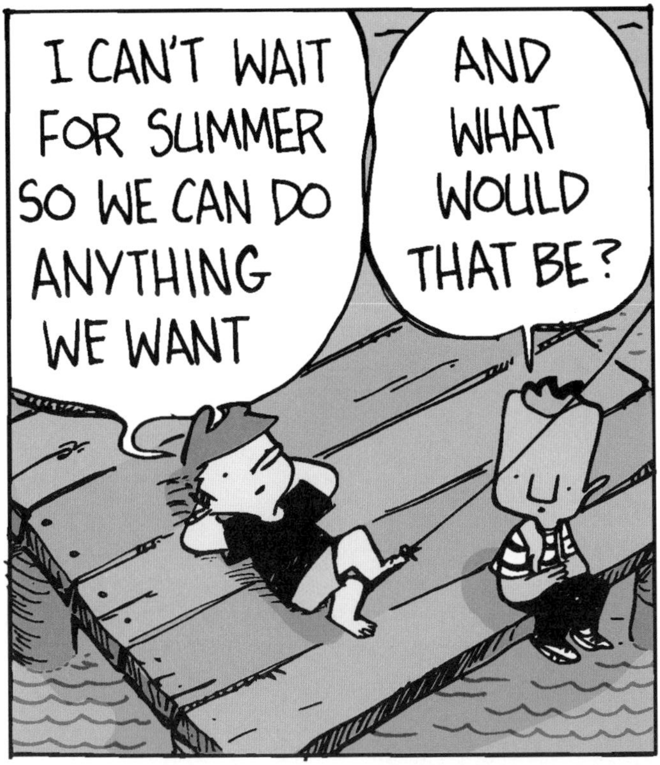
I CAN'T WAIT FOR SUMMER SO WE CAN DO ANYTHING WE WANT
AND WHAT WOULD THAT BE?

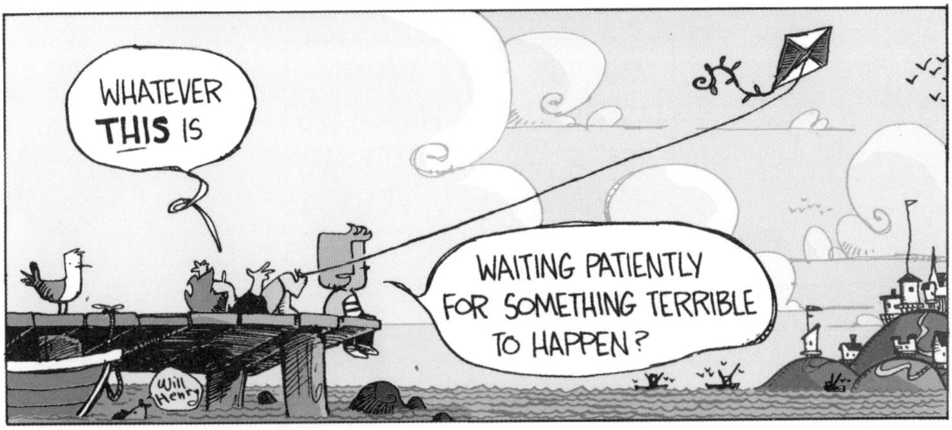
WHATEVER THIS IS
WAITING PATIENTLY FOR SOMETHING TERRIBLE TO HAPPEN?
Will Henry

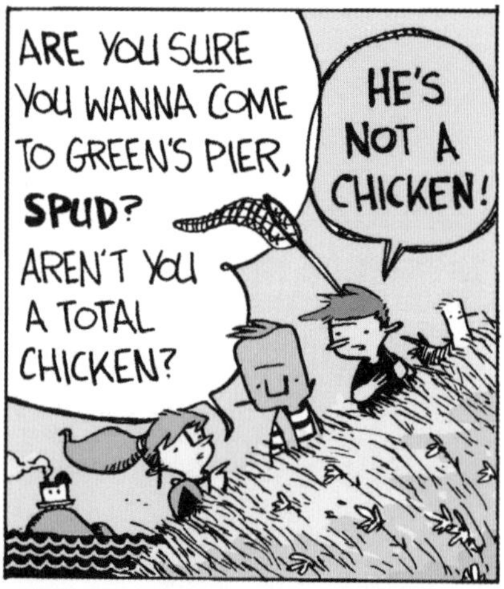
ARE YOU SURE YOU WANNA COME TO GREEN'S PIER, SPUD? AREN'T YOU A TOTAL CHICKEN?
HE'S NOT A CHICKEN!

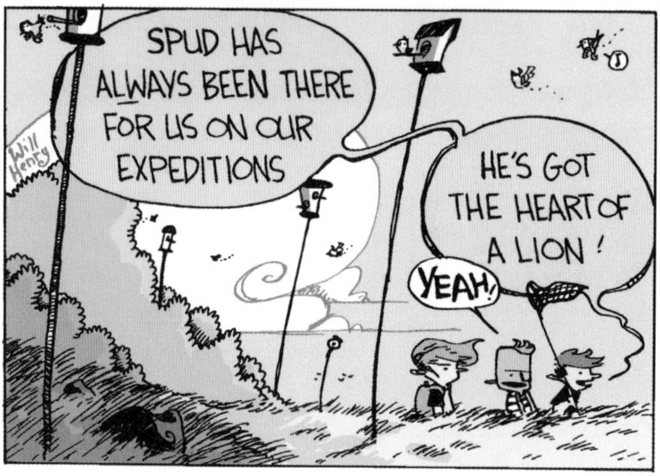
SPUD HAS ALWAYS BEEN THERE FOR US ON OUR EXPEDITIONS
HE'S GOT THE HEART OF A LION!
YEAH!
Will Henry

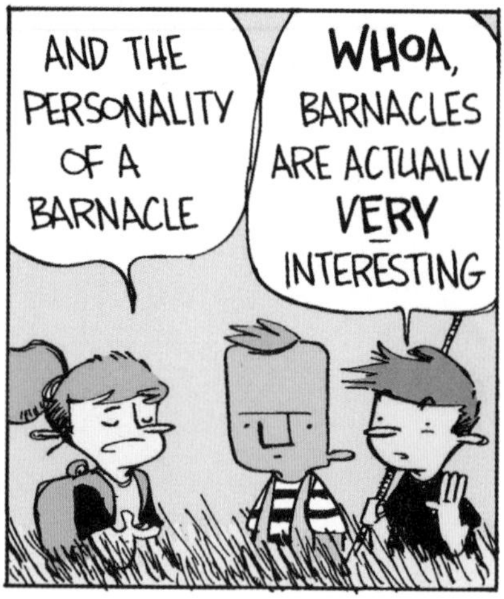
AND THE PERSONALITY OF A BARNACLE
WHOA, BARNACLES ARE ACTUALLY VERY INTERESTING

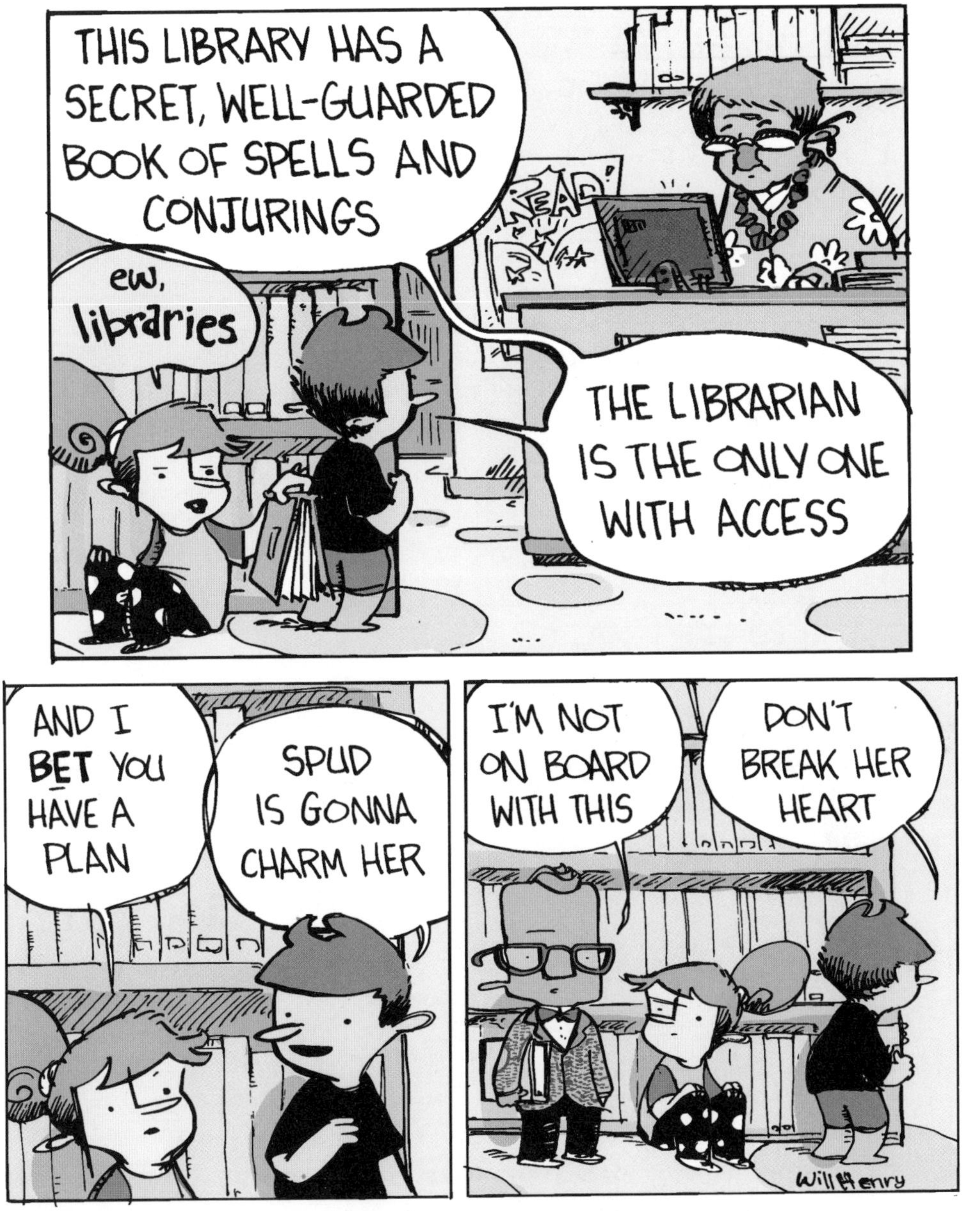
THIS LIBRARY HAS A SECRET, WELL-GUARDED BOOK OF SPELLS AND CONJURINGS
ew, libraries
READ!
THE LIBRARIAN IS THE ONLY ONE WITH ACCESS
AND I BET YOU HAVE A PLAN
SPUD IS GONNA CHARM HER
I'M NOT ON BOARD WITH THIS
DON'T BREAK HER HEART
Will Henry

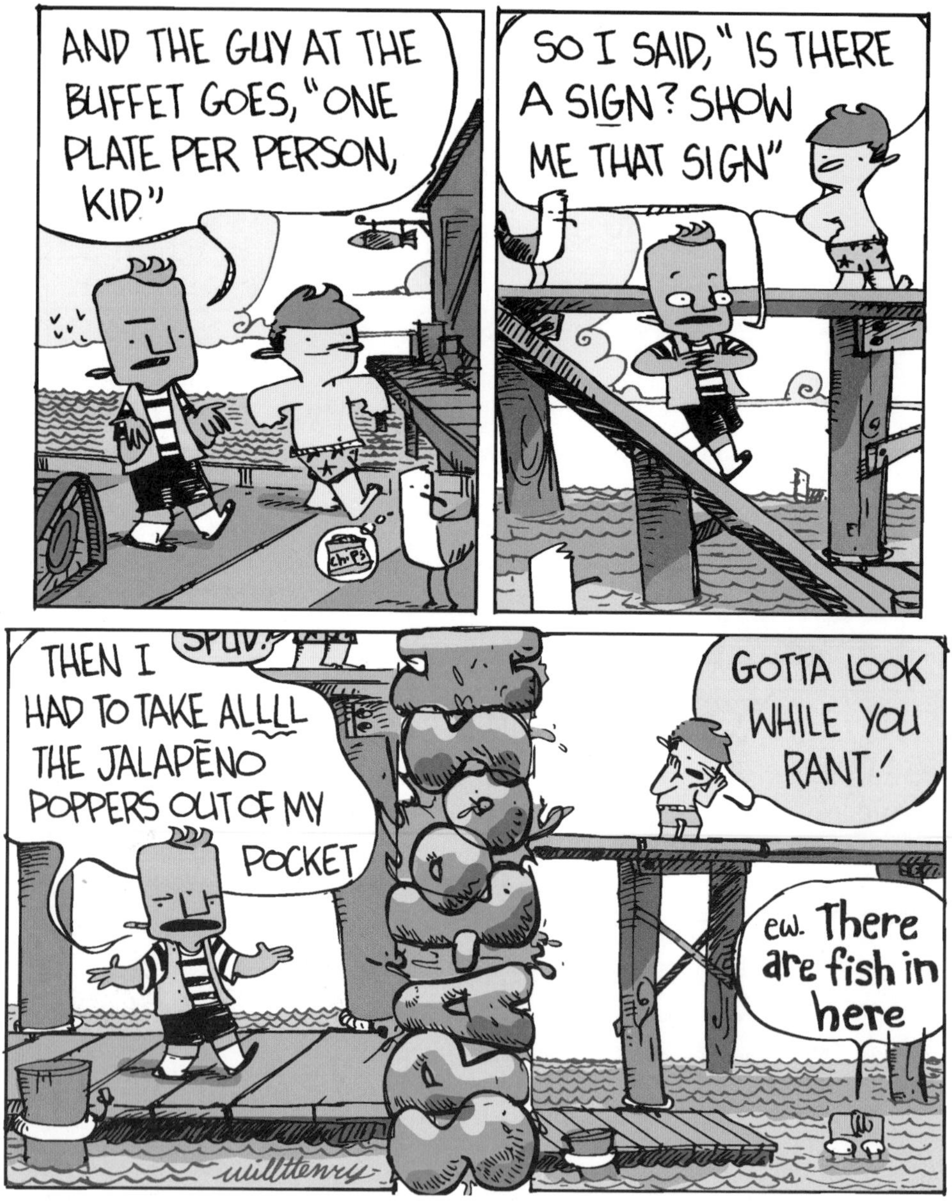
AND THE GUY AT THE BUFFET GOES, "ONE PLATE PER PERSON, KID"
chips
SO I SAID, " IS THERE A SIGN? SHOW ME THAT SIGN"
THEN I HAD TO TAKE ALLLL THE JALAPEÑO POPPERS OUT OF MY POCKET
SPUD!
GOTTA LOOK WHILE YOU RANT!
ew. There are fish in here
willHenry

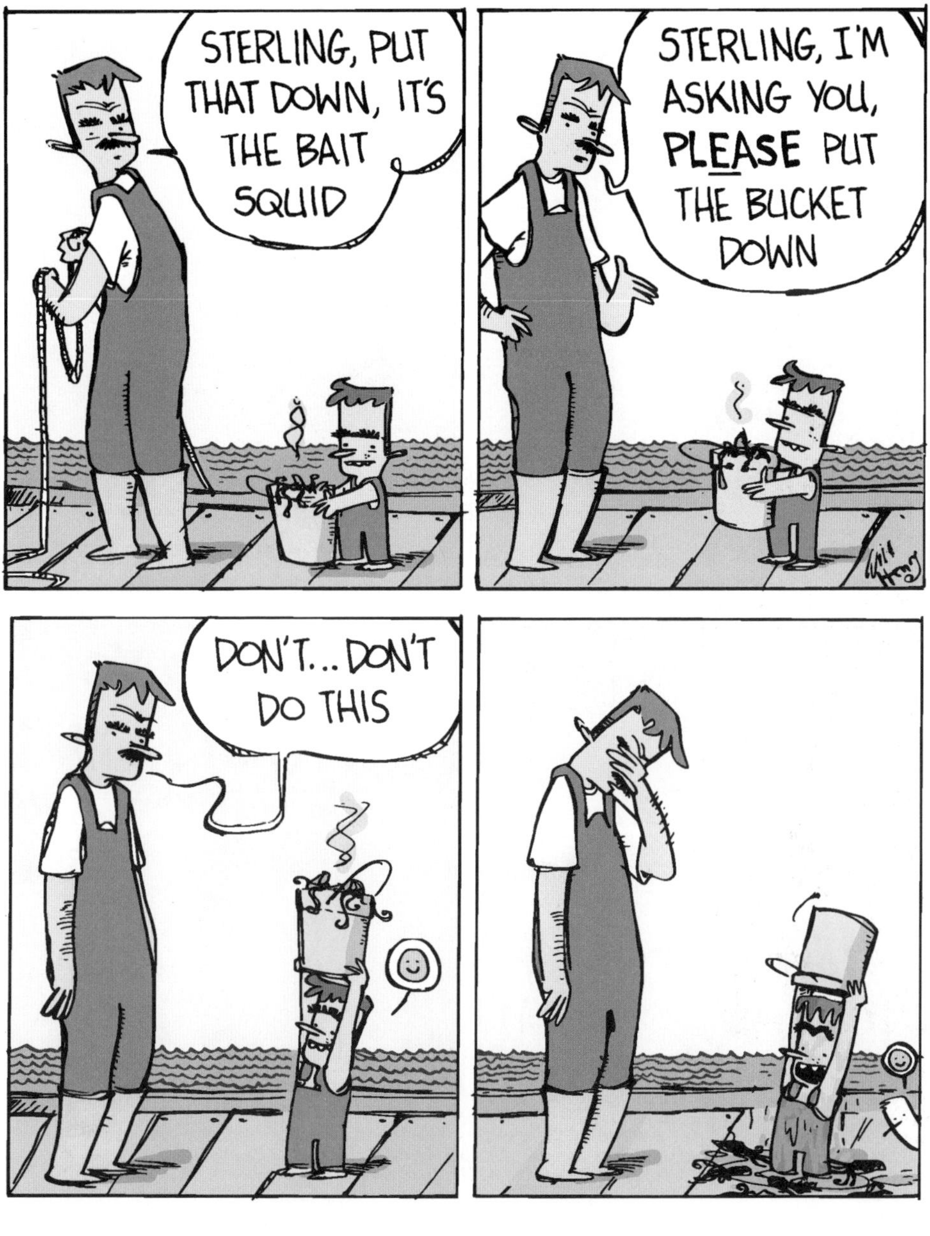
STERLING, PUT THAT DOWN, IT'S THE BAIT SQUID
STERLING, I'M ASKING YOU, **PLEASE** PUT THE BUCKET DOWN
DON'T... DON'T DO THIS

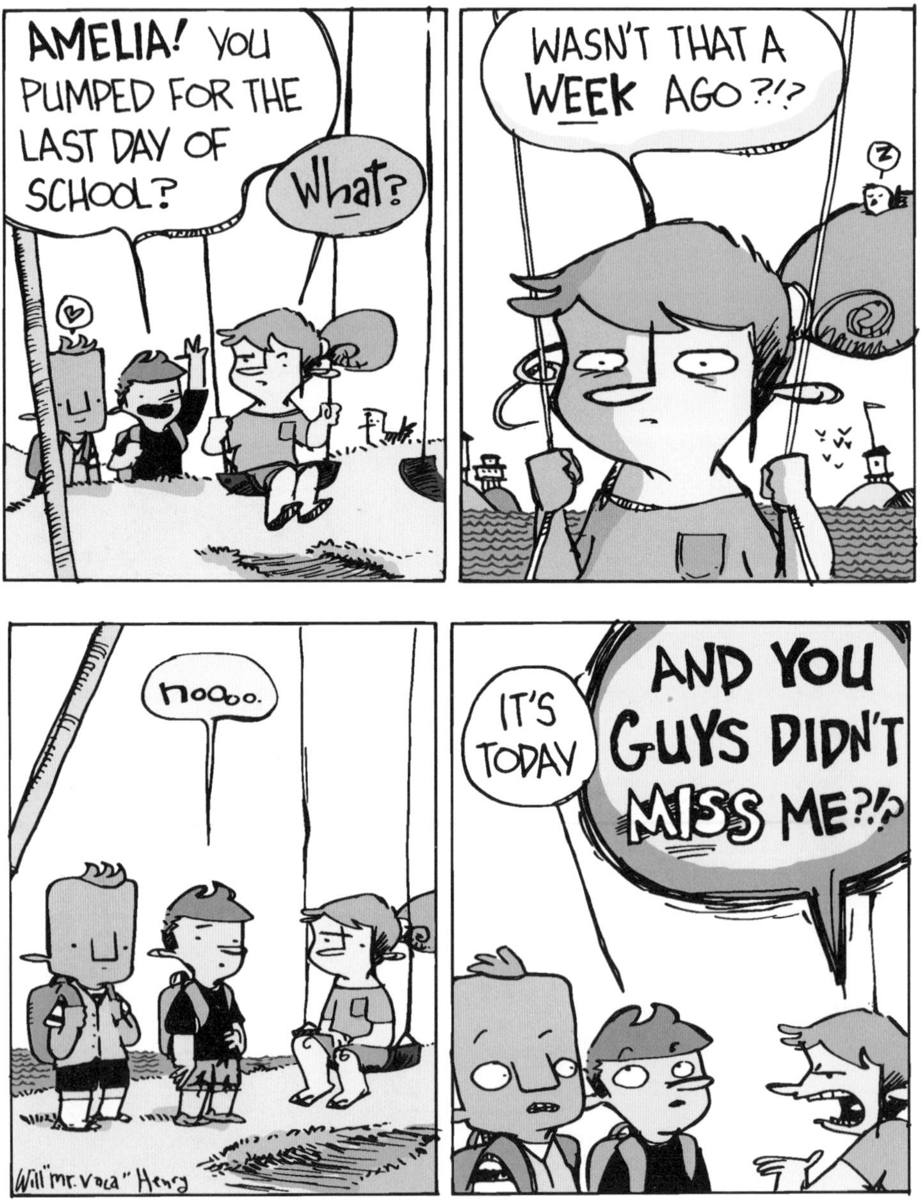
AMELIA! YOU PUMPED FOR THE LAST DAY OF SCHOOL?
What?
WASN'T THAT A WEEK AGO?!?
nooo.
IT'S TODAY
AND YOU GUYS DIDN'T MISS ME?!?
Will "mr. vaca" Henry

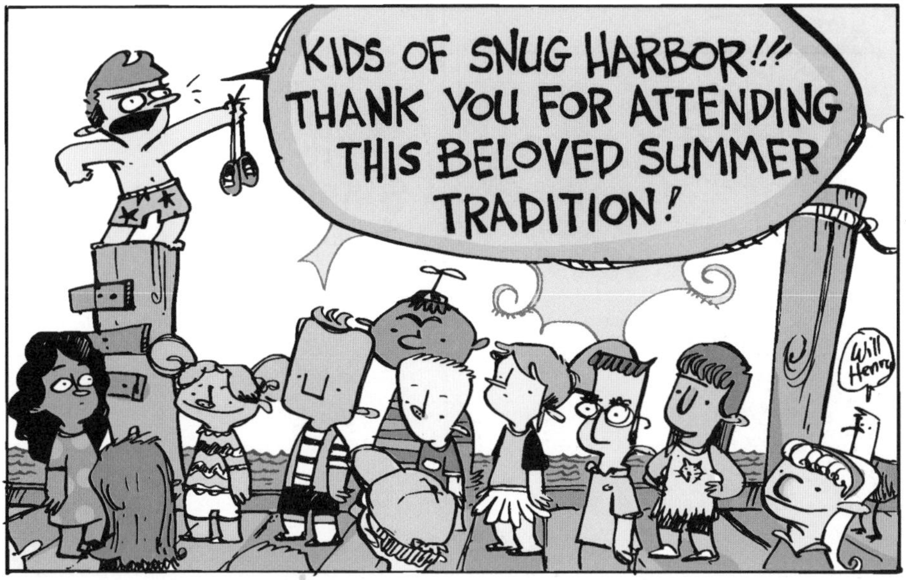
KIDS OF SNUG HARBOR!!!
THANK YOU FOR ATTENDING
THIS BELOVED SUMMER
TRADITION!
Will Henry

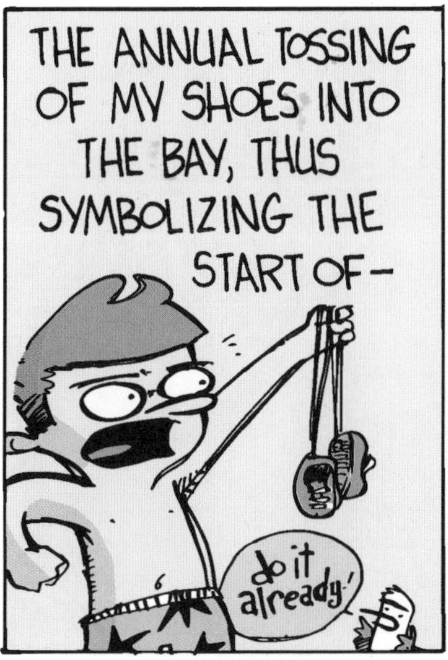
THE ANNUAL TOSSING OF MY SHOES INTO THE BAY, THUS SYMBOLIZING THE START OF–
do it already!

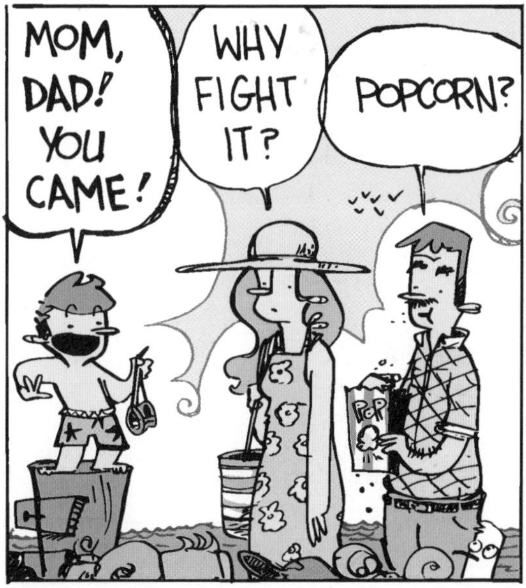
MOM, DAD! YOU CAME!
WHY FIGHT IT?
POPCORN?
POP

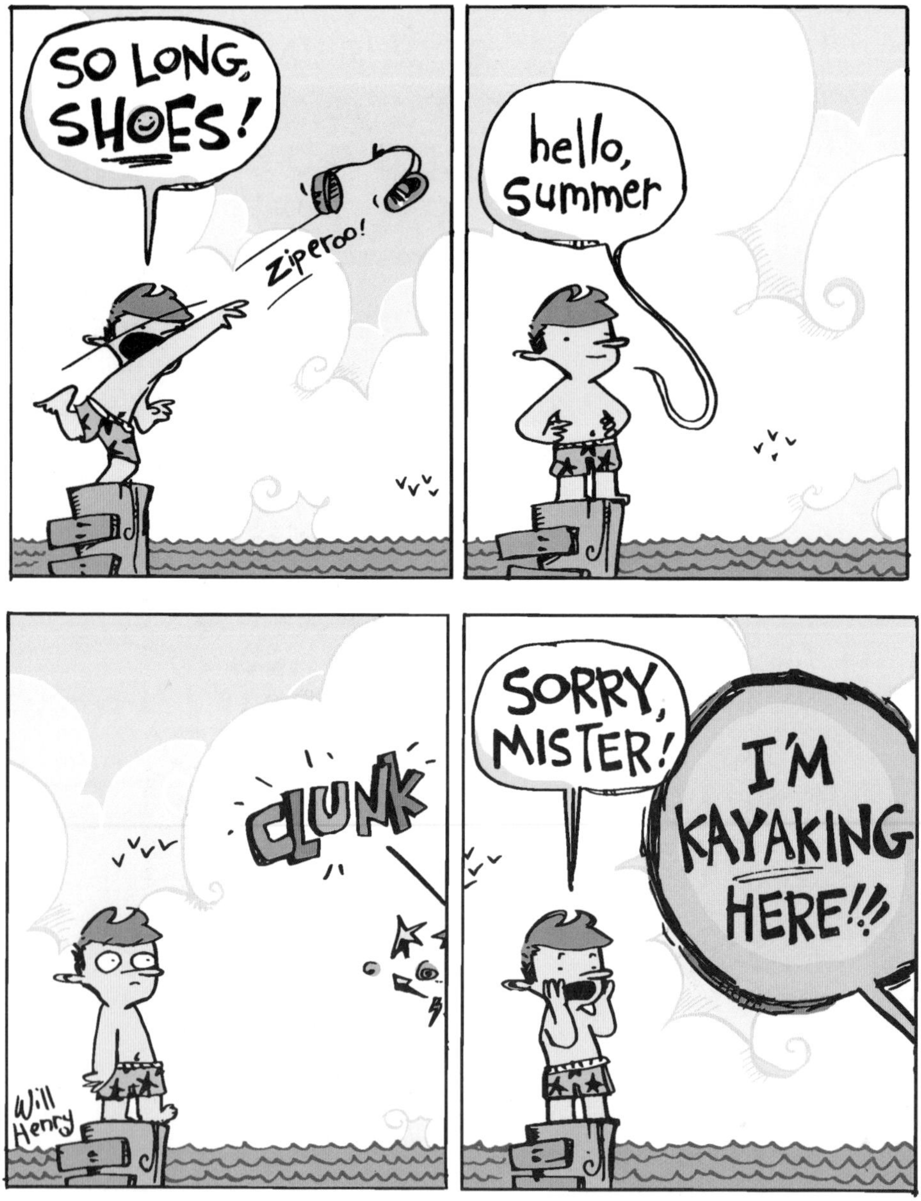
SO LONG, SHOES!
Ziperoo!
hello, Summer
CLUNK
SORRY, MISTER!
I'M KAYAKING HERE!!!
Will Henry

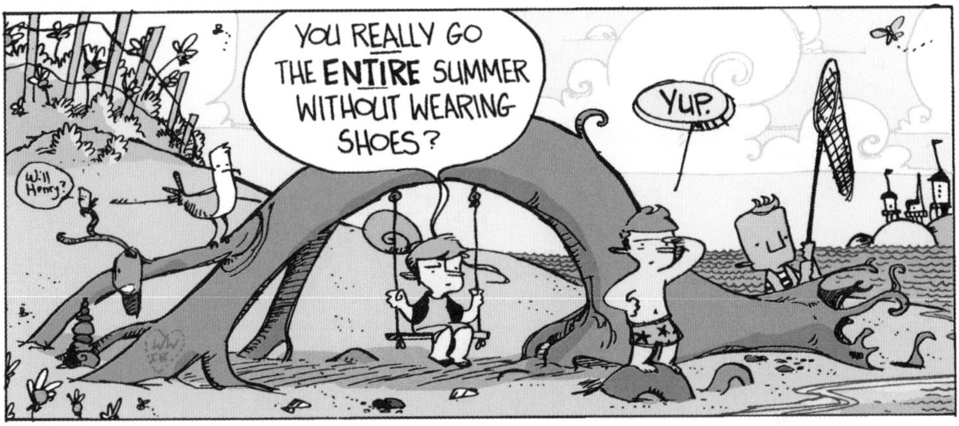
Will Henry?
YOU REALLY GO THE ENTIRE SUMMER WITHOUT WEARING SHOES?
YUP.

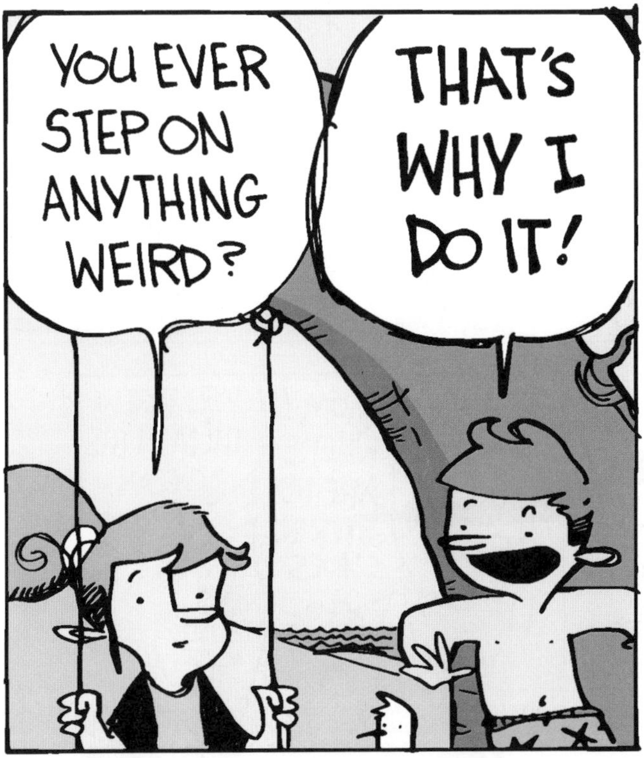
YOU EVER STEP ON ANYTHING WEIRD?
THAT'S WHY I DO IT!

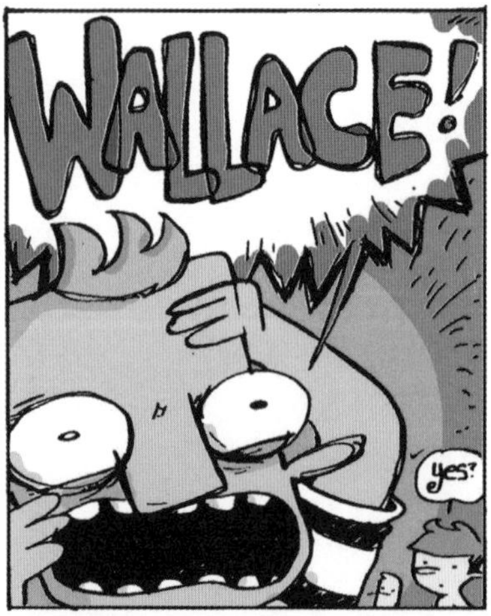
WALLACE!
yes?

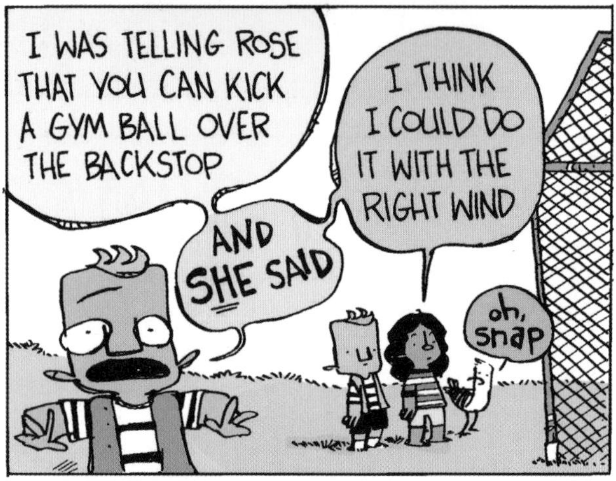
I WAS TELLING ROSE THAT YOU CAN KICK A GYM BALL OVER THE BACKSTOP
AND SHE SAID
I THINK I COULD DO IT WITH THE RIGHT WIND
oh, snap

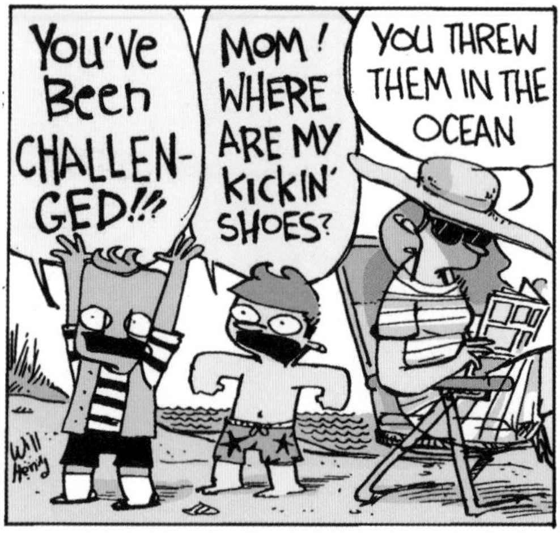
You've Been CHALLEN-GED!!!
MOM! WHERE ARE MY KICKIN' SHOES?
YOU THREW THEM IN THE OCEAN
Will Henry

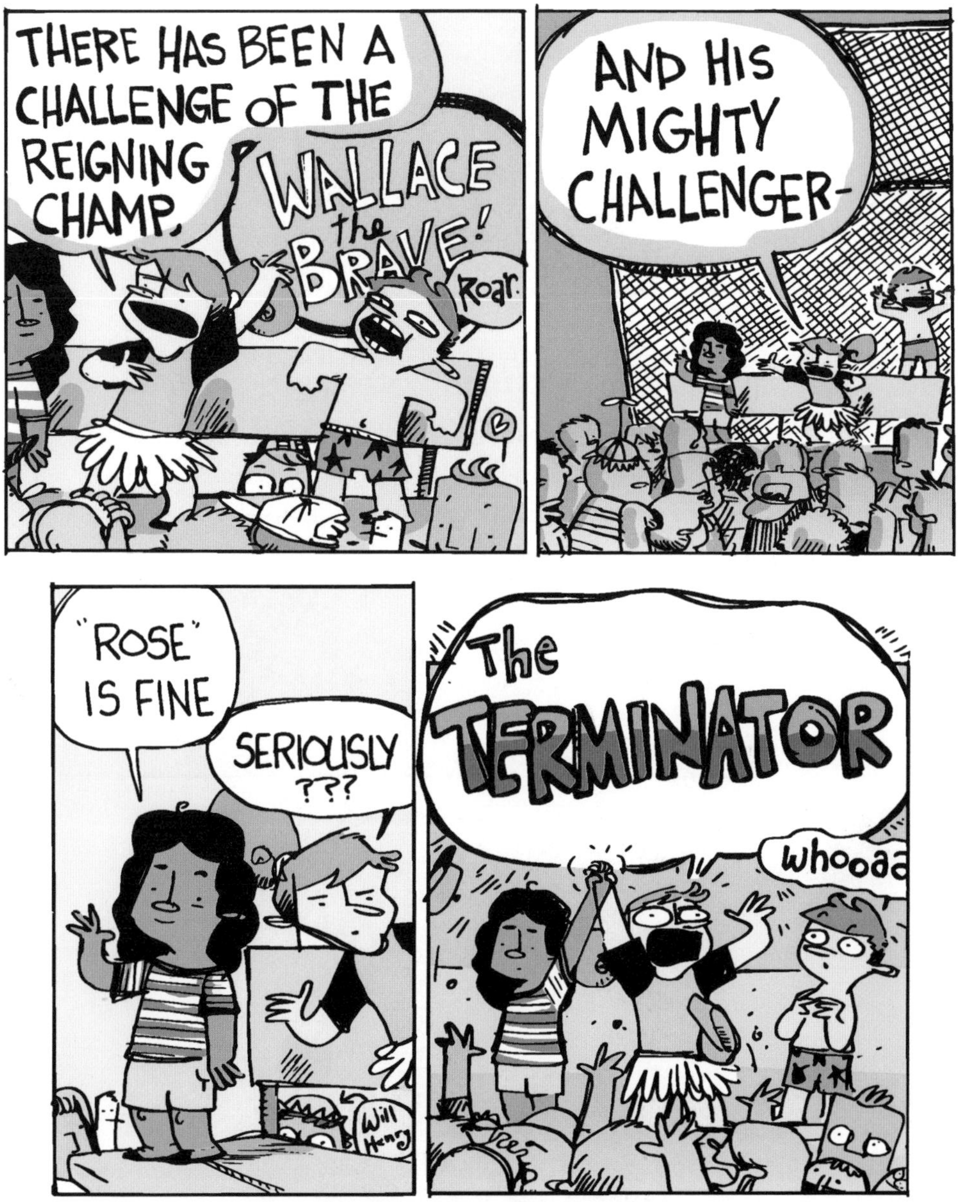
THERE HAS BEEN A CHALLENGE OF THE REIGNING CHAMP,
WALLACE the BRAVE!
Roar.
AND HIS MIGHTY CHALLENGER-
"ROSE" IS FINE
SERIOUSLY ???
Will Henry
The TERMINATOR
whooaa

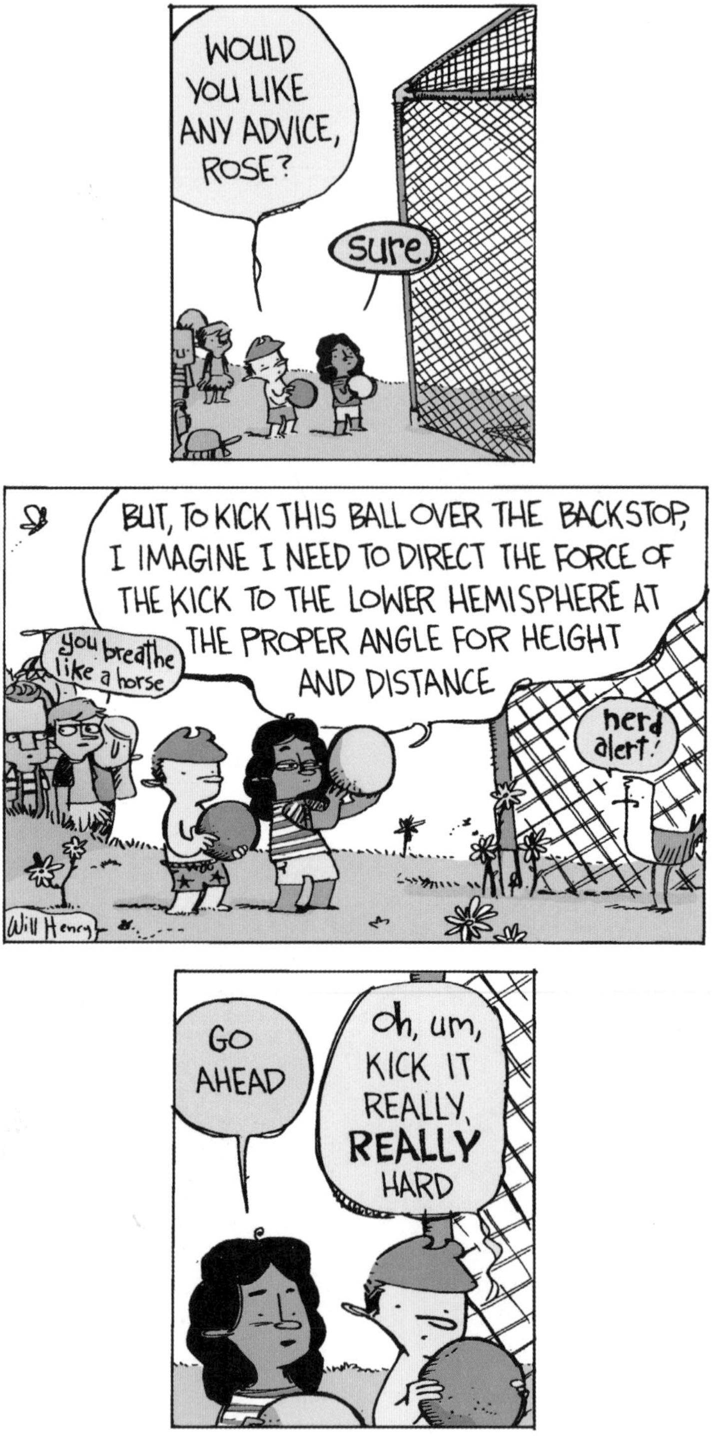
WOULD YOU LIKE ANY ADVICE, ROSE?
sure.
BUT, TO KICK THIS BALL OVER THE BACKSTOP, I IMAGINE I NEED TO DIRECT THE FORCE OF THE KICK TO THE LOWER HEMISPHERE AT THE PROPER ANGLE FOR HEIGHT AND DISTANCE
you breathe like a horse
nerd alert!
Will Henry
GO AHEAD
oh, um, KICK IT REALLY, **REALLY** HARD

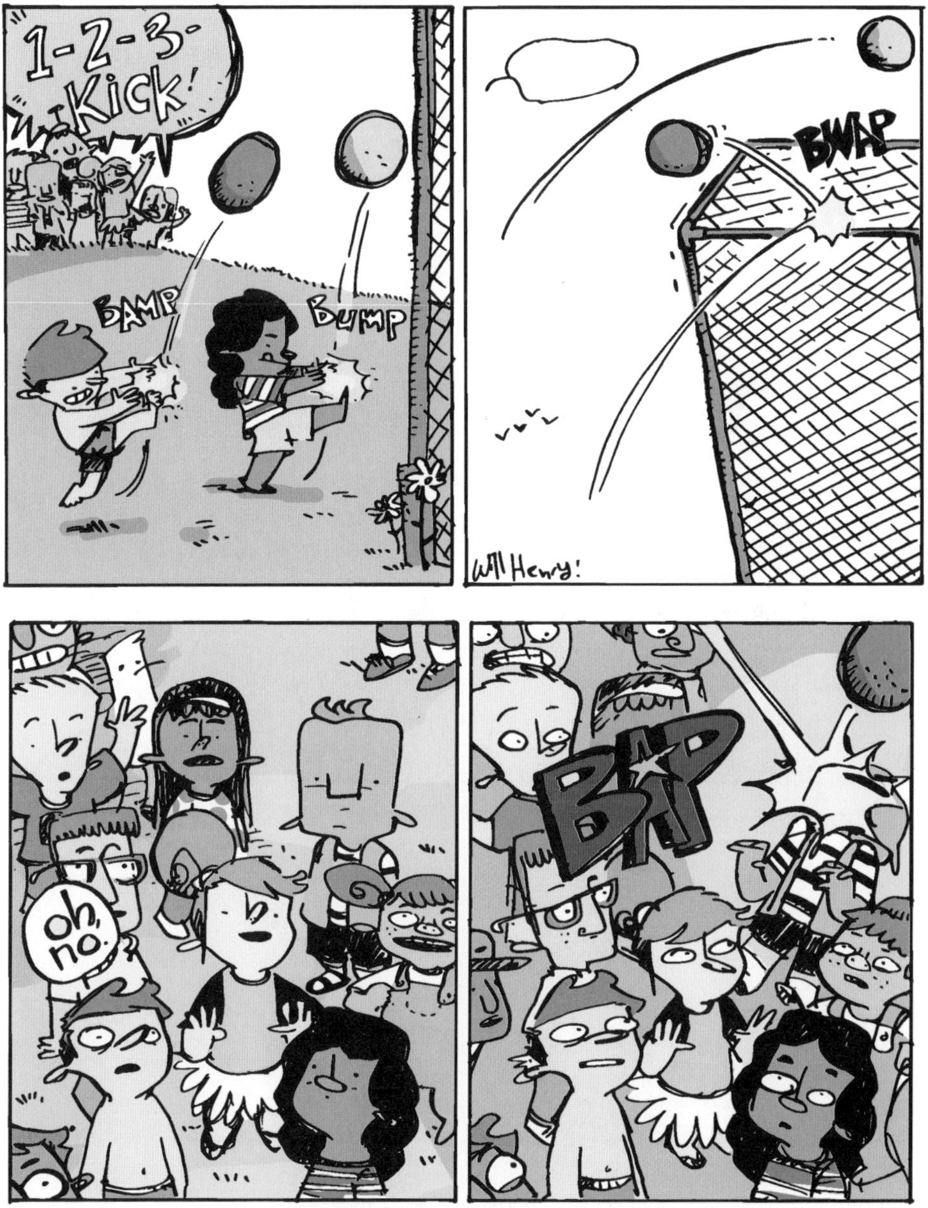
1-2-3-KICK!
BAMP
Bump
BWAP
Will Henry!
oh, no.
BAP

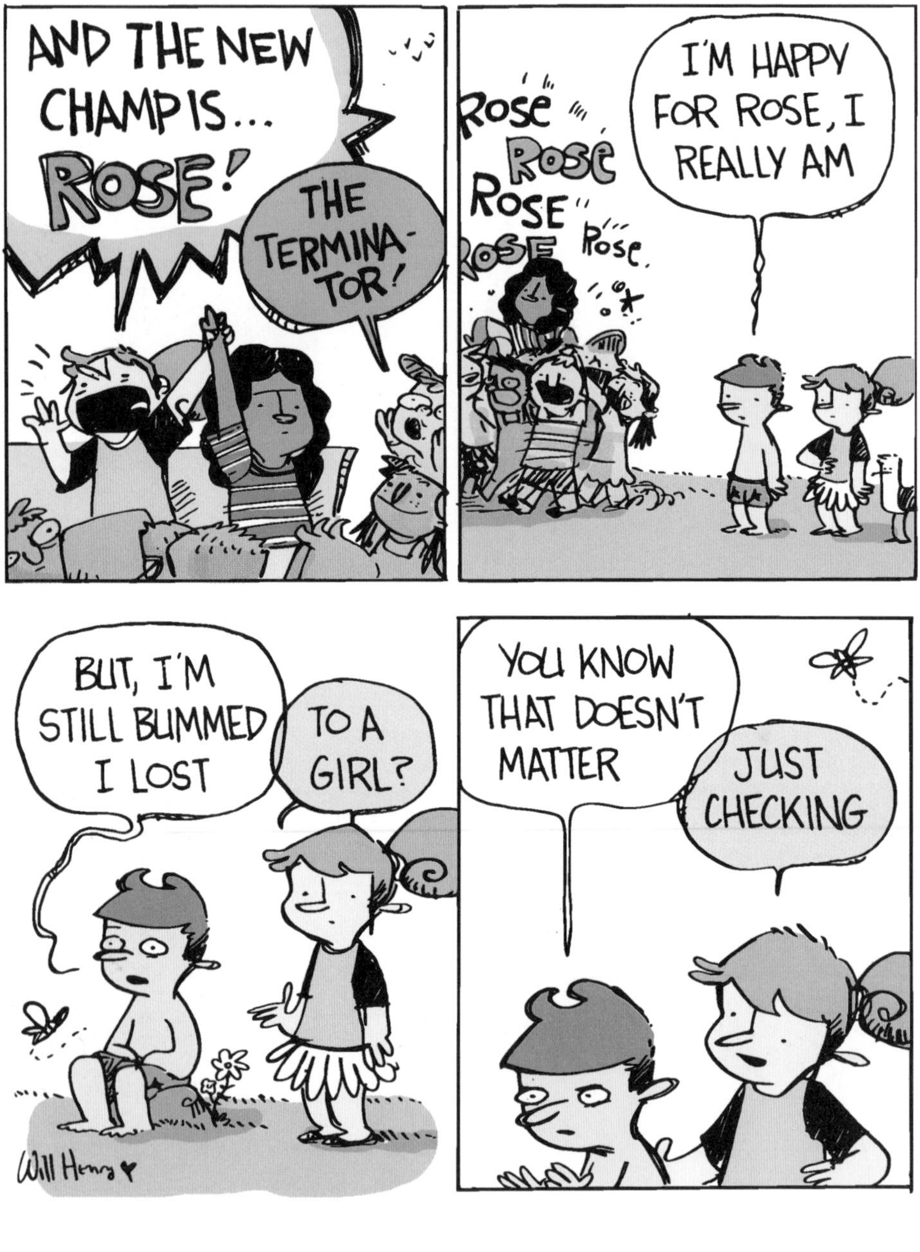
AND THE NEW CHAMP IS... ROSE!
THE TERMINATOR!
ROSE ROSE ROSE ROSE ROSE
I'M HAPPY FOR ROSE, I REALLY AM
BUT, I'M STILL BUMMED I LOST
TO A GIRL?
YOU KNOW THAT DOESN'T MATTER
JUST CHECKING
Will Henry

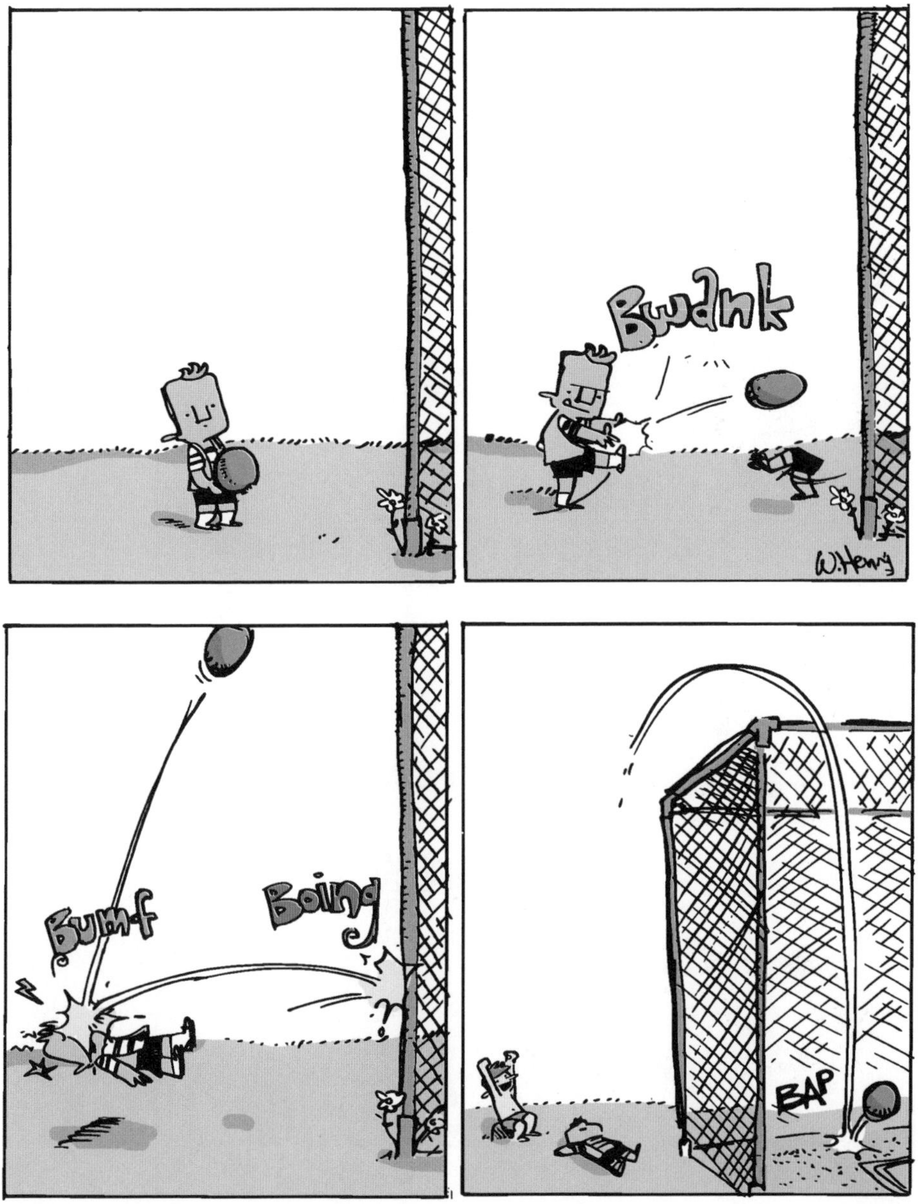
Bwank
W.Henry
Bumf
Boing
BAP

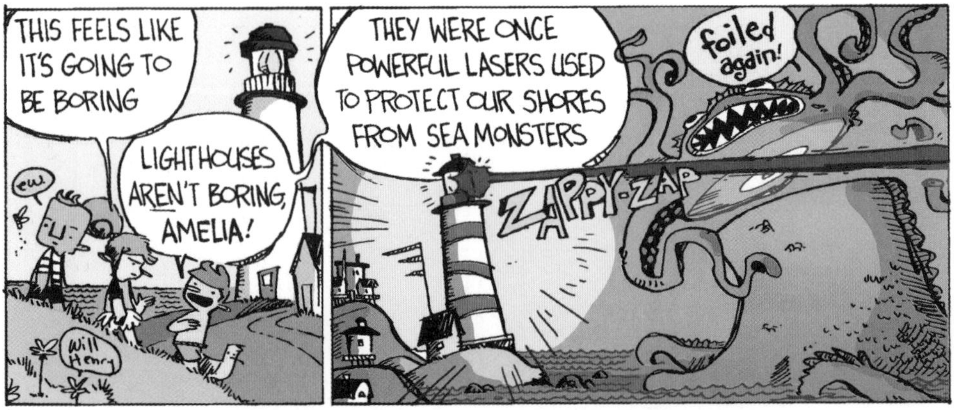
THIS FEELS LIKE IT'S GOING TO BE BORING
ew
LIGHTHOUSES AREN'T BORING, AMELIA!
Will Henry
THEY WERE ONCE POWERFUL LASERS USED TO PROTECT OUR SHORES FROM SEA MONSTERS
foiled again!
ZAPPY-ZAP

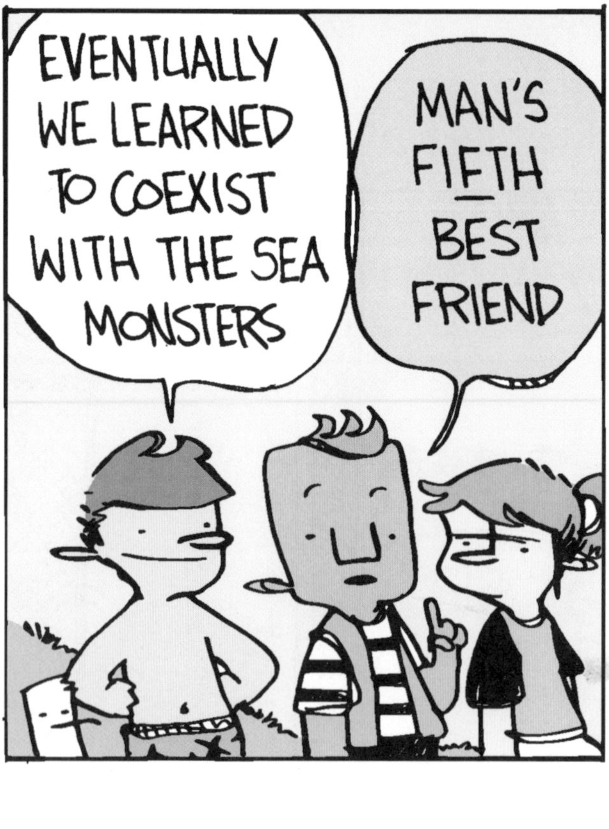
EVENTUALLY WE LEARNED TO COEXIST WITH THE SEA MONSTERS
MAN'S FIFTH BEST FRIEND

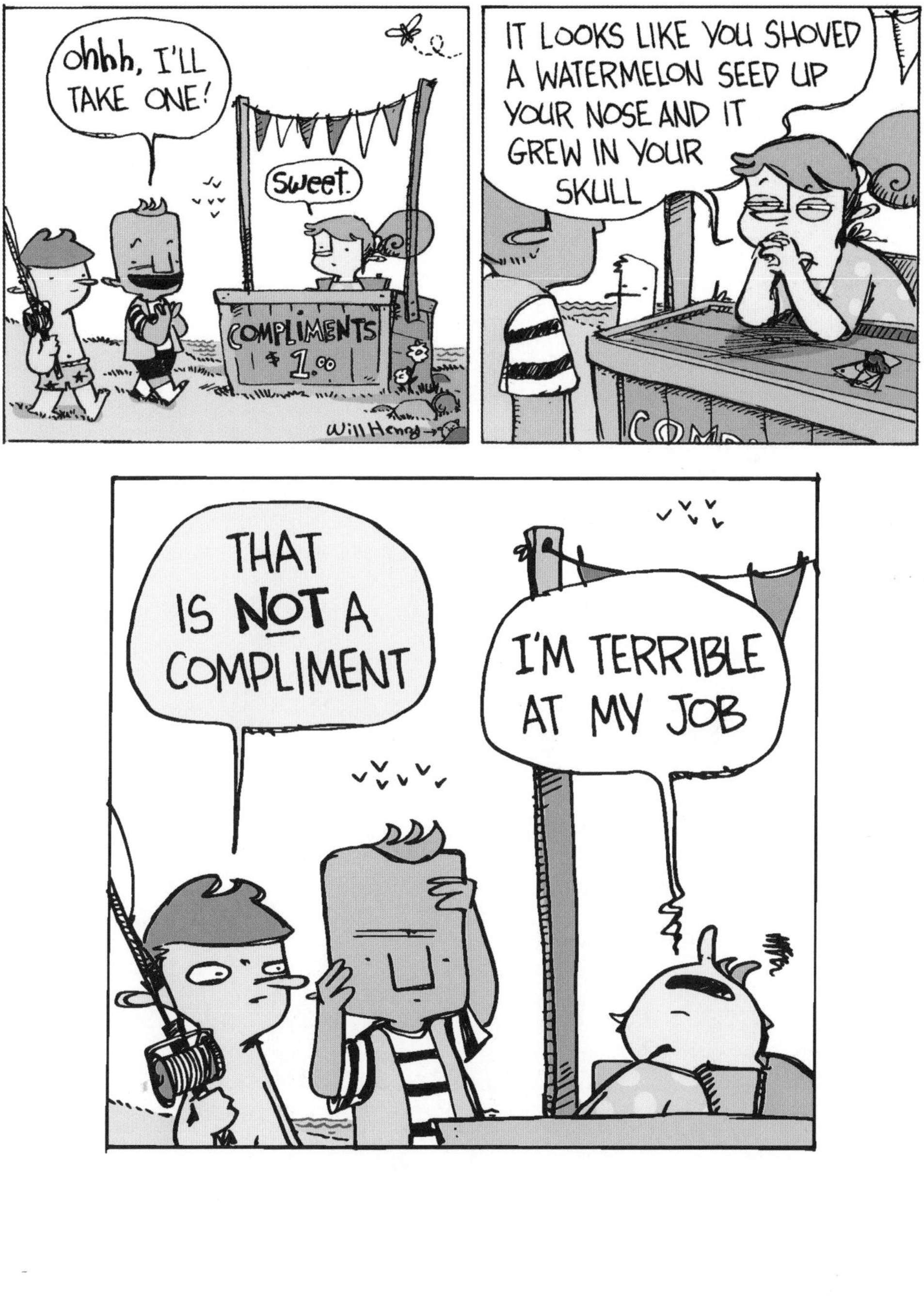
ohhh, I'LL TAKE ONE!
Sweet.
COMPLIMENTS $1.00
Will Henry
IT LOOKS LIKE YOU SHOVED A WATERMELON SEED UP YOUR NOSE AND IT GREW IN YOUR SKULL
THAT IS NOT A COMPLIMENT
I'M TERRIBLE AT MY JOB

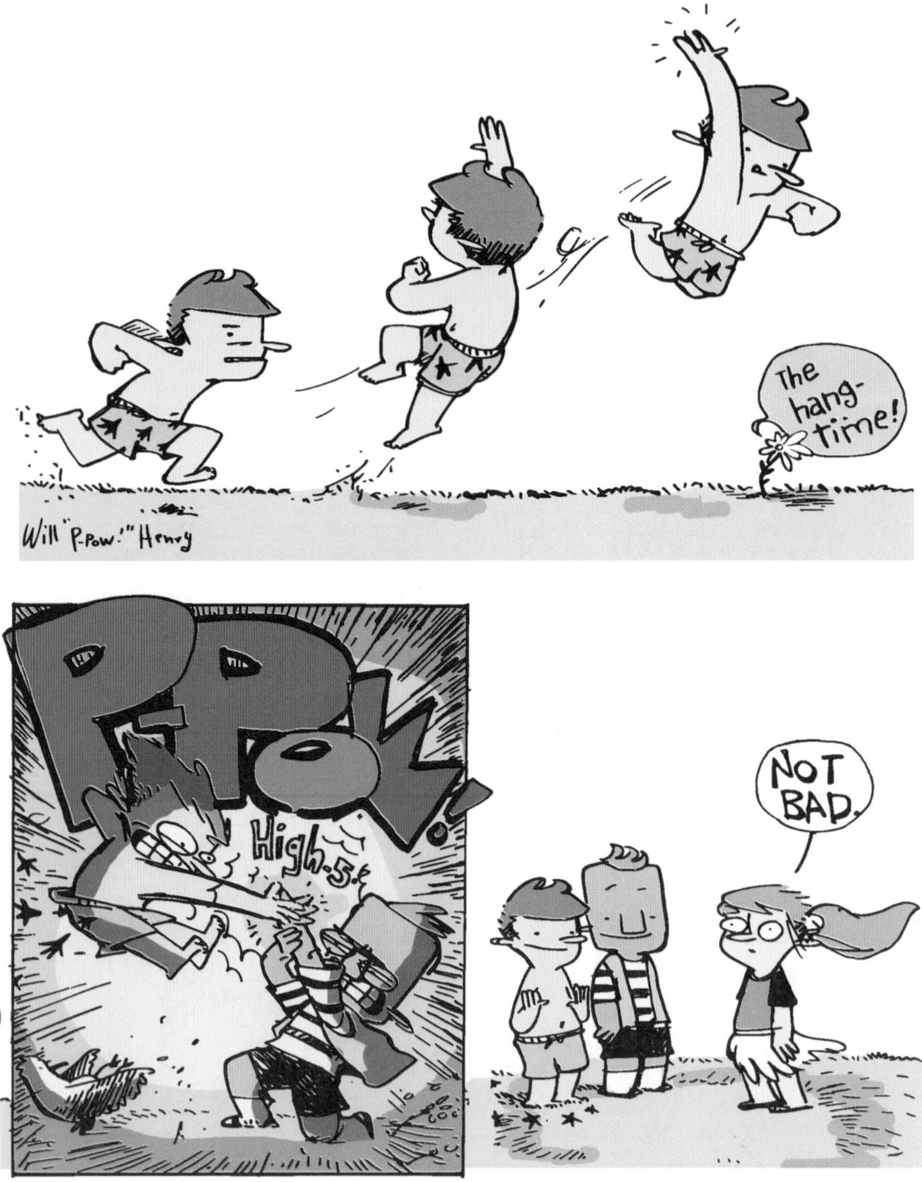
The hang-time!
Will "P-Pow!" Henry
P-POW!
High-5!
NOT BAD.

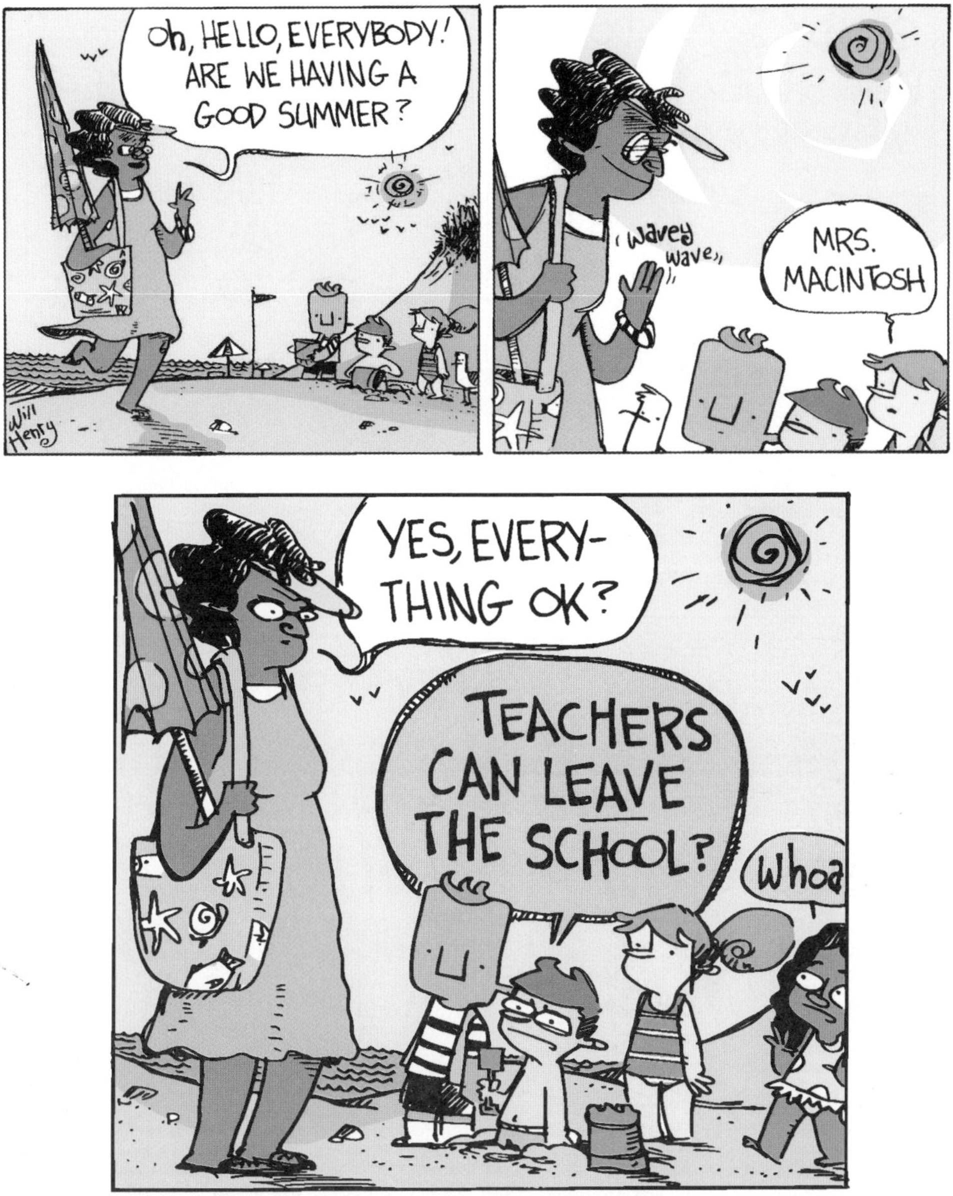
Oh, HELLO, EVERYBODY! ARE WE HAVING A GOOD SUMMER?
Will Henry
MRS. MACINTOSH
wavey wave
YES, EVERY-THING OK?
TEACHERS CAN LEAVE THE SCHOOL?
Whoa

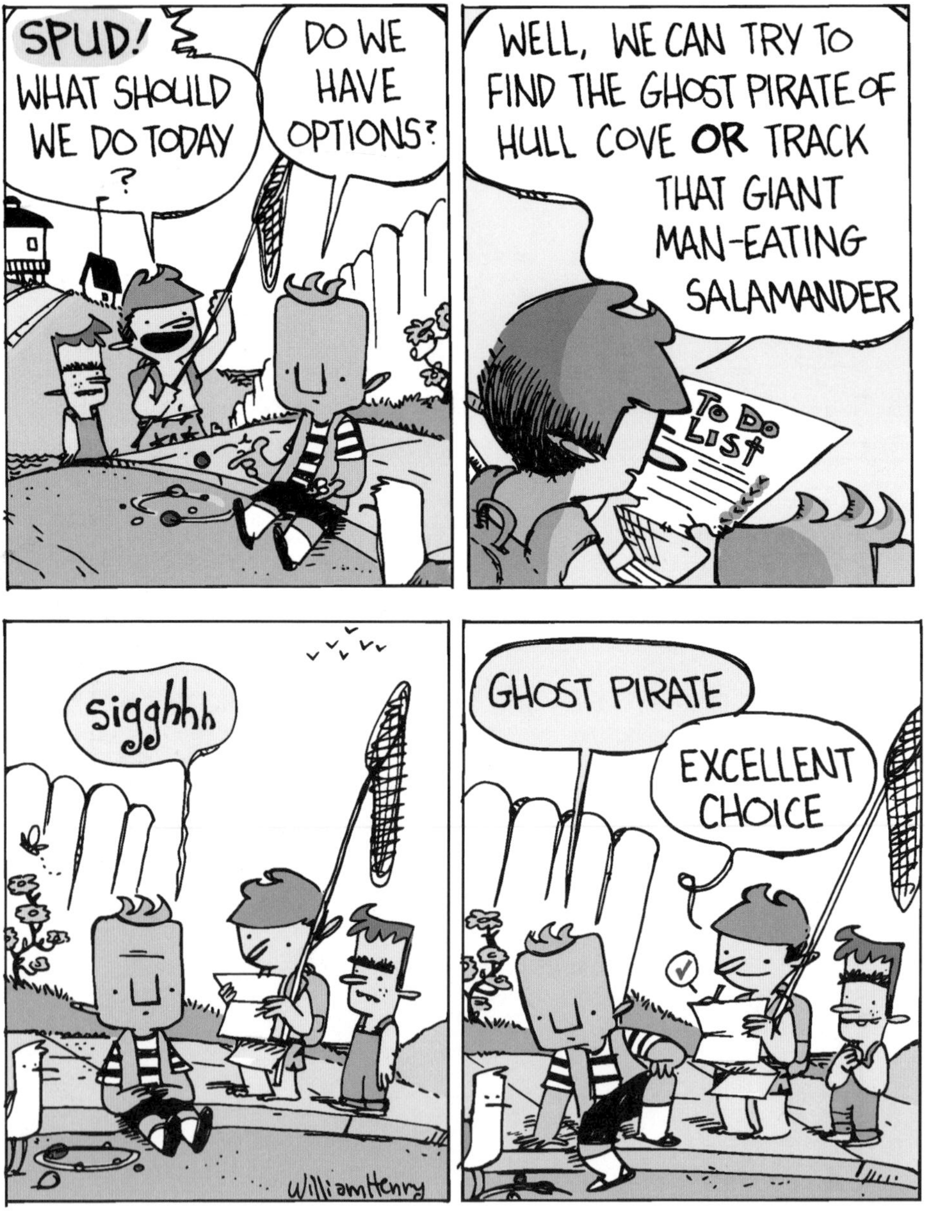
SPUD! WHAT SHOULD WE DO TODAY?
DO WE HAVE OPTIONS?
WELL, WE CAN TRY TO FIND THE GHOST PIRATE OF HULL COVE OR TRACK THAT GIANT MAN-EATING SALAMANDER
TO DO LIST
sigghhh
WilliamHenry
GHOST PIRATE
EXCELLENT CHOICE

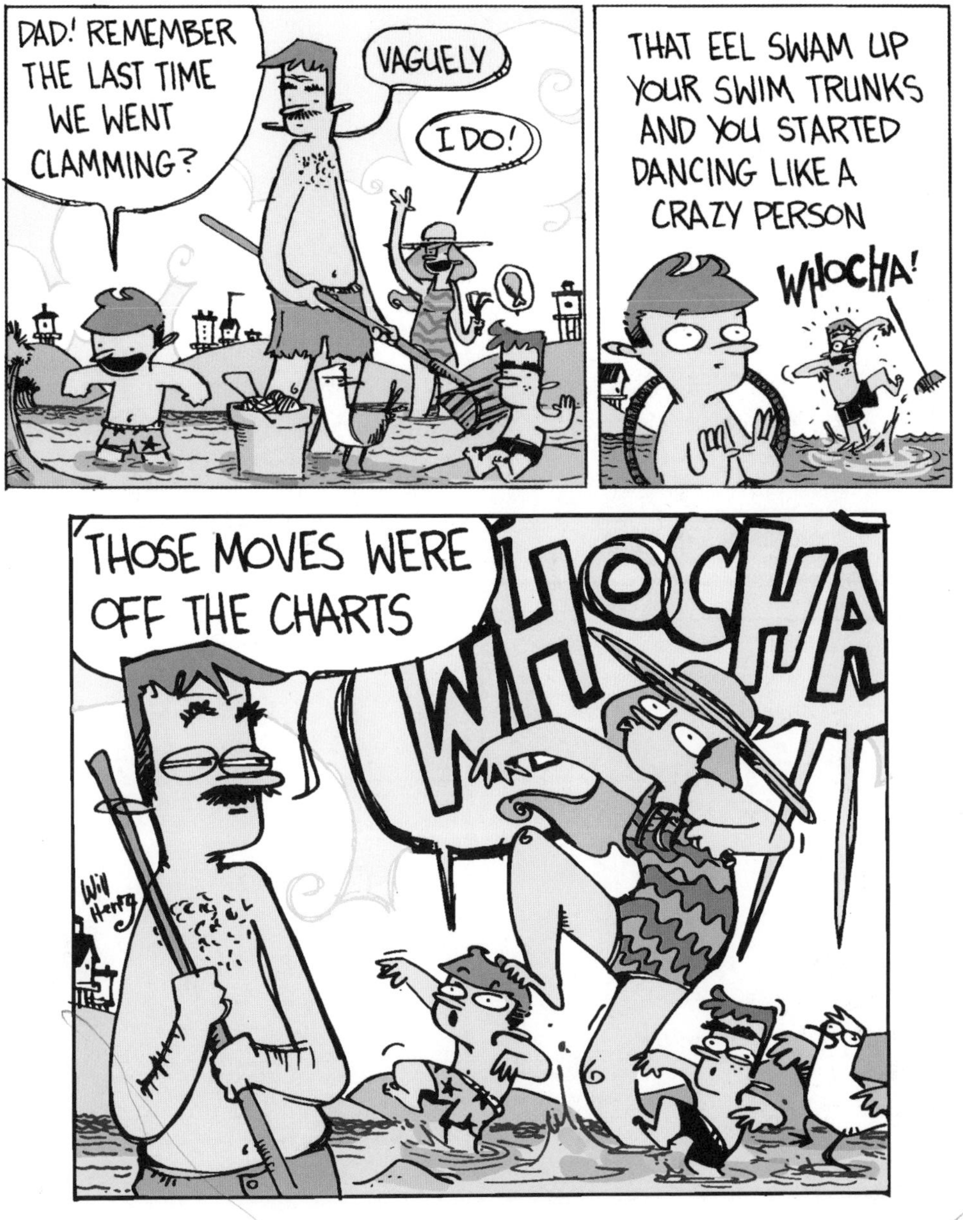
DAD! REMEMBER THE LAST TIME WE WENT CLAMMING?
VAGUELY
I DO!
THAT EEL SWAM UP YOUR SWIM TRUNKS AND YOU STARTED DANCING LIKE A CRAZY PERSON
WHOCHA!
THOSE MOVES WERE OFF THE CHARTS
WHOCHA

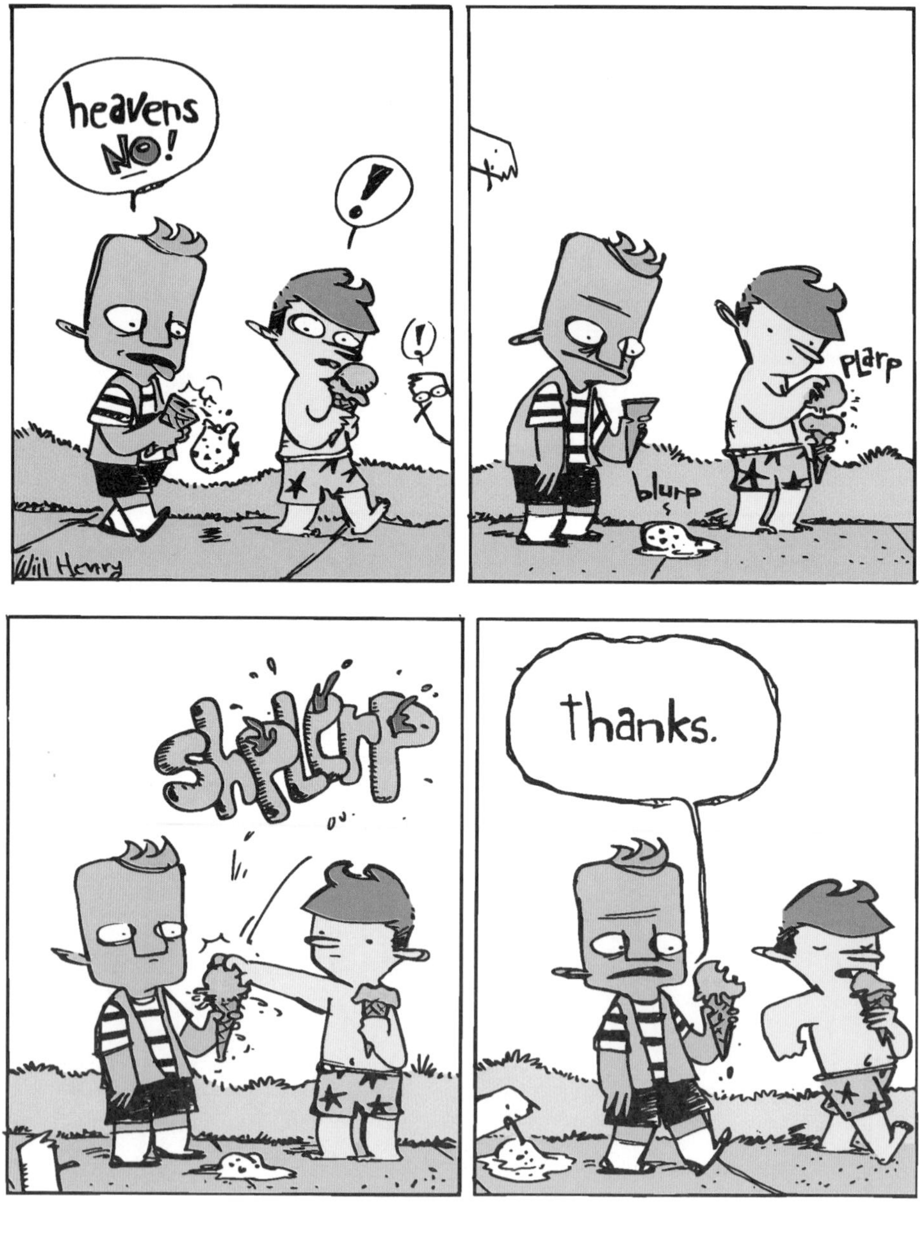
heavens NO!
!
(!)
Will Henry
PLARP
blurp
SHPLURP
thanks.

THAT'S THE CHOCOLATE DANCE...
WE SAVED SOME FOR YOU!
Will Henry!

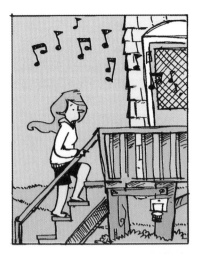

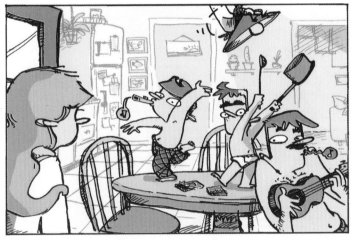

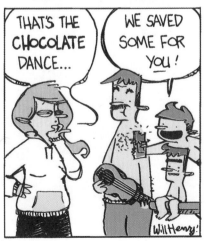

I STILL DON'T UNDERSTAND WHY SPUD IS YOUR BEST FRIEND
I HAD TO REPLACE MY LAST BEST FRIEND
come again?!?
bzz bzz
JOSH LETOURNEAU. HE HAD A TON OF HOCKEY TRADING CARDS AND WAS ABDUCTED BY ALIENS
take the cards
Lucky.
WillHenry
SO, BY DEFAULT ???
NO! BECAUSE SPUD IS AWESOME!!!
I bet Josh was too...

WALLACE, YOU BE A RUNNING BACK
ROSE AND GUNTHER, YOU BE WIDE RECEIVERS
AND SPUD...
SPUD, WHAT DO YOU WANNA BE?
Will Henry!
AN ORTHODONTIST!
I DID NOT KNOW THAT
I KEEP IT PRIVATE
HOW 'BOUT LEFT GOAL POST?

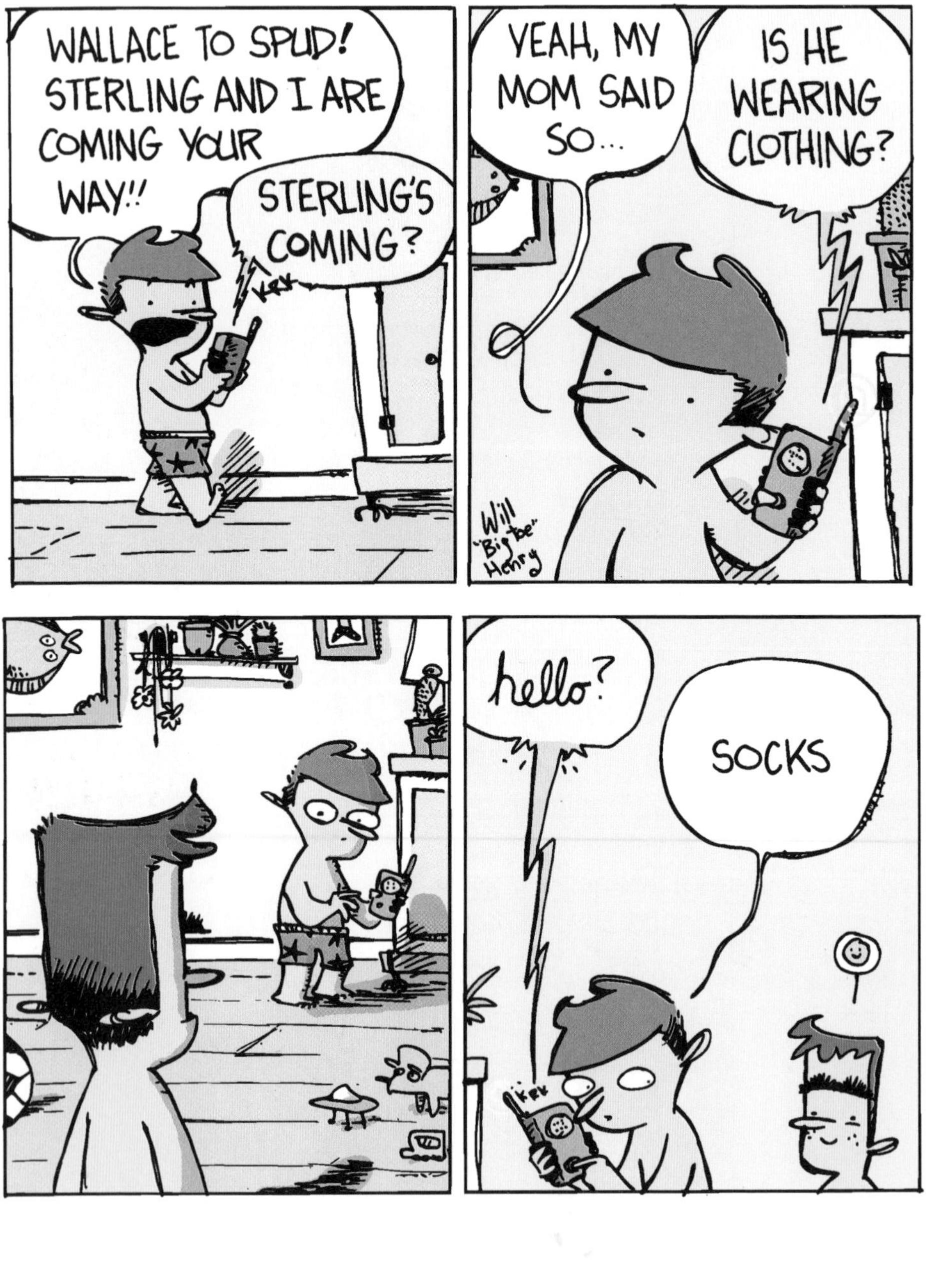
WALLACE TO SPUD! STERLING AND I ARE COMING YOUR WAY!!
STERLING'S COMING?
YEAH, MY MOM SAID SO...
IS HE WEARING CLOTHING?
Will "Big Toe" Henry
hello?
SOCKS

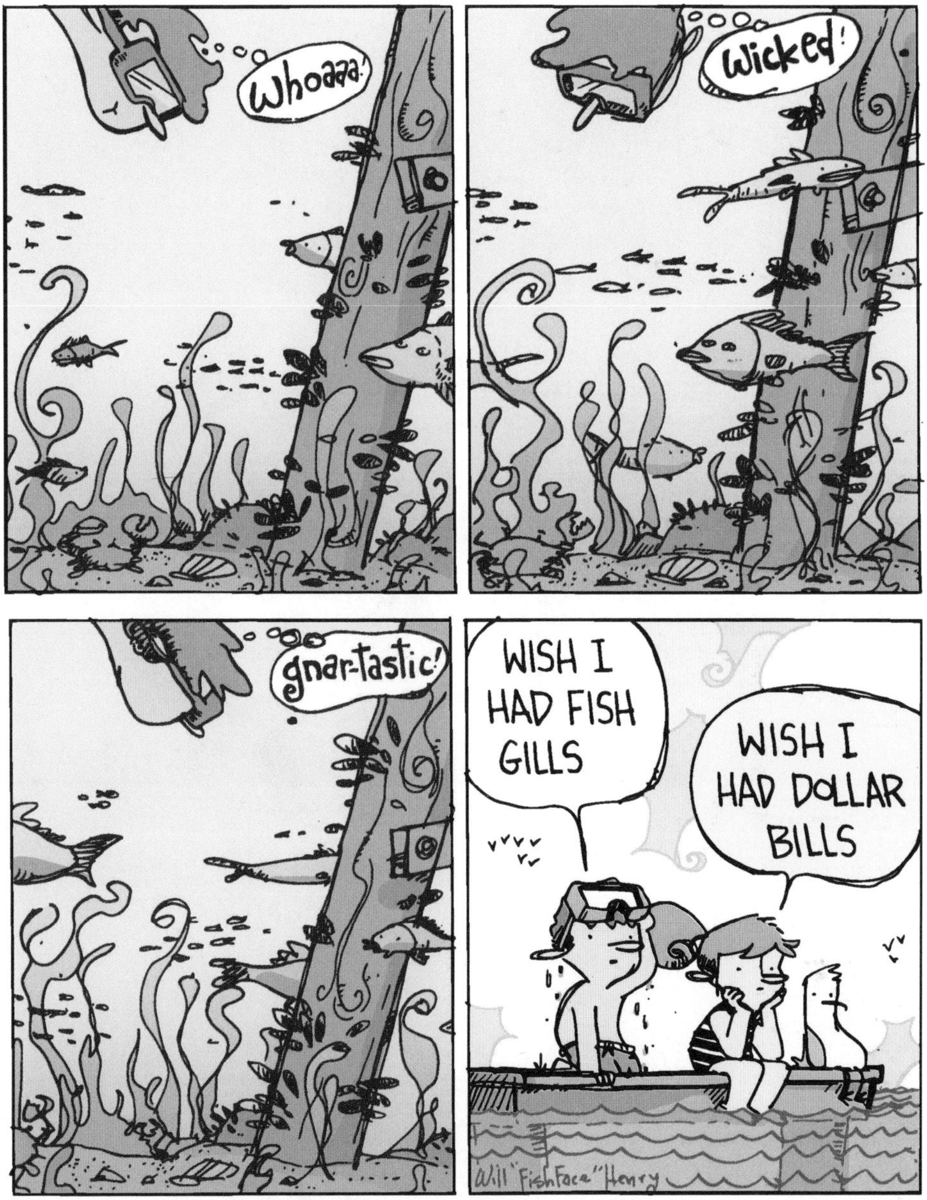
Whoaaa!
Wicked!
gnar-tastic!
WISH I HAD FISH GILLS
WISH I HAD DOLLAR BILLS
Will "FishFace" Henry

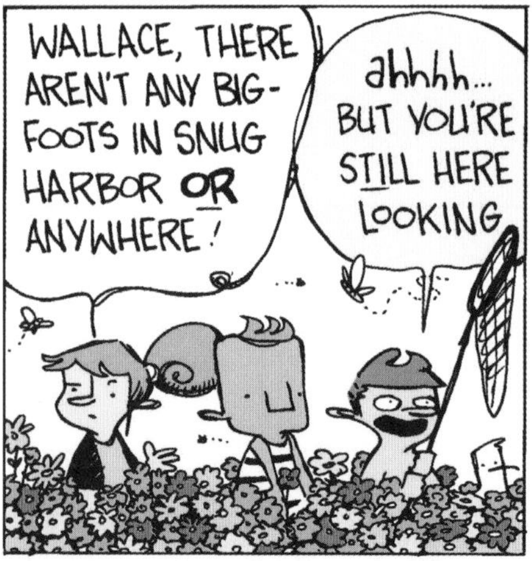
WALLACE, THERE AREN'T ANY BIG-FOOTS IN SNUG HARBOR **OR** ANYWHERE!
ahhhh... BUT YOU'RE STILL HERE LOOKING

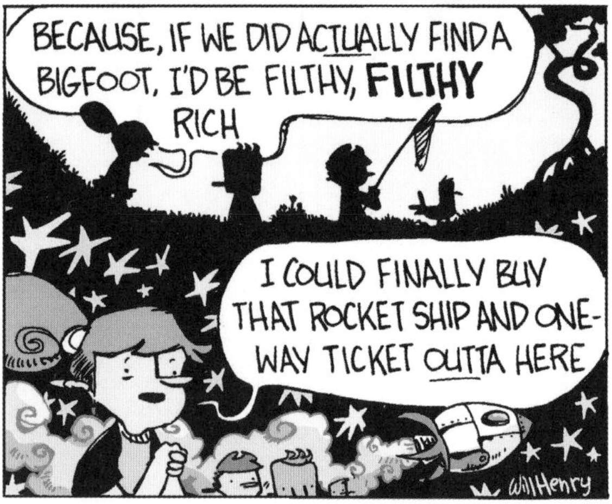
BECAUSE, IF WE DID ACTUALLY FIND A BIGFOOT, I'D BE FILTHY, **FILTHY** RICH
I COULD FINALLY BUY THAT ROCKET SHIP AND ONE-WAY TICKET OUTTA HERE
WillHenry

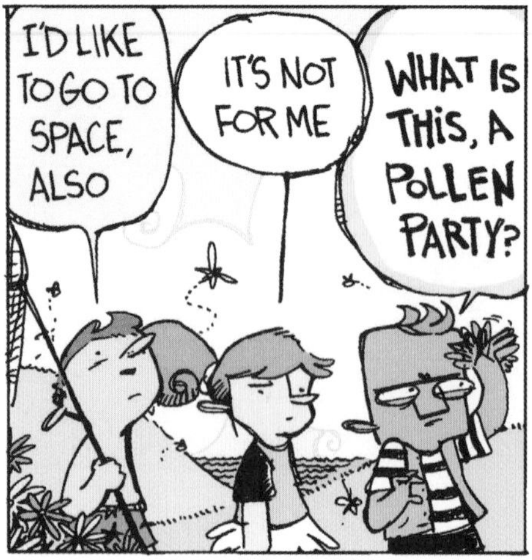
I'D LIKE TO GO TO SPACE, ALSO
IT'S NOT FOR ME
WHAT IS THIS, A POLLEN PARTY?

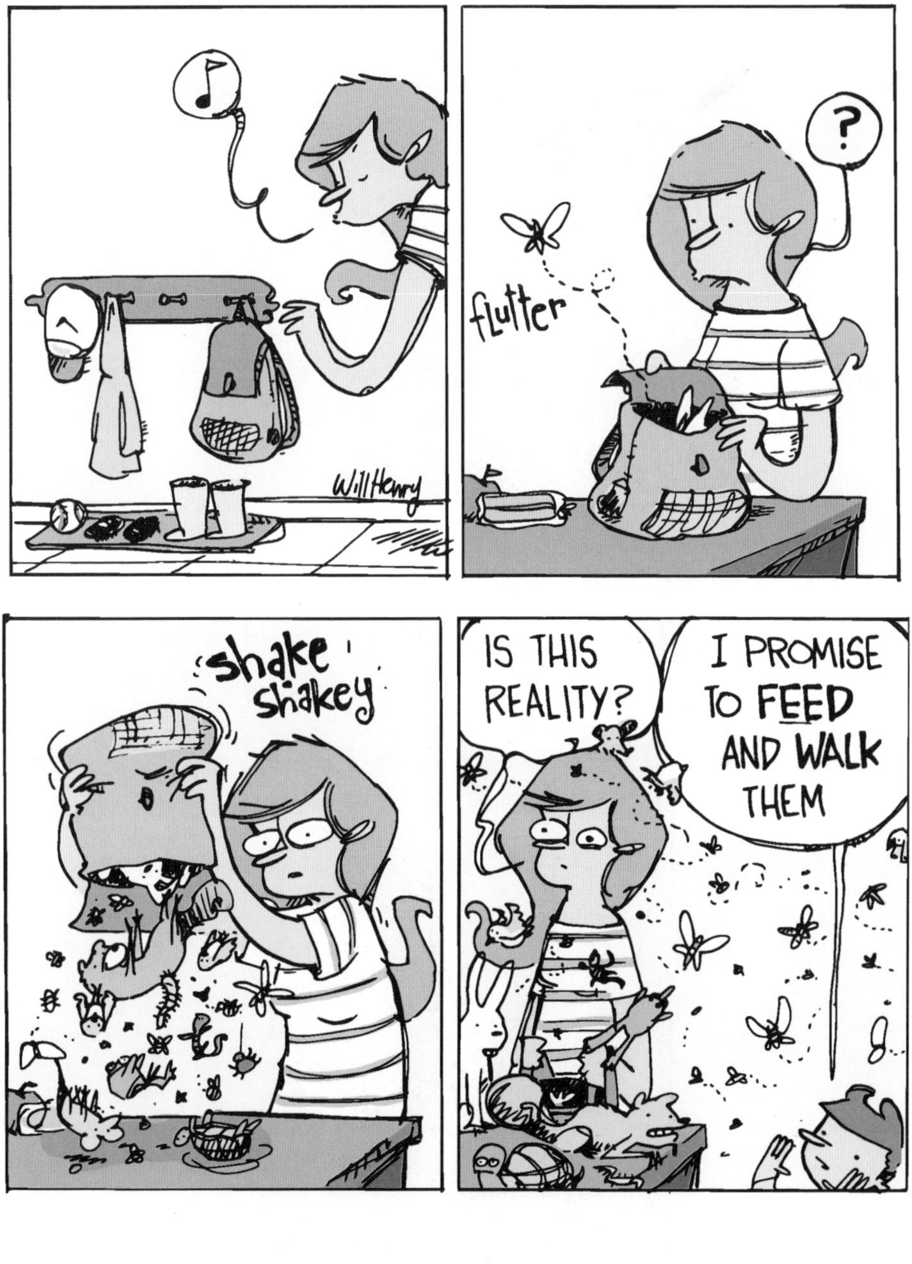
Will Henry
?
flutter
shake
shakey
IS THIS REALITY?
I PROMISE TO FEED AND WALK THEM

SPUD! COME IN, THIS IS WALLACE!
AMELIA SWEARS SHE SAW A BIGFOOT SITTING IN THE OSPREY NEST BY ZEEK'S CREEK. SHE MAY BE PULLING MY CHAIN, BUT THAT'S A CHANCE WE CAN'T TAKE. MEET US BY THE MEADOW IN FIFTEEN. I HAVE A PLAN TO LURE THE SASQUATCH OUT USING DEER URINE. STERLING SAYS HE KNOWS HOW TO GET SOME BUT TO WEAR YOUR WELLIES BECAUSE IT'S GONNA GET MESSY. WALLACE OUT!
sighhh...

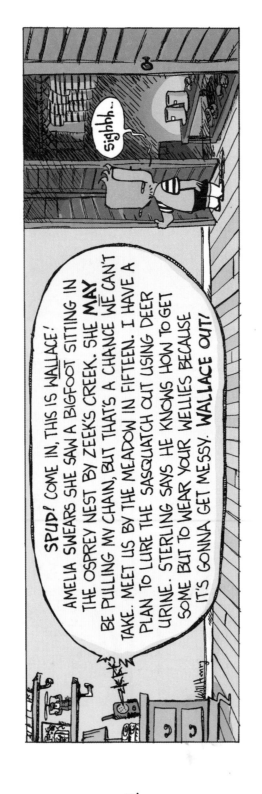

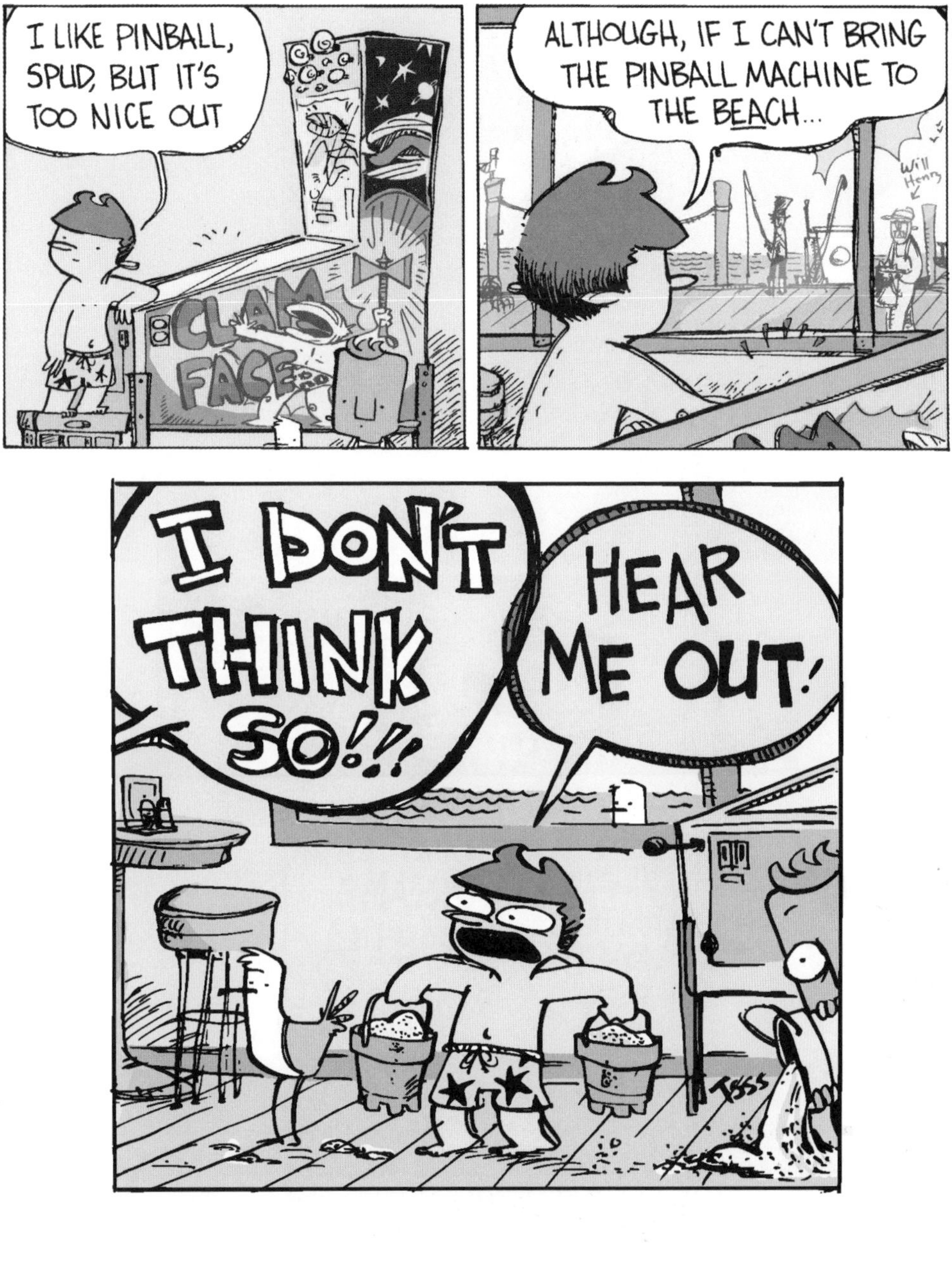
I LIKE PINBALL, SPUD, BUT IT'S TOO NICE OUT
CLAM FACE
ALTHOUGH, IF I CAN'T BRING THE PINBALL MACHINE TO THE BEACH...
Will Henry
I DON'T THINK SO!!!
HEAR ME OUT!

ANYTHING YOU WANNA DO THIS SUMMER ?
nap.
I'D LIKE TO START RANDOMLY THROWING SHAVING CREAM AT PEOPLE
hello
hi
HEY, WHAT BETTER DAY THAN TODAY!
Follow YOUR DREAMS, AMELIA!

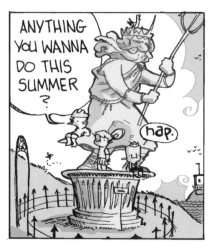

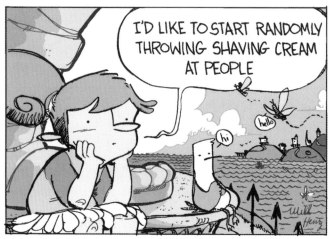

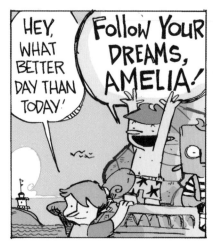

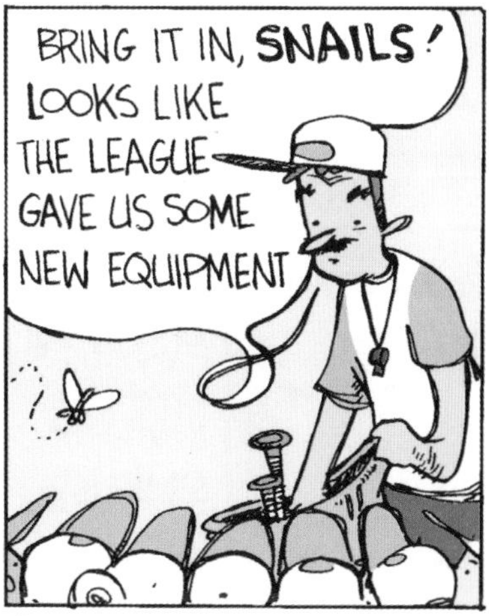
BRING IT IN, **SNAILS**! LOOKS LIKE THE LEAGUE GAVE US SOME NEW EQUIPMENT

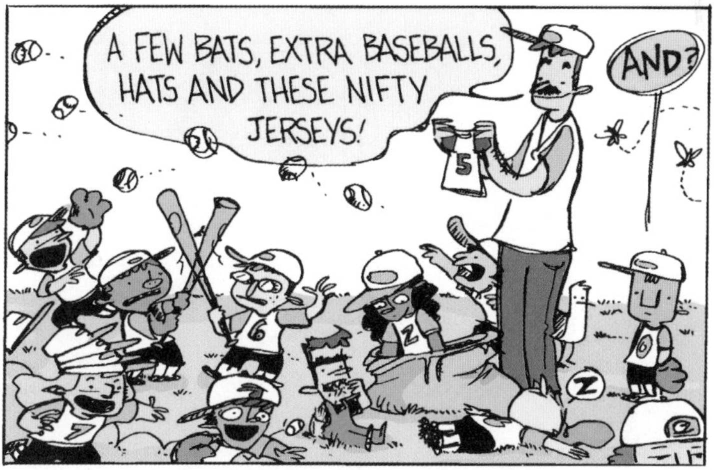
A FEW BATS, EXTRA BASEBALLS, HATS AND THESE NIFTY JERSEYS!
AND?

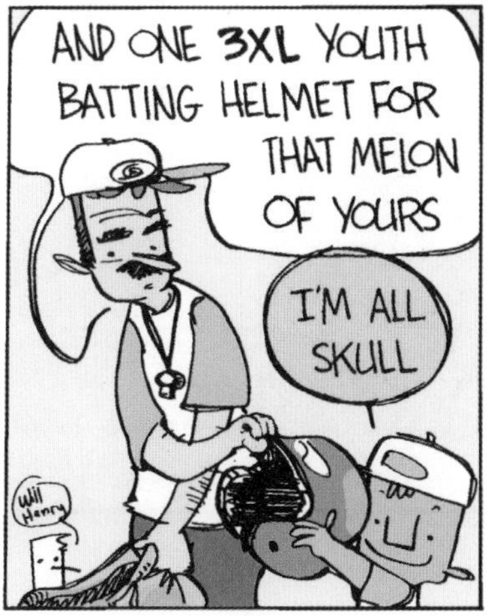
AND ONE **3XL** YOUTH BATTING HELMET FOR THAT MELON OF YOURS
I'M ALL SKULL
Will Henry

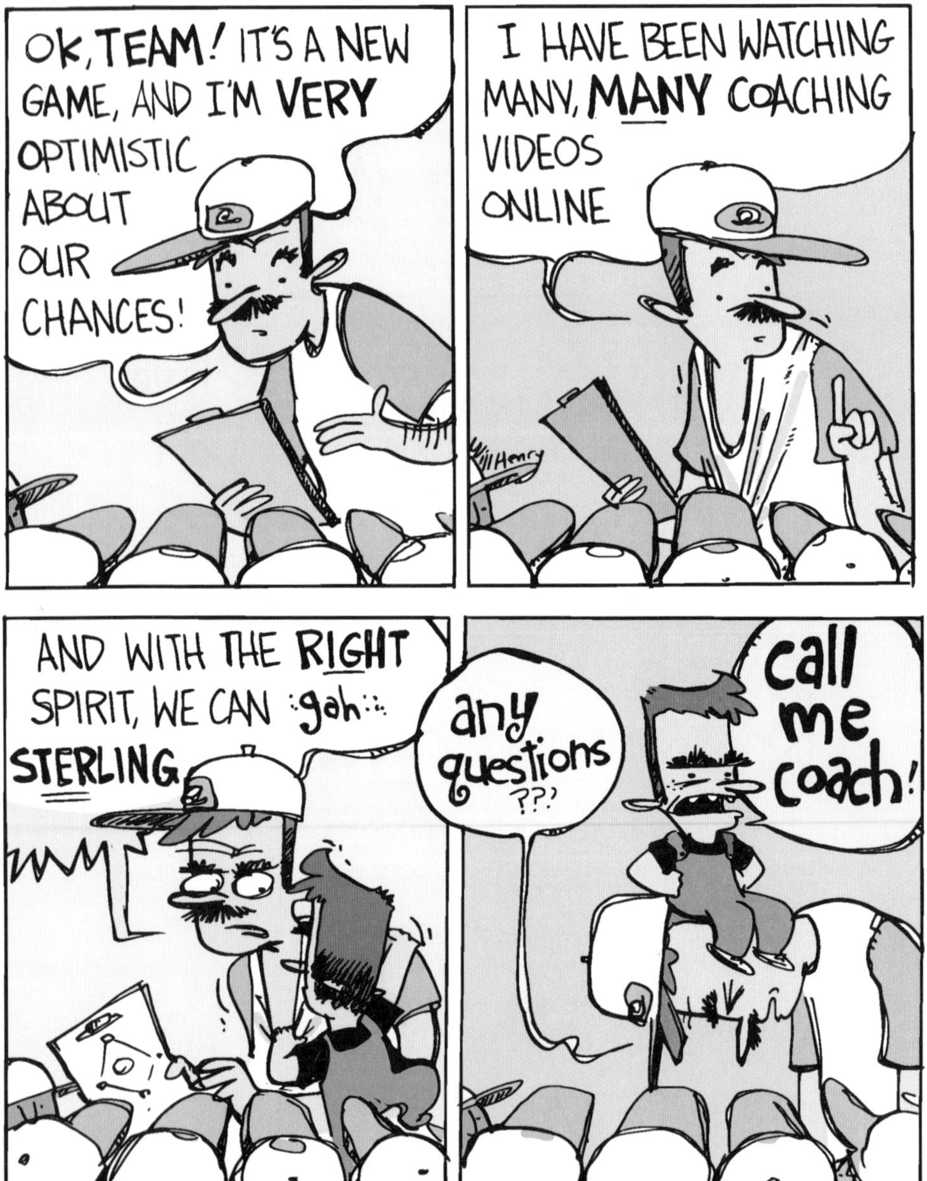
OK, TEAM! IT'S A NEW GAME, AND I'M VERY OPTIMISTIC ABOUT OUR CHANCES!
I HAVE BEEN WATCHING MANY, MANY COACHING VIDEOS ONLINE
AND WITH THE RIGHT SPIRIT, WE CAN :gah:: STERLING
any questions ???
call me coach!

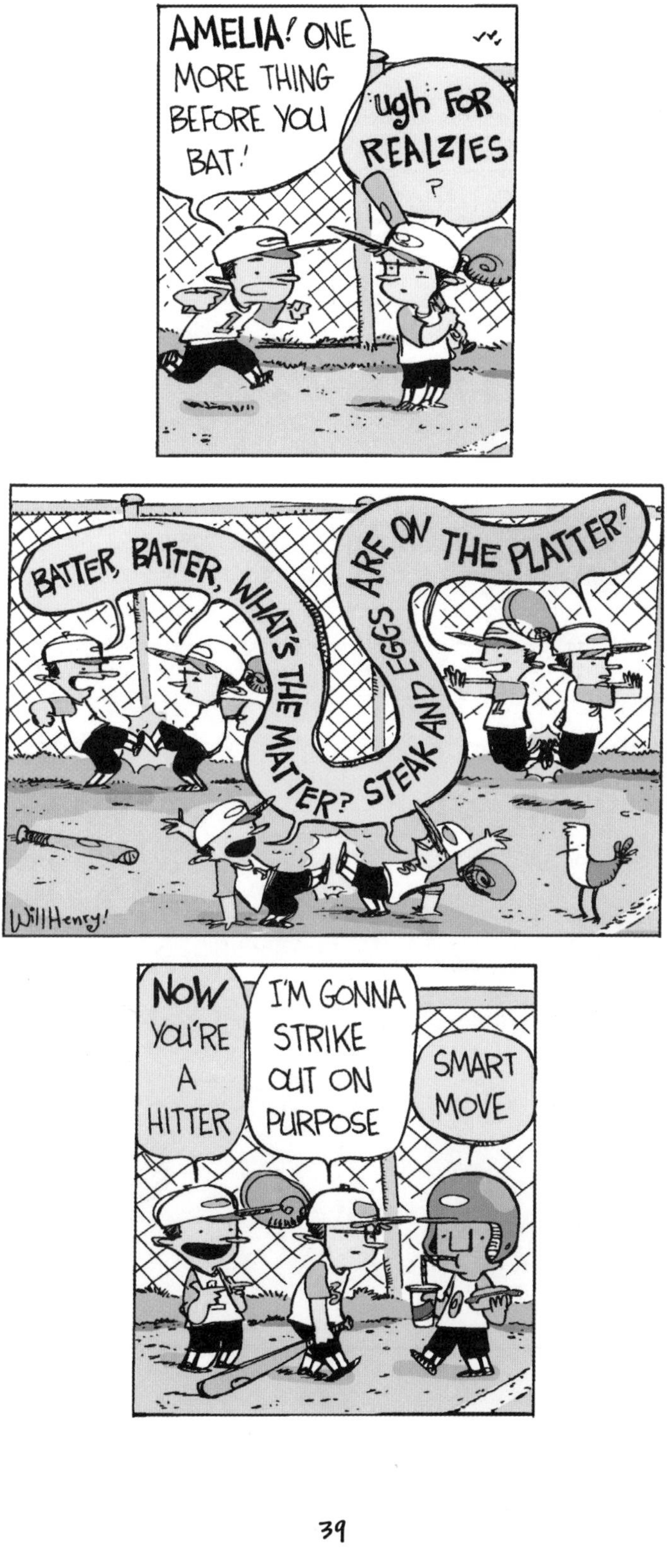
AMELIA! ONE MORE THING BEFORE YOU BAT!
ugh FOR REALZIES?
BATTER, BATTER, WHAT'S THE MATTER? STEAK AND EGGS ARE ON THE PLATTER!
WillHenry!
NOW YOU'RE A HITTER
I'M GONNA STRIKE OUT ON PURPOSE
SMART MOVE

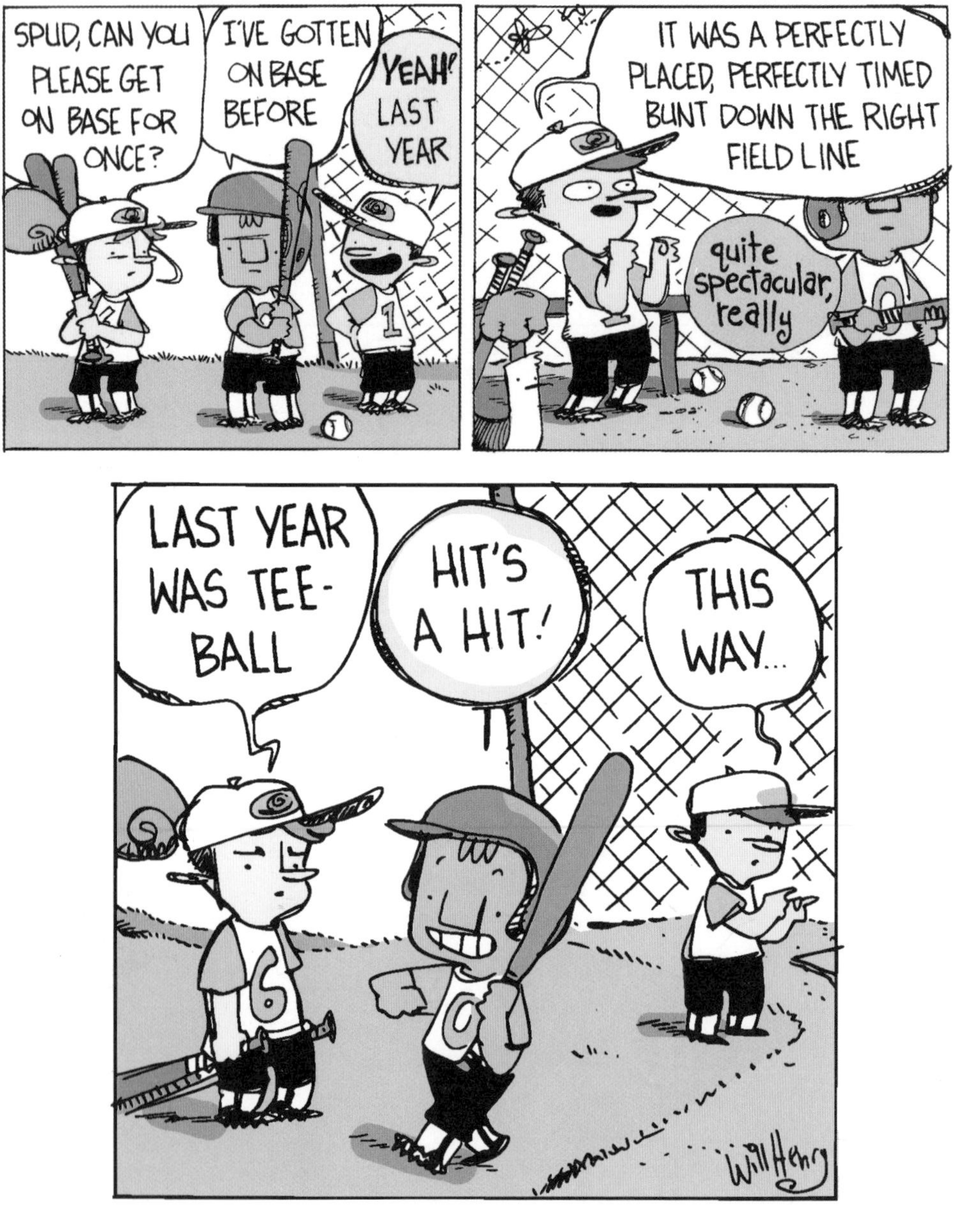
SPUD, CAN YOU PLEASE GET ON BASE FOR ONCE?
I'VE GOTTEN ON BASE BEFORE
YEAH! LAST YEAR
IT WAS A PERFECTLY PLACED, PERFECTLY TIMED BUNT DOWN THE RIGHT FIELD LINE
quite spectacular, really
LAST YEAR WAS TEE-BALL
HIT'S A HIT!
THIS WAY...
Will Henry

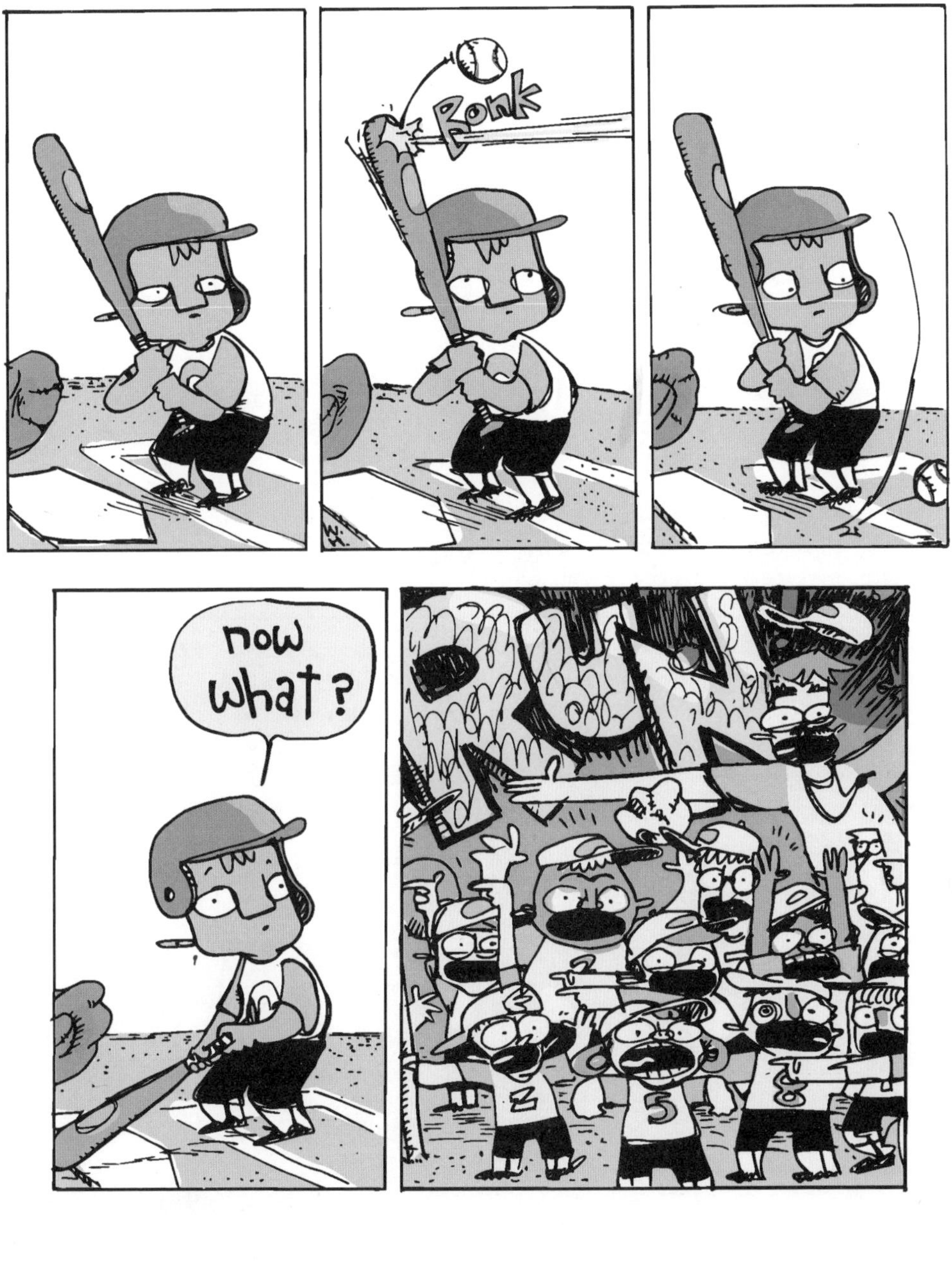
Bonk
now what?
RUN

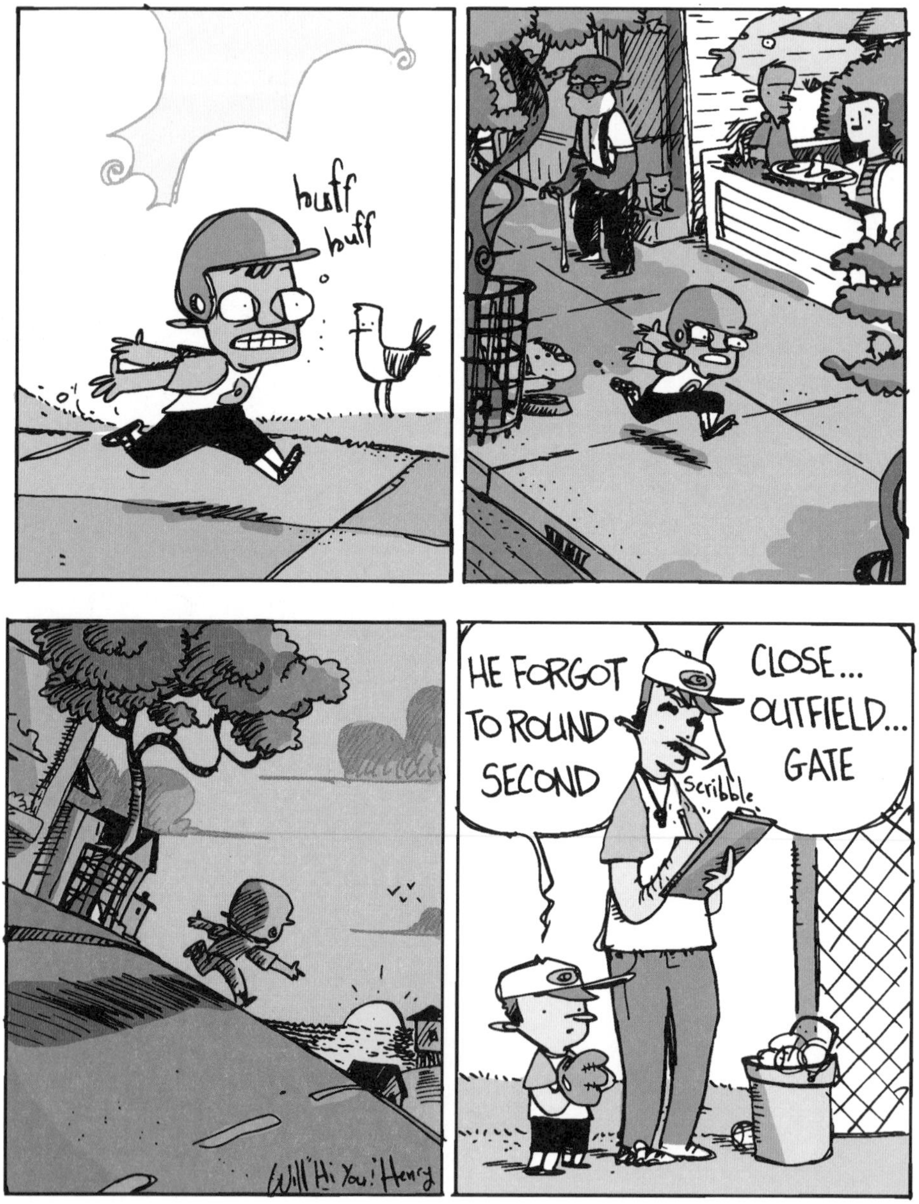
huff
huff
Will "Hi You!" Henry
HE FORGOT TO ROUND SECOND
CLOSE... OUTFIELD... GATE
Scribble

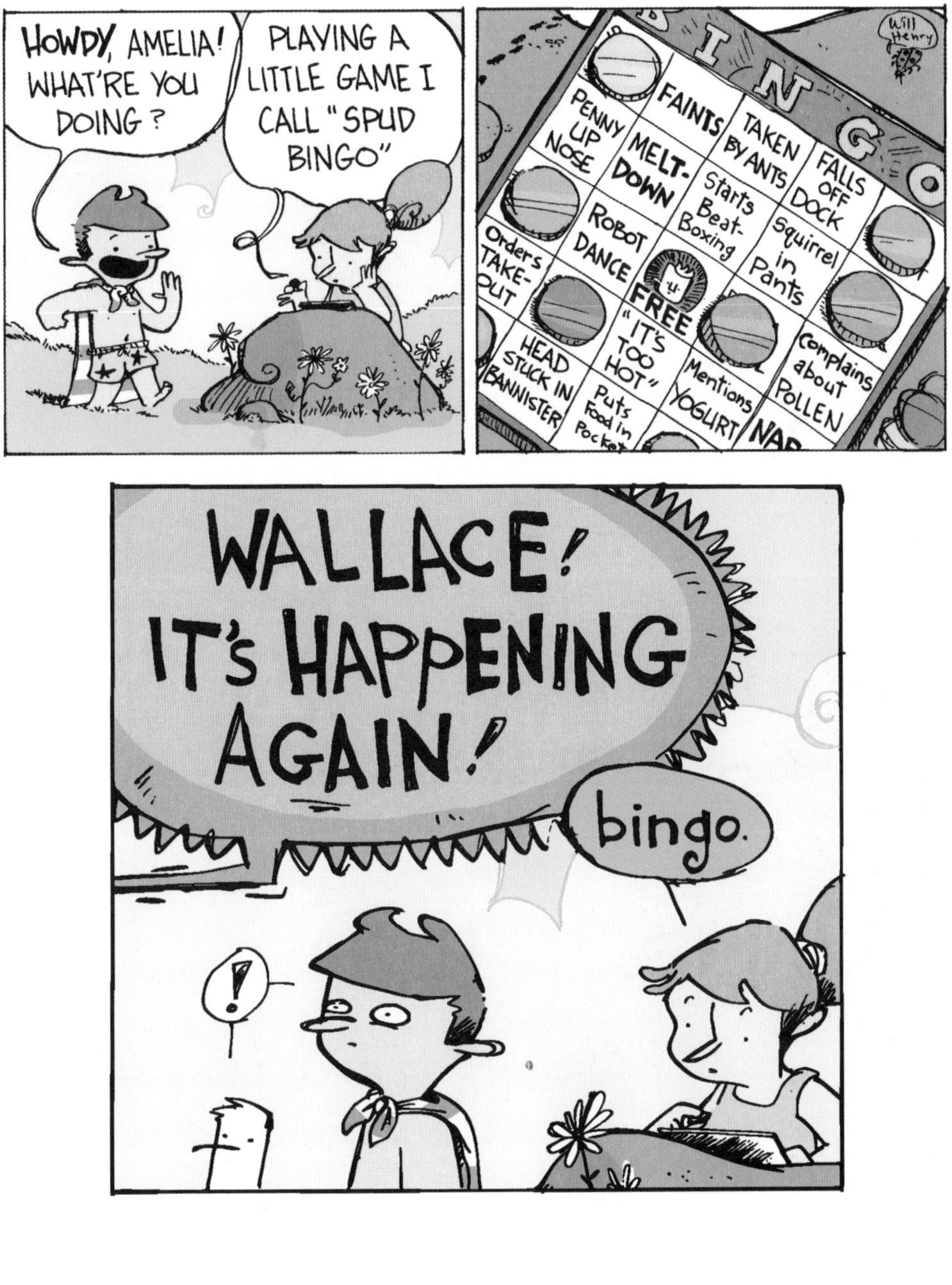
HOWDY, AMELIA! WHAT'RE YOU DOING?
PLAYING A LITTLE GAME I CALL "SPUD BINGO"
BINGO
Will Henry
FAINTS
TAKEN BY ANTS
FALLS OFF DOCK
PENNY UP NOSE
MELT-DOWN
Starts Beat-Boxing
Squirrel in Pants
Orders TAKE-OUT
ROBOT DANCE
FREE
Complains about POLLEN
HEAD STUCK IN BANNISTER
"IT'S TOO HOT"
Mentions YOGURT
Puts Food in Pocket
NAP
WALLACE! IT'S HAPPENING AGAIN!
bingo.
!

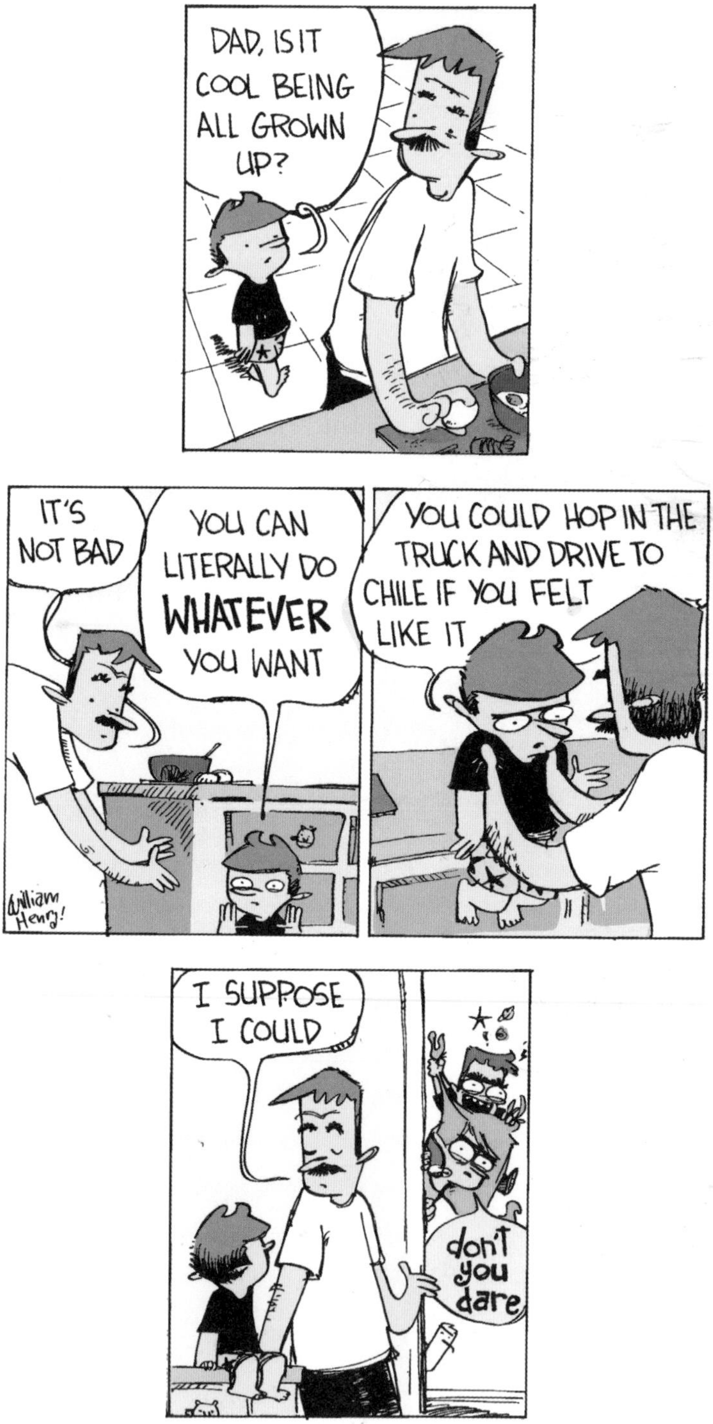
DAD, IS IT COOL BEING ALL GROWN UP?
IT'S NOT BAD
YOU CAN LITERALLY DO **WHATEVER** YOU WANT
William Henry!
YOU COULD HOP IN THE TRUCK AND DRIVE TO CHILE IF YOU FELT LIKE IT
I SUPPOSE I COULD
don't you dare

WALLACE IS GONNA JUMP FARMER BROWN'S AWARD-WINNING MANURE PILE WITH A POGO STICK
AND WE NEED SOMEONE TO LIGHT THE SPARKLERS
BETTER THAN CHECKERS
Will Henry

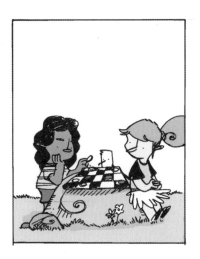

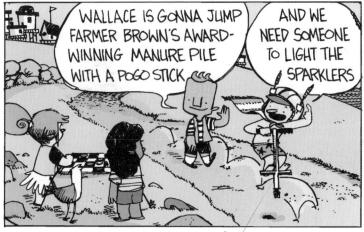

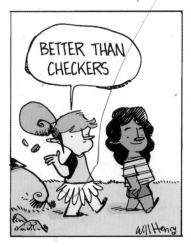

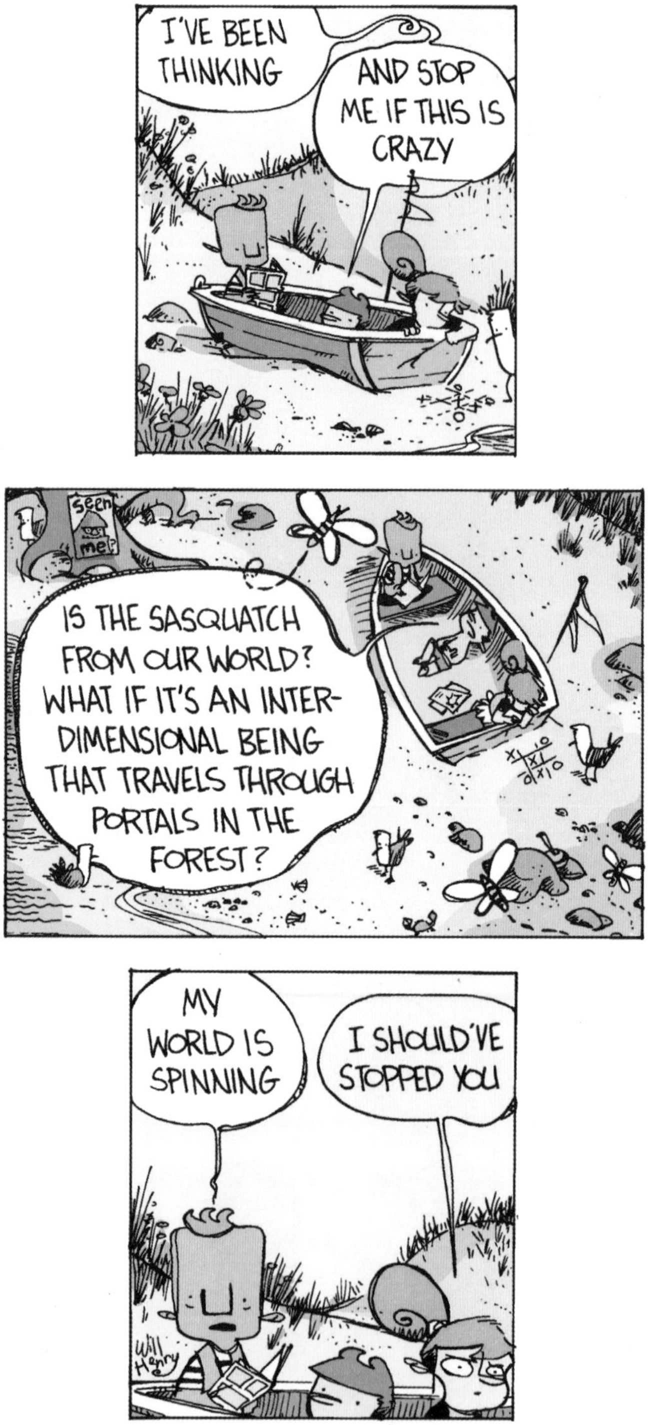
I'VE BEEN THINKING
AND STOP ME IF THIS IS CRAZY
seen me?
IS THE SASQUATCH FROM OUR WORLD? WHAT IF IT'S AN INTER-DIMENSIONAL BEING THAT TRAVELS THROUGH PORTALS IN THE FOREST?
MY WORLD IS SPINNING
I SHOULD'VE STOPPED YOU
Will Henry

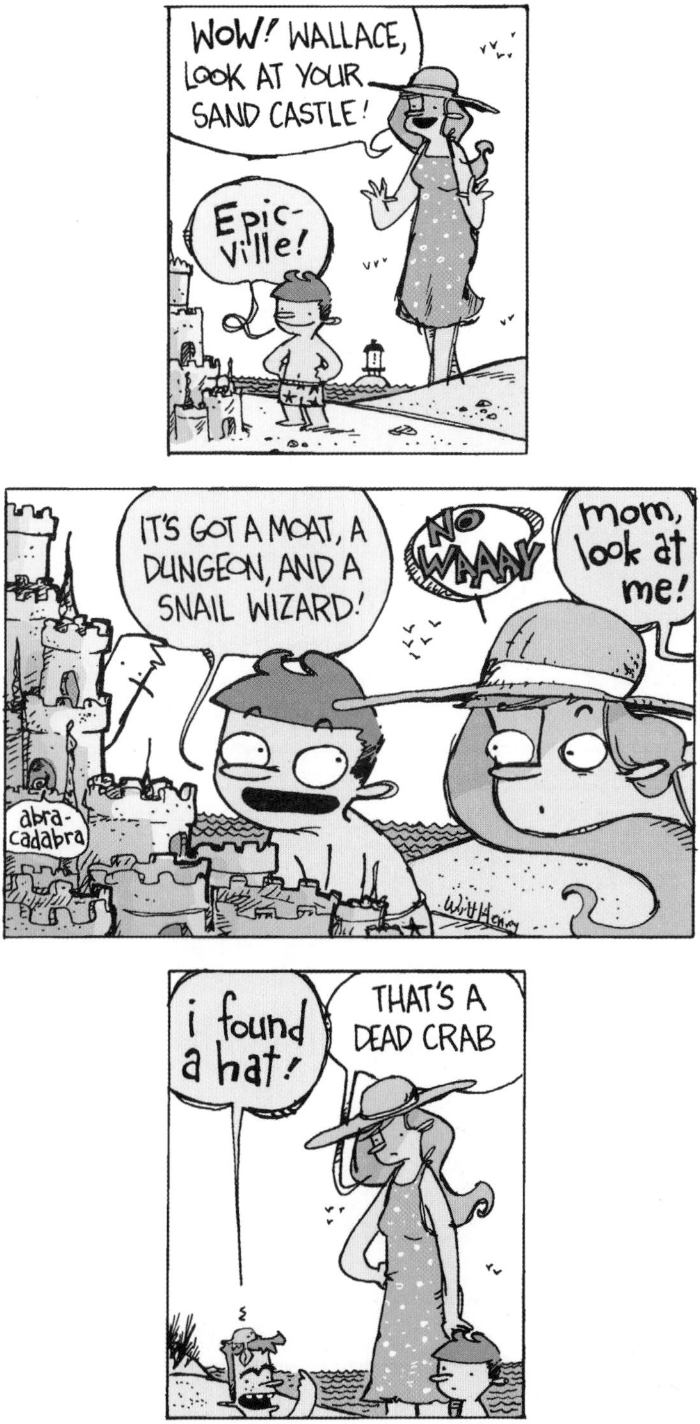
WOW! WALLACE, LOOK AT YOUR SAND CASTLE!
Epic-ville!
IT'S GOT A MOAT, A DUNGEON, AND A SNAIL WIZARD!
abra-cadabra
NO WAAAY
mom, look at me!
i found a hat!
THAT'S A DEAD CRAB

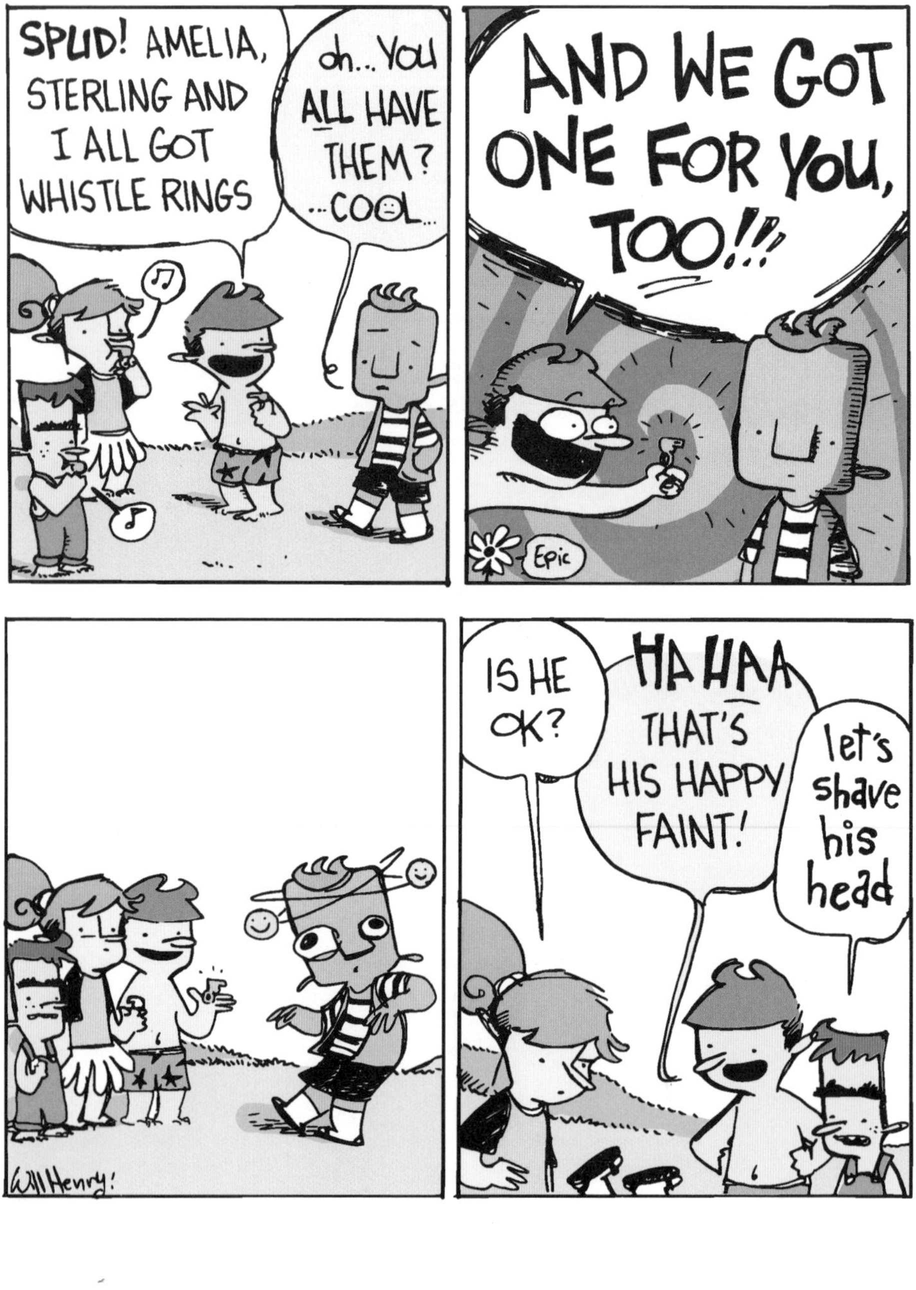
SPUD! AMELIA, STERLING AND I ALL GOT WHISTLE RINGS
oh... YOU ALL HAVE THEM? ...COOL...
AND WE GOT ONE FOR YOU, TOO!!!
Epic
Will Henry!
IS HE OK?
HA HAA THAT'S HIS HAPPY FAINT!
let's shave his head

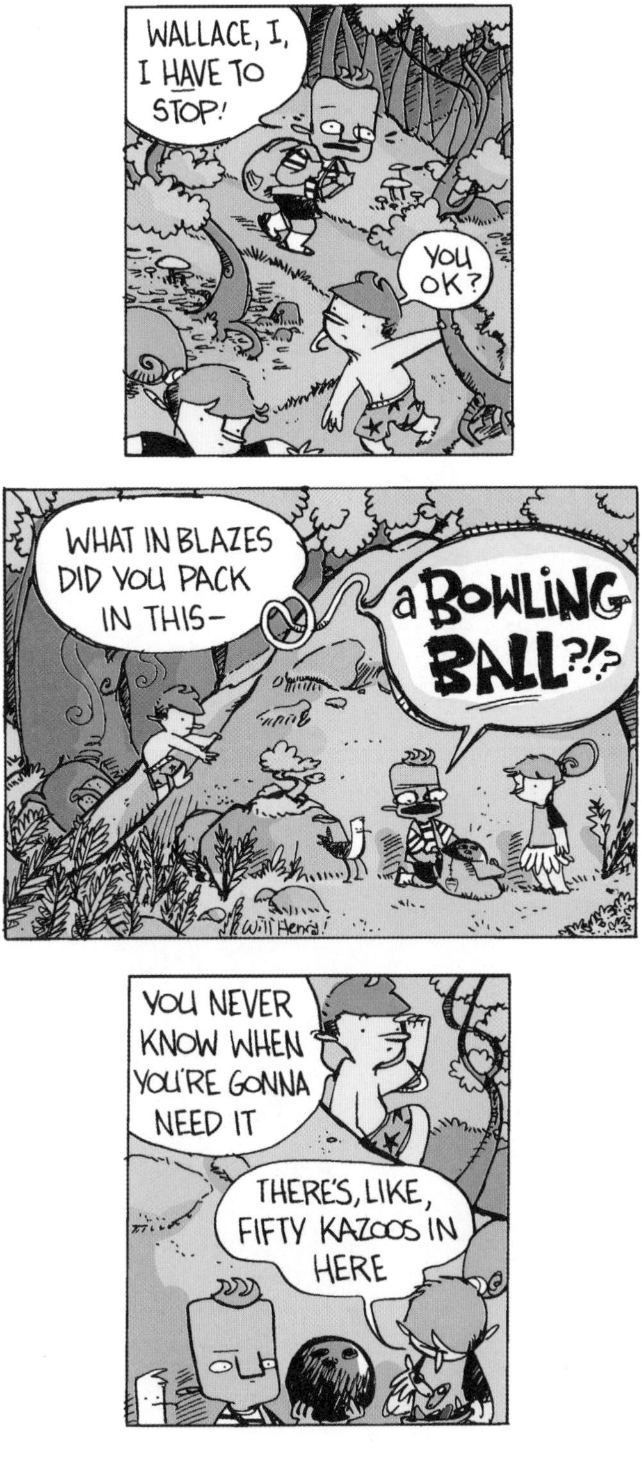
WALLACE, I, I HAVE TO STOP!
YOU OK?
WHAT IN BLAZES DID YOU PACK IN THIS-
a BOWLING BALL?!?
Will Henry!
YOU NEVER KNOW WHEN YOU'RE GONNA NEED IT
THERE'S, LIKE, FIFTY KAZOOS IN HERE

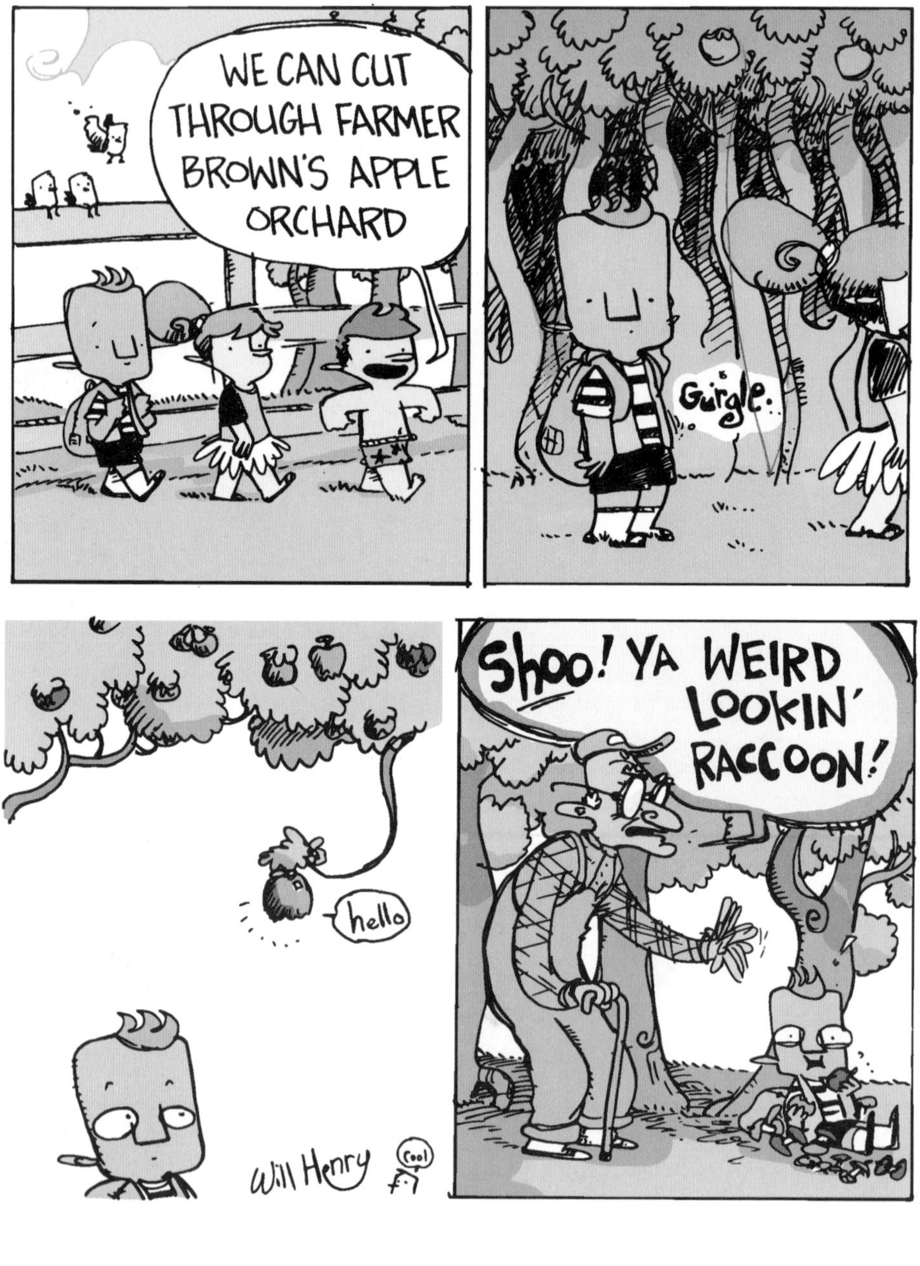
WE CAN CUT THROUGH FARMER BROWN'S APPLE ORCHARD
Gurgle.
hello
Will Henry
cool
Shoo! YA WEIRD LOOKIN' RACCOON!

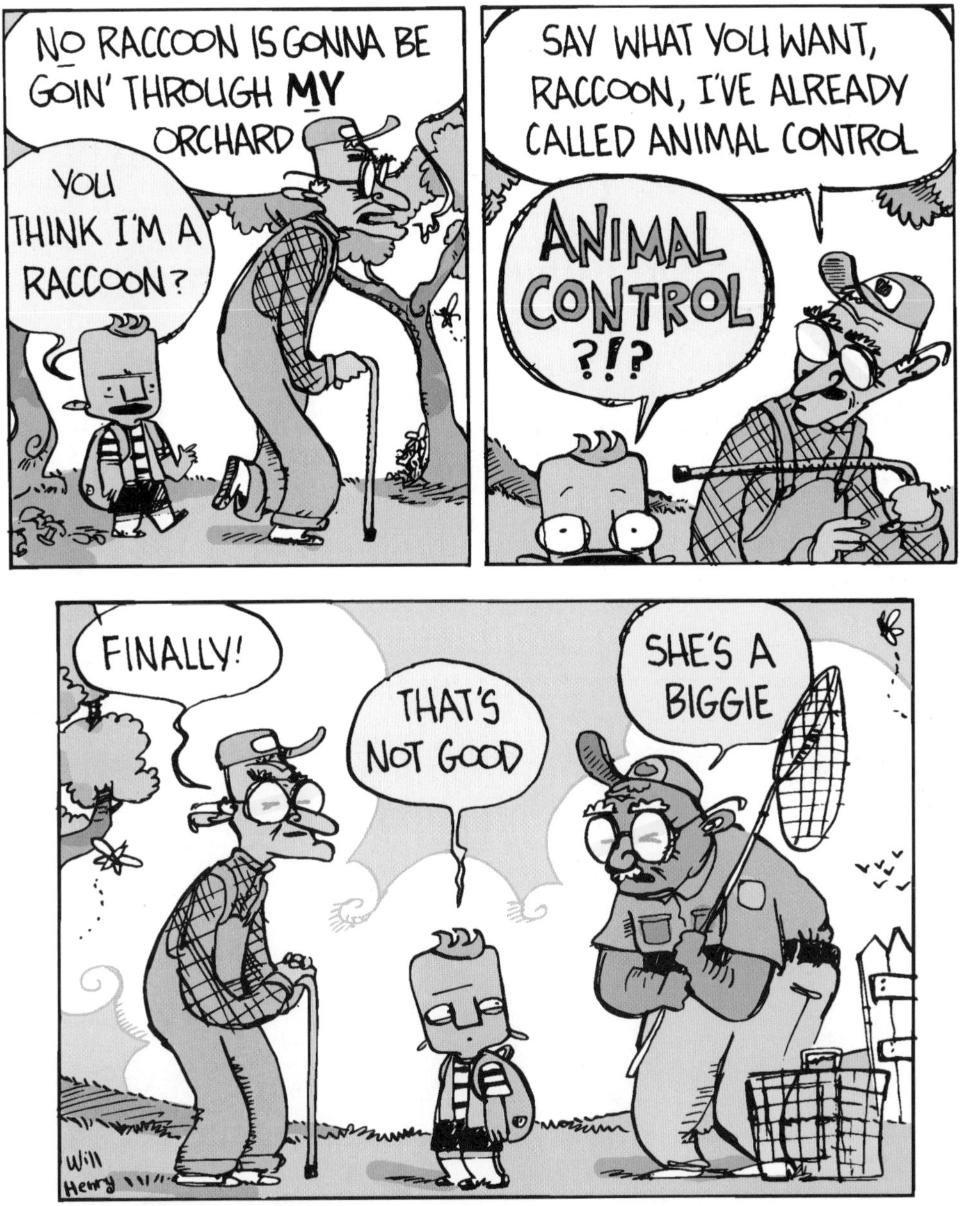
NO RACCOON IS GONNA BE GOIN' THROUGH MY ORCHARD
YOU THINK I'M A RACCOON?
SAY WHAT YOU WANT, RACCOON, I'VE ALREADY CALLED ANIMAL CONTROL
ANIMAL CONTROL ?!?
FINALLY!
THAT'S NOT GOOD
SHE'S A BIGGIE
Will Henry

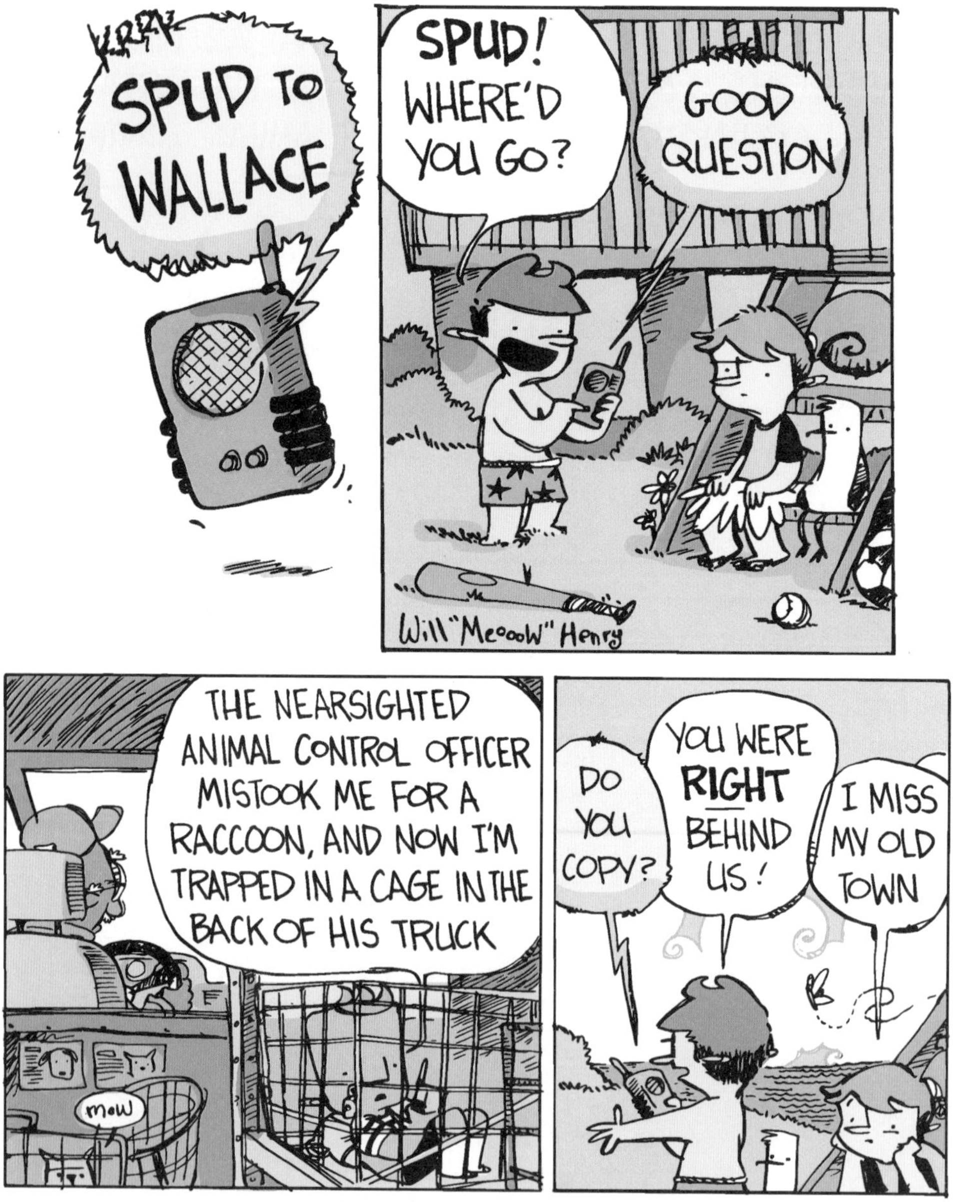
SPUD TO WALLACE
SPUD! WHERE'D YOU GO?
GOOD QUESTION
Will "Meooow" Henry
THE NEARSIGHTED ANIMAL CONTROL OFFICER MISTOOK ME FOR A RACCOON, AND NOW I'M TRAPPED IN A CAGE IN THE BACK OF HIS TRUCK
mow
DO YOU COPY?
YOU WERE RIGHT BEHIND US!
I MISS MY OLD TOWN

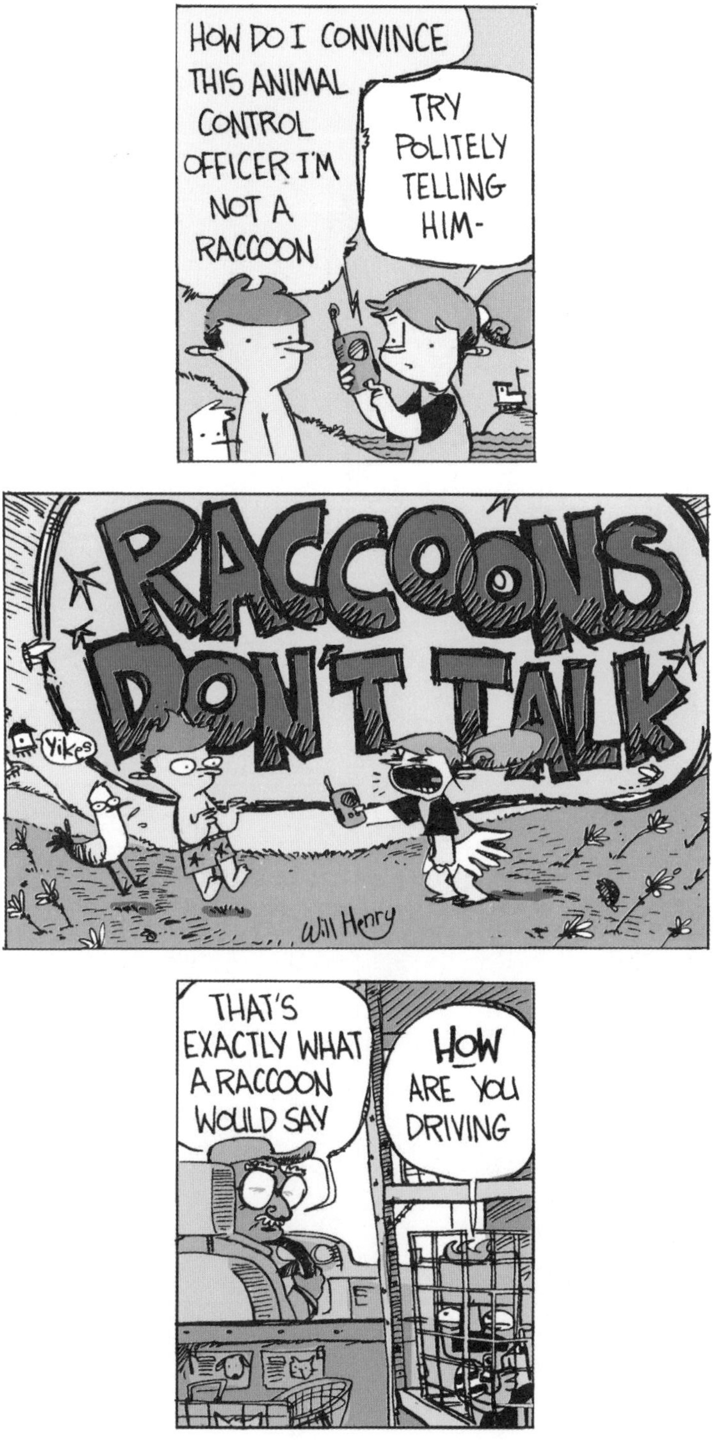
HOW DO I CONVINCE THIS ANIMAL CONTROL OFFICER I'M NOT A RACCOON
TRY POLITELY TELLING HIM-
RACCOONS DON'T TALK
yikes
Will Henry
THAT'S EXACTLY WHAT A RACCOON WOULD SAY
HOW ARE YOU DRIVING

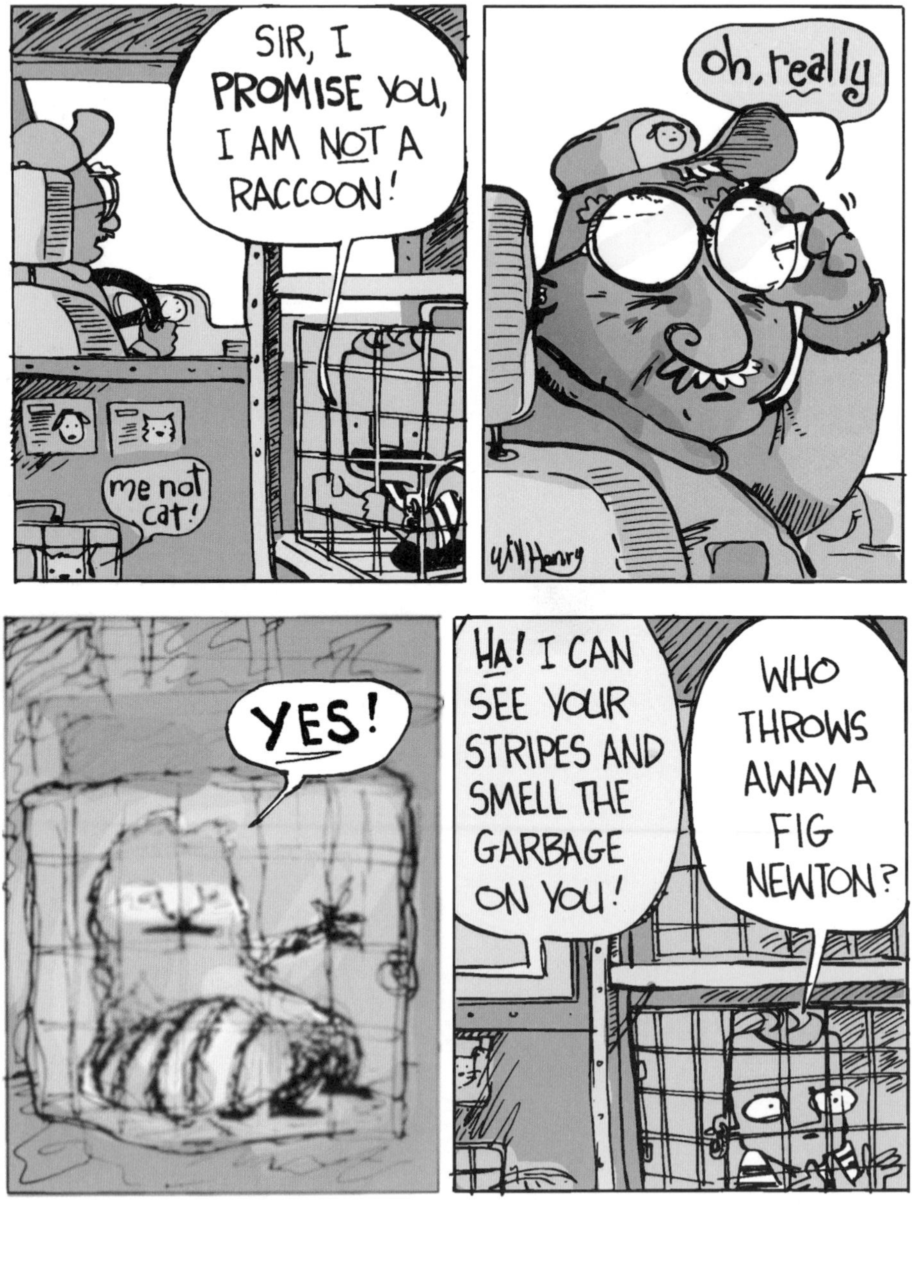
SIR, I PROMISE YOU, I AM NOT A RACCOON!
me not cat!
oh, really
Will Henry
YES!
HA! I CAN SEE YOUR STRIPES AND SMELL THE GARBAGE ON YOU!
WHO THROWS AWAY A FIG NEWTON?

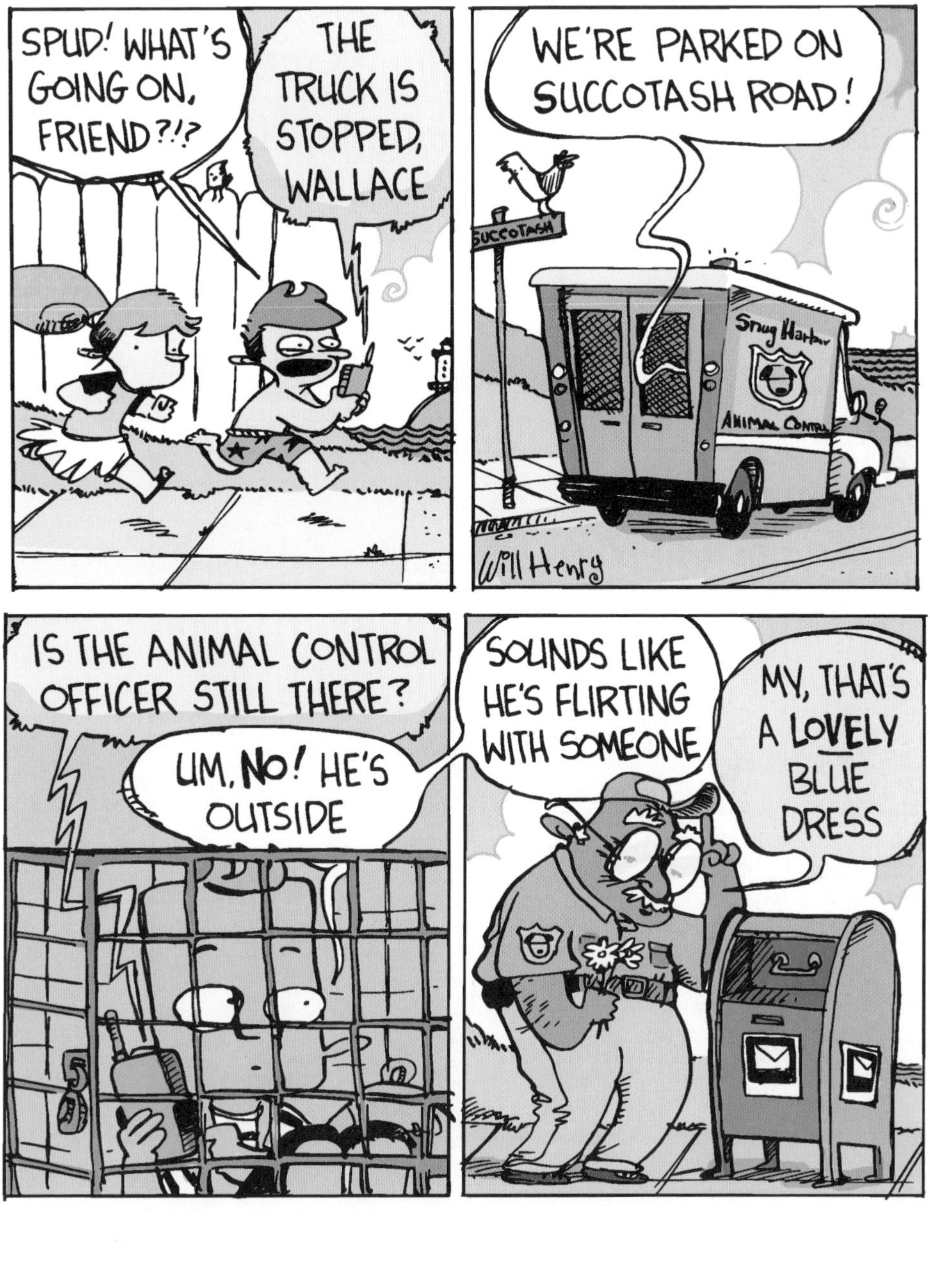
SPUD! WHAT'S GOING ON, FRIEND?!?
THE TRUCK IS STOPPED, WALLACE
WE'RE PARKED ON SUCCOTASH ROAD!
SUCCOTASH
Snug Harbor
Will Henry
IS THE ANIMAL CONTROL OFFICER STILL THERE?
UM, NO! HE'S OUTSIDE
SOUNDS LIKE HE'S FLIRTING WITH SOMEONE
MY, THAT'S A LOVELY BLUE DRESS

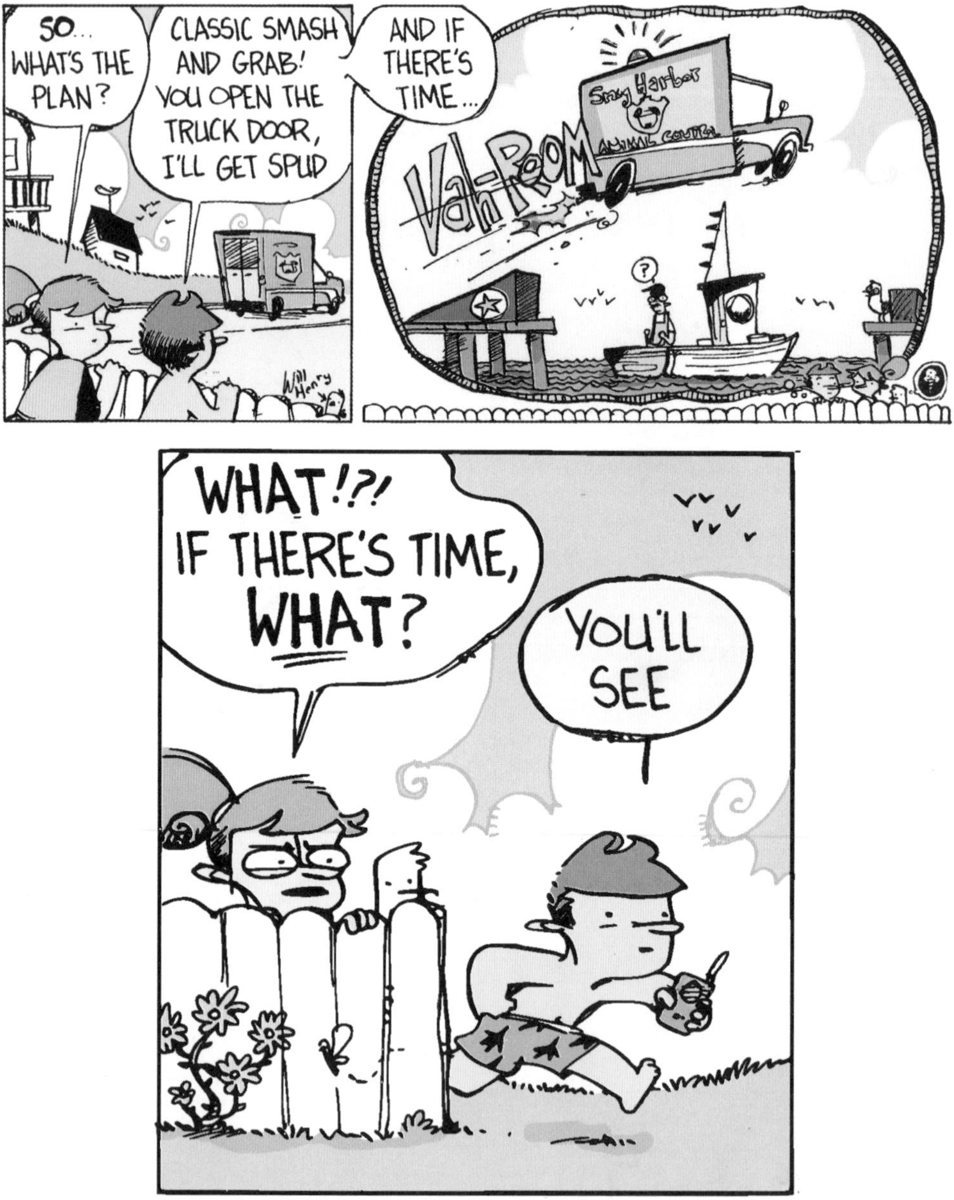
SO... WHAT'S THE PLAN?
CLASSIC SMASH AND GRAB! YOU OPEN THE TRUCK DOOR, I'LL GET SPUD
AND IF THERE'S TIME...
VAH-ROOM
WHAT!?! IF THERE'S TIME, WHAT?
YOU'LL SEE

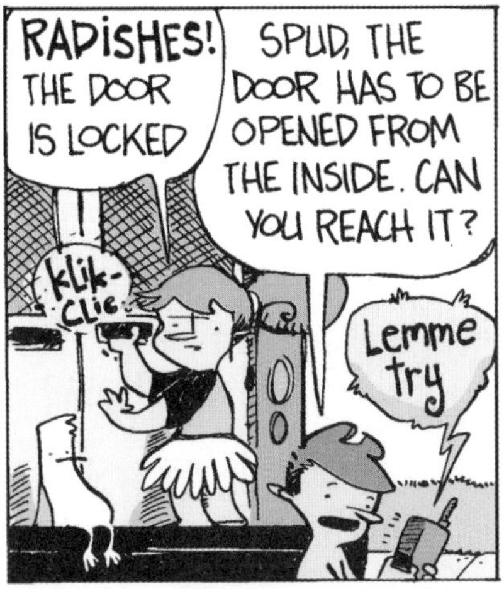
RADISHES! THE DOOR IS LOCKED
SPUD, THE DOOR HAS TO BE OPENED FROM THE INSIDE. CAN YOU REACH IT?
klik-clic
Lemme try

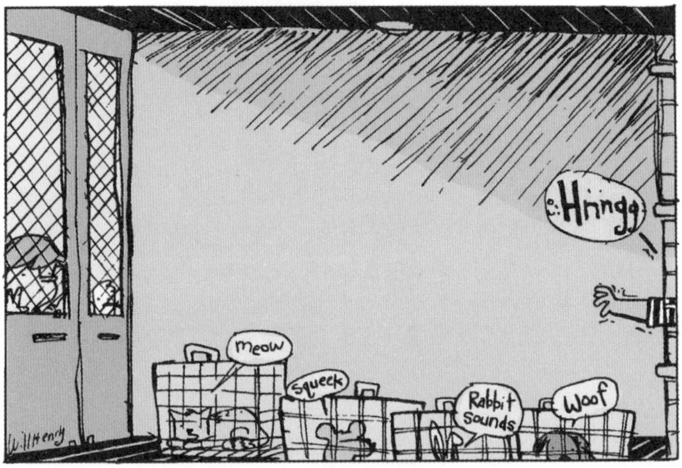
Hrnngg
meow
squeek
Rabbit sounds
woof
WillHenry

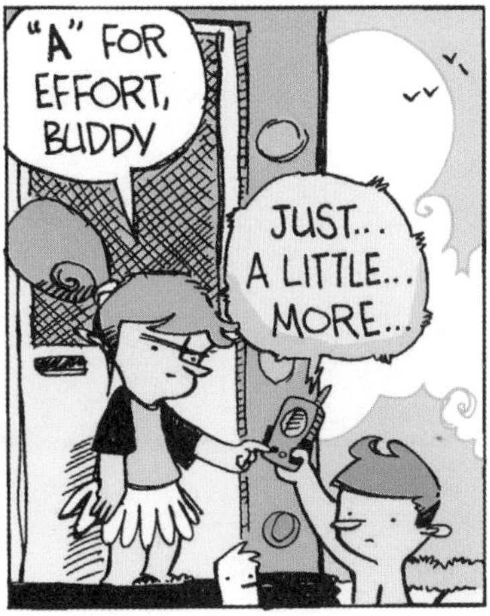
"A" FOR EFFORT, BUDDY
JUST... A LITTLE... MORE...

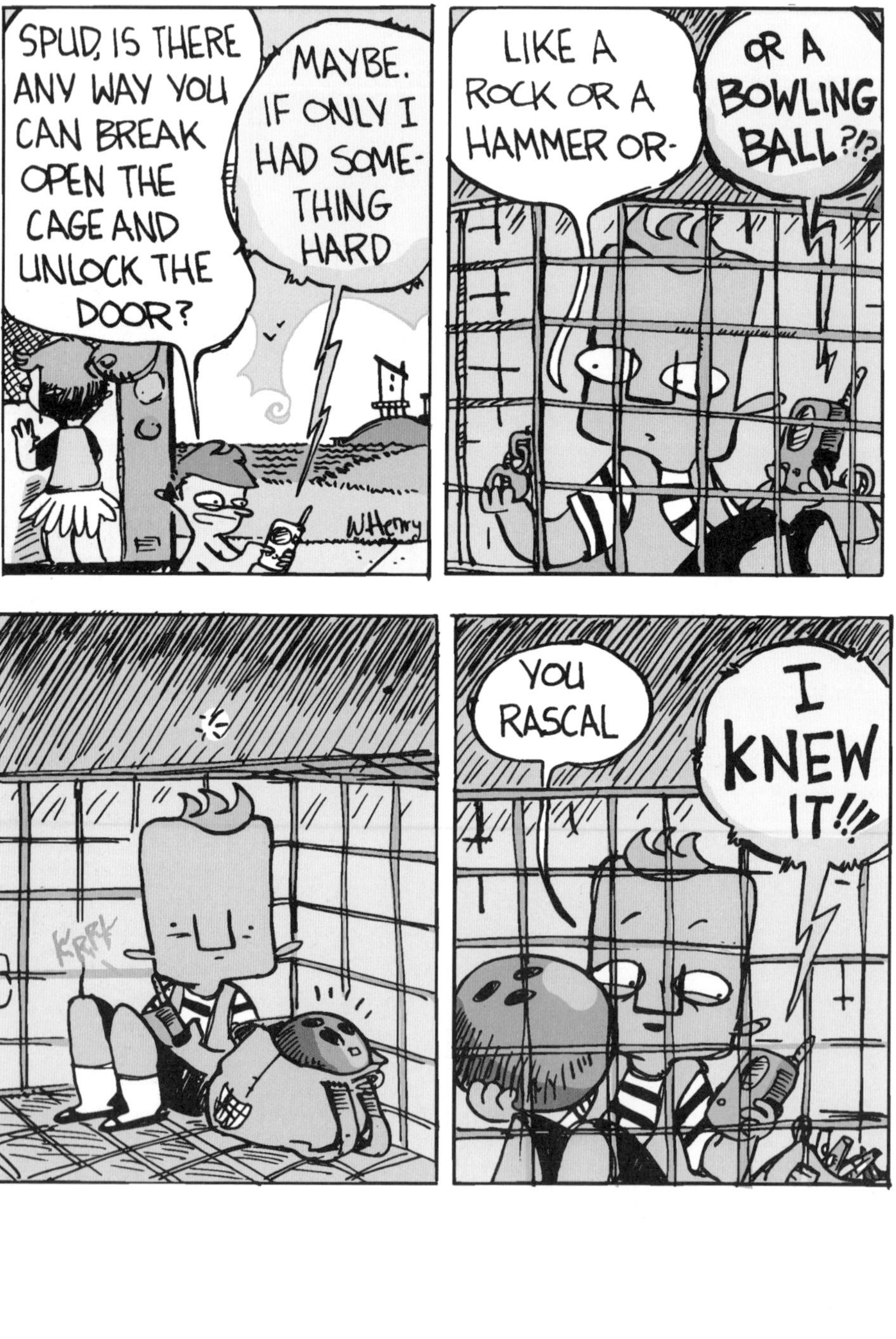
SPUD, IS THERE ANY WAY YOU CAN BREAK OPEN THE CAGE AND UNLOCK THE DOOR?
MAYBE. IF ONLY I HAD SOME-THING HARD
W.Henry
LIKE A ROCK OR A HAMMER OR-
OR A BOWLING BALL?!?
KRRK
YOU RASCAL
I KNEW IT!!!

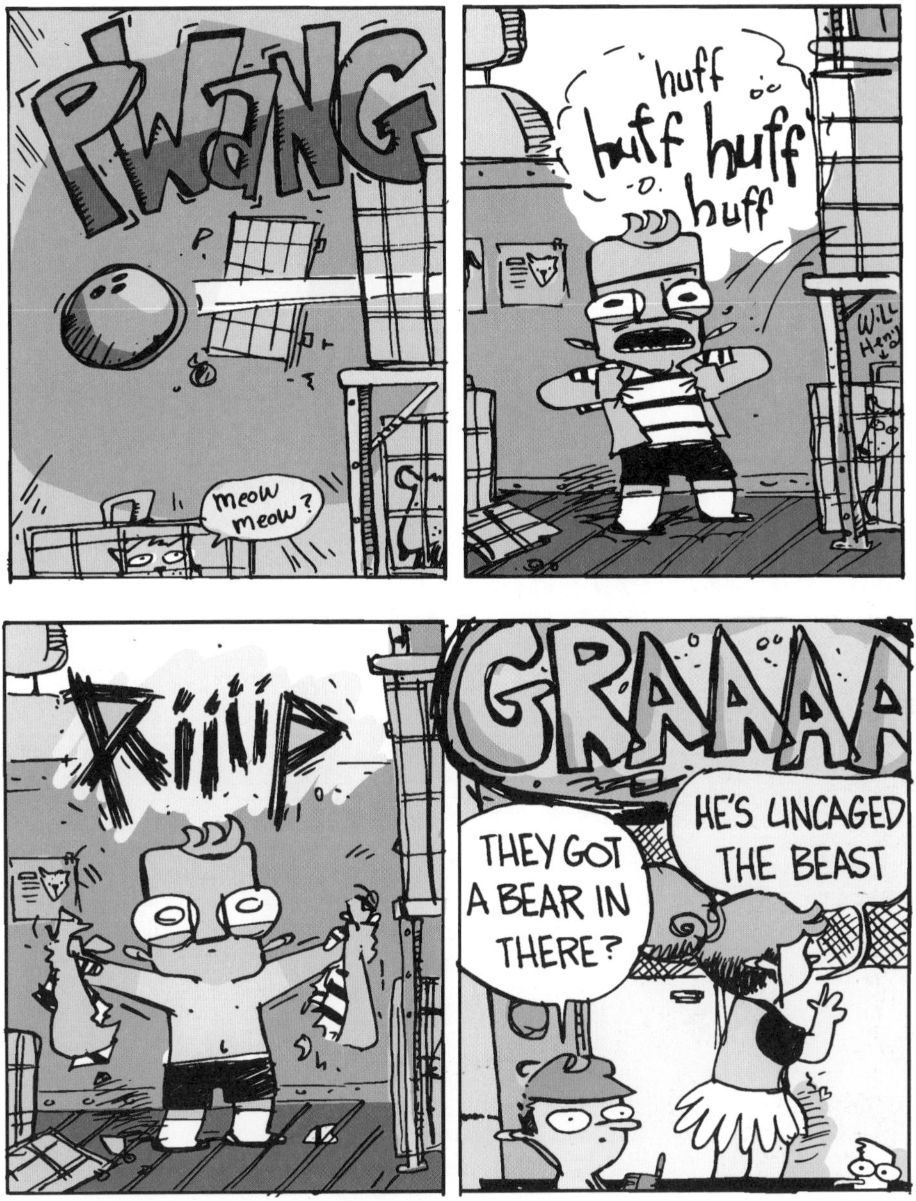
PWANG
meow meow?
huff
huff huff
huff
W.LL Henry
RIIIP
GRAAAA
THEY GOT A BEAR IN THERE?
HE'S UNCAGED THE BEAST

HA HA! I FEEL SO ALIVE! NOW WHAT?
I DUNNO, GO HOME AND HAVE DINNER?
SOUNDS LIKE AN INVITE!
IT IS NOT.
I'LL PROBABLY TAKE THIS BOWLING BALL AND BUST OPEN THE REST OF THE CAGES
VERY GOOD!
SEE YA TOMORROW!
CLANG
Will "Save The Animals" Henry

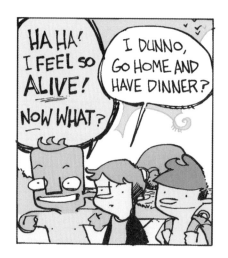

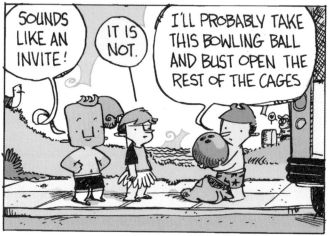

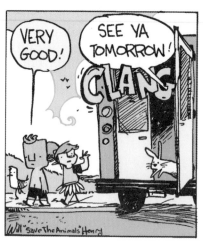

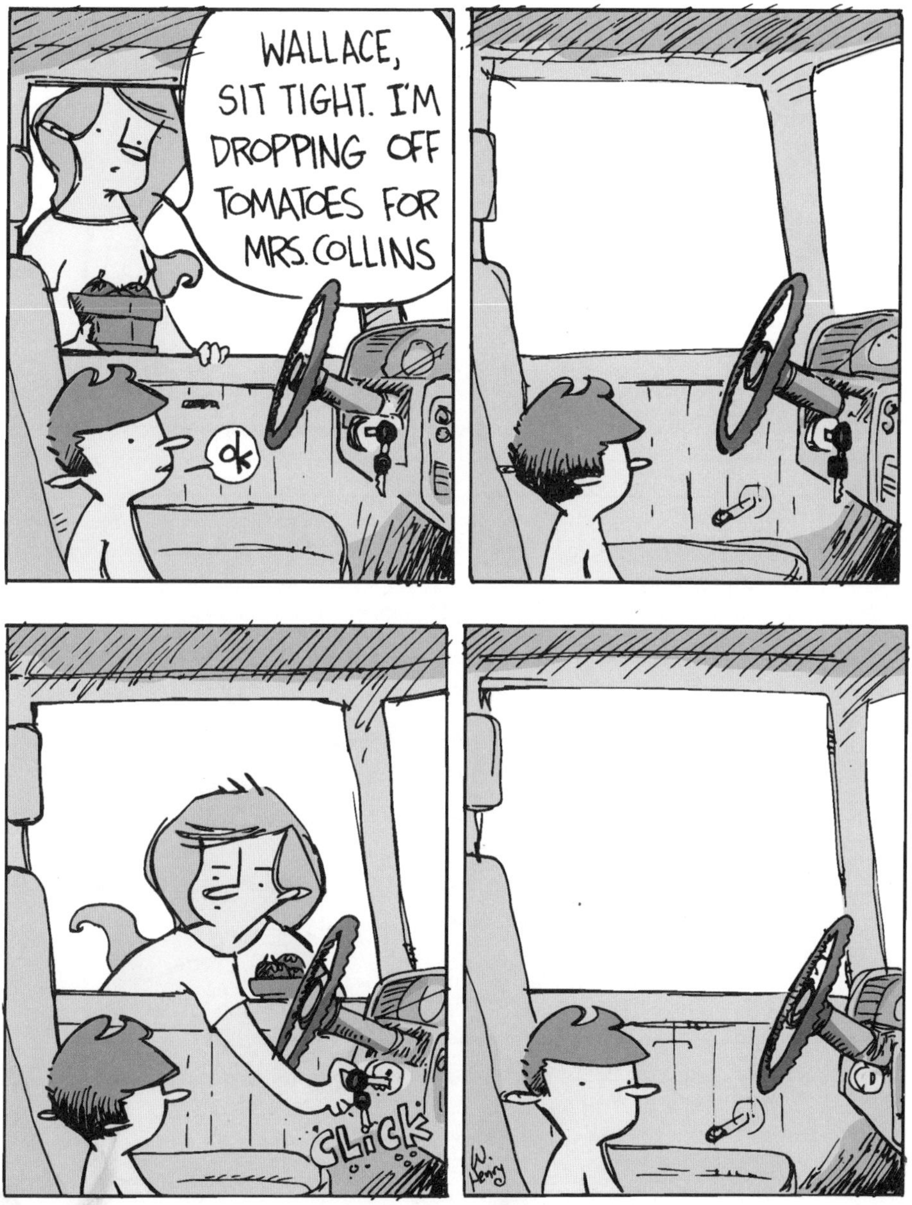
WALLACE, SIT TIGHT. I'M DROPPING OFF TOMATOES FOR MRS. COLLINS
ok
CLICK
W. Henry

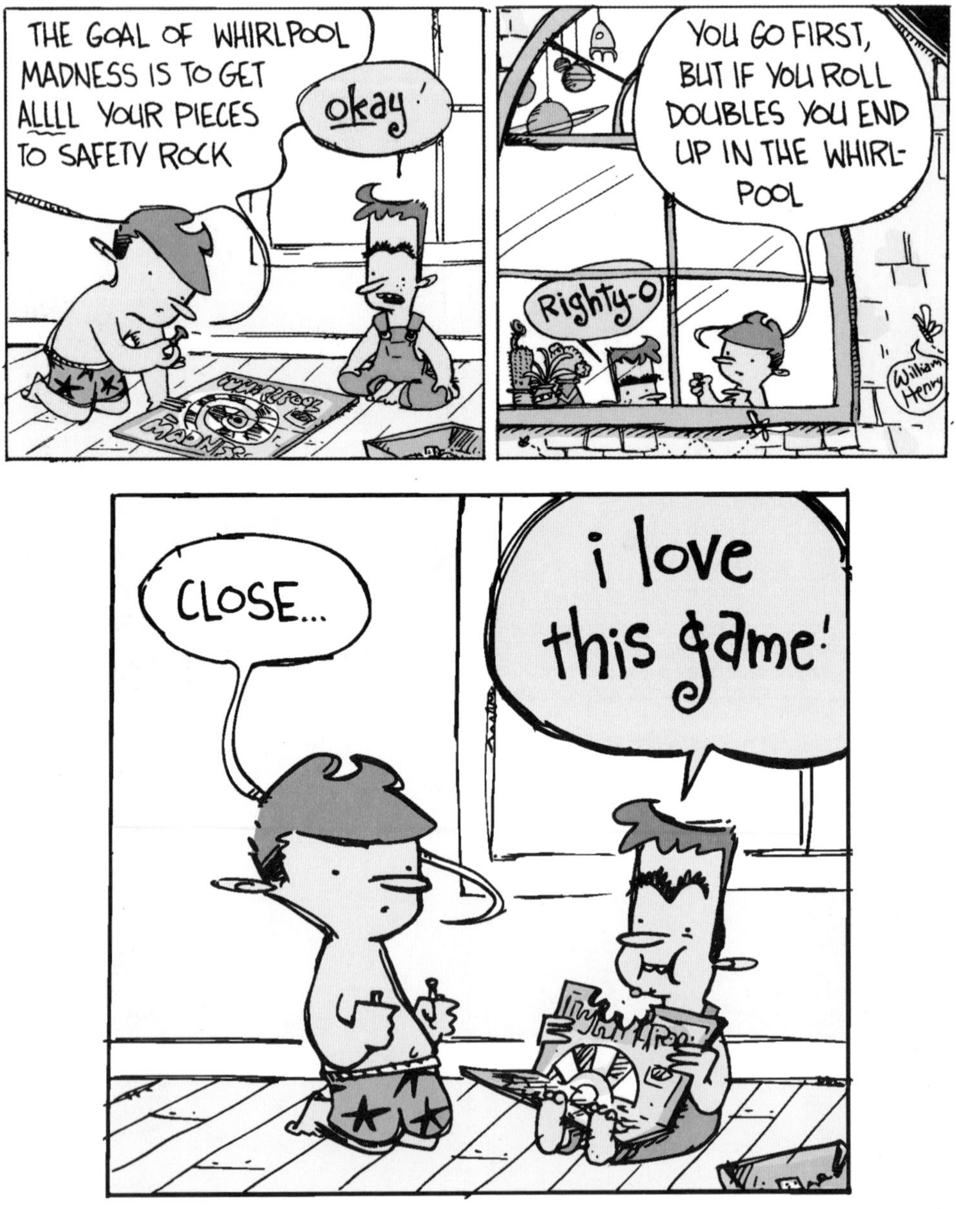
THE GOAL OF WHIRLPOOL MADNESS IS TO GET ALLLL YOUR PIECES TO SAFETY ROCK
okay!
YOU GO FIRST, BUT IF YOU ROLL DOUBLES YOU END UP IN THE WHIRL-POOL
Righty-O
William Henry
CLOSE...
i love this game!

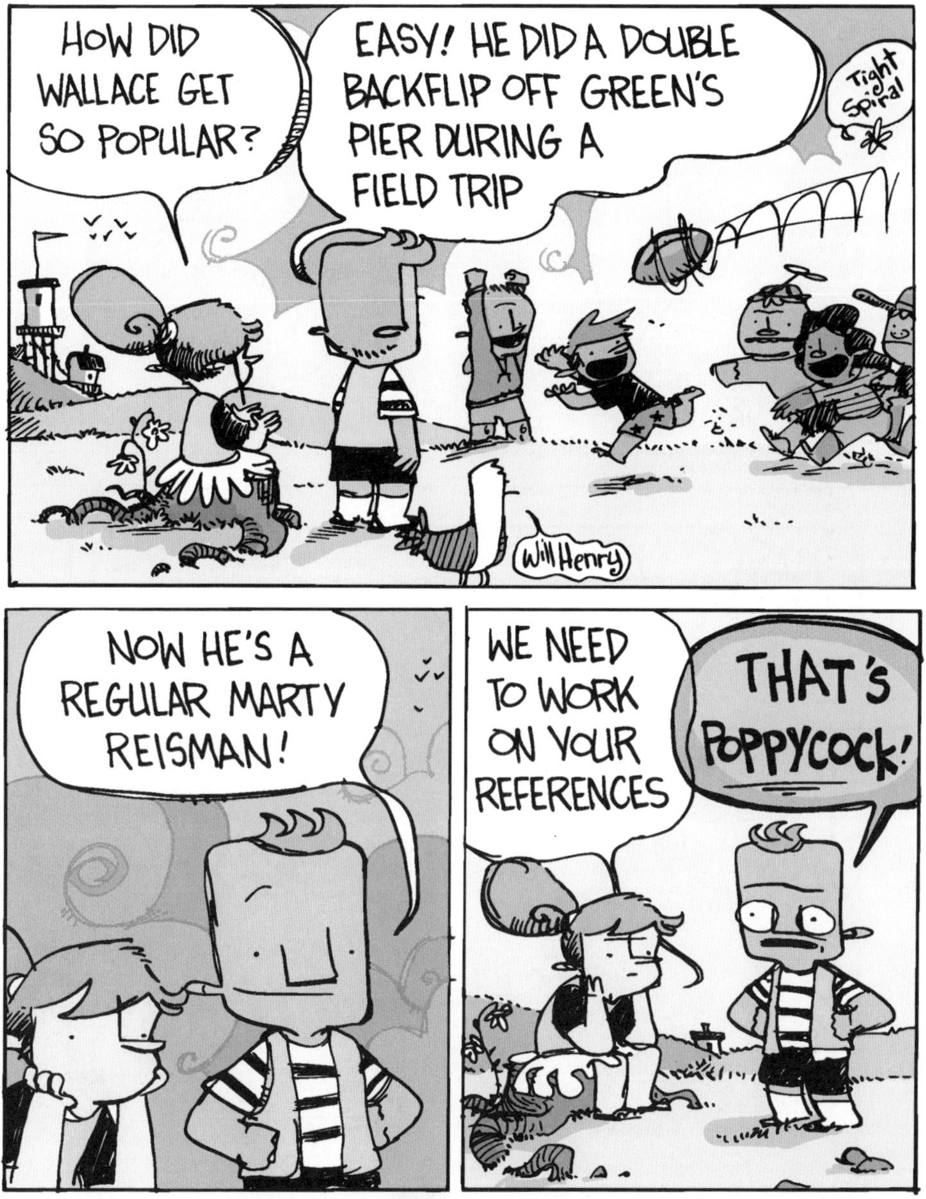
HOW DID WALLACE GET SO POPULAR?
EASY! HE DID A DOUBLE BACKFLIP OFF GREEN'S PIER DURING A FIELD TRIP
Tight Spiral
Will Henry
NOW HE'S A REGULAR MARTY REISMAN!
WE NEED TO WORK ON YOUR REFERENCES
THAT'S POPPYCOCK!

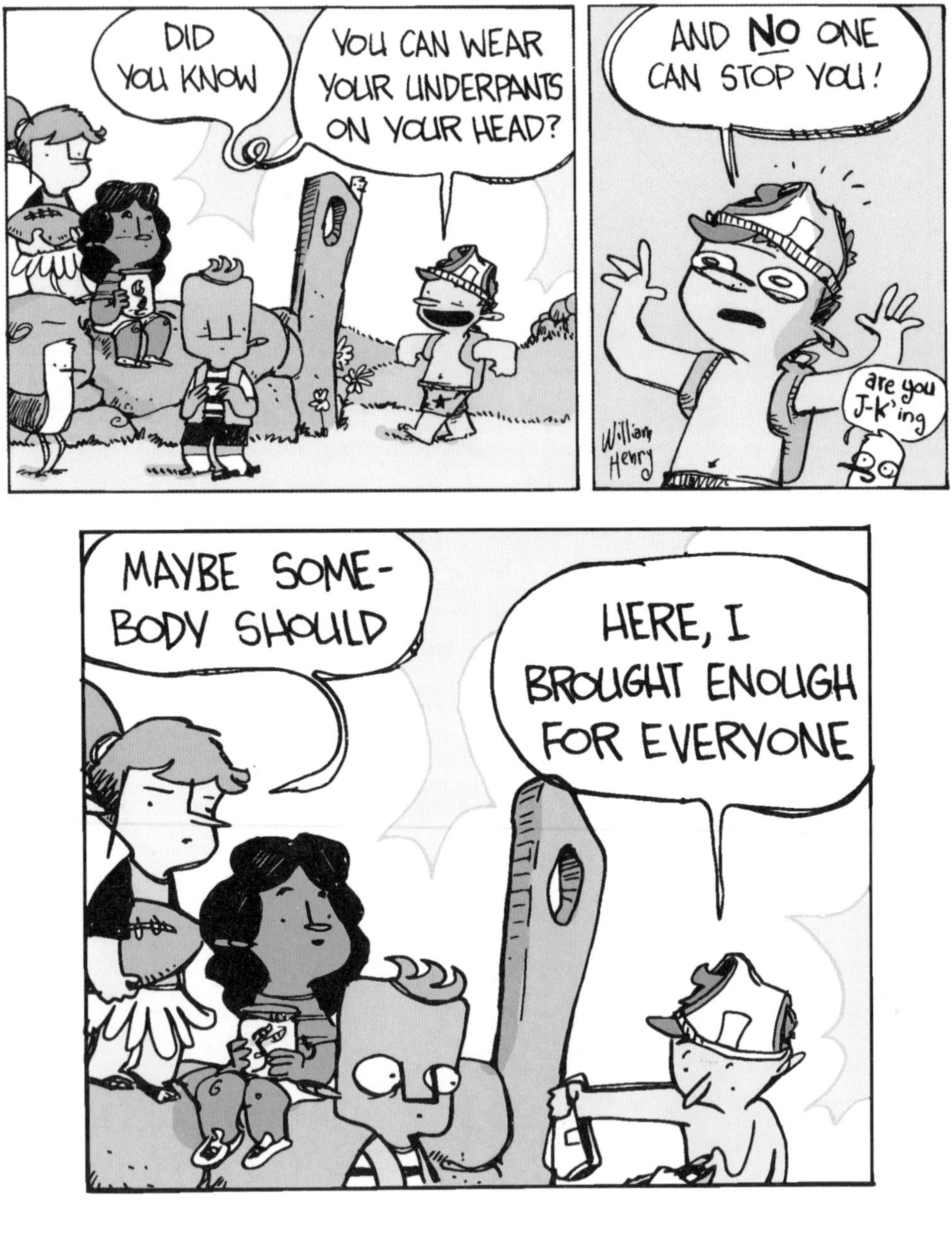
DID YOU KNOW
YOU CAN WEAR YOUR UNDERPANTS ON YOUR HEAD?
AND NO ONE CAN STOP YOU!
are you J-K'ing
William Henry
MAYBE SOME-BODY SHOULD
HERE, I BROUGHT ENOUGH FOR EVERYONE

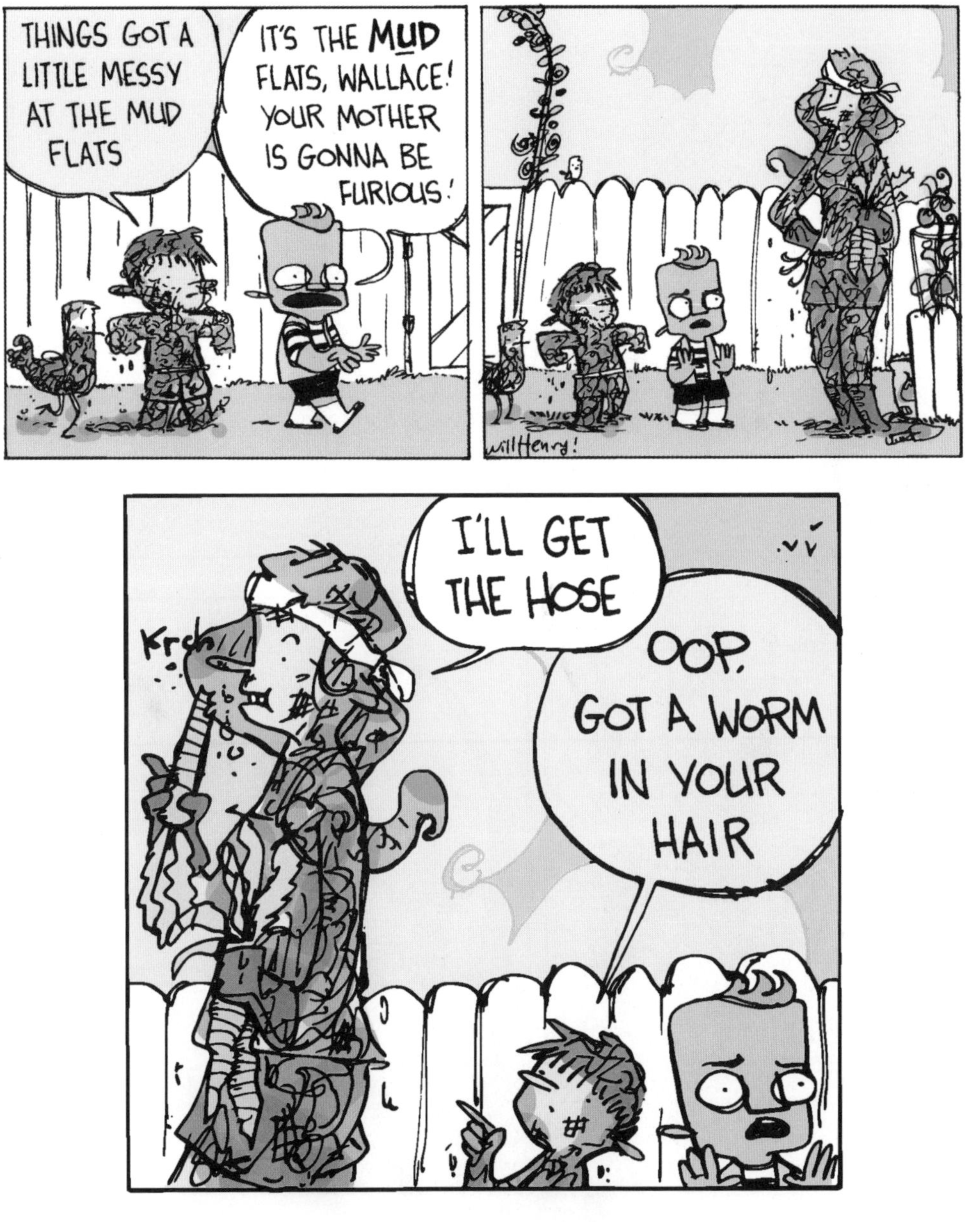
THINGS GOT A LITTLE MESSY AT THE MUD FLATS
IT'S THE MUD FLATS, WALLACE! YOUR MOTHER IS GONNA BE FURIOUS!
willHenry!
Krch
I'LL GET THE HOSE
OOP. GOT A WORM IN YOUR HAIR

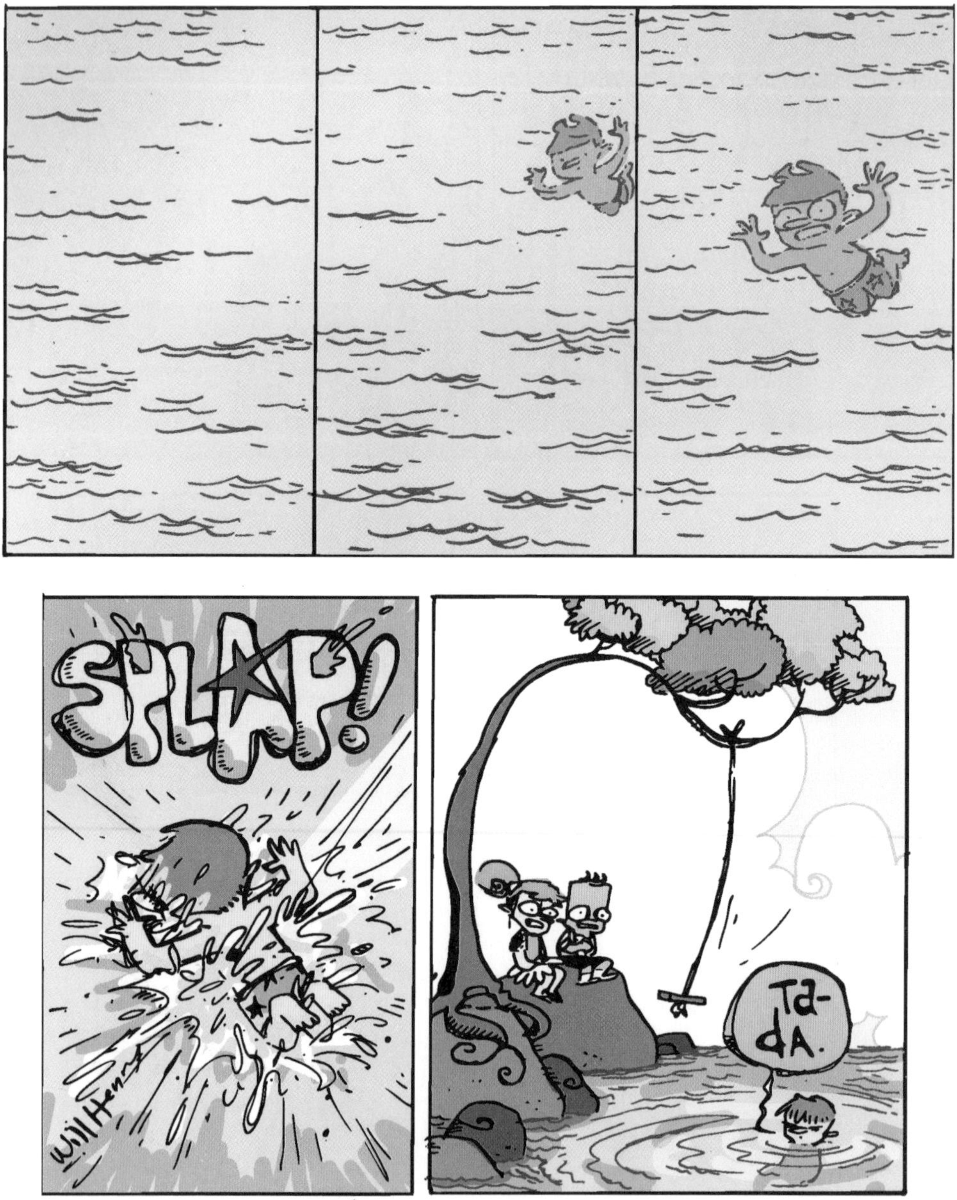
SPLAP!
Will Henry
Ta-da.

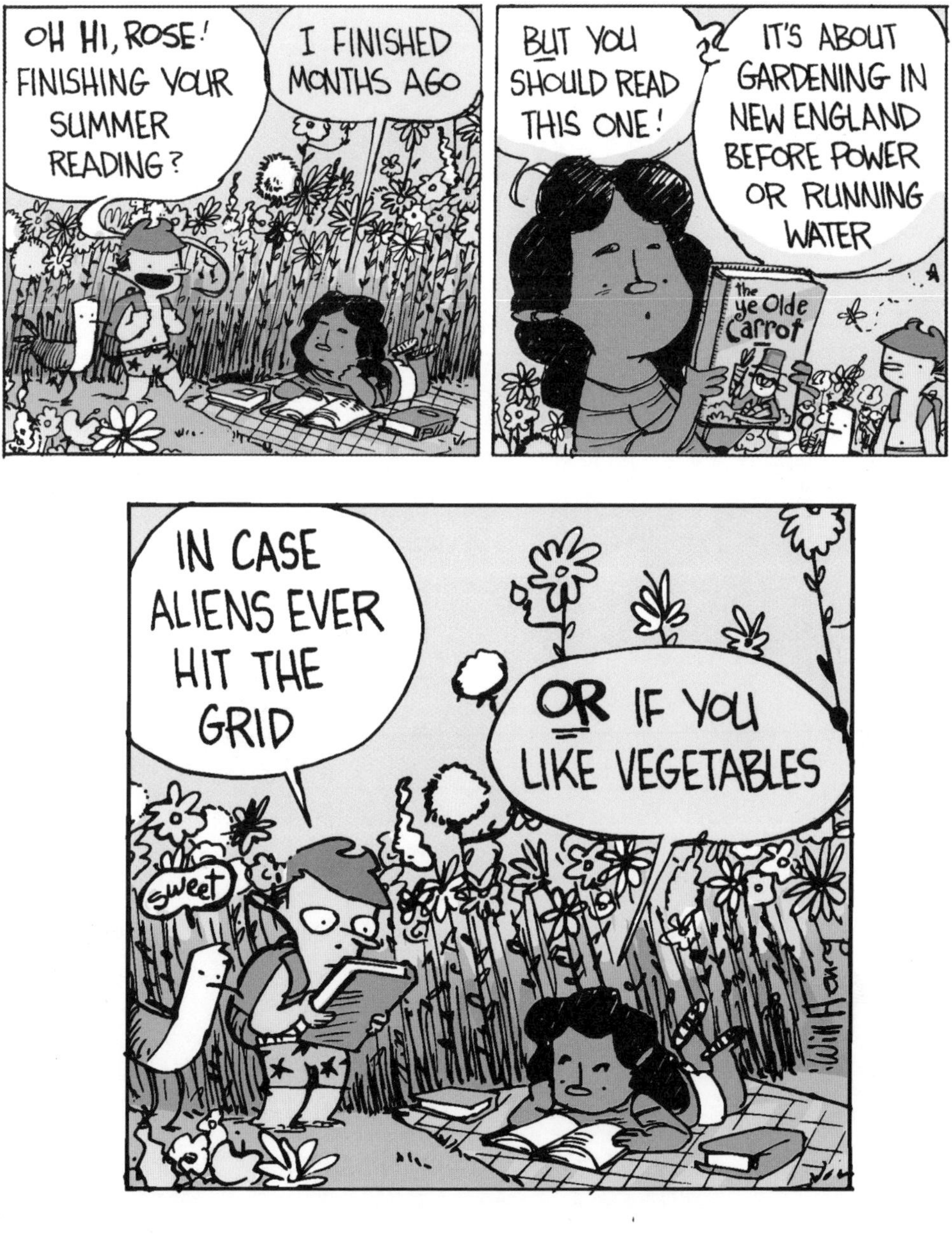
OH HI, ROSE! FINISHING YOUR SUMMER READING?
I FINISHED MONTHS AGO
BUT YOU SHOULD READ THIS ONE!
IT'S ABOUT GARDENING IN NEW ENGLAND BEFORE POWER OR RUNNING WATER
the ye Olde Carrot
IN CASE ALIENS EVER HIT THE GRID
OR IF YOU LIKE VEGETABLES
sweet
Will Henry

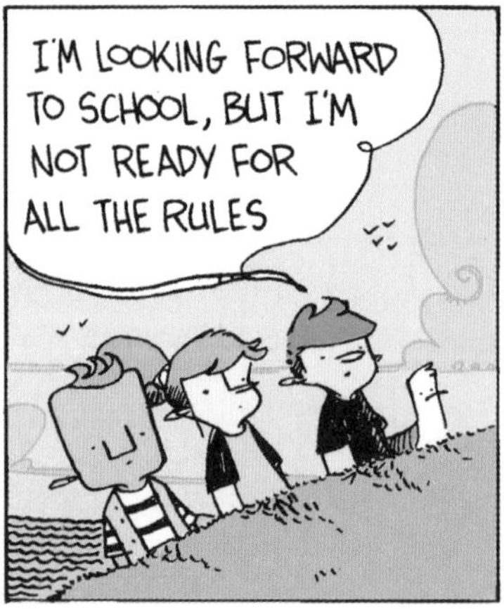
I'M LOOKING FORWARD TO SCHOOL, BUT I'M NOT READY FOR ALL THE RULES

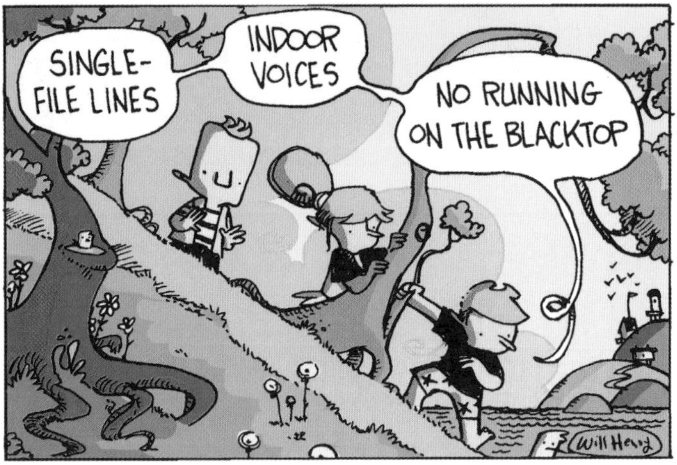
SINGLE-FILE LINES
INDOOR VOICES
NO RUNNING ON THE BLACKTOP

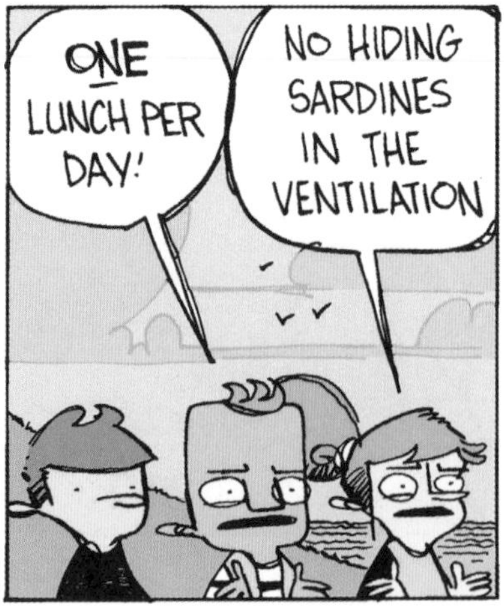
ONE LUNCH PER DAY!
NO HIDING SARDINES IN THE VENTILATION

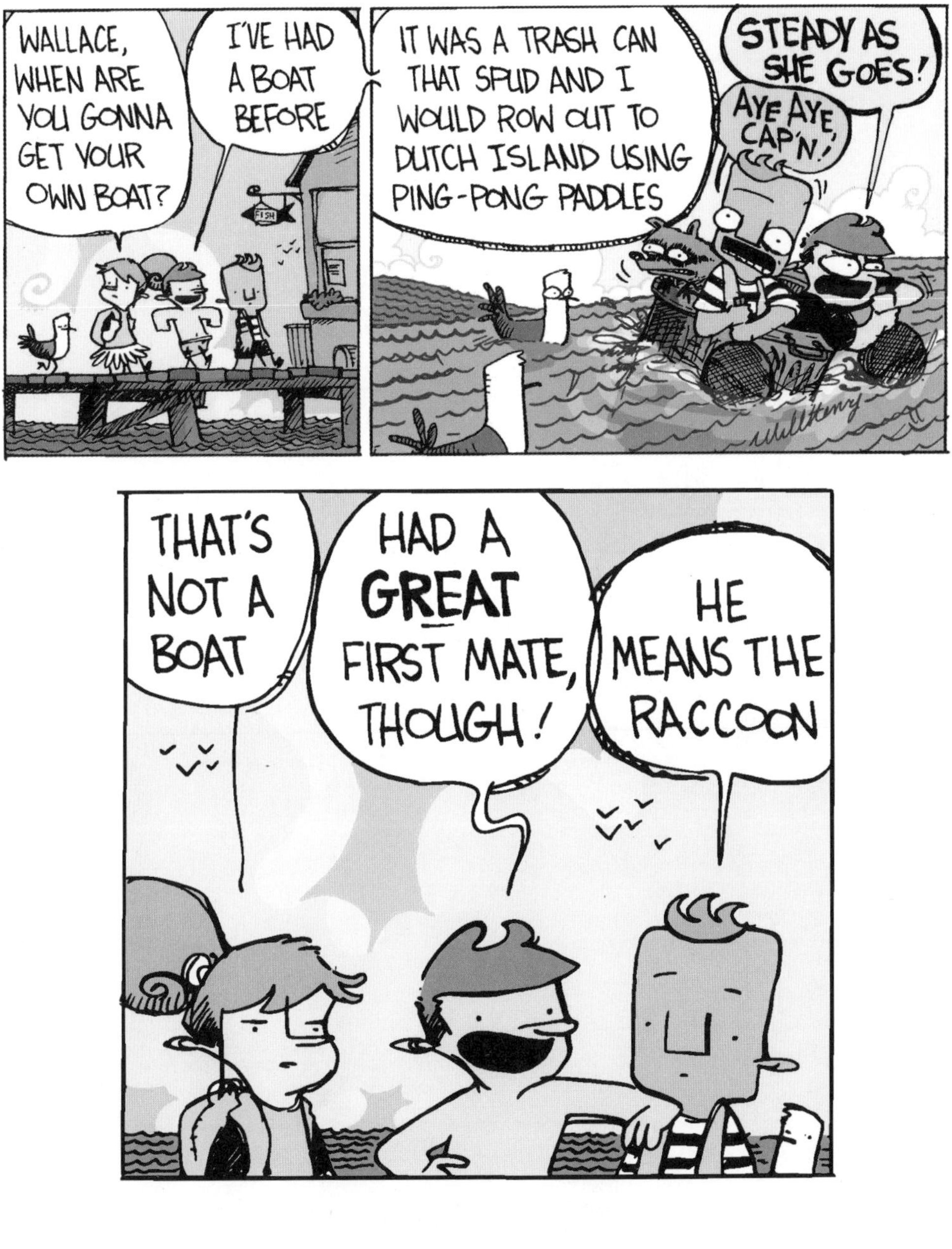

WALLACE, WHEN ARE YOU GONNA GET YOUR OWN BOAT?
I'VE HAD A BOAT BEFORE
IT WAS A TRASH CAN THAT SPUD AND I WOULD ROW OUT TO DUTCH ISLAND USING PING-PONG PADDLES
STEADY AS SHE GOES!
AYE AYE, CAP'N!
FISH
THAT'S NOT A BOAT
HAD A GREAT FIRST MATE, THOUGH!
HE MEANS THE RACCOON

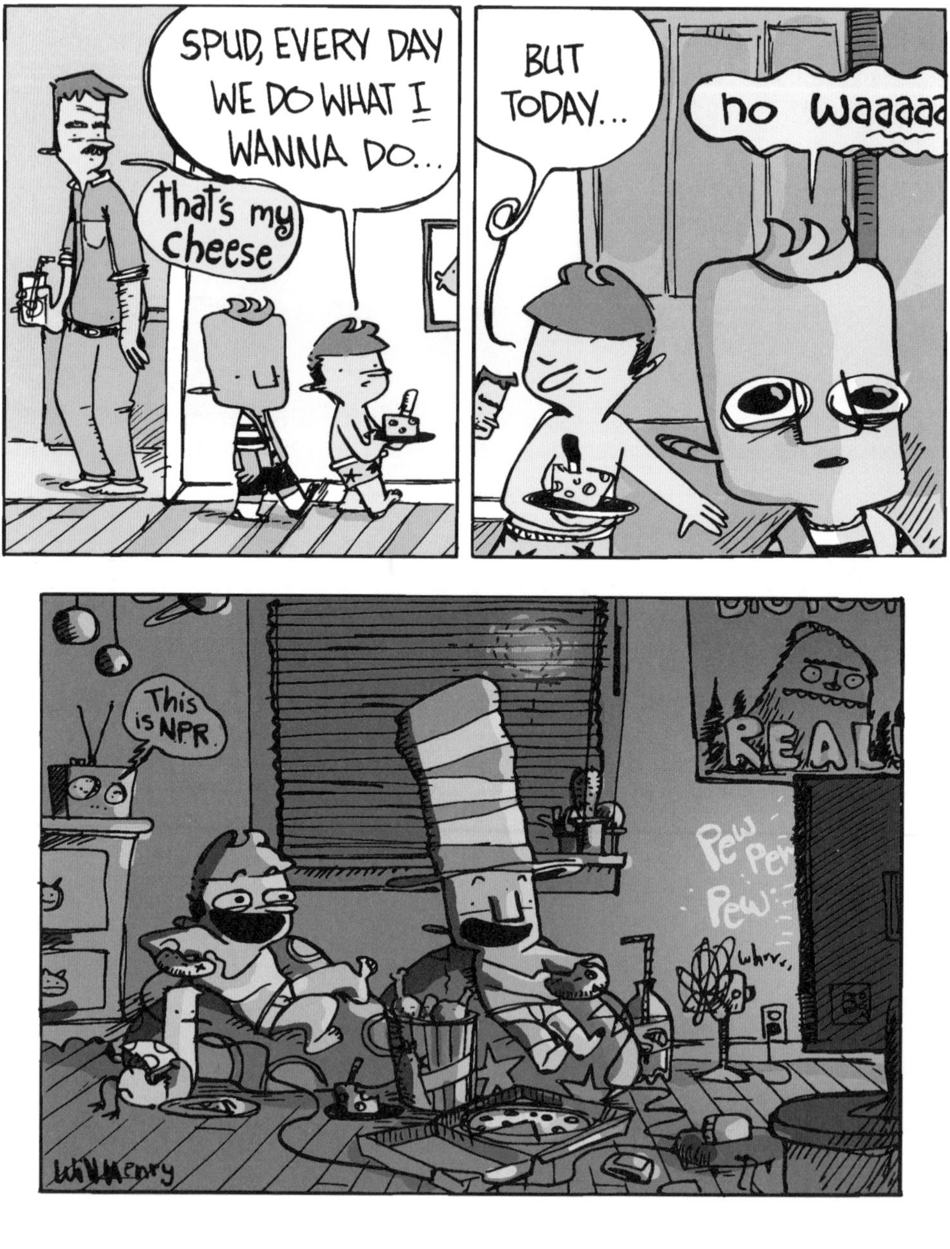
SPUD, EVERY DAY WE DO WHAT I WANNA DO...
that's my cheese
BUT TODAY...
no waaaaa
This is NPR.
REAL
Pew Pew Pew

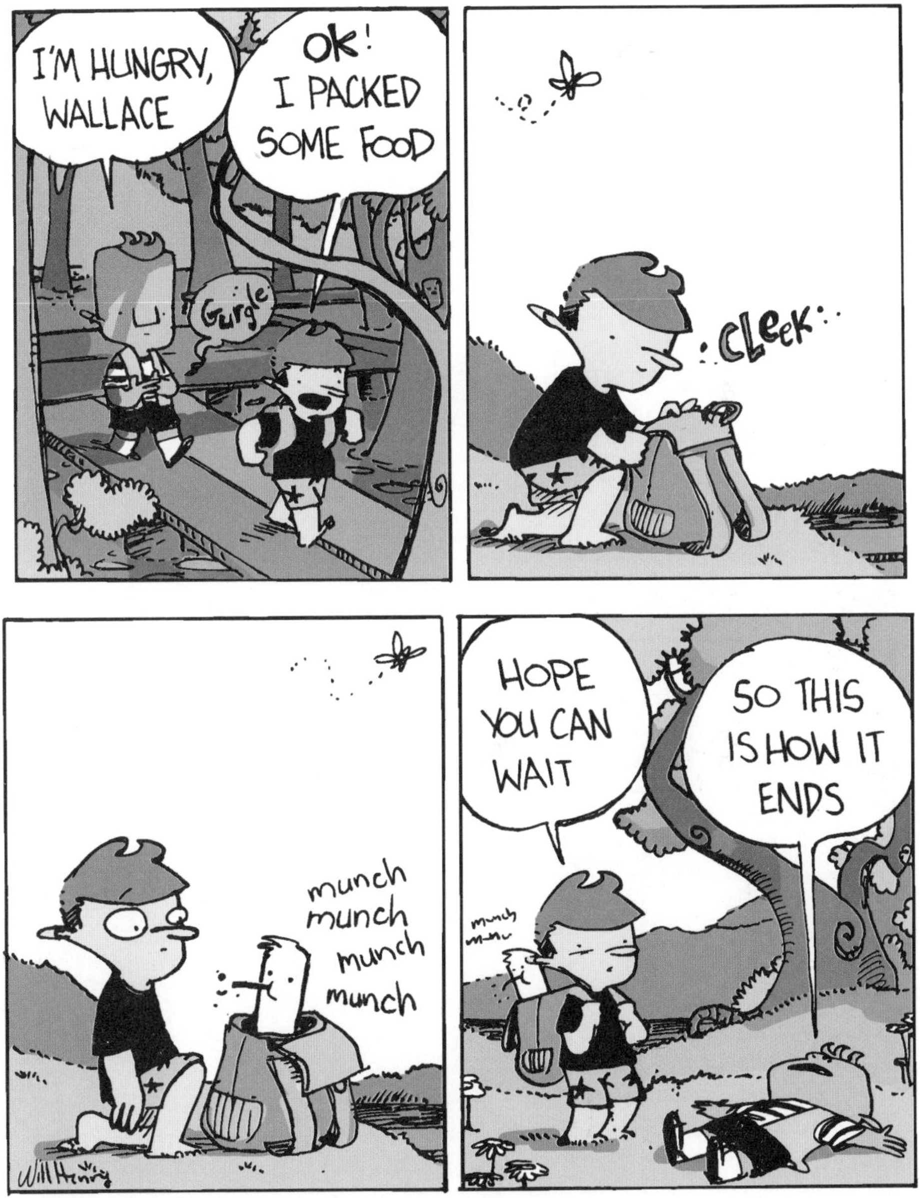
I'M HUNGRY, WALLACE
OK! I PACKED SOME FOOD
Gurgle
CLEEK
munch munch munch munch
Will Henry
HOPE YOU CAN WAIT
SO THIS IS HOW IT ENDS

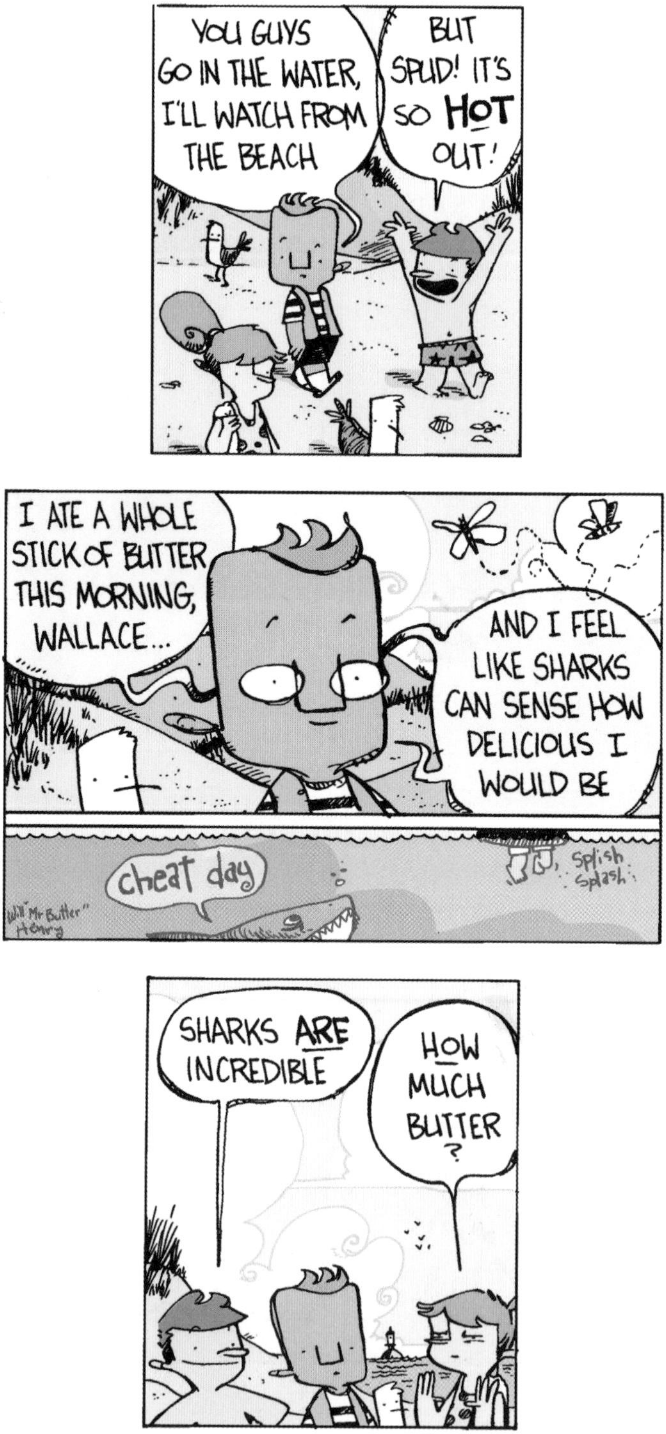
YOU GUYS GO IN THE WATER, I'LL WATCH FROM THE BEACH
BUT SPUD! IT'S SO HOT OUT!
I ATE A WHOLE STICK OF BUTTER THIS MORNING, WALLACE...
AND I FEEL LIKE SHARKS CAN SENSE HOW DELICIOUS I WOULD BE
cheat day
Splish Splash
Will "Mr Butter" Henry
SHARKS ARE INCREDIBLE
HOW MUCH BUTTER?

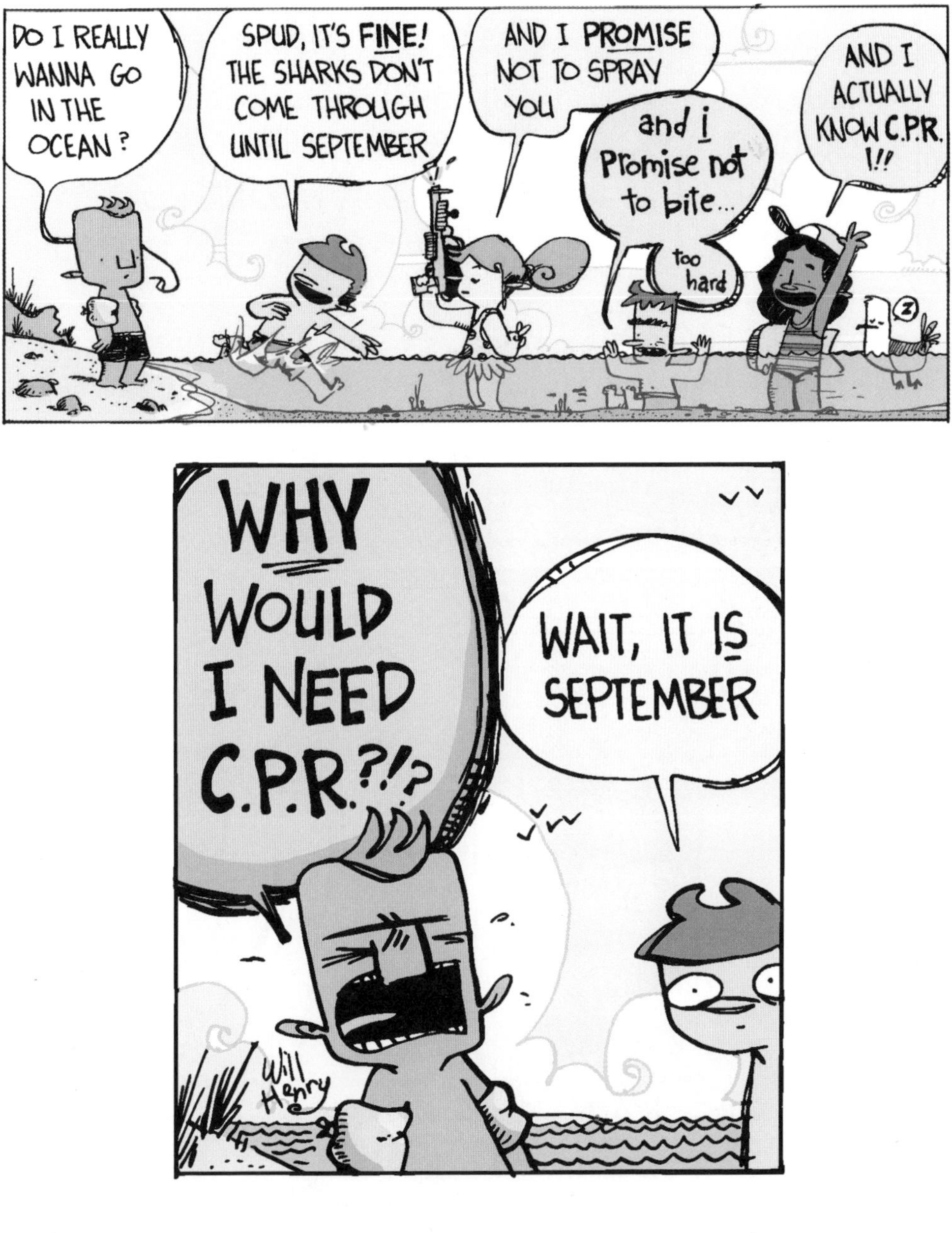
DO I REALLY WANNA GO IN THE OCEAN ?
SPUD, IT'S FINE! THE SHARKS DON'T COME THROUGH UNTIL SEPTEMBER
AND I PROMISE NOT TO SPRAY YOU
and i Promise not to bite...
too hard
AND I ACTUALLY KNOW C.P.R. !!!
WHY WOULD I NEED C.P.R.?!?
WAIT, IT IS SEPTEMBER
Will Henry

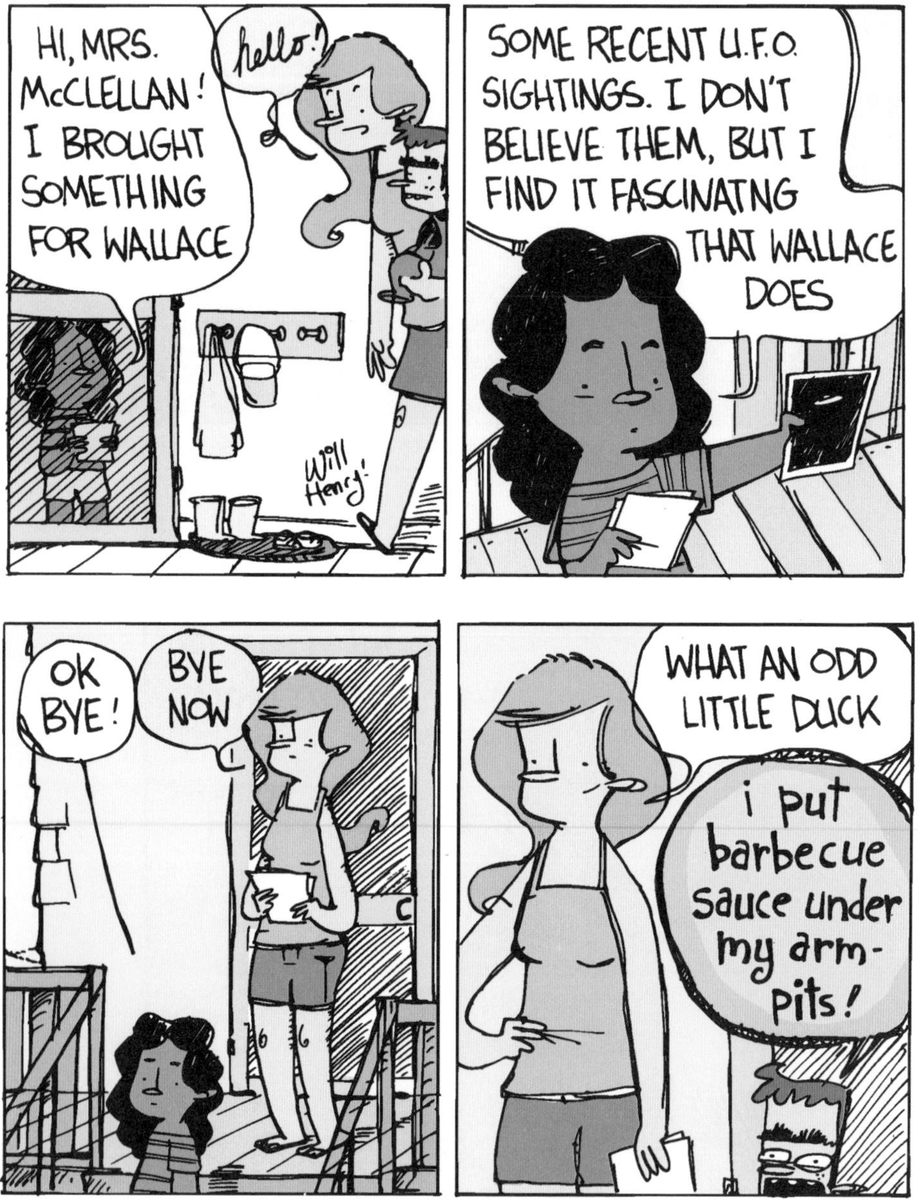
HI, MRS. McCLELLAN! I BROUGHT SOMETHING FOR WALLACE
hello!
Will Henry!
SOME RECENT U.F.O. SIGHTINGS. I DON'T BELIEVE THEM, BUT I FIND IT FASCINATNG THAT WALLACE DOES
OK BYE!
BYE NOW
WHAT AN ODD LITTLE DUCK
i put barbecue sauce under my arm-pits!

I WISH MORE PEOPLE CARRIED AROUND ROTTEN VEGETABLES
Will "Human Cabbage" Henry
LIKE IN MEDIEVAL TIMES, WHEN YOU ALWAYS HAD SOMETHING TO THROW AT PEOPLE
ouch-eth
I HAVE SOME KETCHUP PACKETS
IF I DIDN'T LIKE YOU -BOOM- CABBAGE TO THE FACE!

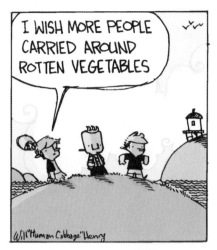

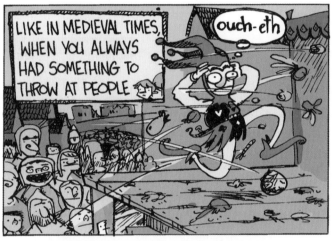

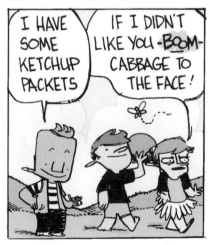

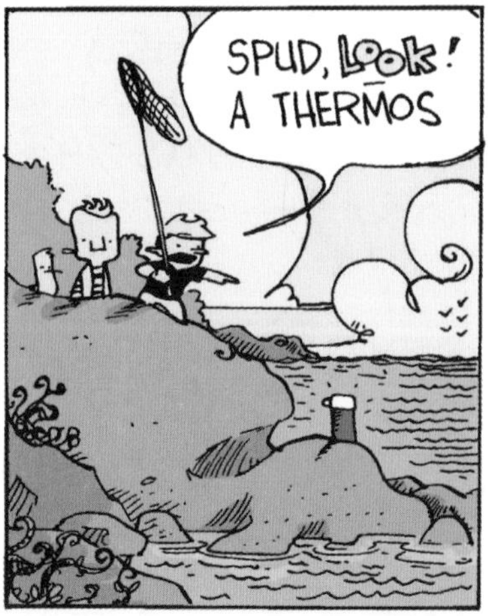
SPUD, LOOK! A THERMOS

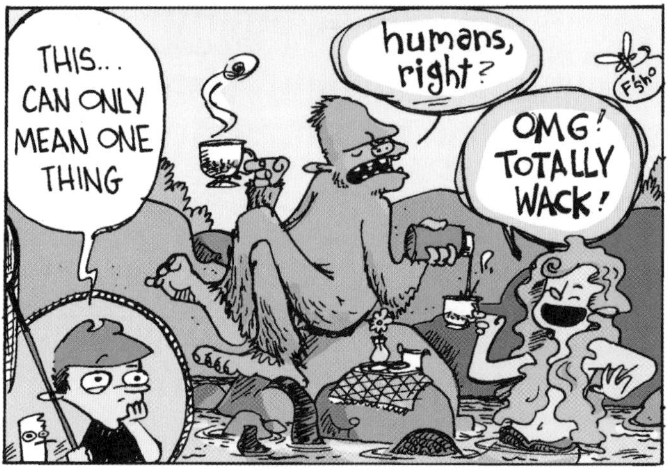
THIS... CAN ONLY MEAN ONE THING
humans, right?
F'sho
OMG! TOTALLY WACK!

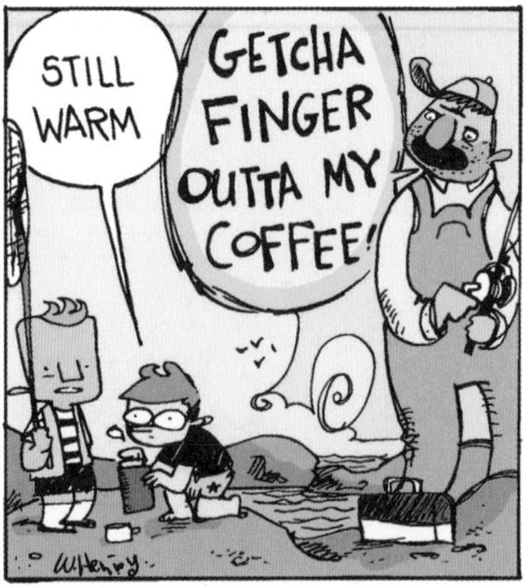
STILL WARM
GETCHA FINGER OUTTA MY COFFEE!

YOU GUYS FIND ANY BEACH GLASS?
POCKETS FULL
BEACH GLASS COMES FROM MERMAIDS
THEY COUGH IT UP LIKE HAIRBALLS, AND THE CURRENTS BRING IT TO SHORE
HEACK
ew.
yuck
Will Henry!
WHY AM I TOUCHING THESE?
REALLY?!? DID THEY FART OUT THESE ROCKS?

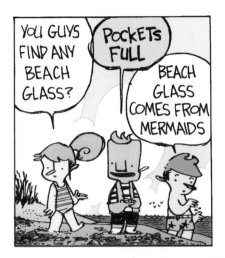

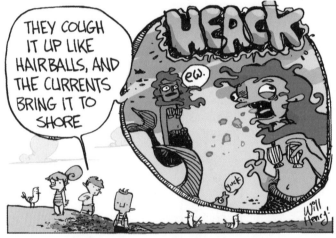

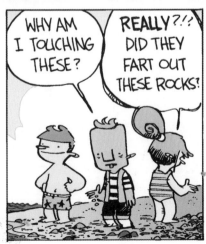

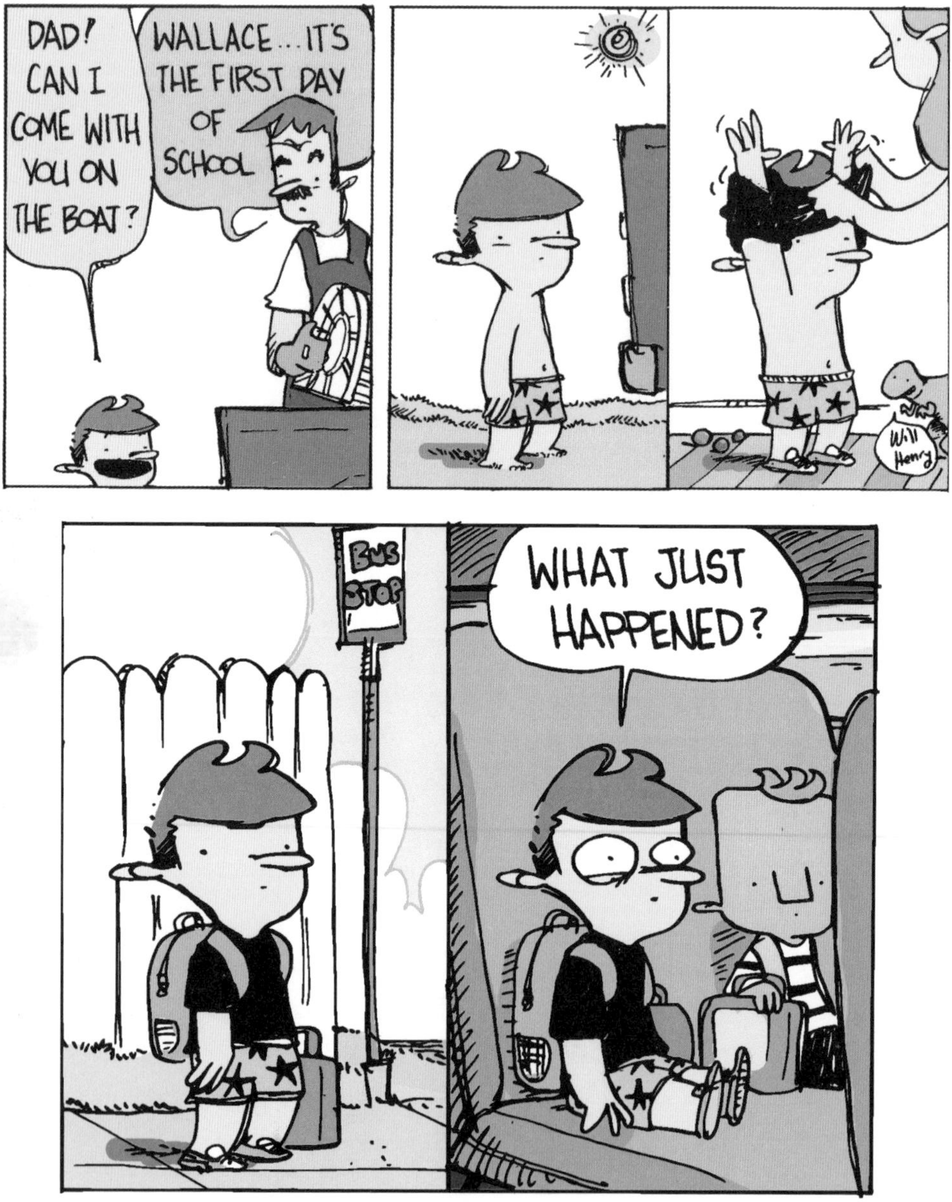
DAD! CAN I COME WITH YOU ON THE BOAT?
WALLACE... IT'S THE FIRST DAY OF SCHOOL
Will Henry
BUS STOP
WHAT JUST HAPPENED?

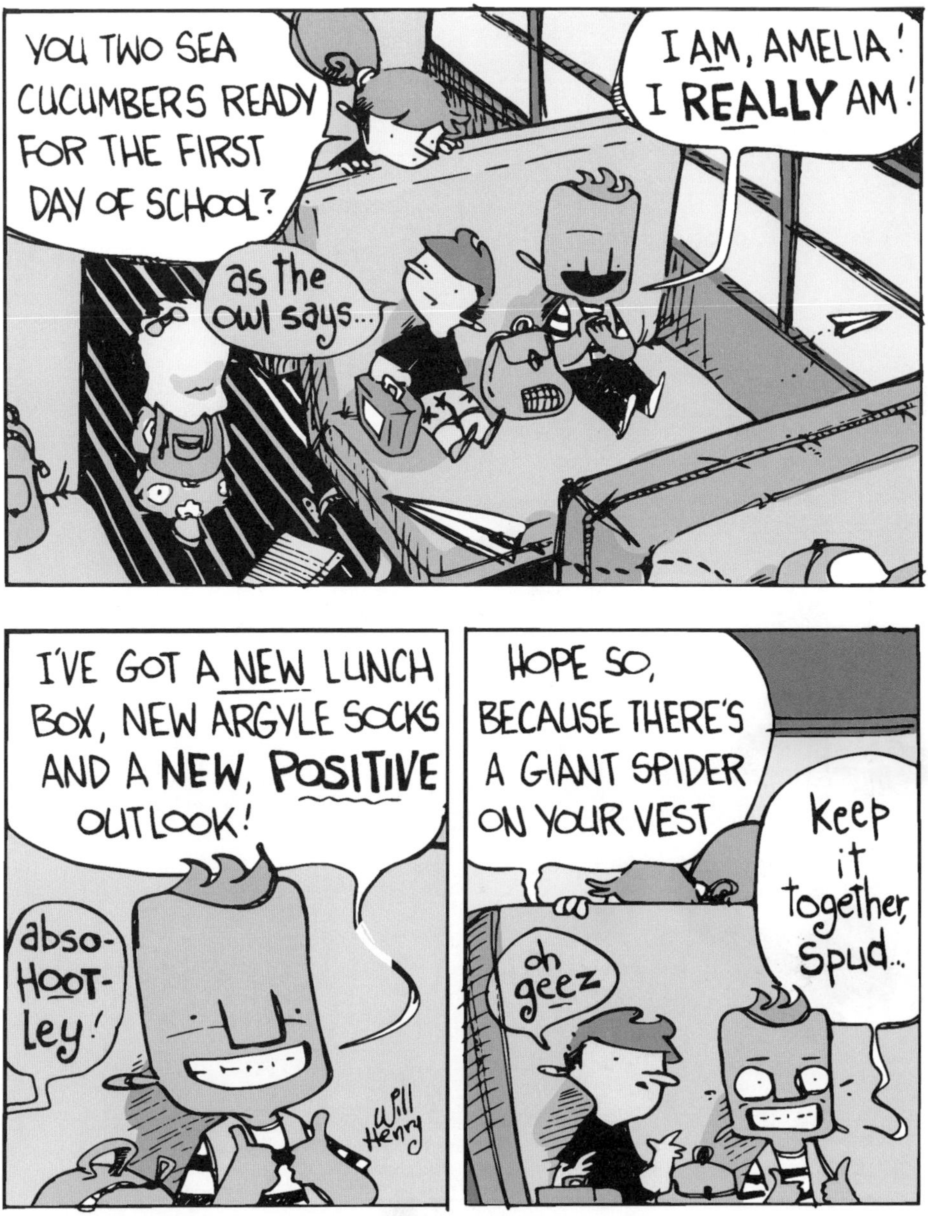

YOU TWO SEA CUCUMBERS READY FOR THE FIRST DAY OF SCHOOL?
I AM, AMELIA! I REALLY AM!
as the owl says...
I'VE GOT A NEW LUNCH BOX, NEW ARGYLE SOCKS AND A NEW, POSITIVE OUTLOOK!
abso-HOOT-ley!
Will Henry
HOPE SO, BECAUSE THERE'S A GIANT SPIDER ON YOUR VEST
Keep it together, Spud...
oh geez

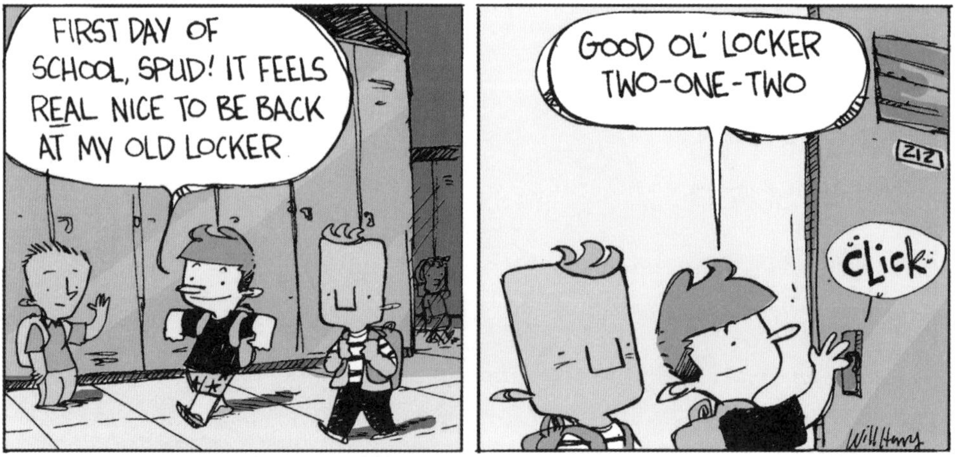
FIRST DAY OF SCHOOL, SPUD! IT FEELS REAL NICE TO BE BACK AT MY OLD LOCKER
GOOD OL' LOCKER TWO-ONE-TWO
212
CLICK
Will Henry

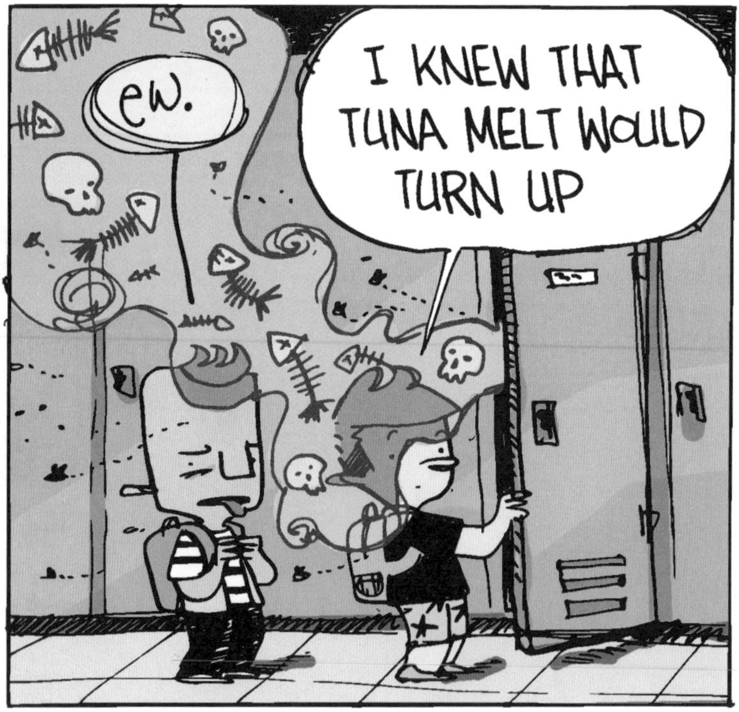
ew.
I KNEW THAT TUNA MELT WOULD TURN UP

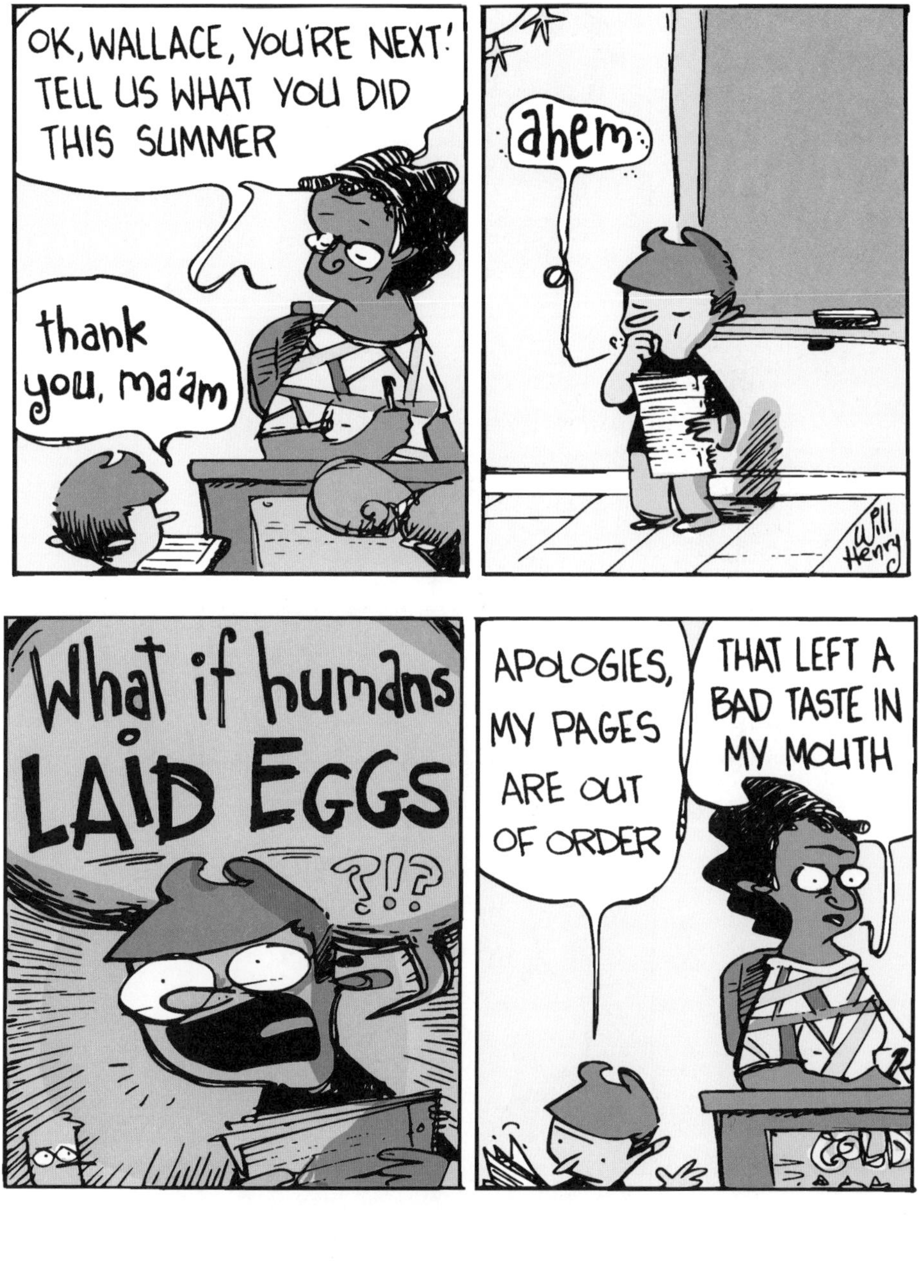
OK, WALLACE, YOU'RE NEXT! TELL US WHAT YOU DID THIS SUMMER
thank you, ma'am
ahem
Will Henry
What if humans LAID EGGS
?!?
APOLOGIES, MY PAGES ARE OUT OF ORDER
THAT LEFT A BAD TASTE IN MY MOUTH

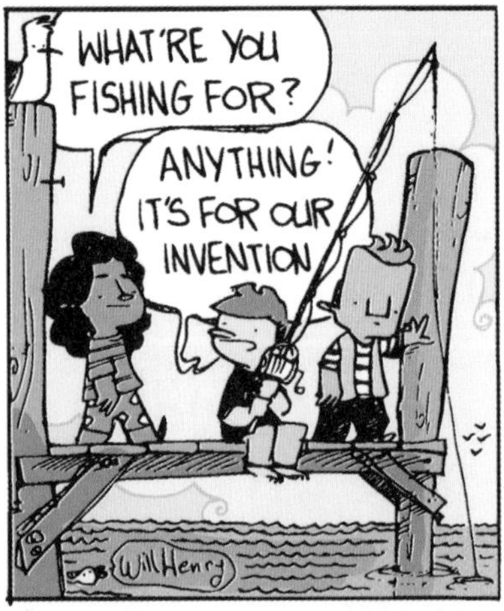
WHAT'RE YOU FISHING FOR?
ANYTHING! IT'S FOR OUR INVENTION
Will Henry

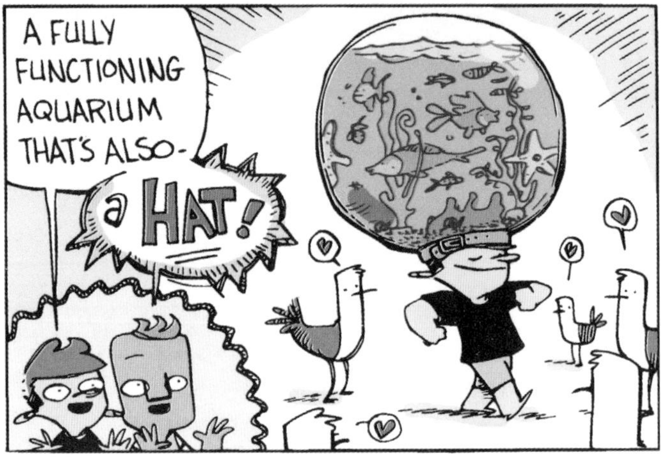
A FULLY FUNCTIONING AQUARIUM THAT'S ALSO-
a HAT!

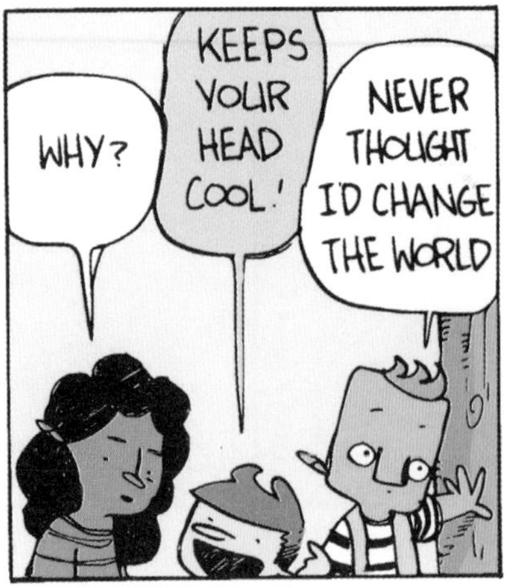
WHY?
KEEPS YOUR HEAD COOL!
NEVER THOUGHT I'D CHANGE THE WORLD

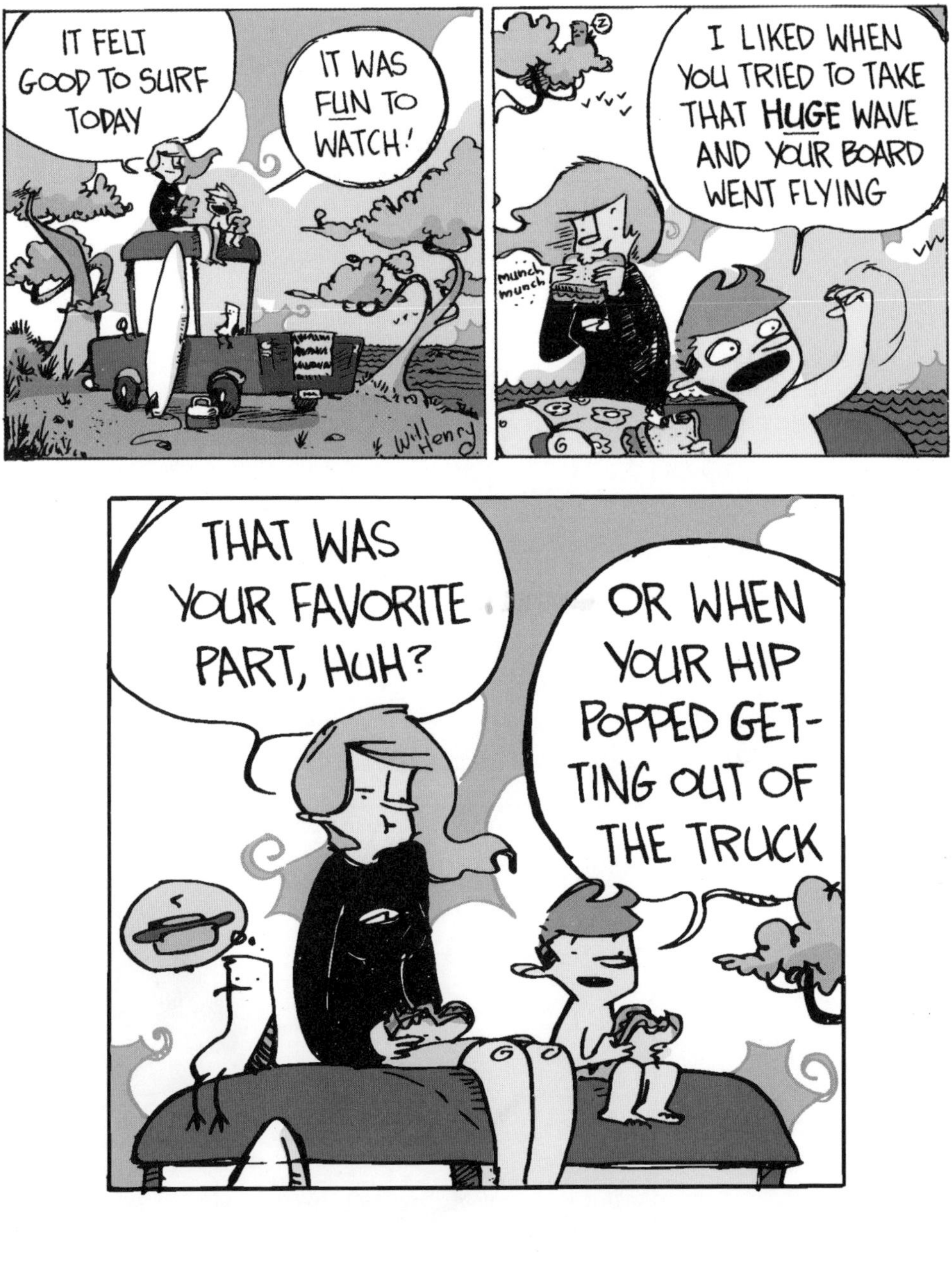
IT FELT GOOD TO SURF TODAY
IT WAS FUN TO WATCH!
Will Henry
I LIKED WHEN YOU TRIED TO TAKE THAT HUGE WAVE AND YOUR BOARD WENT FLYING
munch munch
THAT WAS YOUR FAVORITE PART, HUH?
OR WHEN YOUR HIP POPPED GET-TING OUT OF THE TRUCK

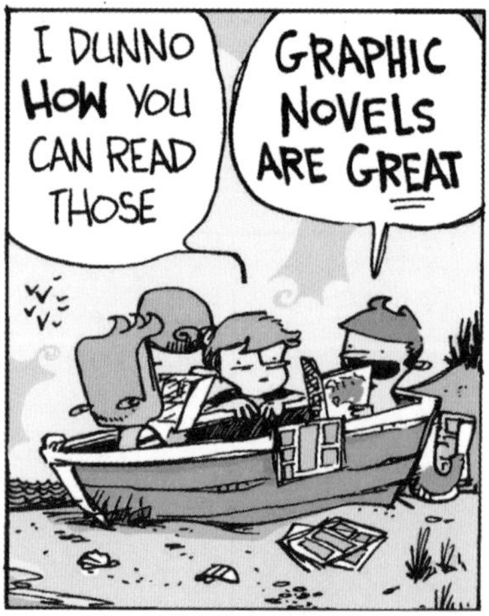
I DUNNO HOW YOU CAN READ THOSE
GRAPHIC NOVELS ARE GREAT

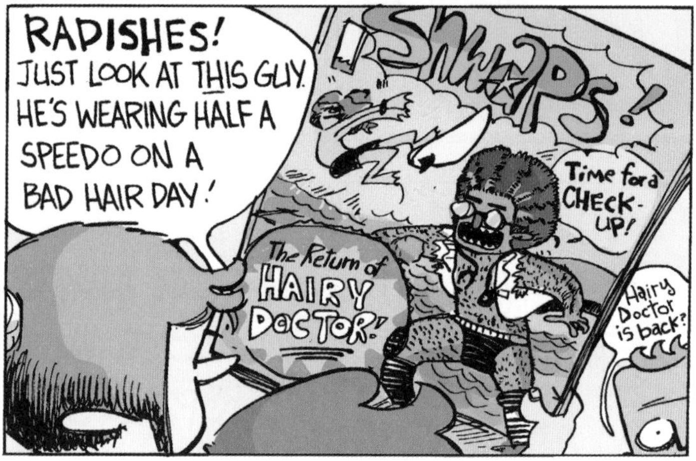
RADISHES! JUST LOOK AT THIS GUY. HE'S WEARING HALF A SPEEDO ON A BAD HAIR DAY!
SHWAPS!
Time for a CHECK-UP!
The Return of HAIRY DOCTOR!
Hairy Doctor is back?

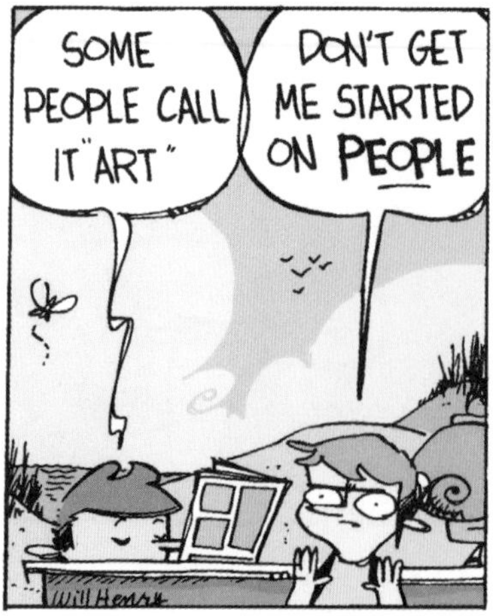
SOME PEOPLE CALL IT "ART"
DON'T GET ME STARTED ON PEOPLE
Will Henry

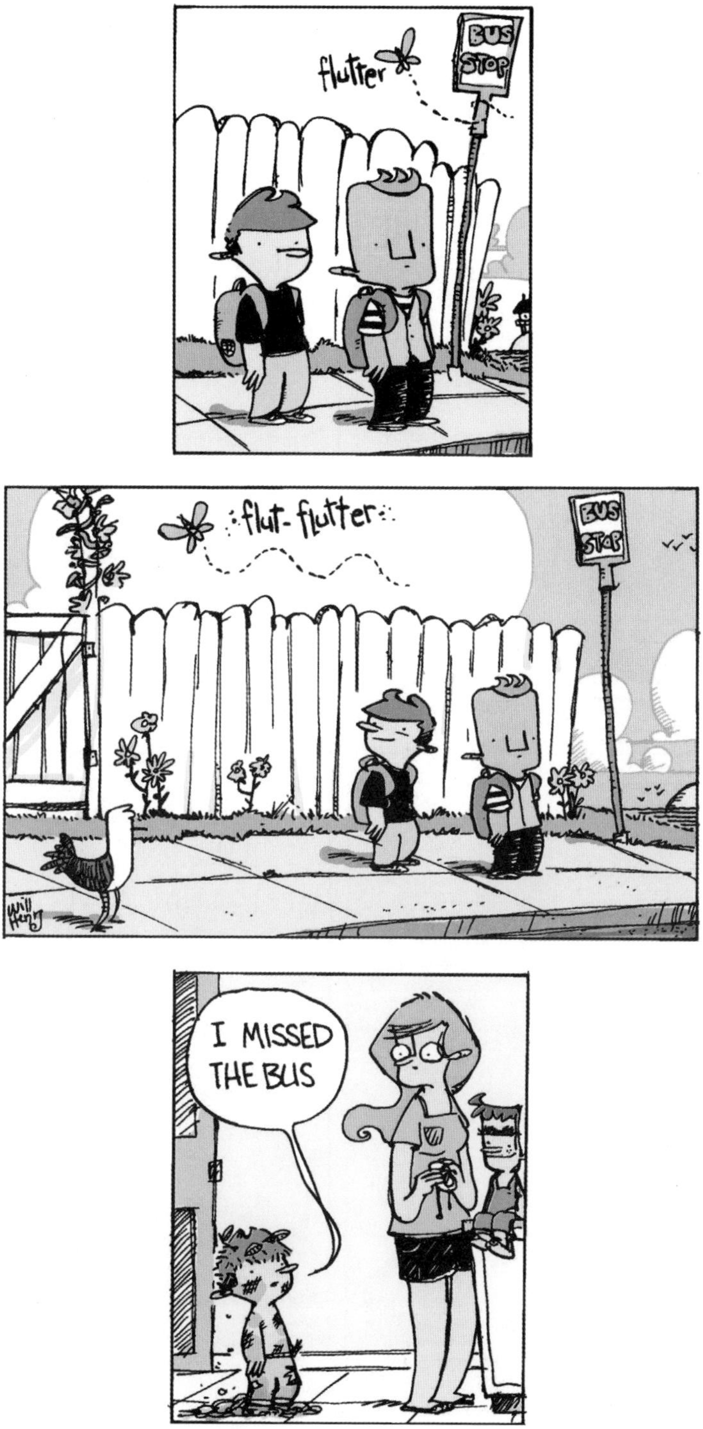
flutter
BUS STOP
flut-flutter
BUS STOP
Will Henry
I MISSED THE BUS

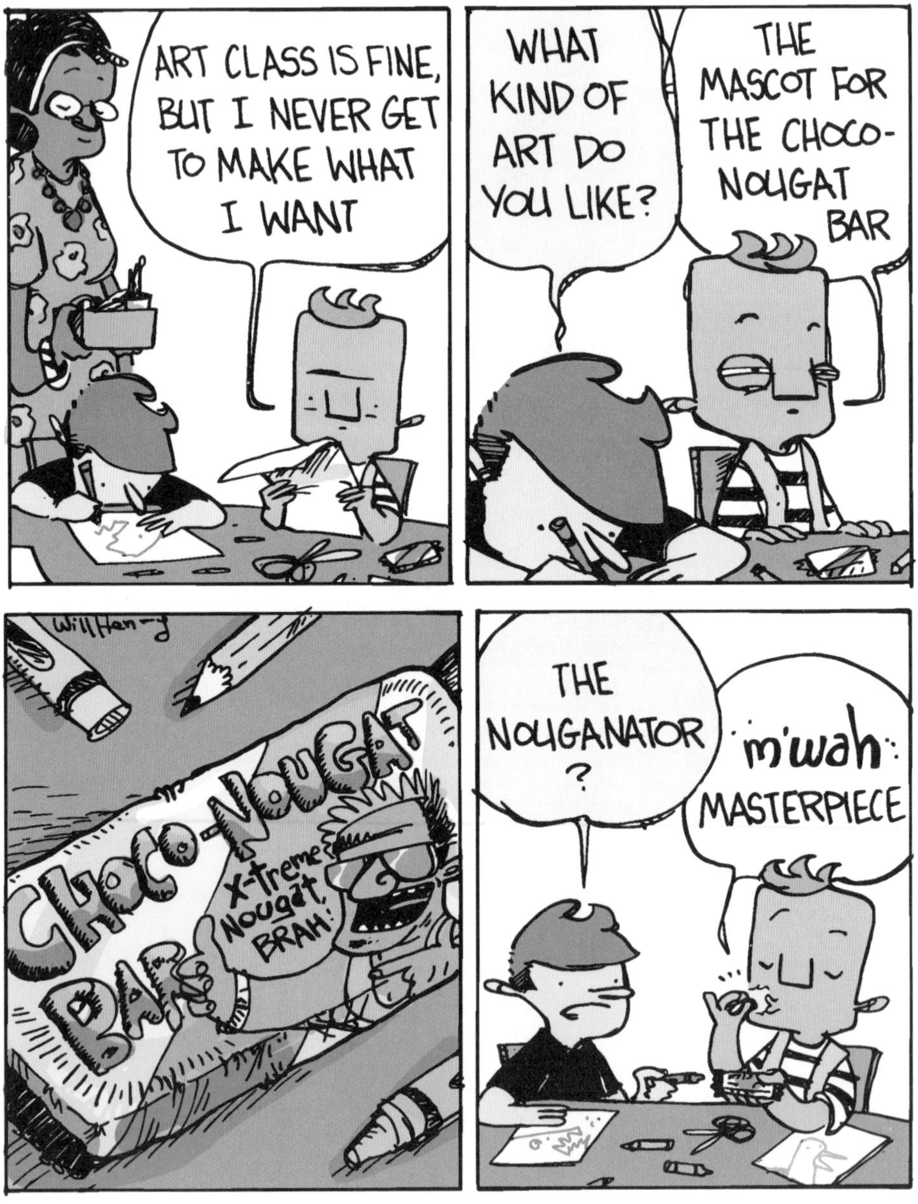
ART CLASS IS FINE, BUT I NEVER GET TO MAKE WHAT I WANT
WHAT KIND OF ART DO YOU LIKE?
THE MASCOT FOR THE CHOCO-NOUGAT BAR
Will Henry
CHOCO-NOUGAT BAR
X-treme Nougat, BRAH!
THE NOUGANATOR?
m'wah
MASTERPIECE

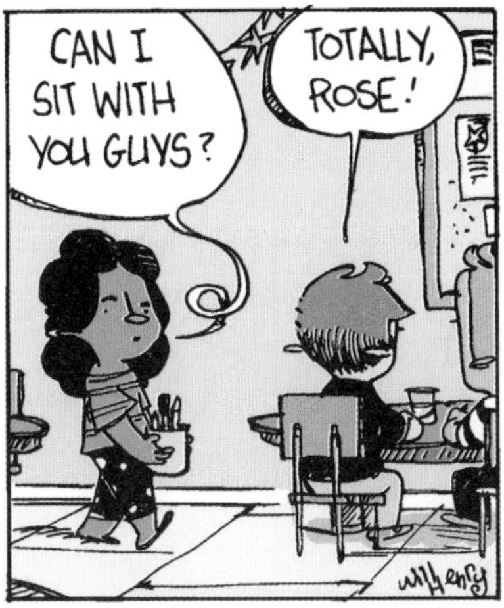
CAN I SIT WITH YOU GUYS?
TOTALLY, ROSE!

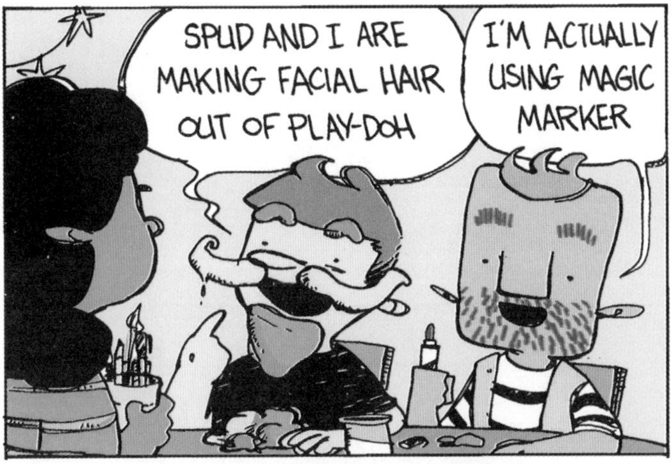
SPUD AND I ARE MAKING FACIAL HAIR OUT OF PLAY-DOH
I'M ACTUALLY USING MAGIC MARKER

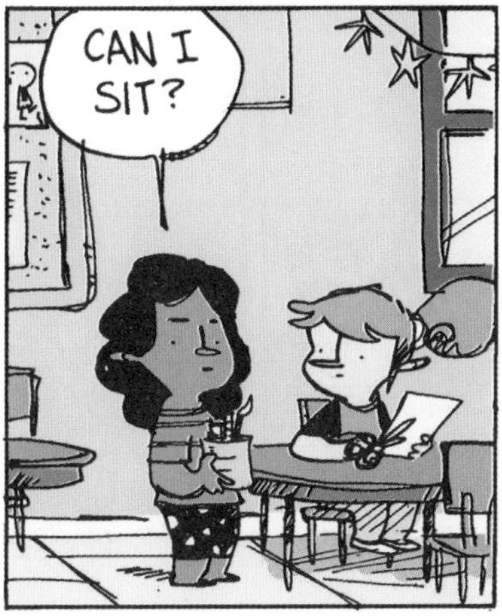
CAN I SIT?

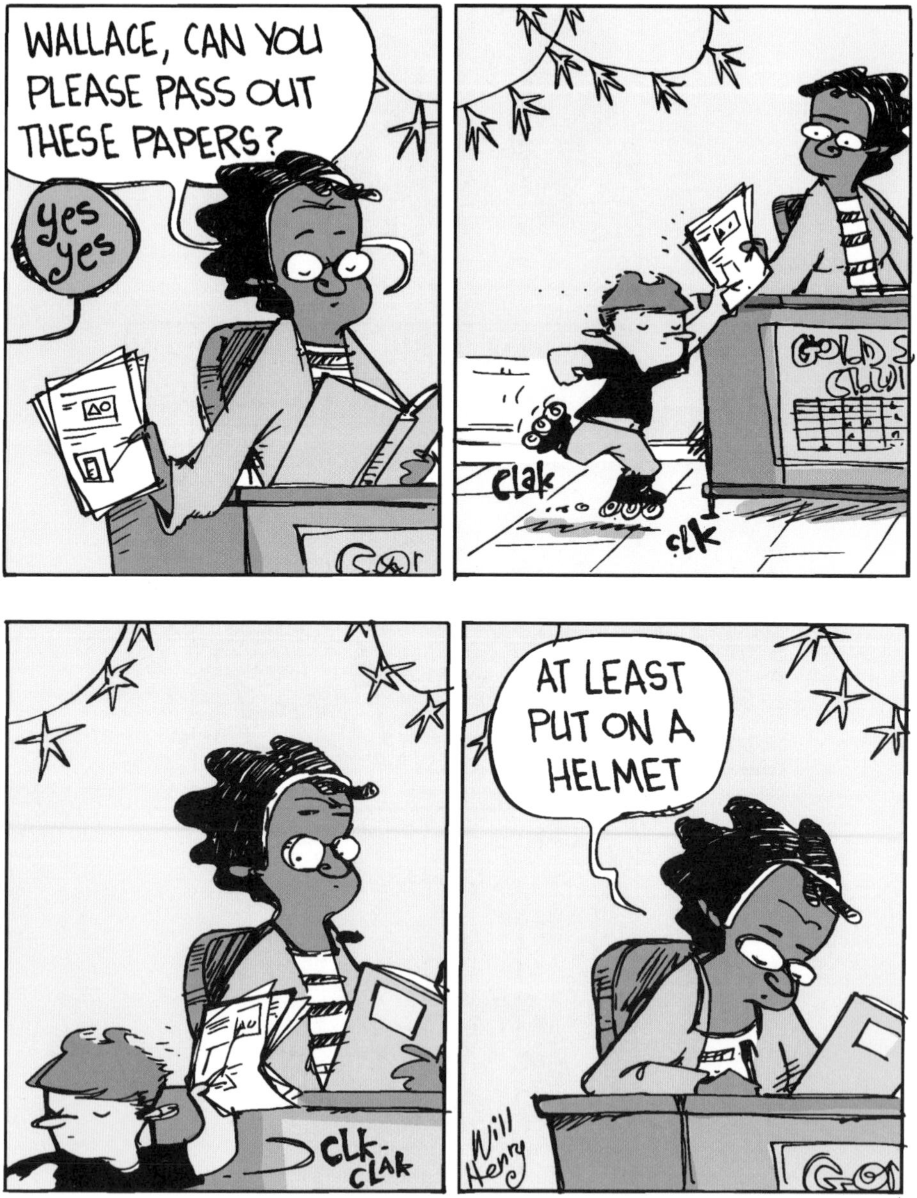
WALLACE, CAN YOU PLEASE PASS OUT THESE PAPERS?
yes yes
CLAK
CLK
CLK-CLAK
AT LEAST PUT ON A HELMET
Will Henry

SPUD, COME IN, SPUD! WE'RE WAITING FOR YA OUTSIDE
HE'S NOT PICKING UP...
I'M GOIN' IN!
TO SPUD'S HOUSE?
Will Henry
I'VE NEVER BEEN IN SPUD'S HOUSE
DON'T LOOK **DIRECTLY** AT THE PUPPETS

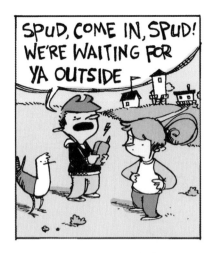

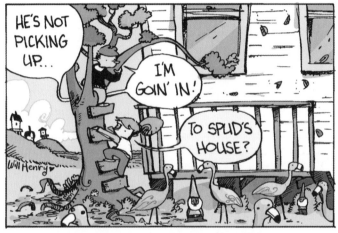

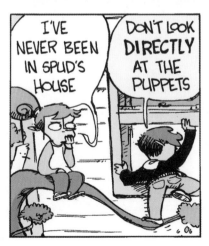

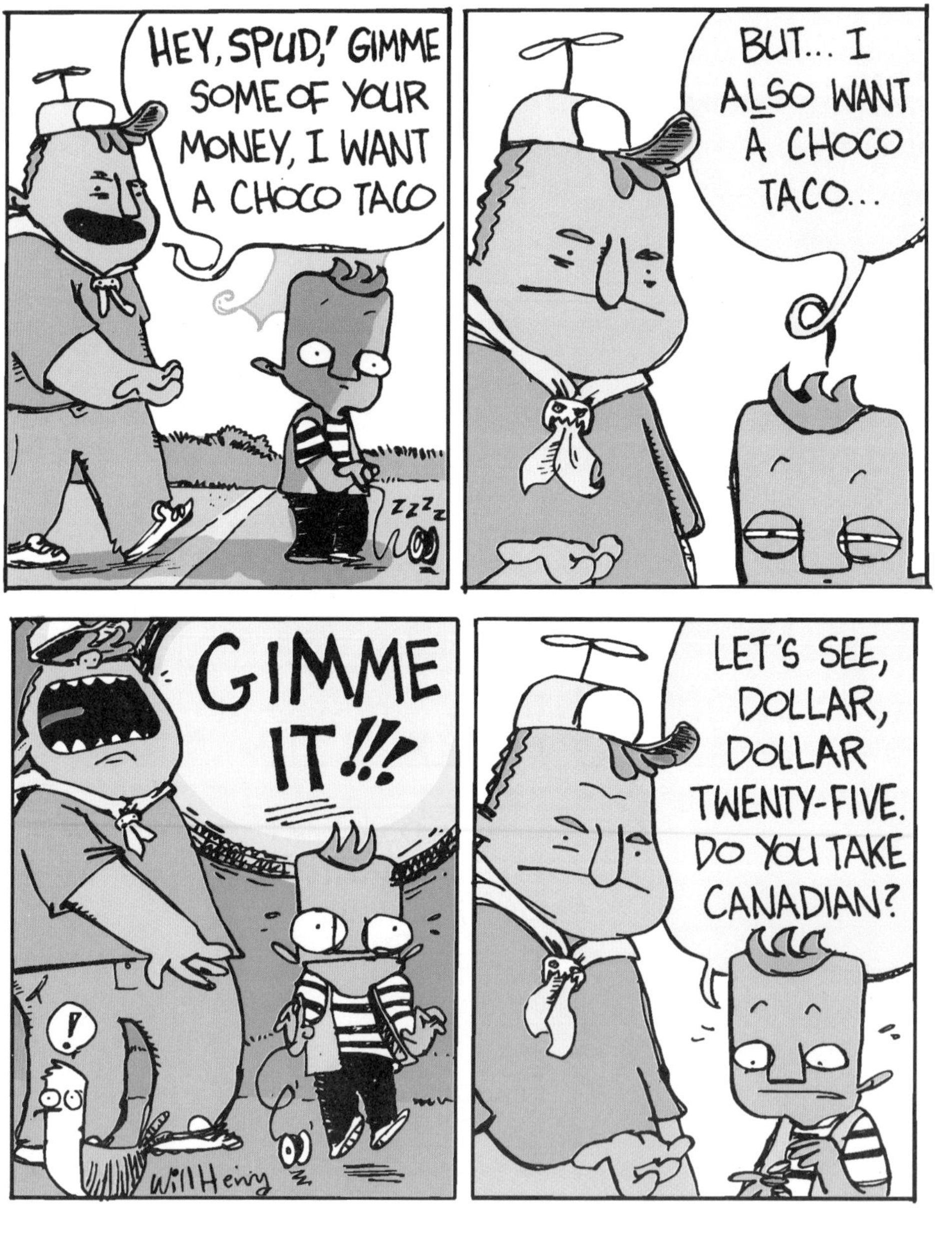
HEY, SPUD! GIMME SOME OF YOUR MONEY, I WANT A CHOCO TACO
ZZZZ
BUT... I ALSO WANT A CHOCO TACO...
GIMME IT!!!
!
Will Henry
LET'S SEE, DOLLAR, DOLLAR TWENTY-FIVE. DO YOU TAKE CANADIAN?

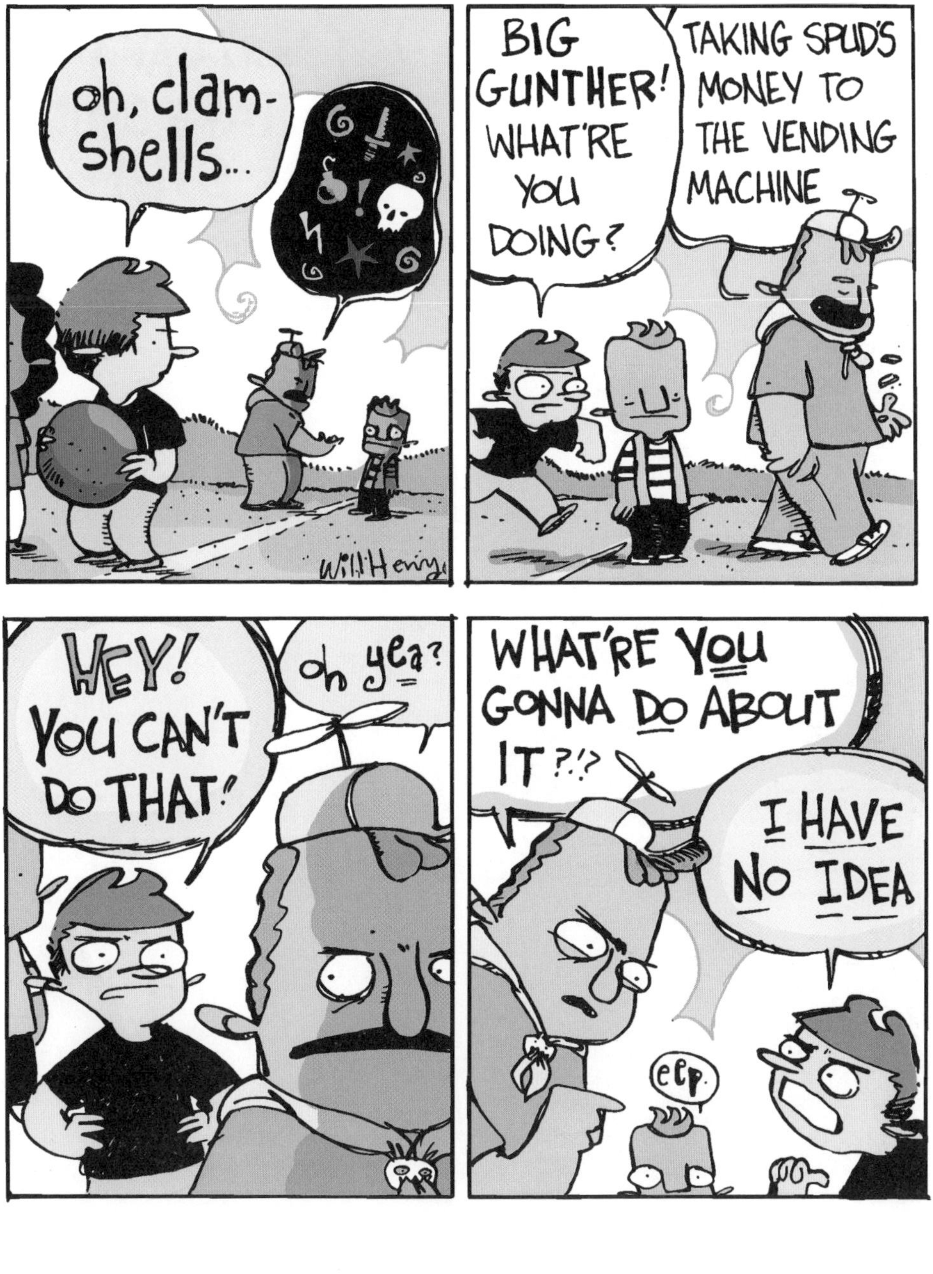
oh, clam-shells...
BIG GUNTHER! WHAT'RE YOU DOING?
TAKING SPUD'S MONEY TO THE VENDING MACHINE
HEY! YOU CAN'T DO THAT!
oh yea?
WHAT'RE YOU GONNA DO ABOUT IT?!?
I HAVE NO IDEA
eep.
Will Henry

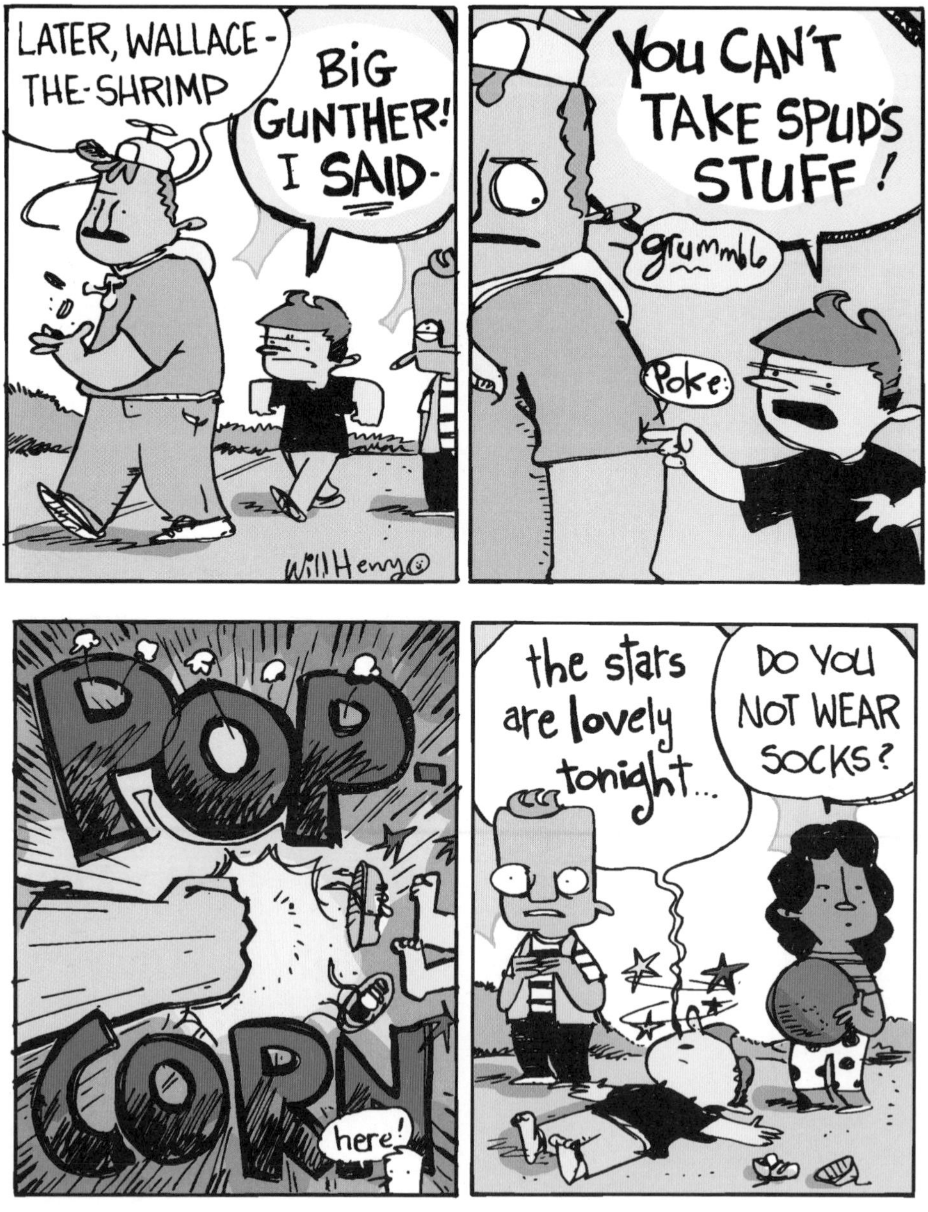
LATER, WALLACE-THE-SHRIMP
BIG GUNTHER! I SAID-
Will Henry
YOU CAN'T TAKE SPUD'S STUFF!
grummbb
Poke
POP-CORN
here!
the stars are lovely tonight...
DO YOU NOT WEAR SOCKS?

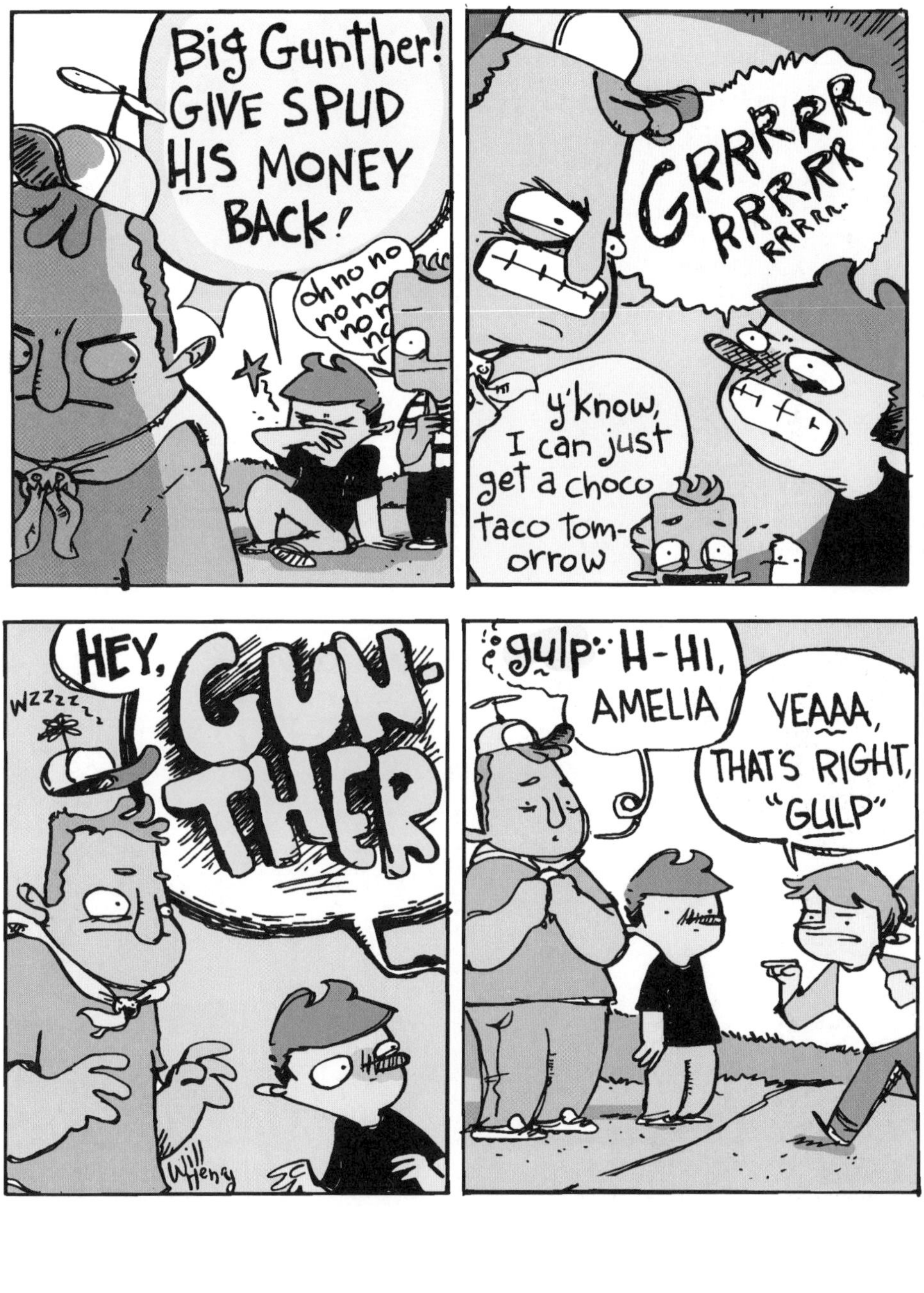
Big Gunther! GIVE SPUD HIS MONEY BACK!
oh no no no no no no
GRRRRR RRRRR RRRRR..
y'know, I can just get a choco taco tom-orrow
HEY, GUN-THER
WZZZZZ
Will Henry
gulp H-HI, AMELIA
YEAAA, THAT'S RIGHT, "GULP"

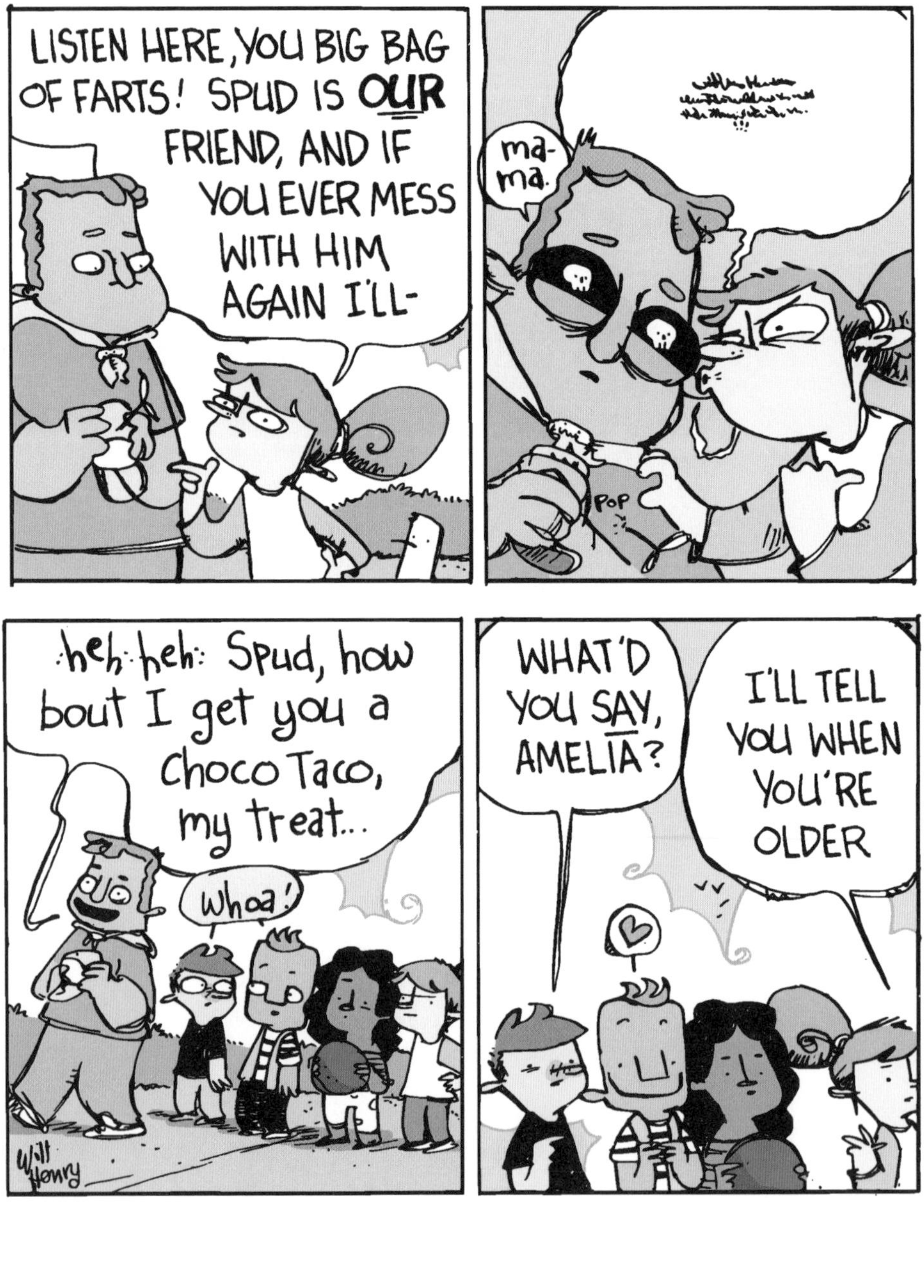
LISTEN HERE, YOU BIG BAG OF FARTS! SPUD IS OUR FRIEND, AND IF YOU EVER MESS WITH HIM AGAIN I'LL-
ma-ma.
POP
:heh: heh: Spud, how bout I get you a Choco Taco, my treat...
Whoa!
Will Henry
WHAT'D YOU SAY, AMELIA?
I'LL TELL YOU WHEN YOU'RE OLDER

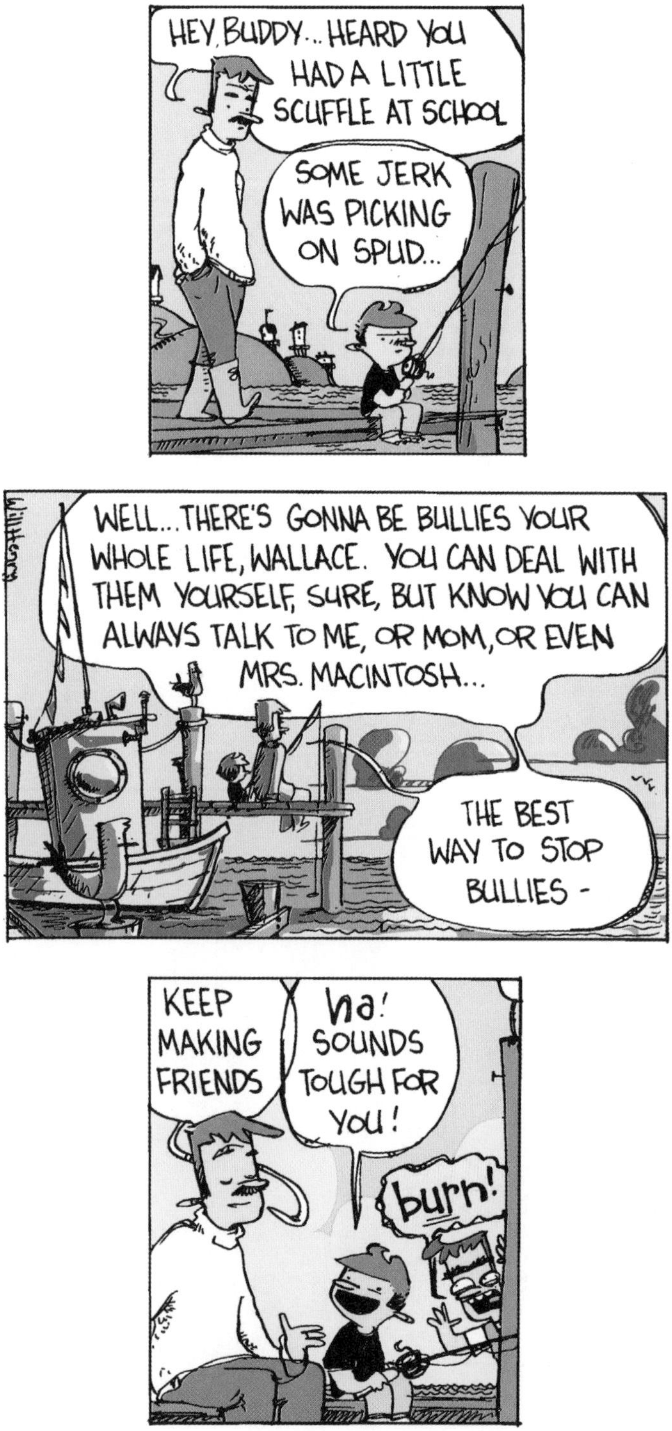
HEY, BUDDY... HEARD YOU HAD A LITTLE SCUFFLE AT SCHOOL
SOME JERK WAS PICKING ON SPUD...
WELL... THERE'S GONNA BE BULLIES YOUR WHOLE LIFE, WALLACE. YOU CAN DEAL WITH THEM YOURSELF, SURE, BUT KNOW YOU CAN ALWAYS TALK TO ME, OR MOM, OR EVEN MRS. MACINTOSH...
THE BEST WAY TO STOP BULLIES -
KEEP MAKING FRIENDS
ha! SOUNDS TOUGH FOR YOU!
burn!

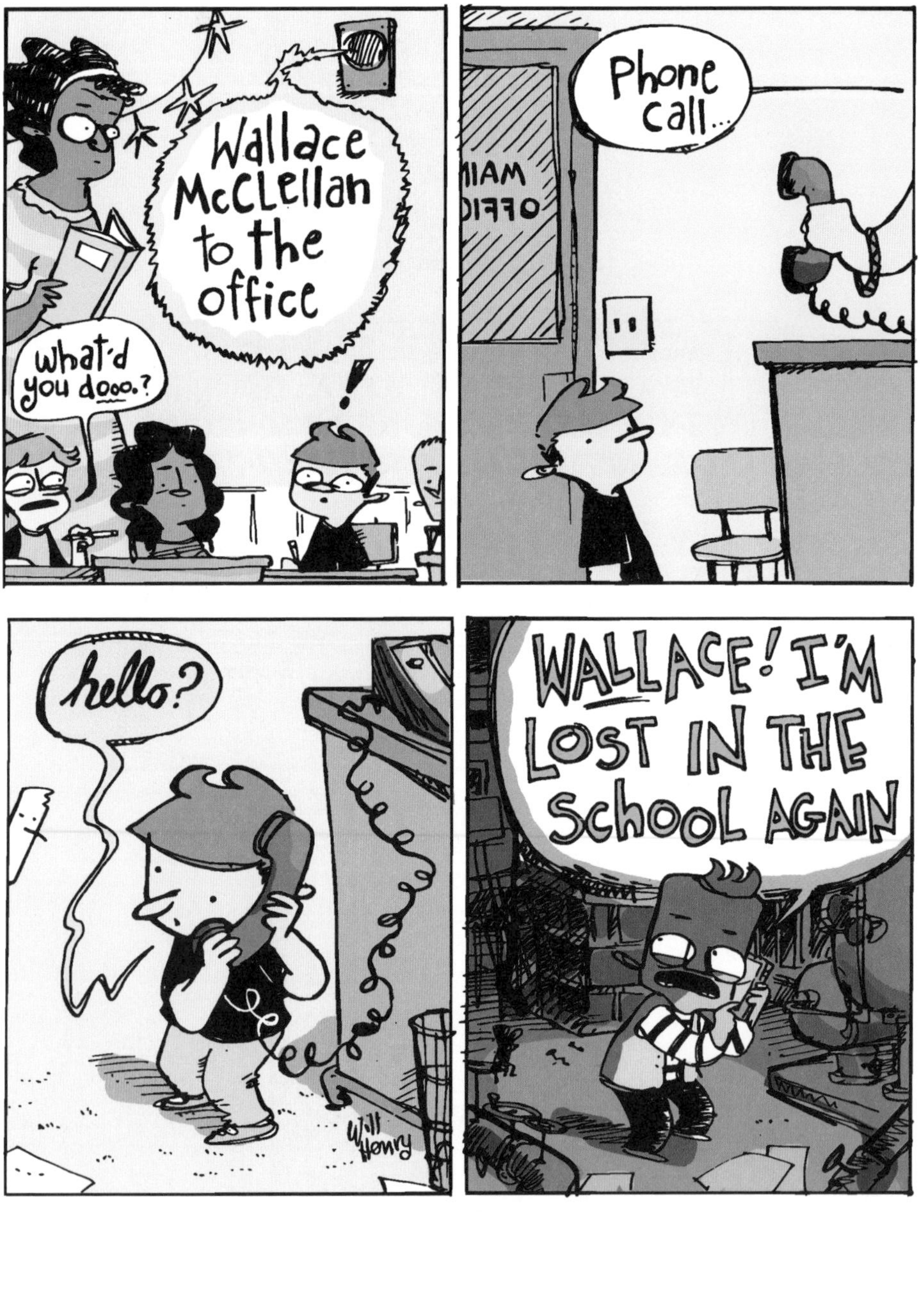
Wallace McClellan to the office
what'd you dooo..?
!
Phone call...
MAIN OFFICE
hello?
Will Henry
WALLACE! I'M LOST IN THE SCHOOL AGAIN

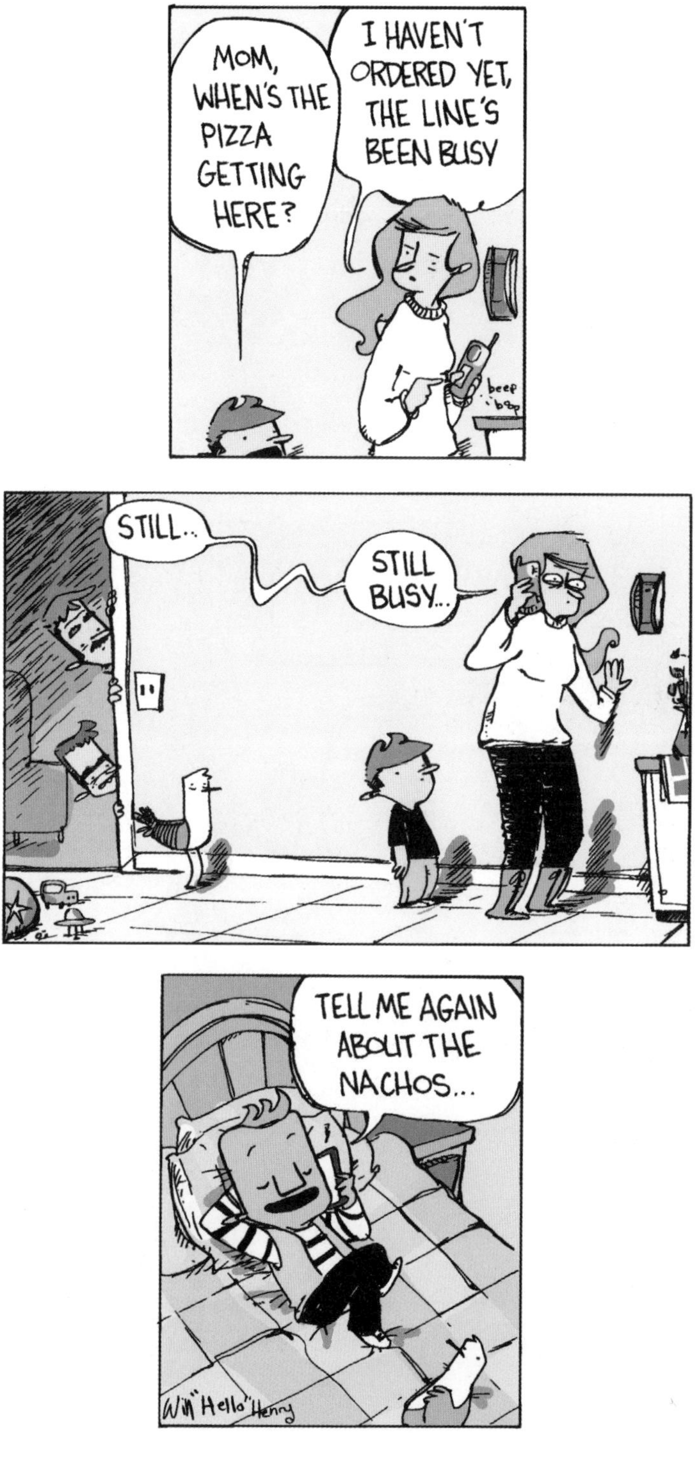
MOM, WHEN'S THE PIZZA GETTING HERE?
I HAVEN'T ORDERED YET, THE LINE'S BEEN BUSY
beep bop
STILL..
STILL BUSY...
TELL ME AGAIN ABOUT THE NACHOS...
Will "Hello" Henry

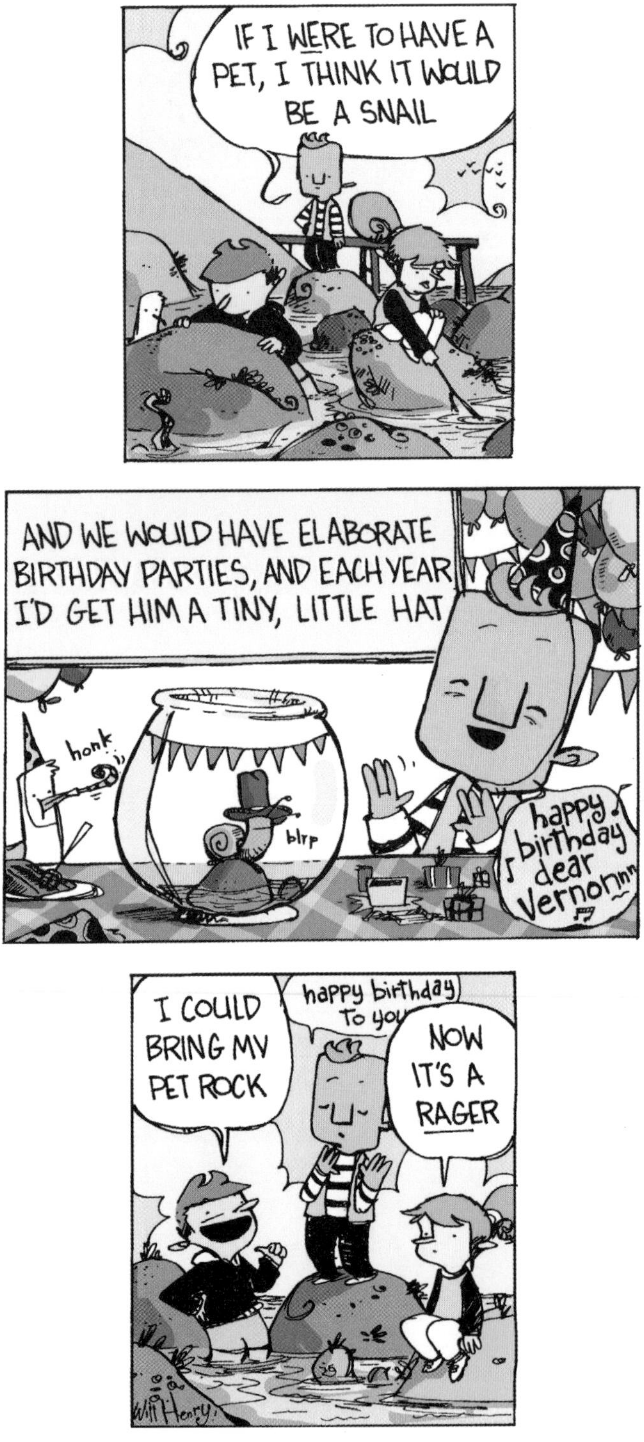
IF I WERE TO HAVE A PET, I THINK IT WOULD BE A SNAIL
AND WE WOULD HAVE ELABORATE BIRTHDAY PARTIES, AND EACH YEAR I'D GET HIM A TINY, LITTLE HAT
honk
blrp
happy birthday dear Vernonnn
I COULD BRING MY PET ROCK
happy birthday To you
NOW IT'S A RAGER
Will Henry

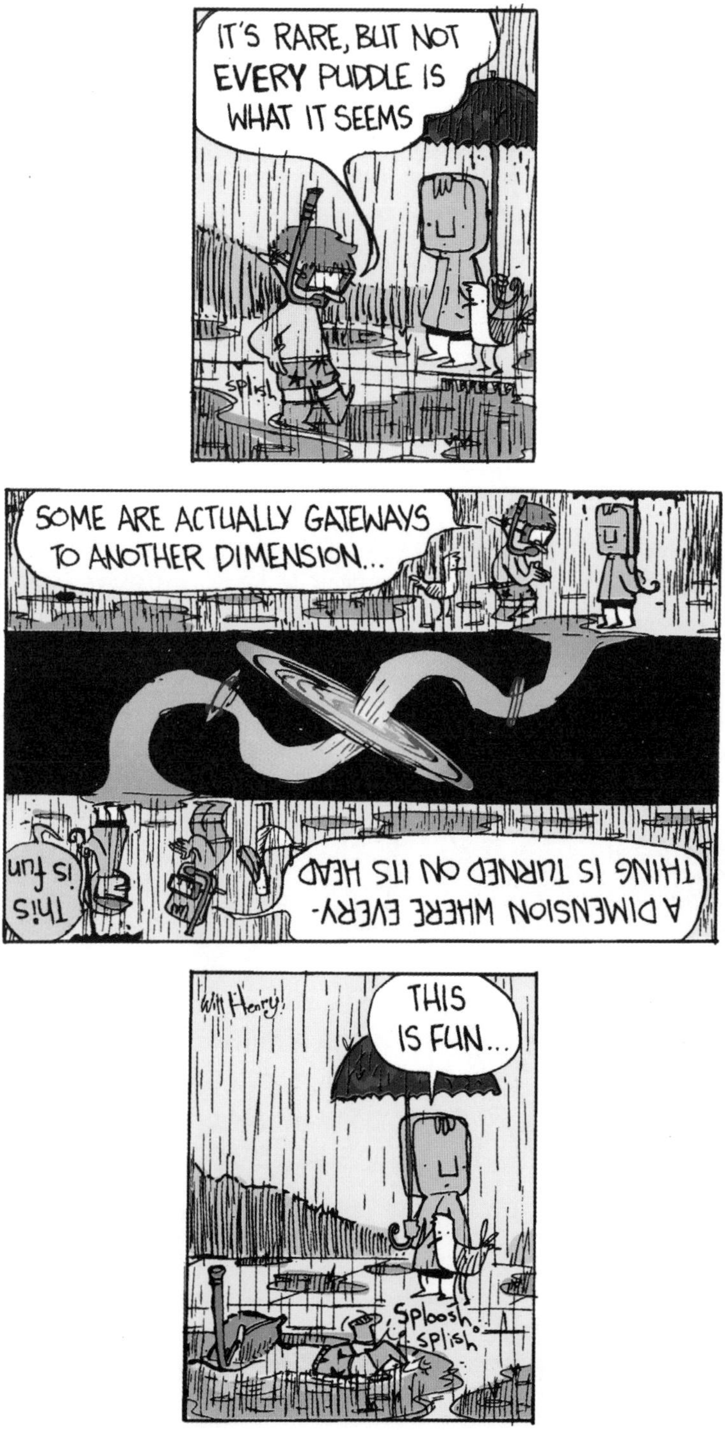
IT'S RARE, BUT NOT EVERY PUDDLE IS WHAT IT SEEMS
splish
SOME ARE ACTUALLY GATEWAYS TO ANOTHER DIMENSION...
A DIMENSION WHERE EVERY-THING IS TURNED ON ITS HEAD
This is fun
Will Henry!
THIS IS FUN...
Sploosh
splish

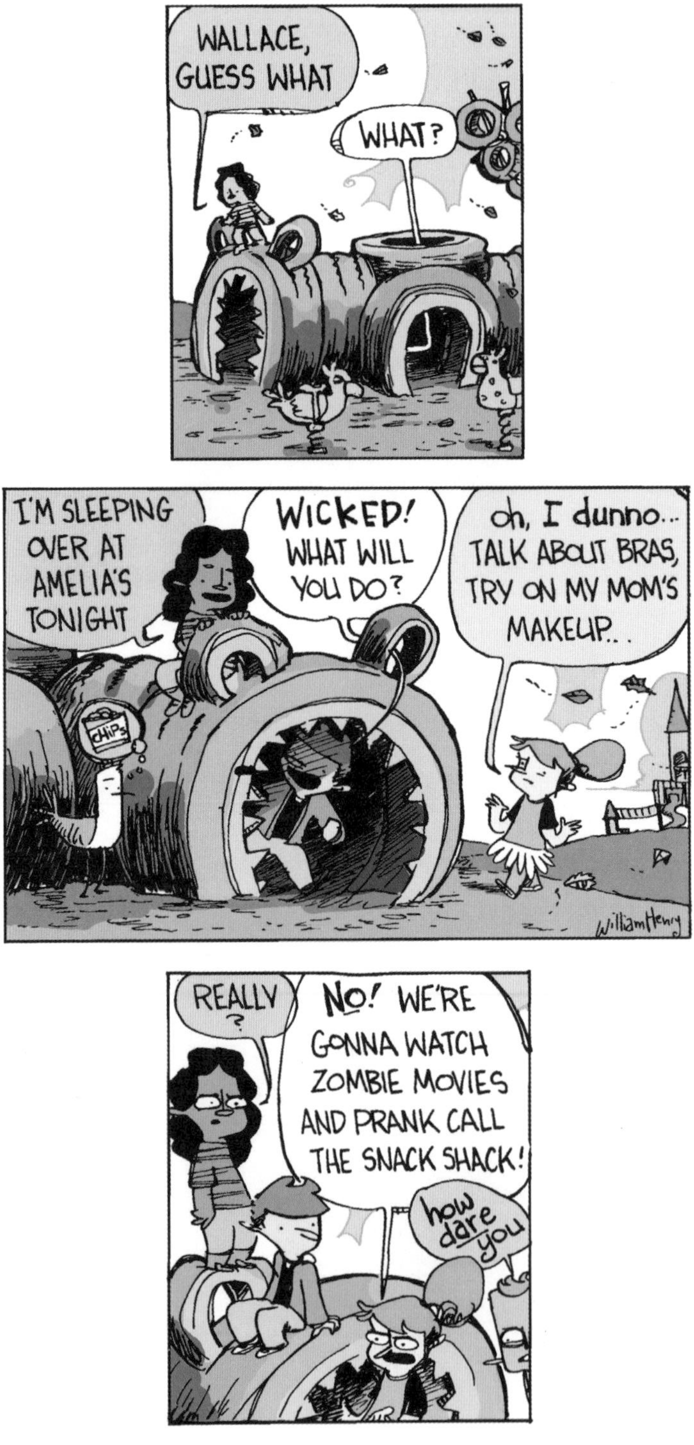
WALLACE, GUESS WHAT
WHAT?
I'M SLEEPING OVER AT AMELIA'S TONIGHT
CHIPS
WICKED! WHAT WILL YOU DO?
oh, I dunno... TALK ABOUT BRAS, TRY ON MY MOM'S MAKEUP...
William Henry
REALLY?
NO! WE'RE GONNA WATCH ZOMBIE MOVIES AND PRANK CALL THE SNACK SHACK!
how dare you

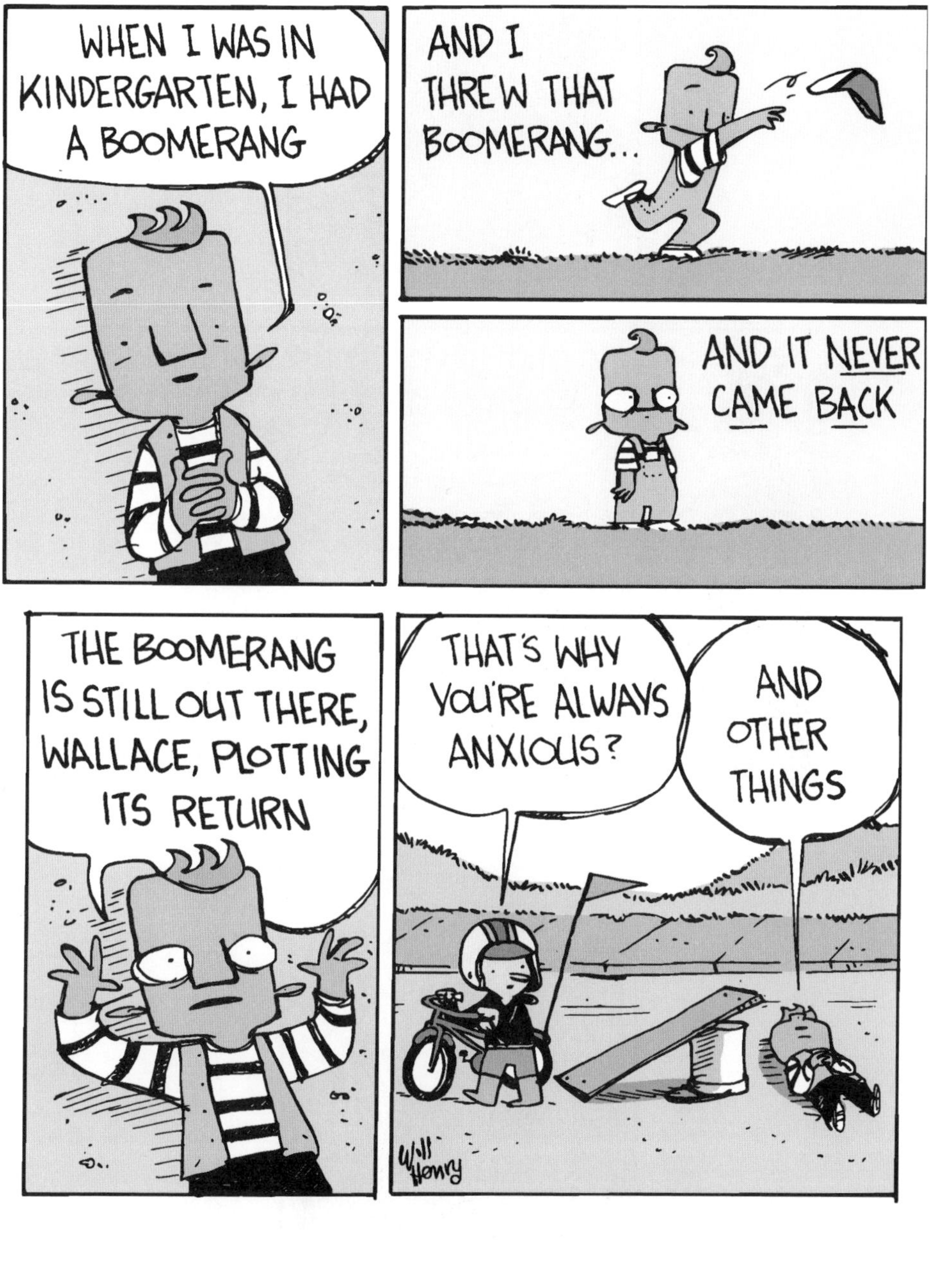
WHEN I WAS IN KINDERGARTEN, I HAD A BOOMERANG
AND I THREW THAT BOOMERANG...
AND IT NEVER CAME BACK
THE BOOMERANG IS STILL OUT THERE, WALLACE, PLOTTING ITS RETURN
THAT'S WHY YOU'RE ALWAYS ANXIOUS?
AND OTHER THINGS
Will Henry

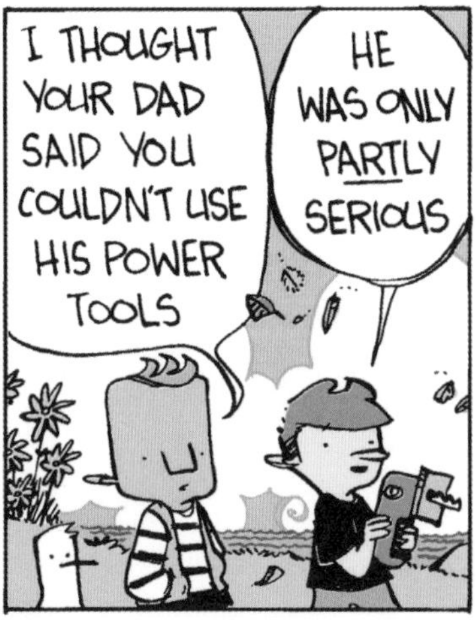
I THOUGHT YOUR DAD SAID YOU COULDN'T USE HIS POWER TOOLS
HE WAS ONLY PARTLY SERIOUS

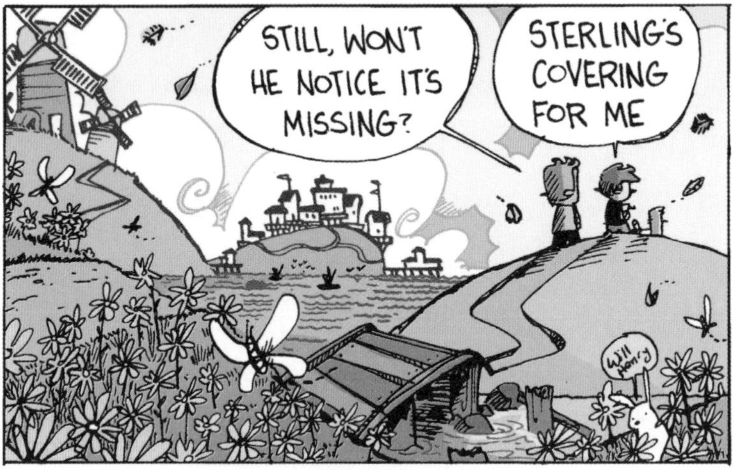
STILL, WON'T HE NOTICE IT'S MISSING?
STERLING'S COVERING FOR ME

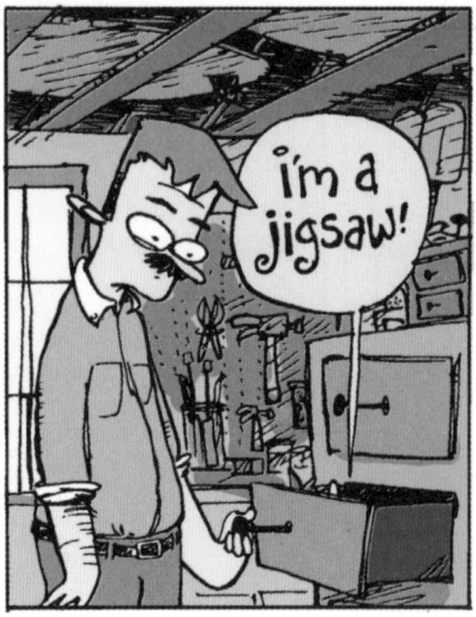
i'm a jigsaw!

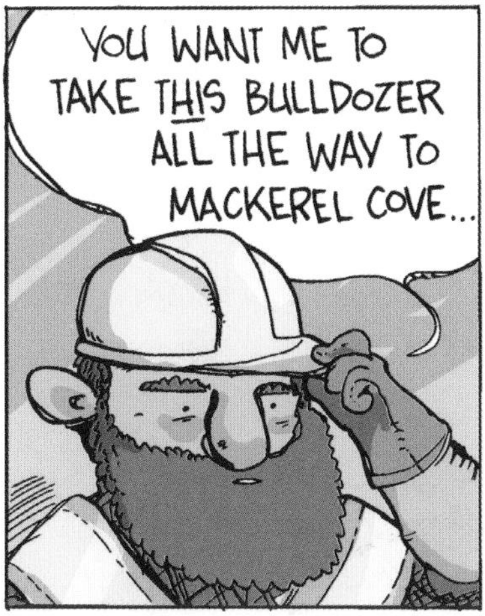
YOU WANT ME TO TAKE THIS BULLDOZER ALL THE WAY TO MACKEREL COVE...

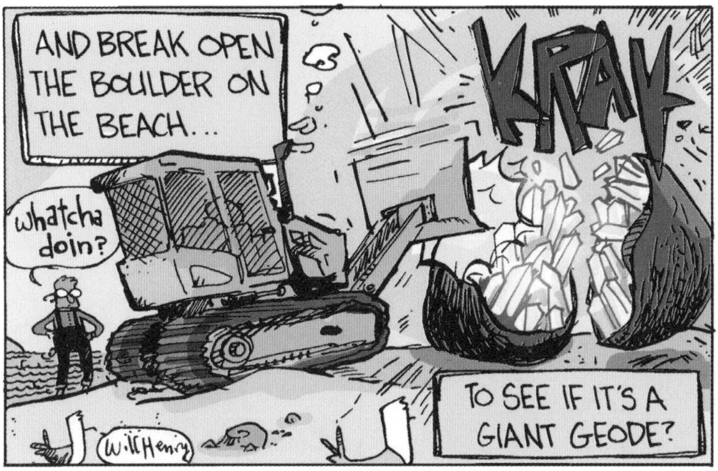
AND BREAK OPEN THE BOULDER ON THE BEACH...
KRAK
whatcha doin?
TO SEE IF IT'S A GIANT GEODE?
WillHenry

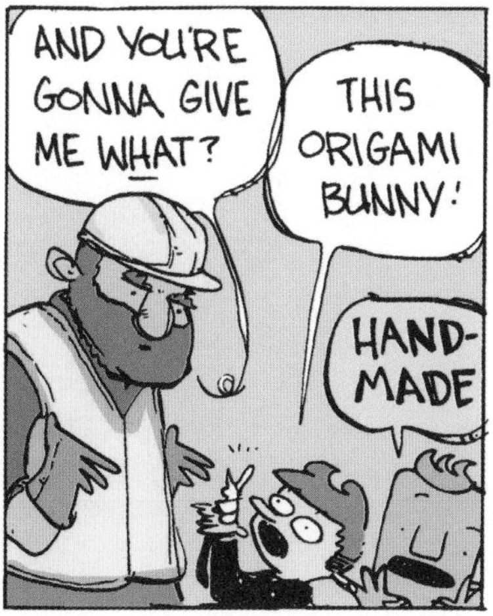
AND YOU'RE GONNA GIVE ME WHAT?
THIS ORIGAMI BUNNY!
HAND-MADE

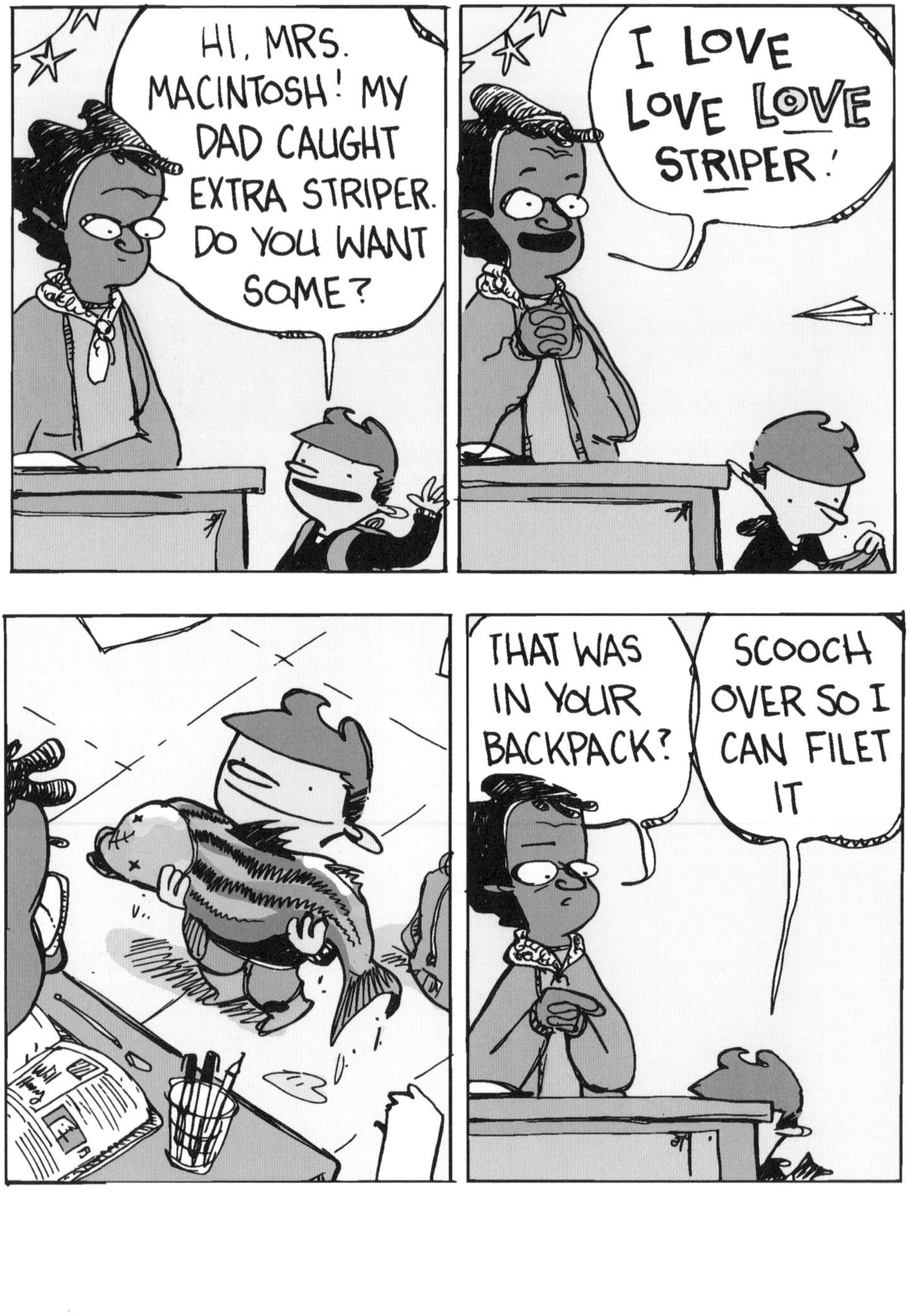
HI, MRS. MACINTOSH! MY DAD CAUGHT EXTRA STRIPER. DO YOU WANT SOME?
I LOVE LOVE LOVE STRIPER!
THAT WAS IN YOUR BACKPACK?
SCOOCH OVER SO I CAN FILET IT

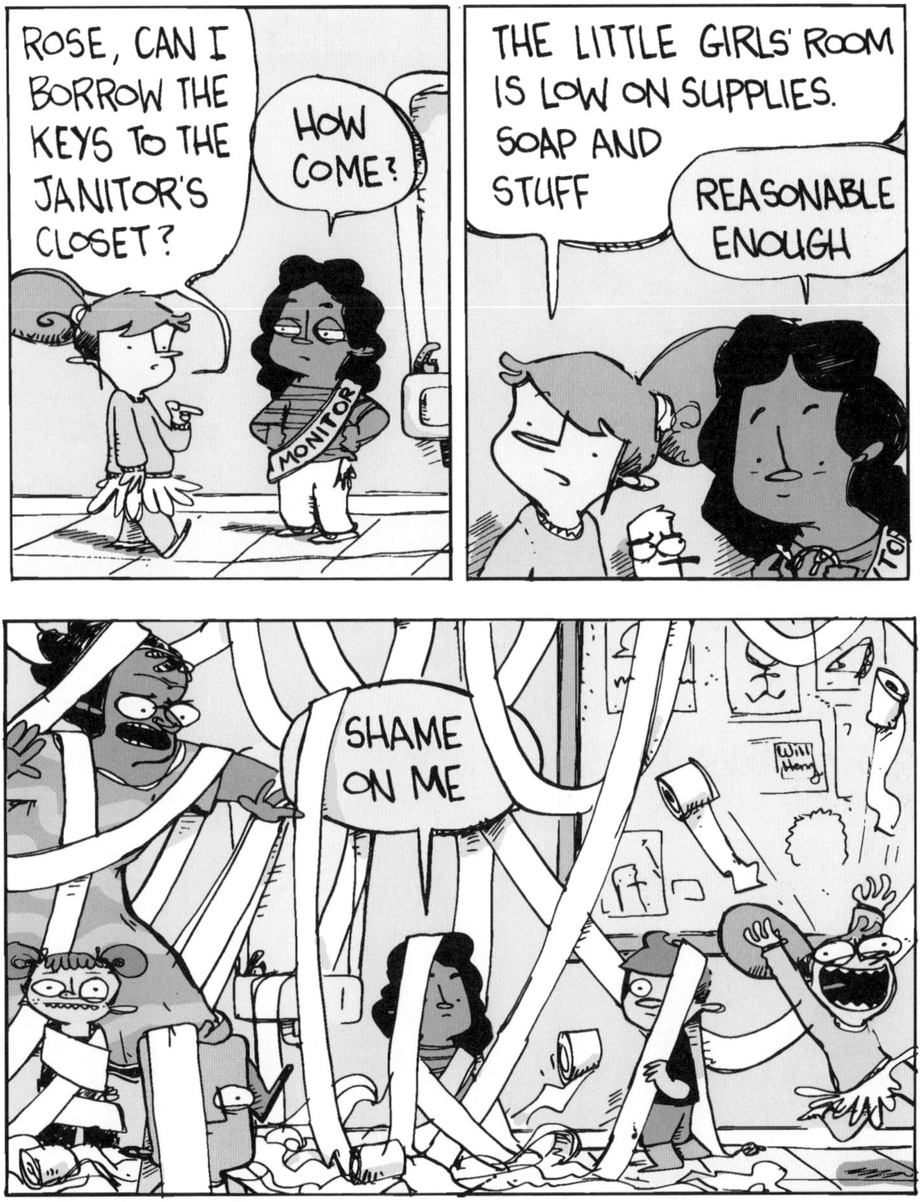
ROSE, CAN I BORROW THE KEYS TO THE JANITOR'S CLOSET?
HOW COME?
MONITOR
THE LITTLE GIRLS' ROOM IS LOW ON SUPPLIES. SOAP AND STUFF
REASONABLE ENOUGH
SHAME ON ME

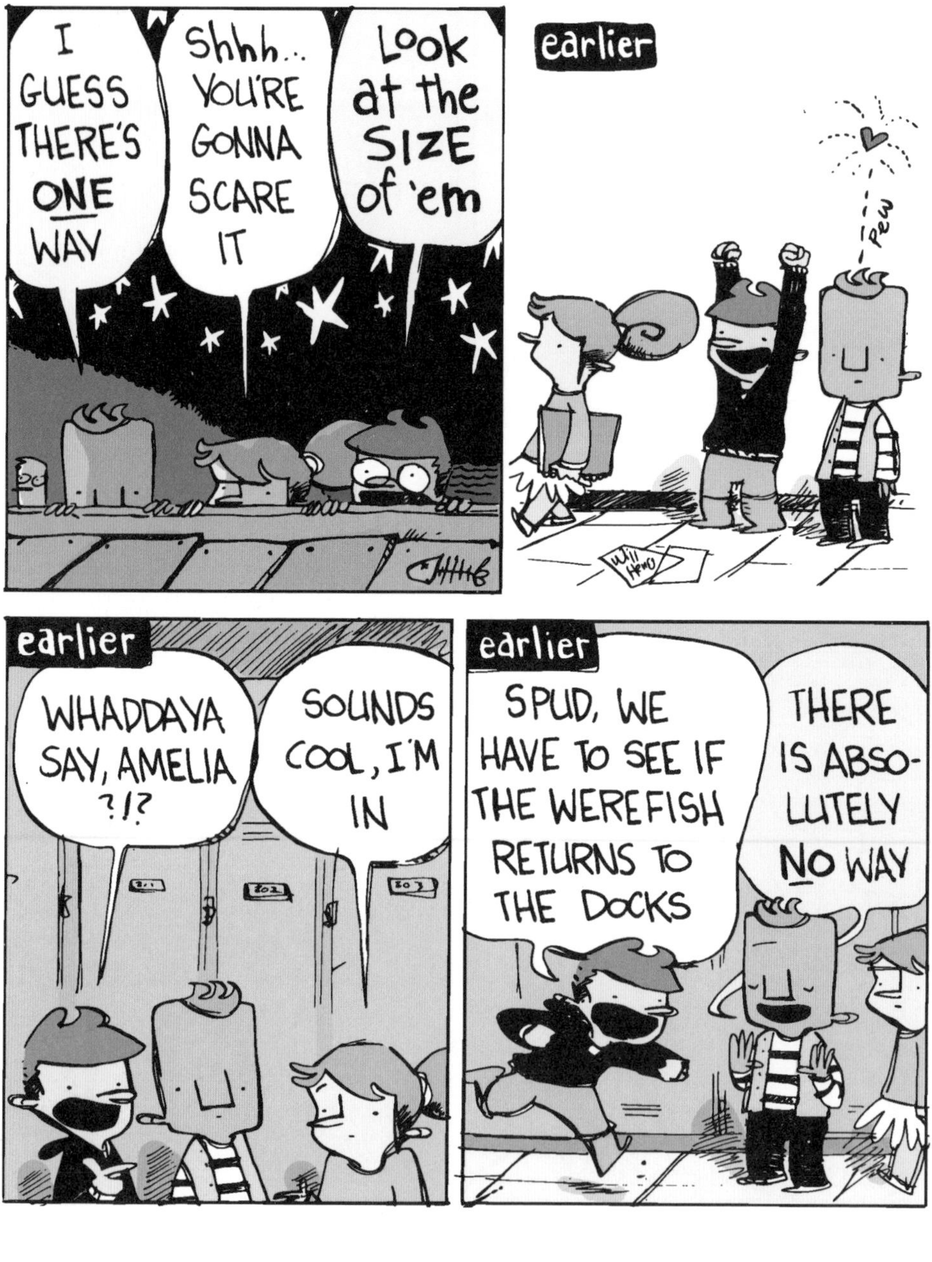
I GUESS THERE'S ONE WAY
Shhh... YOU'RE GONNA SCARE IT
Look at the SIZE of 'em
earlier
PEW
earlier
WHADDAYA SAY, AMELIA ?!?
SOUNDS COOL, I'M IN
earlier
SPUD, WE HAVE TO SEE IF THE WEREFISH RETURNS TO THE DOCKS
THERE IS ABSO-LUTELY NO WAY

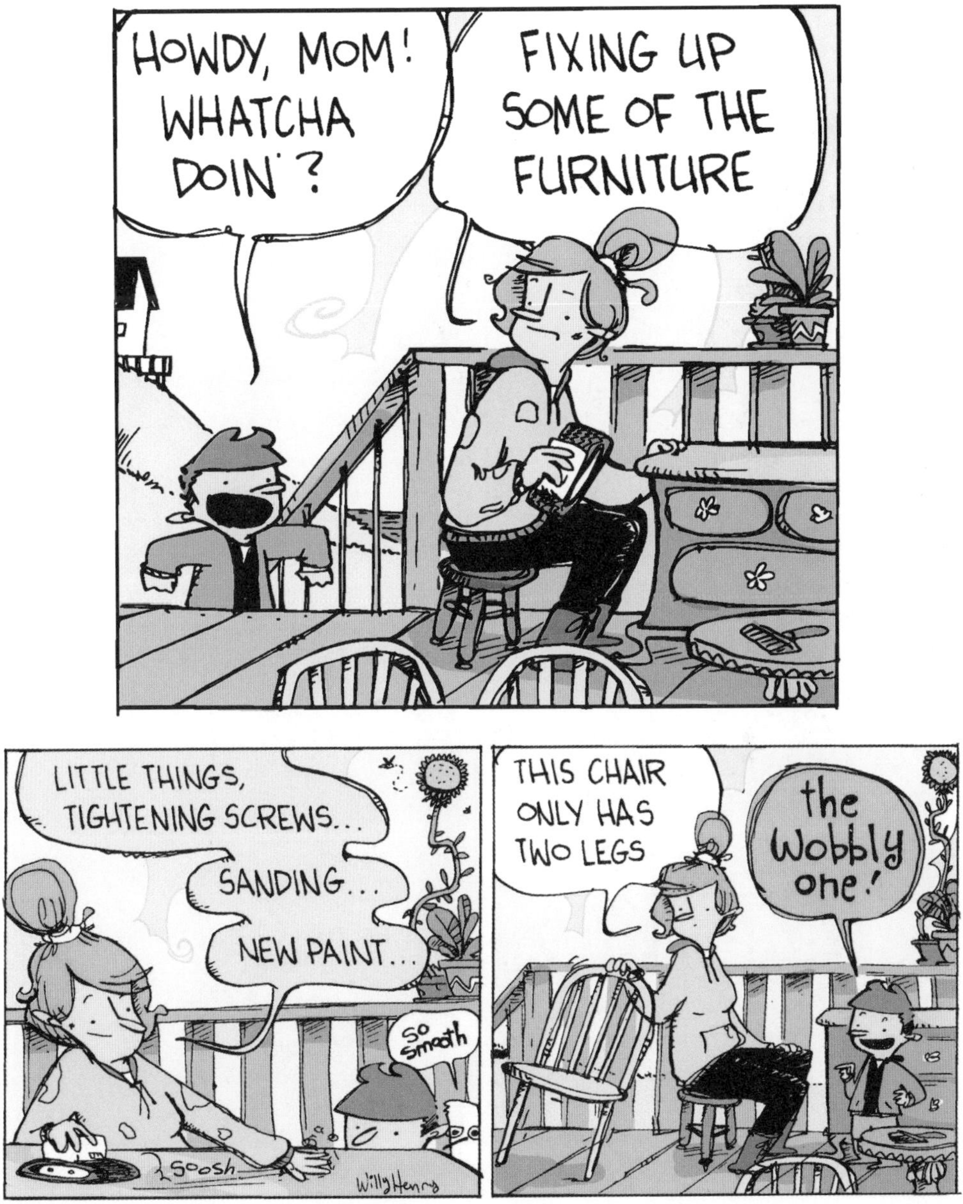
HOWDY, MOM! WHATCHA DOIN'?
FIXING UP SOME OF THE FURNITURE
LITTLE THINGS, TIGHTENING SCREWS...
SANDING...
NEW PAINT...
so smooth
soosh
Willy Henry
THIS CHAIR ONLY HAS TWO LEGS
the Wobbly one!

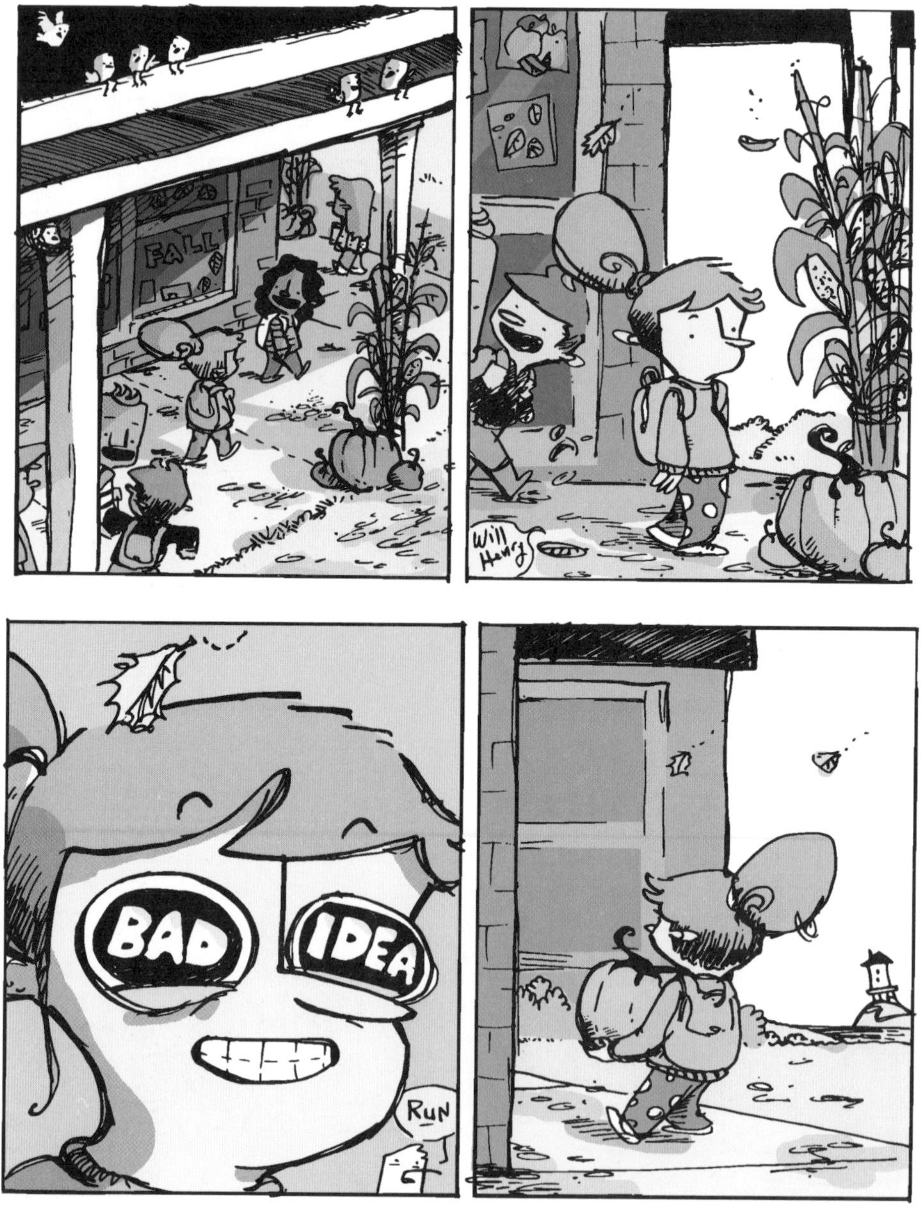
FALL
Will Henry
BAD IDEA
RUN

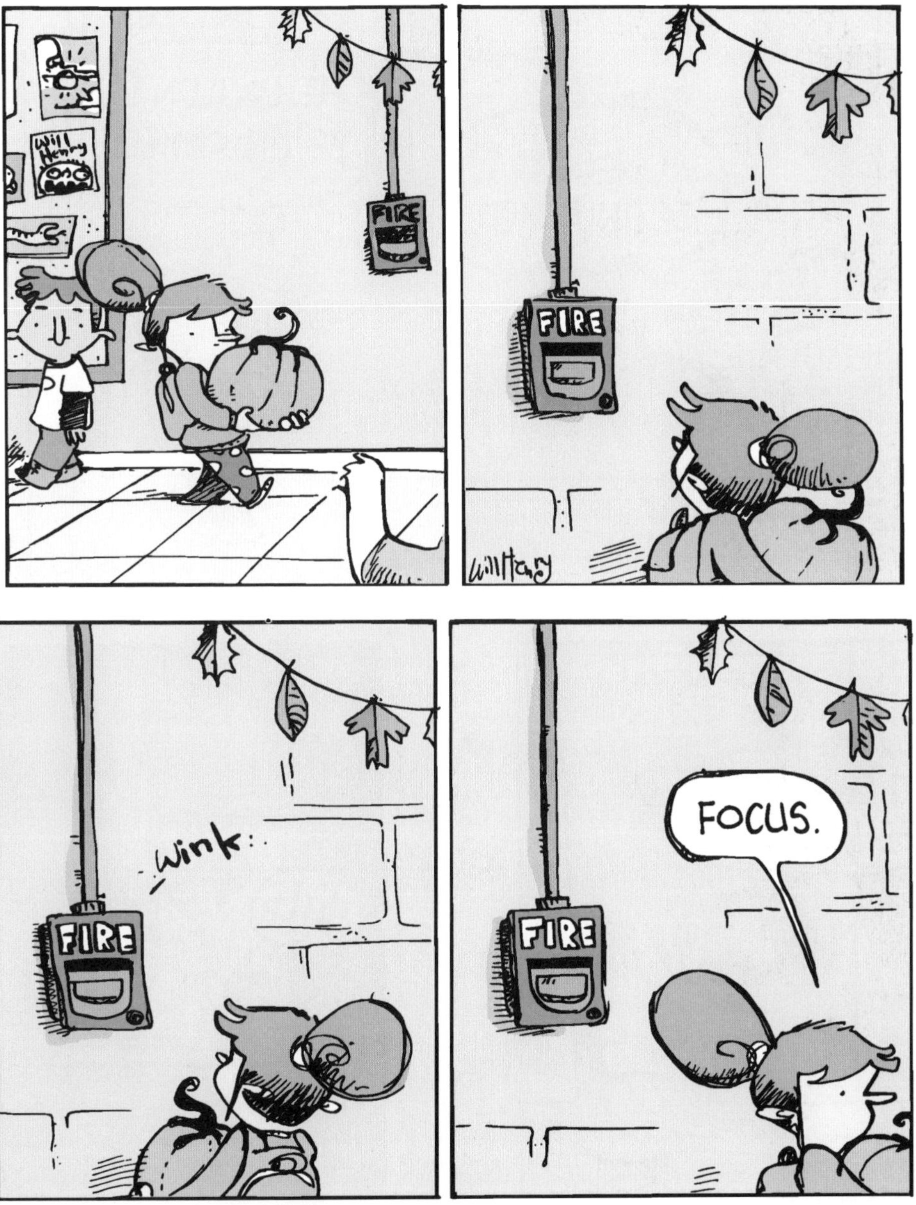
Will Henry
FIRE
FIRE
Will Henry
FIRE
wink
FIRE
FOCUS.

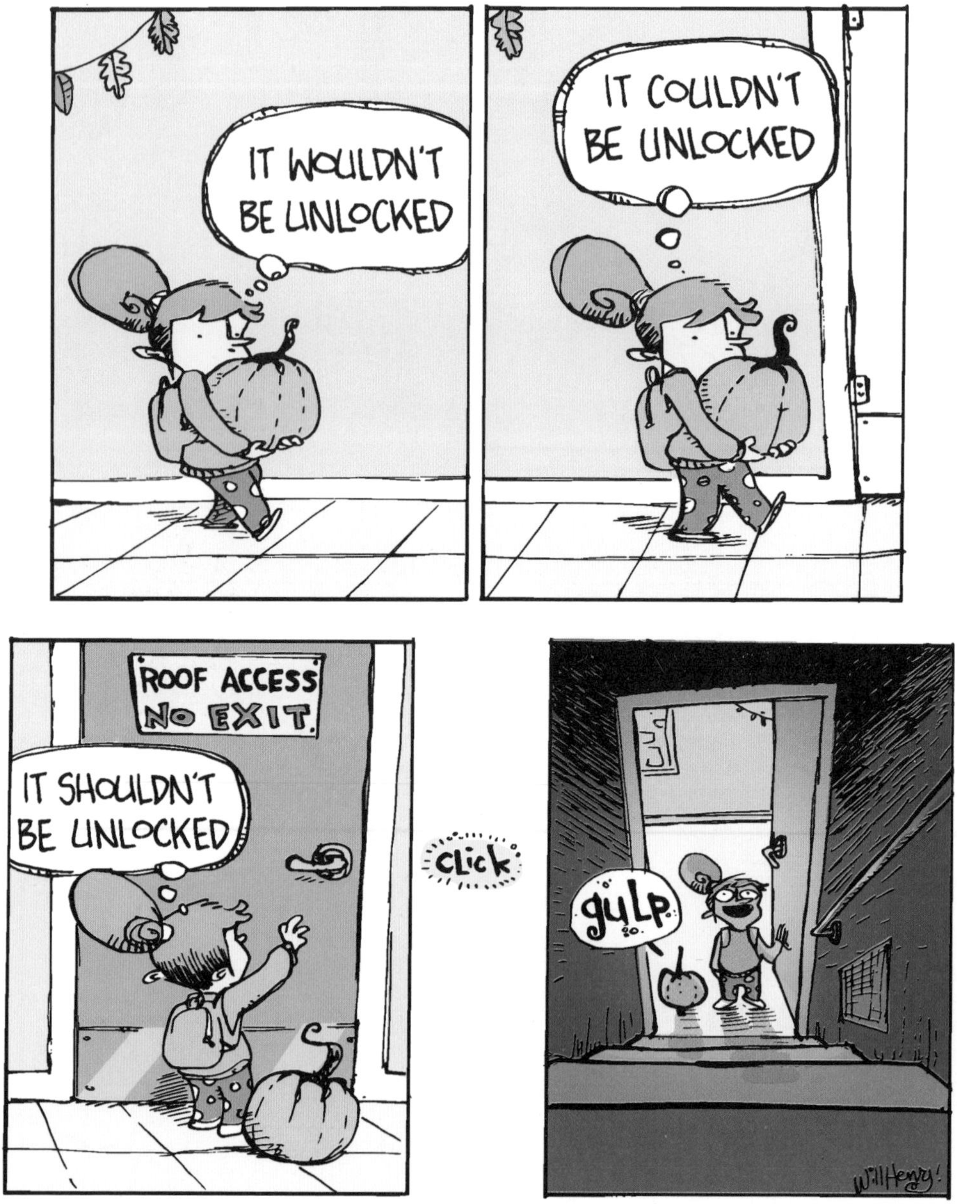
IT WOULDN'T BE UNLOCKED
IT COULDN'T BE UNLOCKED
ROOF ACCESS
NO EXIT
IT SHOULDN'T BE UNLOCKED
CLICK
gulp
Will Henry!

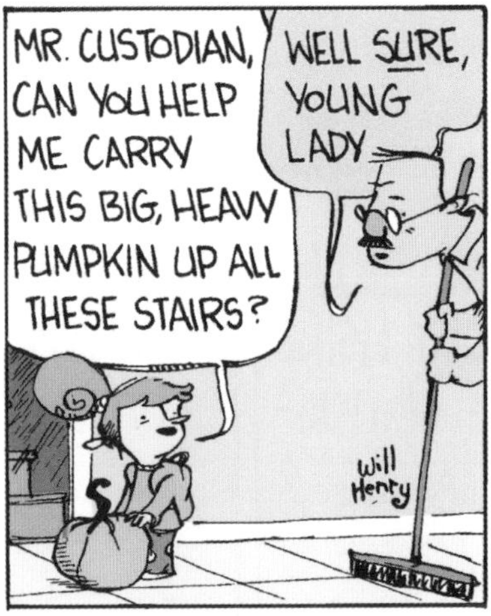
MR. CUSTODIAN, CAN YOU HELP ME CARRY THIS BIG, HEAVY PUMPKIN UP ALL THESE STAIRS?
WELL SURE, YOUNG LADY
Will Henry

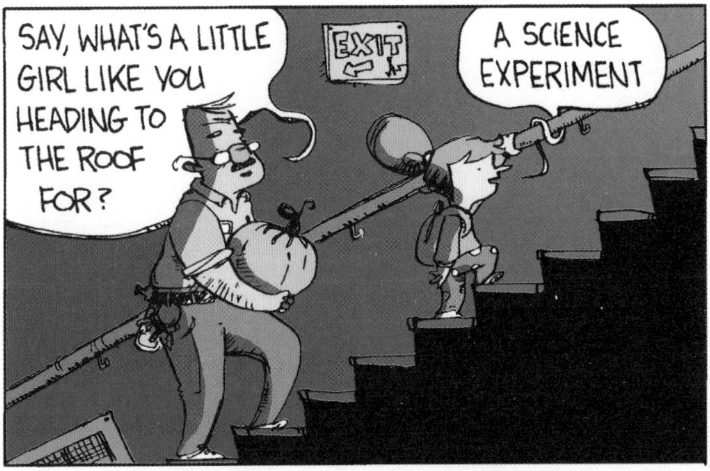
SAY, WHAT'S A LITTLE GIRL LIKE YOU HEADING TO THE ROOF FOR?
EXIT
A SCIENCE EXPERIMENT

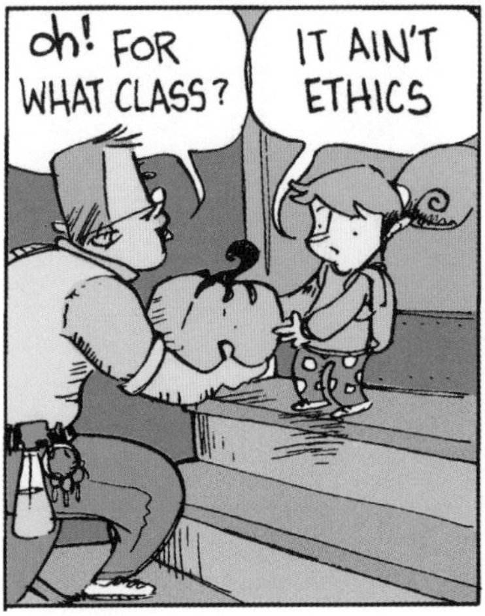
oh! FOR WHAT CLASS?
IT AIN'T ETHICS

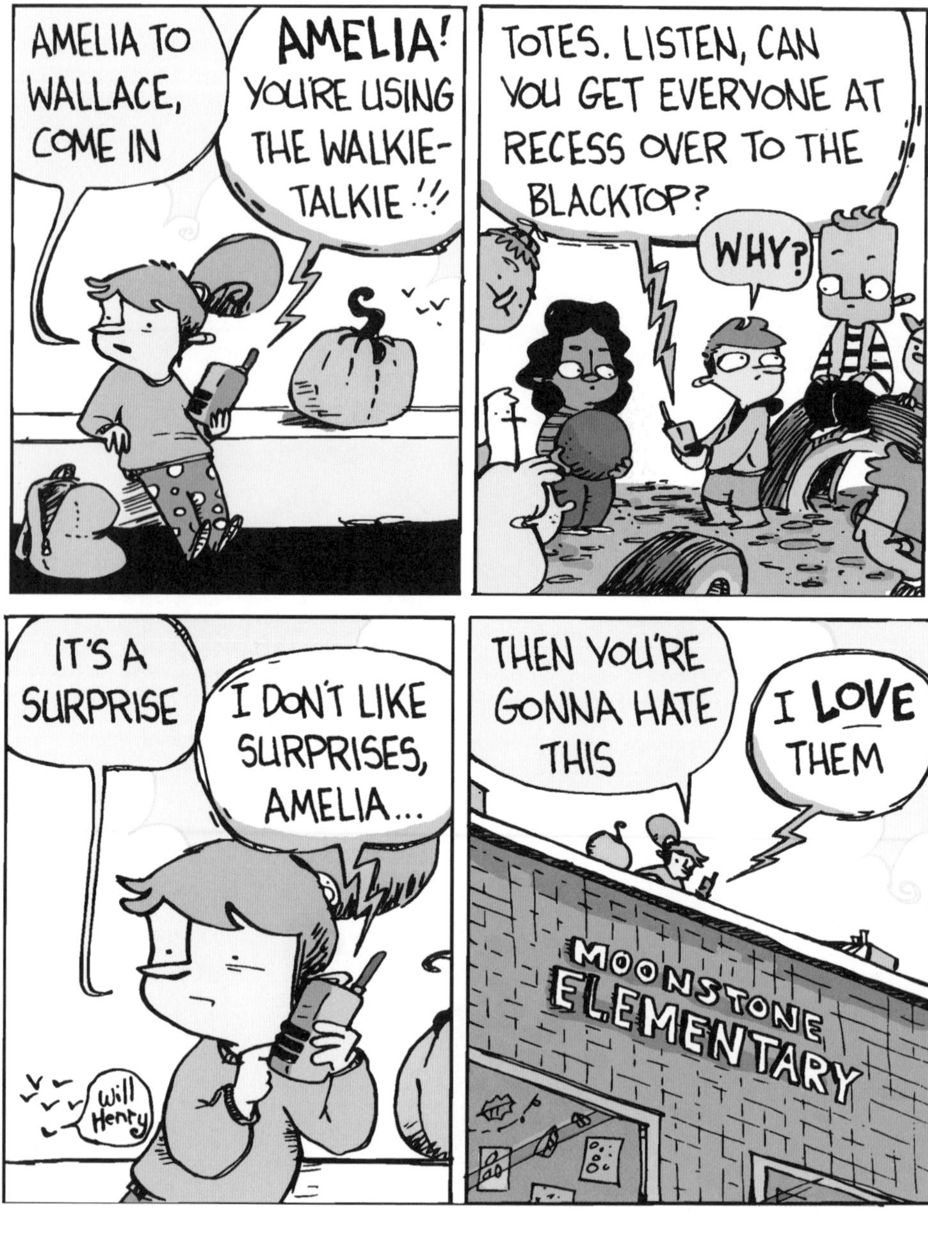
AMELIA TO WALLACE, COME IN
AMELIA! YOU'RE USING THE WALKIE-TALKIE!!
TOTES. LISTEN, CAN YOU GET EVERYONE AT RECESS OVER TO THE BLACKTOP?
WHY?
IT'S A SURPRISE
I DON'T LIKE SURPRISES, AMELIA...
Will Henry
THEN YOU'RE GONNA HATE THIS
I LOVE THEM
MOONSTONE ELEMENTARY

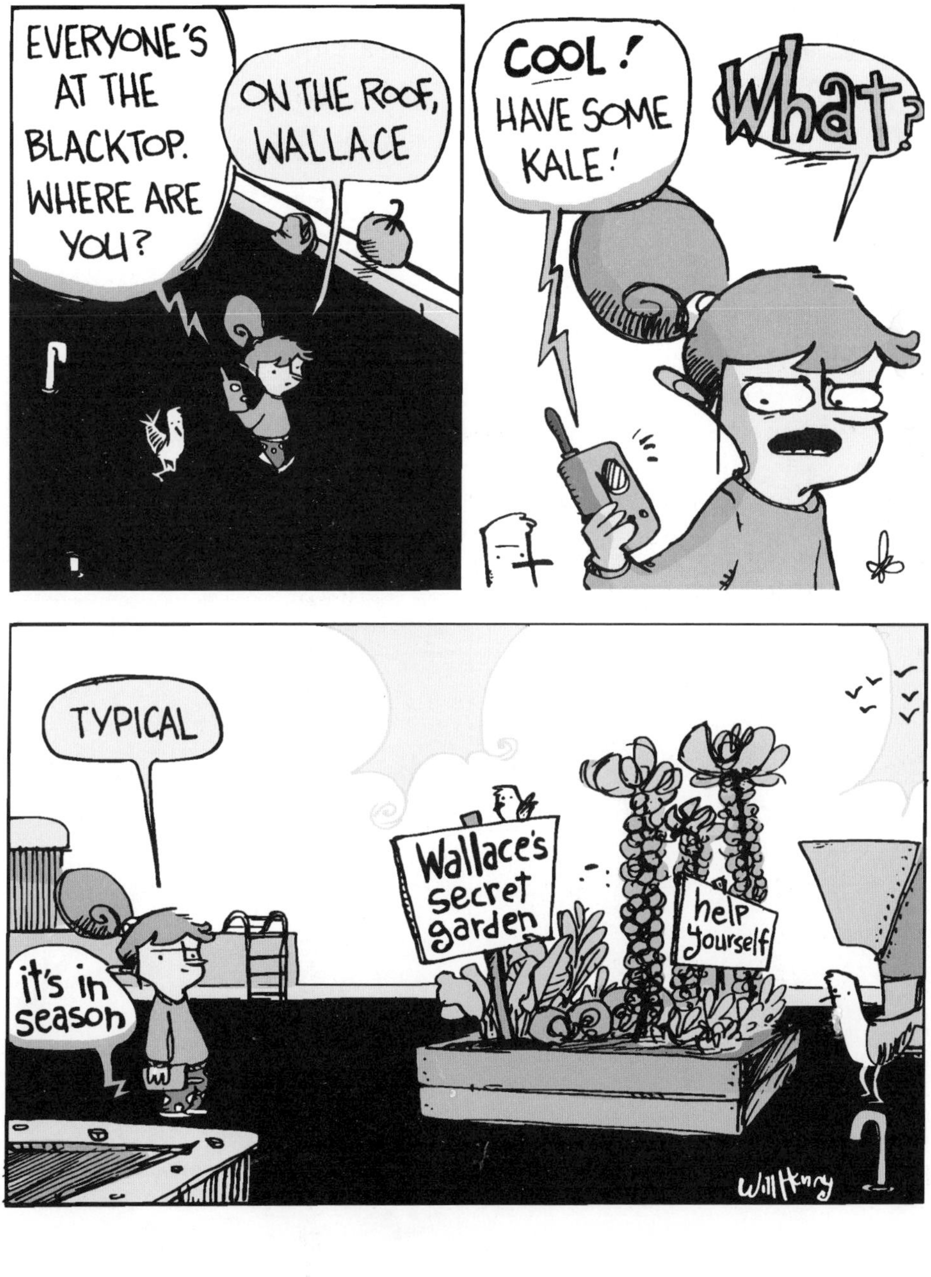
EVERYONE'S AT THE BLACKTOP. WHERE ARE YOU?
ON THE ROOF, WALLACE
COOL! HAVE SOME KALE!
What?
TYPICAL
it's in season
Wallace's secret garden
help yourself
Will Henry

AMELIA, SPUD WANTS TO TALK TO YOU, OVER
I WROTE YOU A POEM
AMELIA, oh AMELIA, YOUR HAIR IS SO RED-
Will Henry
I THINK YOU'RE A COOL PERSON-
screek
LET'S EAT GARLIC BREAD

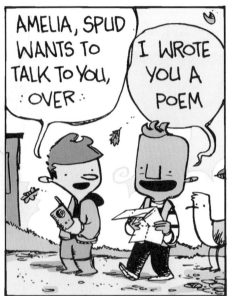

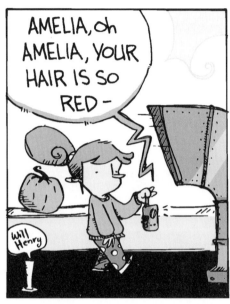

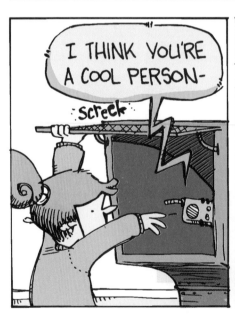

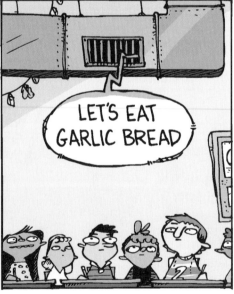

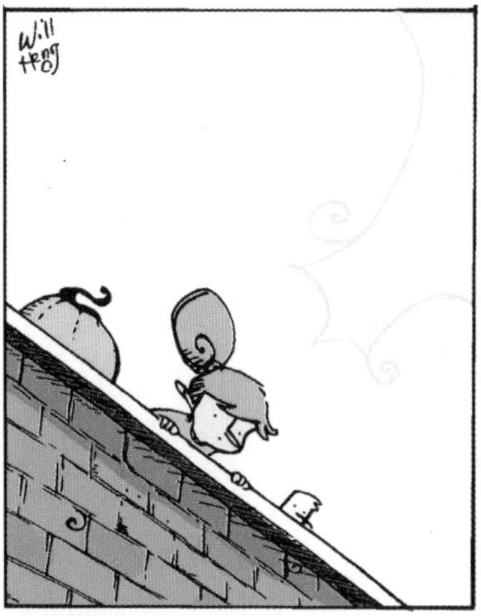

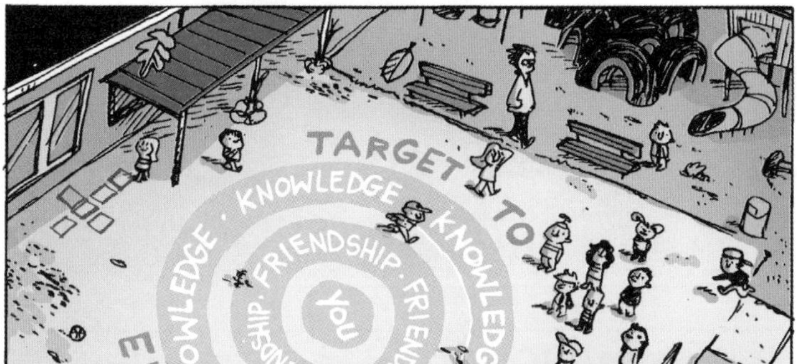
TARGET TO EDUCATION
KNOWLEDGE · KNOWLEDGE · KNOWLEDGE · KNOWLEDGE
FRIENDSHIP · FRIENDSHIP · FRIENDSHIP · FRIENDSHIP
YOU

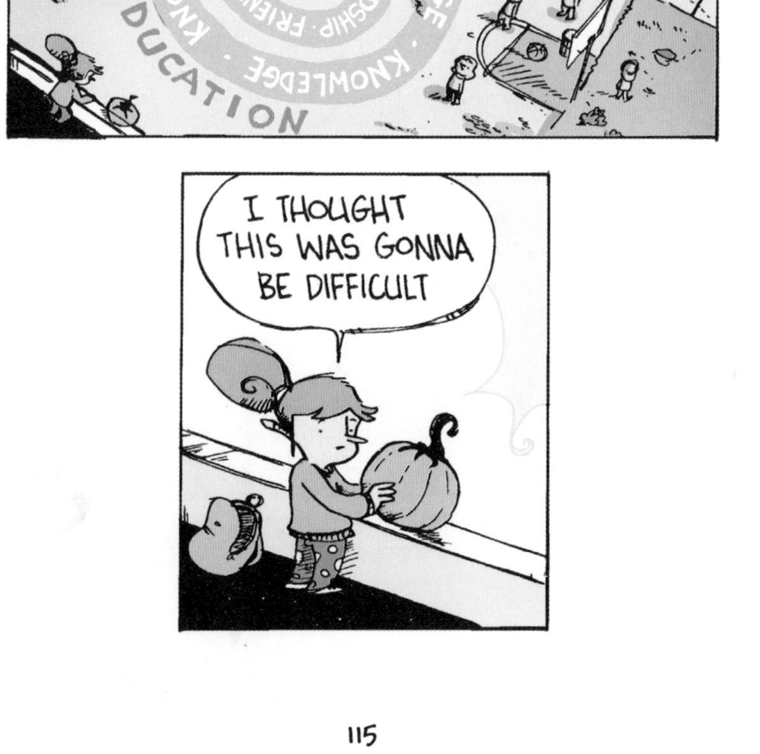
I THOUGHT THIS WAS GONNA BE DIFFICULT

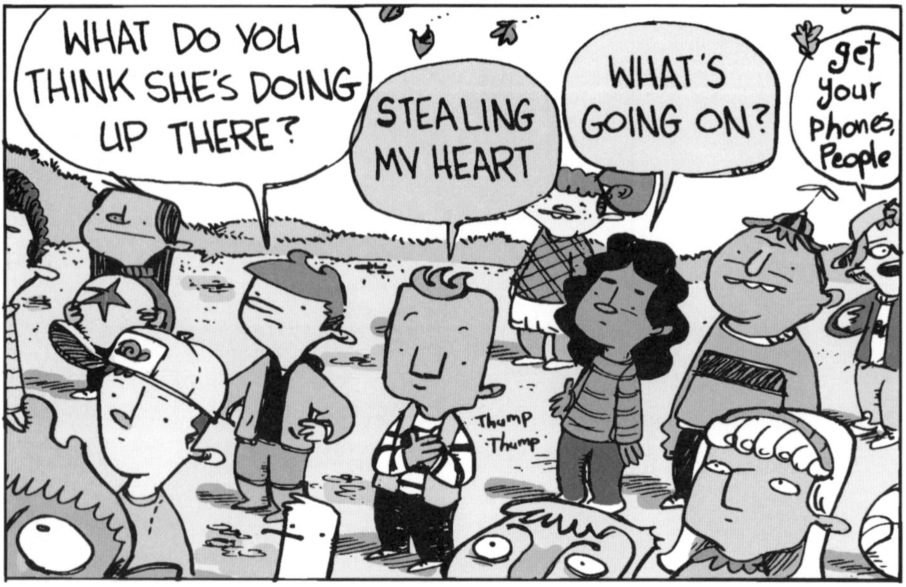
WHAT DO YOU THINK SHE'S DOING UP THERE?
STEALING MY HEART
WHAT'S GOING ON?
get your Phones, People
Thump Thump

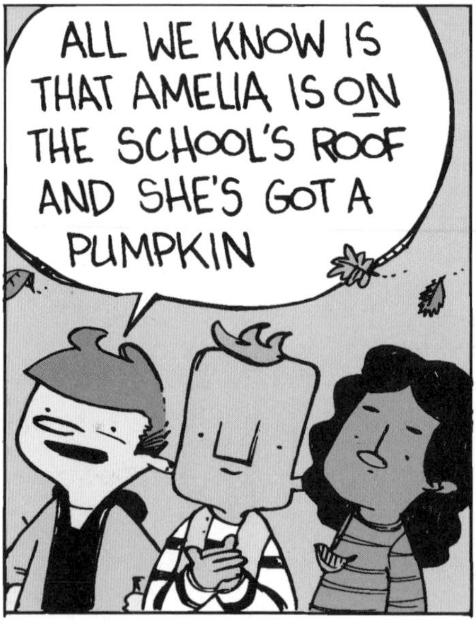
ALL WE KNOW IS THAT AMELIA IS ON THE SCHOOL'S ROOF AND SHE'S GOT A PUMPKIN

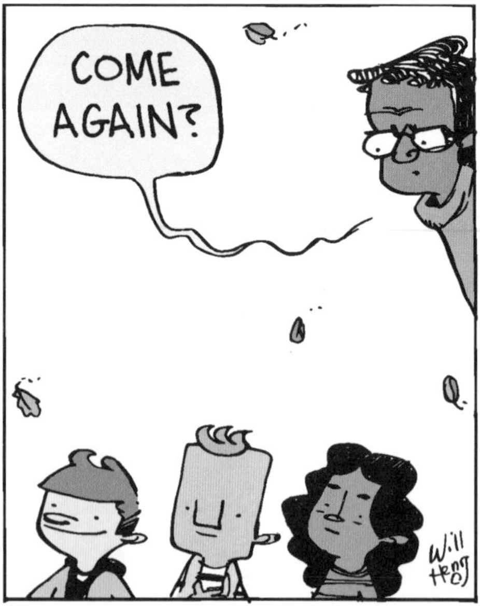
COME AGAIN?
Will Henry

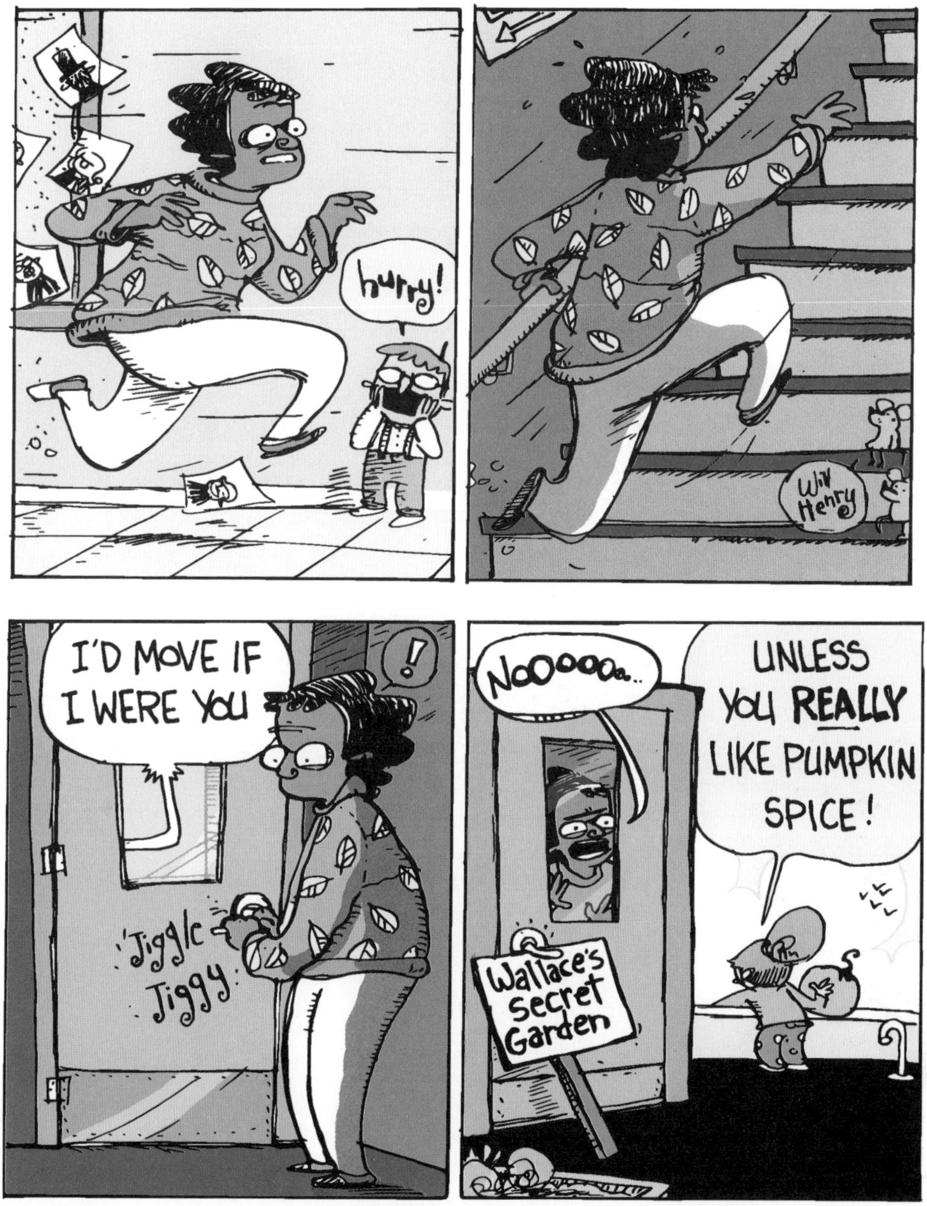

hurry!
Will Henry
I'D MOVE IF I WERE YOU
!
Jiggle Jiggy
NoOooo...
UNLESS YOU REALLY LIKE PUMPKIN SPICE!
Wallace's Secret Garden

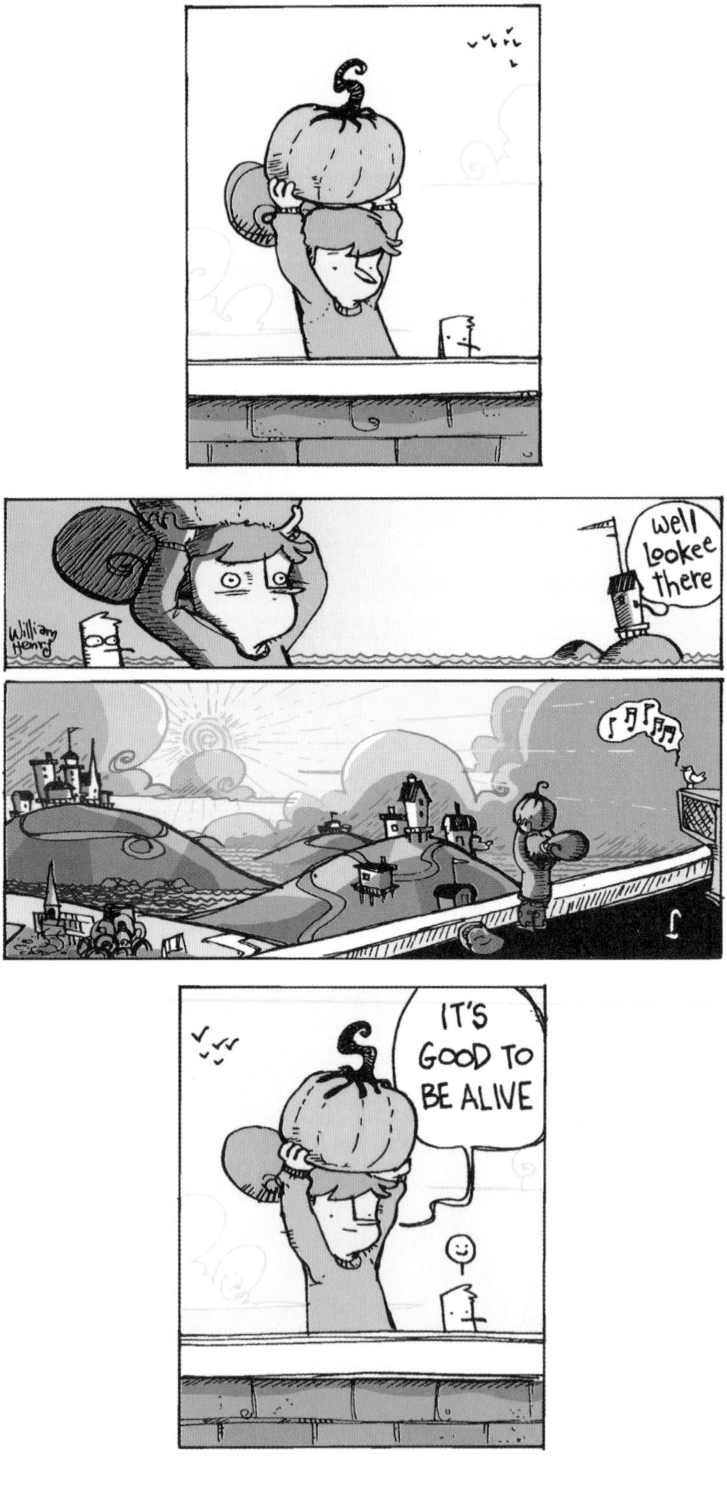
well Lookee there
William Henry
IT'S GOOD TO BE ALIVE

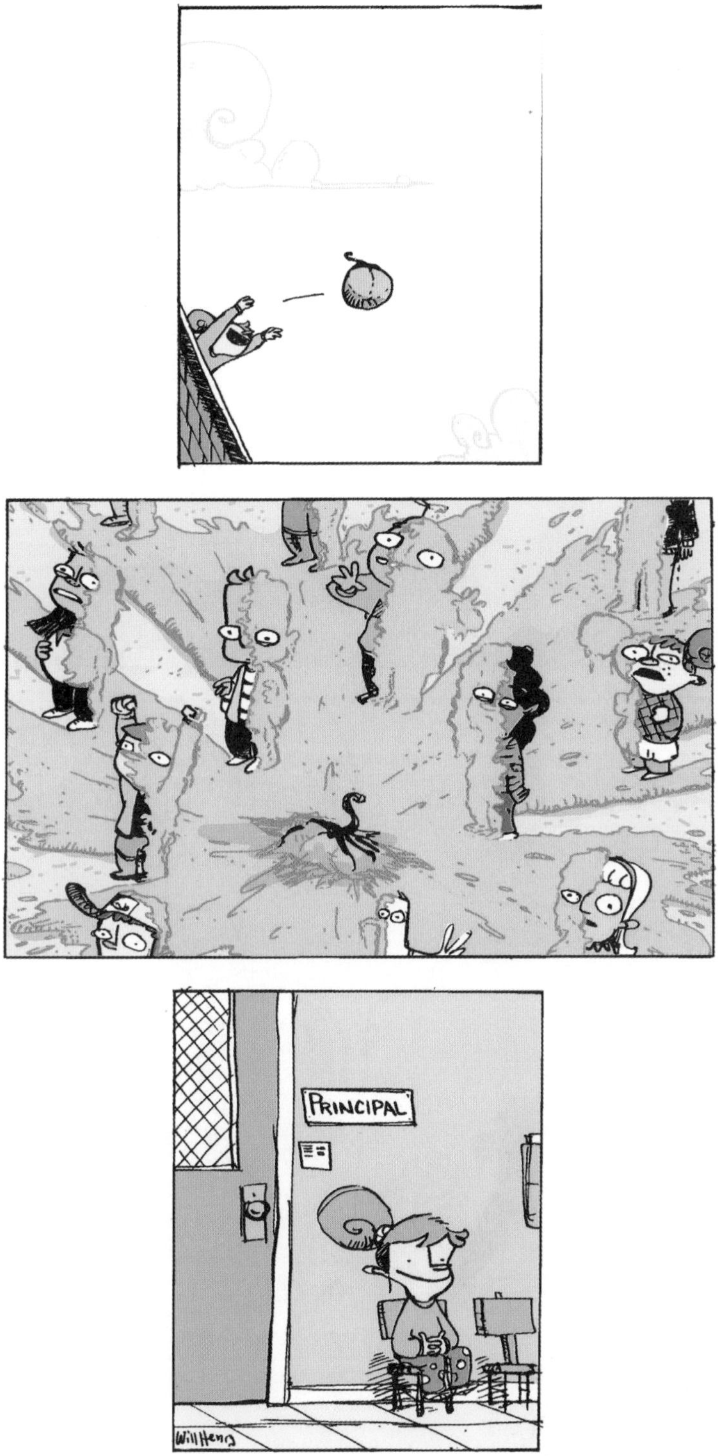
PRINCIPAL
Will Henry

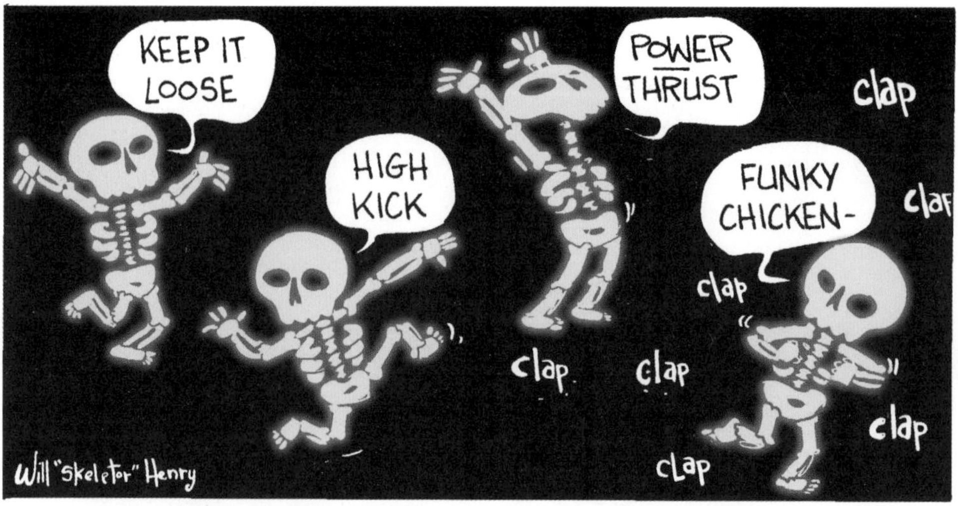
KEEP IT LOOSE
HIGH KICK
POWER THRUST
clap
FUNKY CHICKEN-
clap
clap
clap
clap
clap
clap
Will "skeletor" Henry

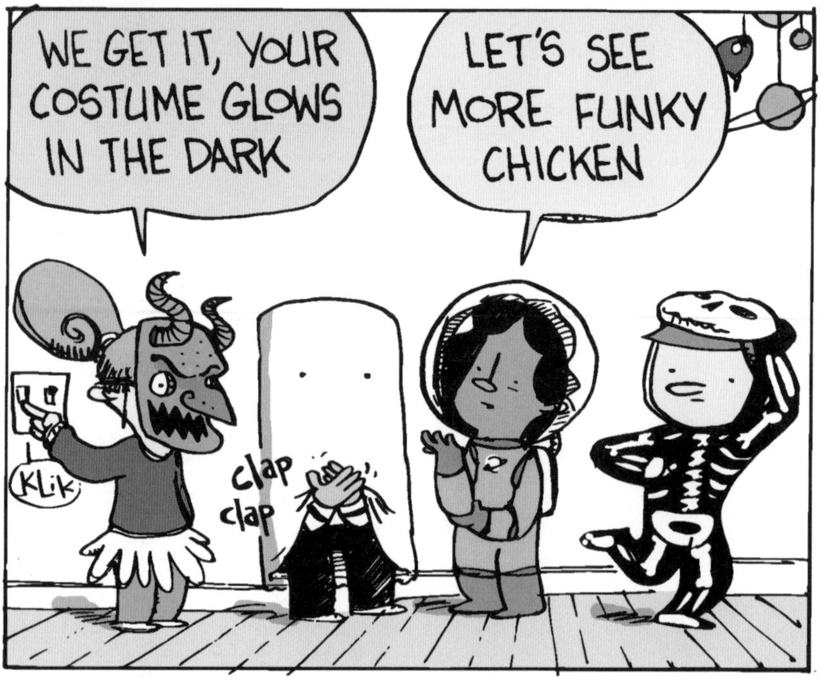
WE GET IT, YOUR COSTUME GLOWS IN THE DARK
LET'S SEE MORE FUNKY CHICKEN
KLIK
clap
clap

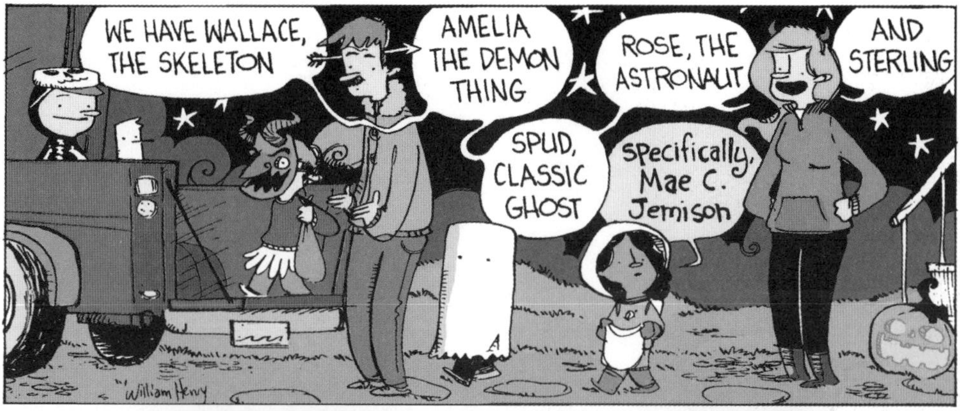

WE HAVE WALLACE, THE SKELETON
AMELIA THE DEMON THING
SPUD, CLASSIC GHOST
ROSE, THE ASTRONAUT
Specifically, Mae C. Jemison
AND STERLING
William Henry

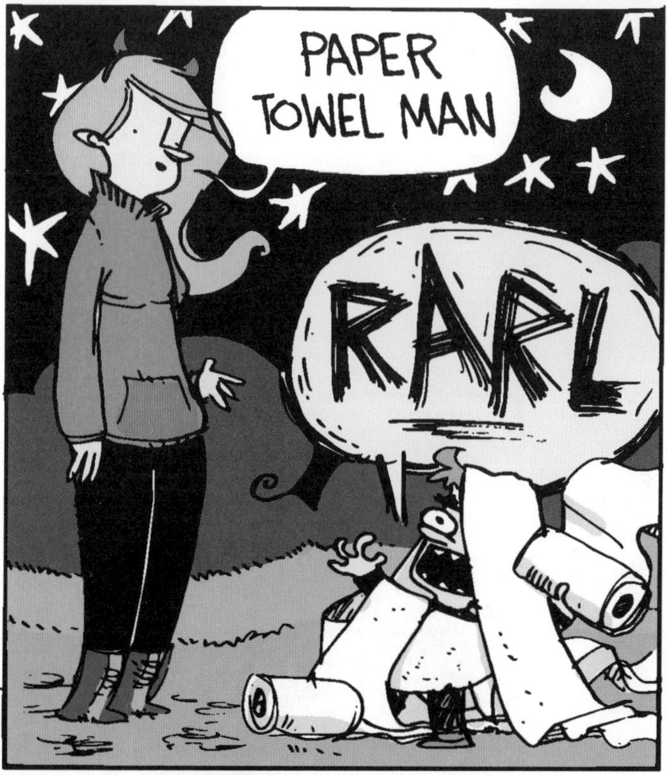

PAPER TOWEL MAN
RARL

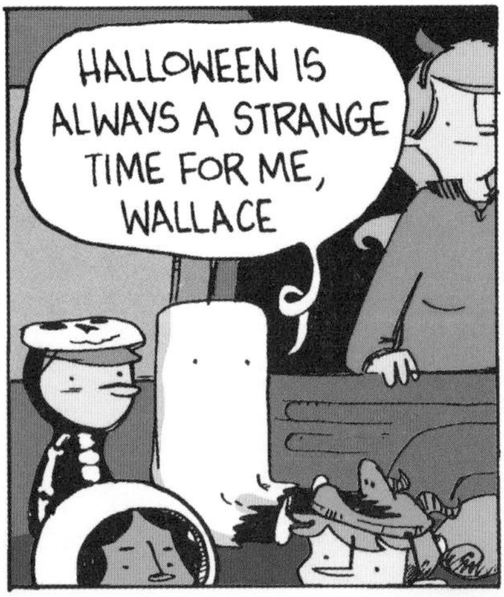
HALLOWEEN IS ALWAYS A STRANGE TIME FOR ME, WALLACE

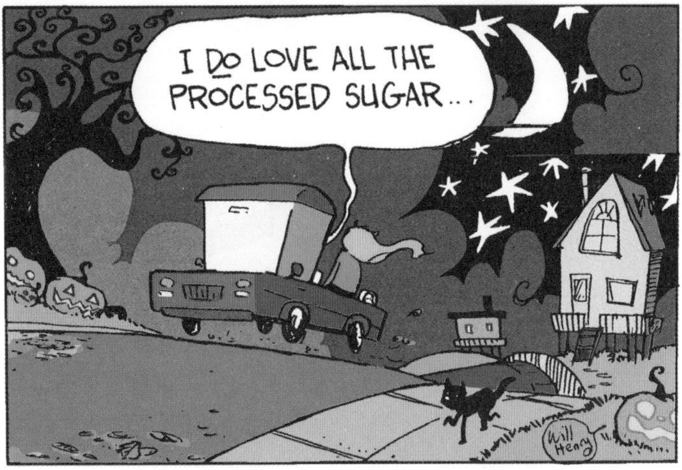
I DO LOVE ALL THE PROCESSED SUGAR...
Will Henry

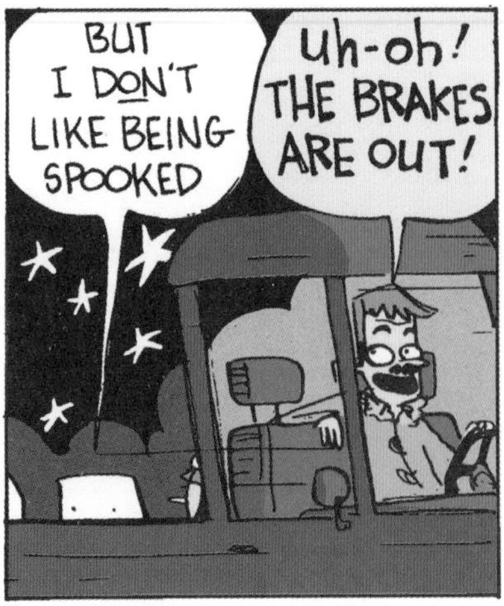
BUT I DON'T LIKE BEING SPOOKED
uh-oh! THE BRAKES ARE OUT!

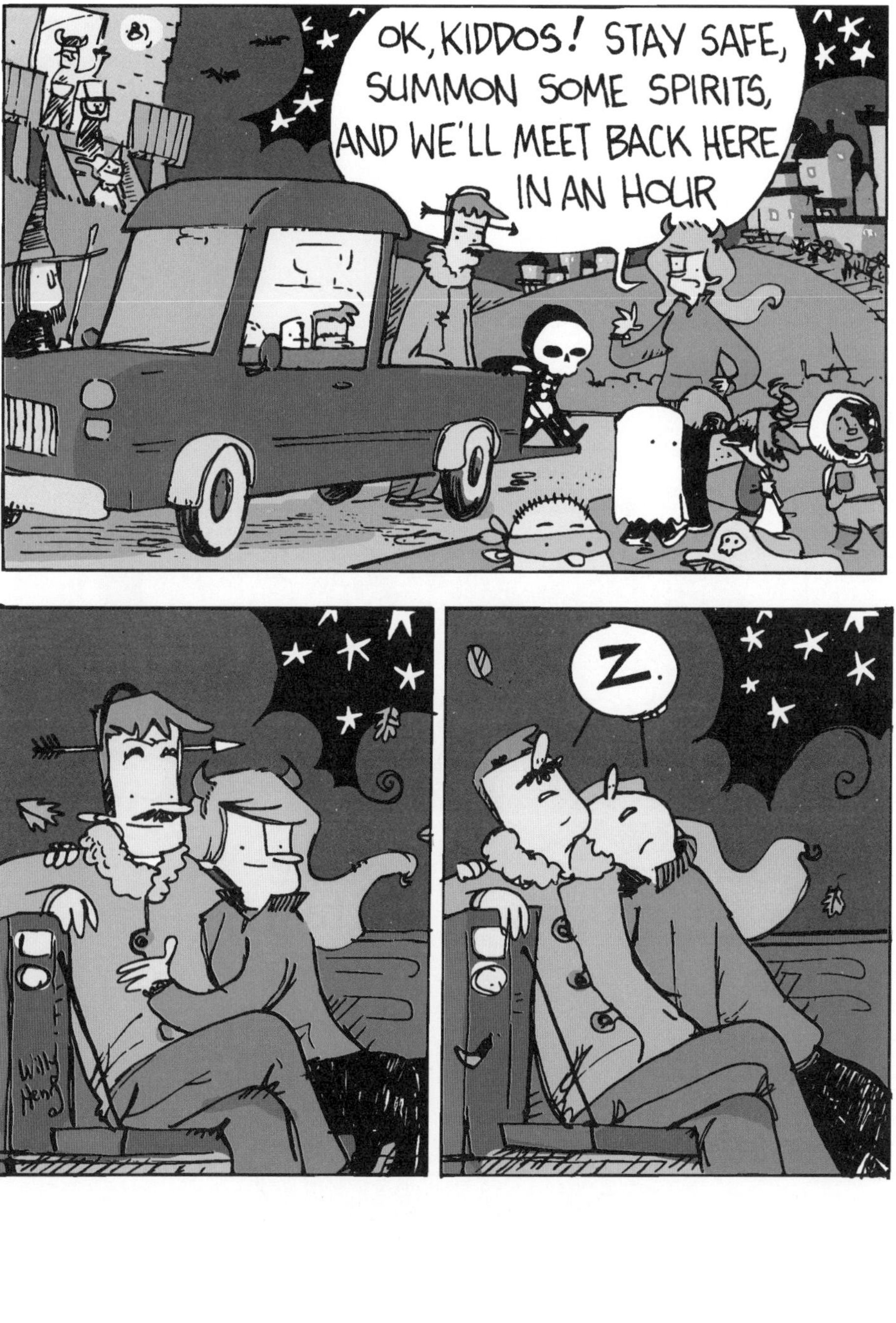
OK, KIDDOS! STAY SAFE, SUMMON SOME SPIRITS, AND WE'LL MEET BACK HERE IN AN HOUR
Z.

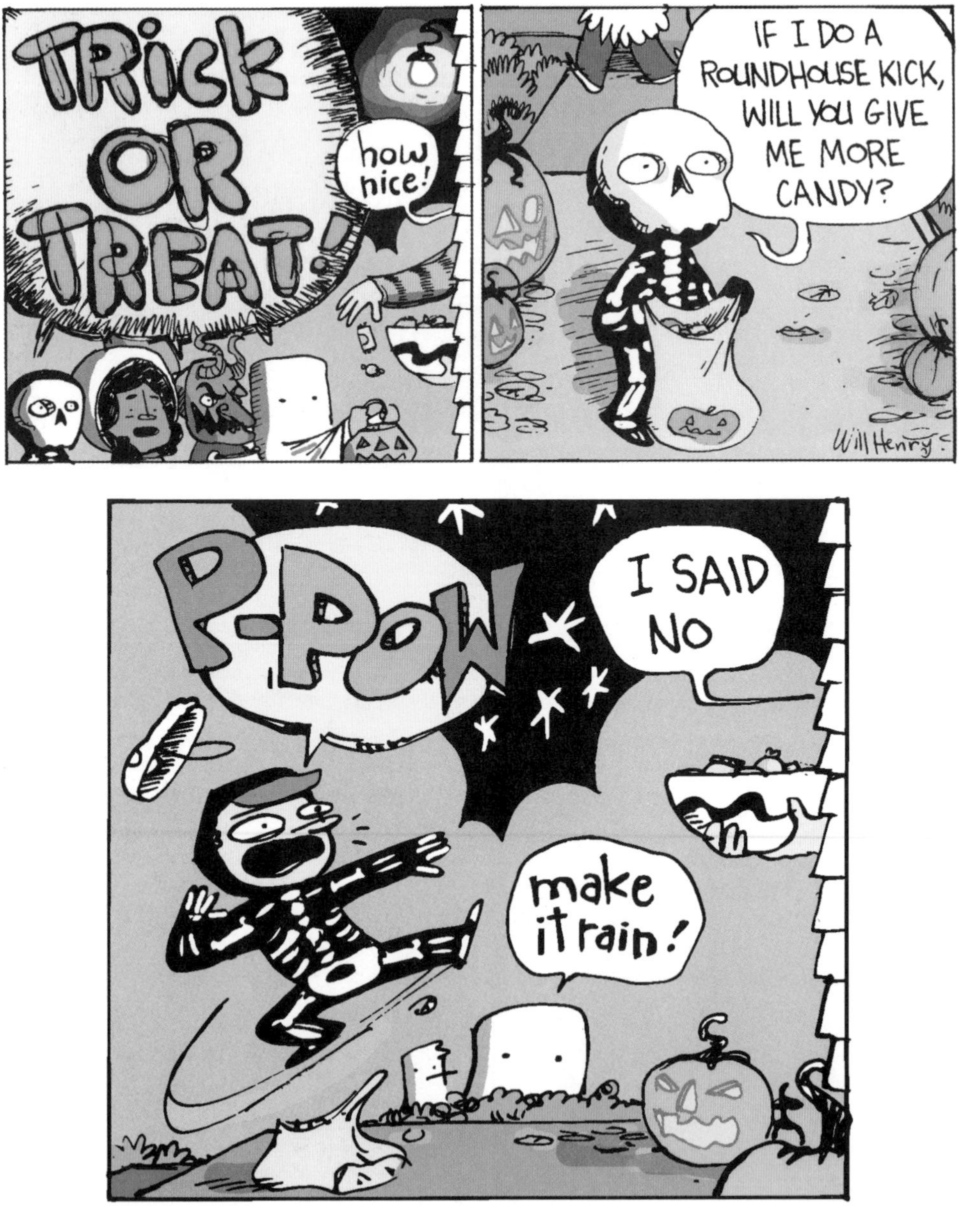
TRICK OR TREAT!
how nice!
IF I DO A ROUNDHOUSE KICK, WILL YOU GIVE ME MORE CANDY?
Will Henry
P-POW
I SAID NO
make it rain!

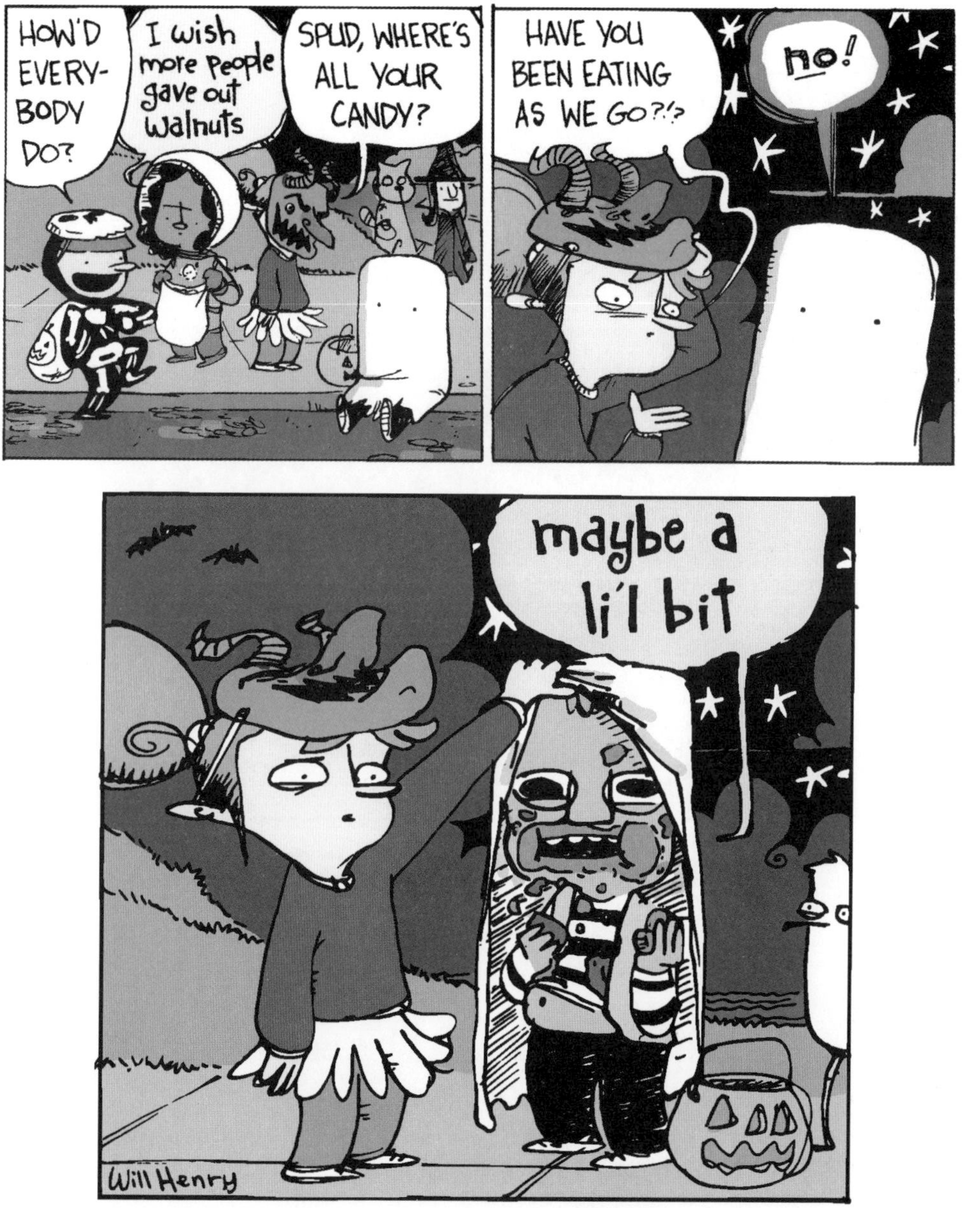
HOW'D EVERY-BODY DO?
I wish more people gave out walnuts
SPUD, WHERE'S ALL YOUR CANDY?
HAVE YOU BEEN EATING AS WE GO?!?
no!
maybe a li'l bit
Will Henry

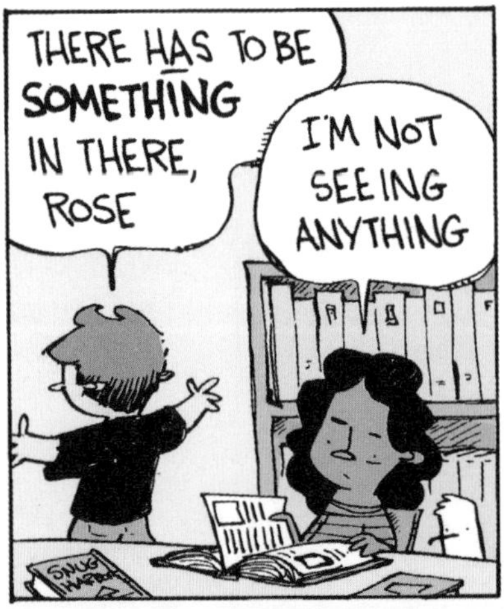
THERE HAS TO BE SOMETHING IN THERE, ROSE
I'M NOT SEEING ANYTHING

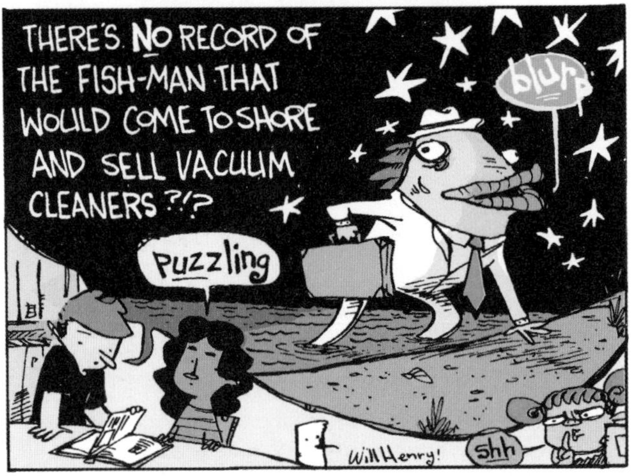
THERE'S NO RECORD OF THE FISH-MAN THAT WOULD COME TO SHORE AND SELL VACUUM CLEANERS ?!?
blurp
puzzling
shh
Will Henry!

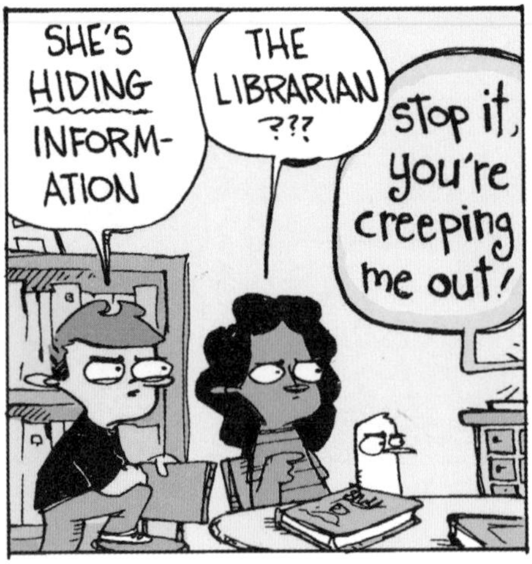
SHE'S HIDING INFORMATION
THE LIBRARIAN ???
stop it, you're creeping me out!

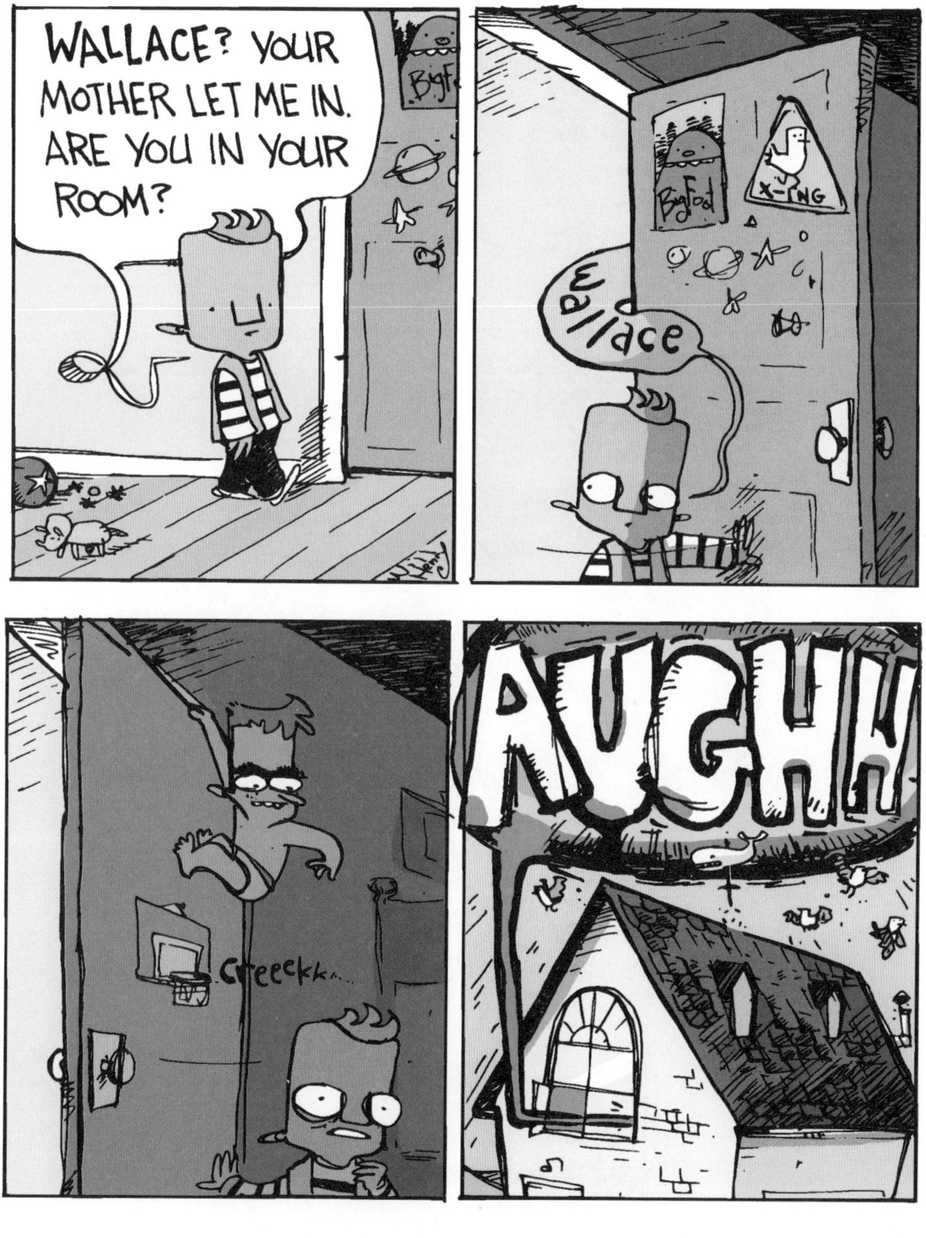
WALLACE? YOUR MOTHER LET ME IN. ARE YOU IN YOUR ROOM?
BigFoot
X-ING
Wallace
Creeekk...
AUGHH

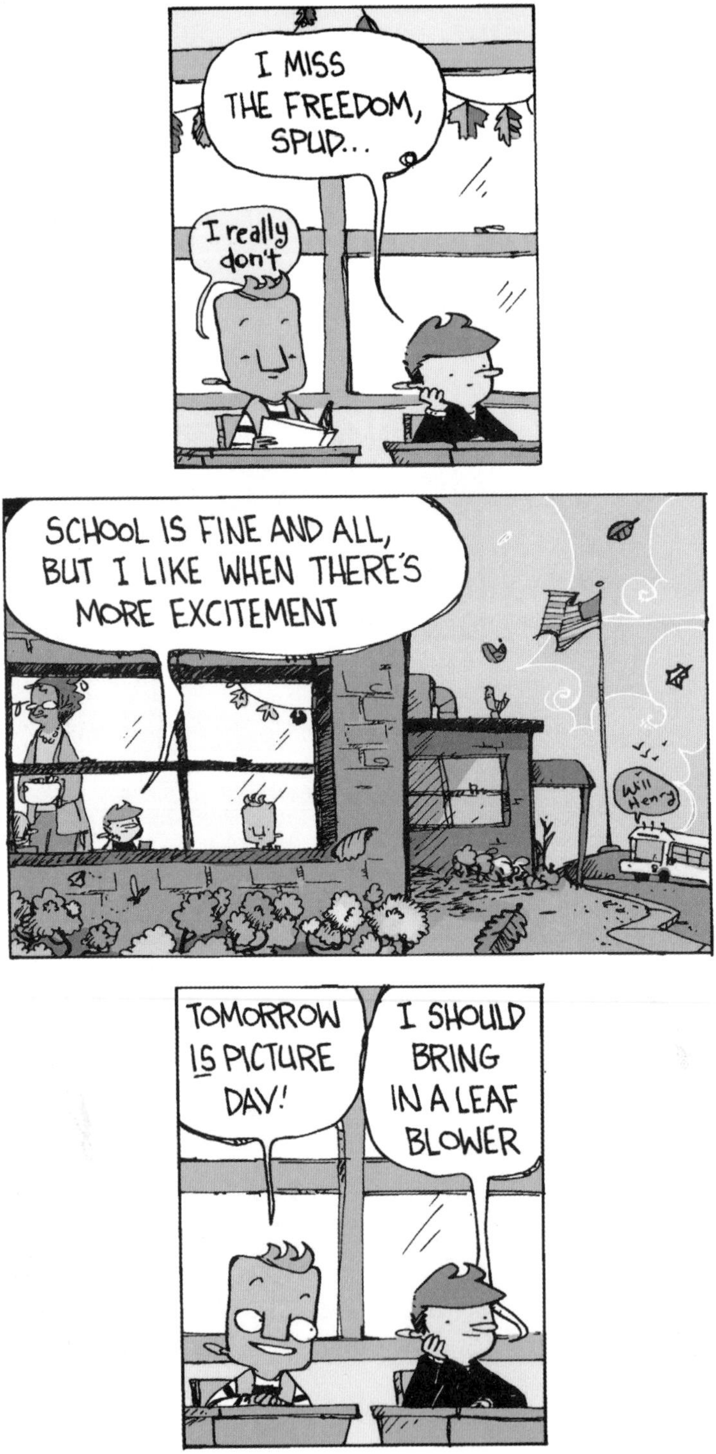
I MISS THE FREEDOM, SPUD...
I really don't
SCHOOL IS FINE AND ALL, BUT I LIKE WHEN THERE'S MORE EXCITEMENT
Will Henry
TOMORROW IS PICTURE DAY!
I SHOULD BRING IN A LEAF BLOWER

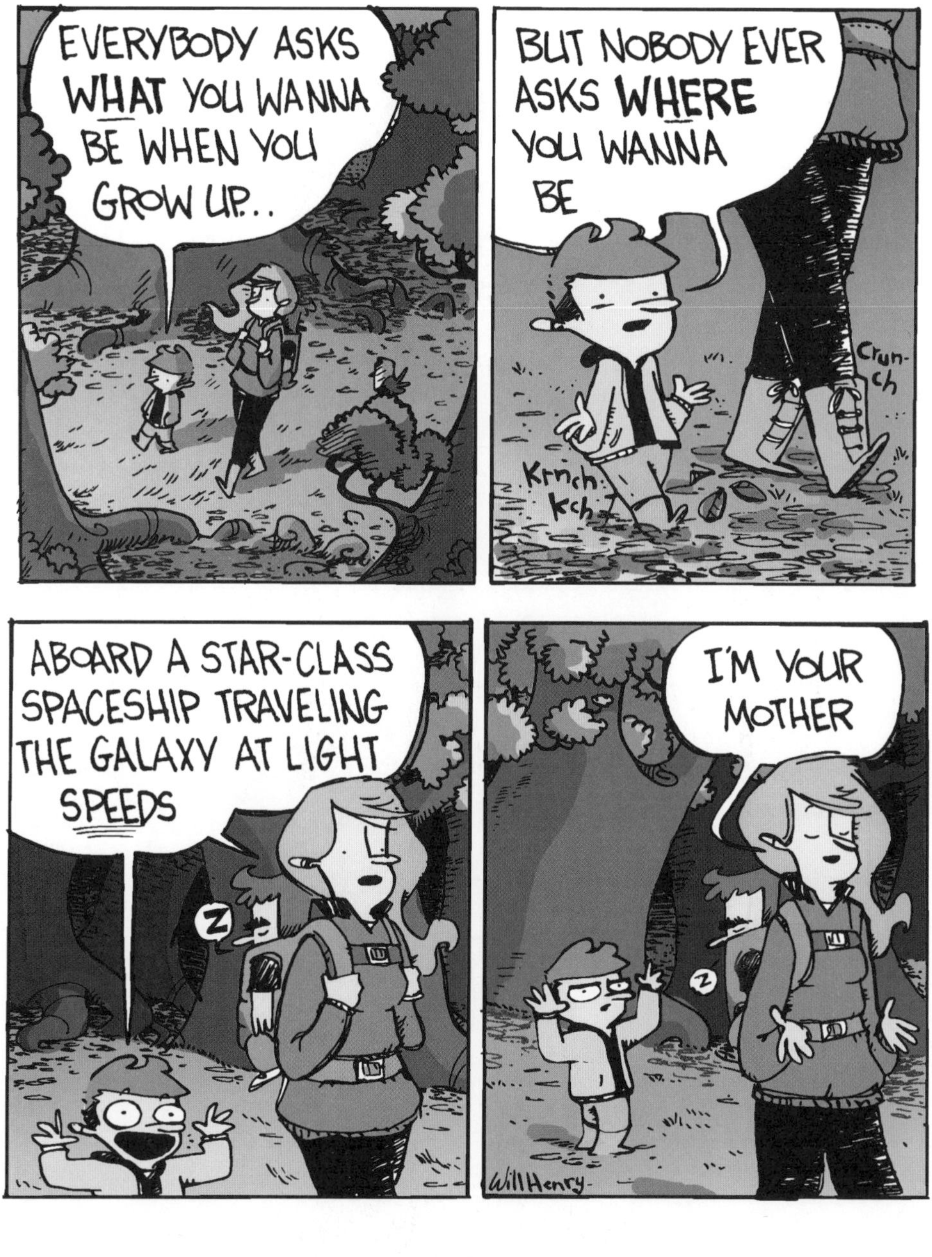
EVERYBODY ASKS WHAT YOU WANNA BE WHEN YOU GROW UP...
BUT NOBODY EVER ASKS WHERE YOU WANNA BE
Krnch Kch
Crun-ch
ABOARD A STAR-CLASS SPACESHIP TRAVELING THE GALAXY AT LIGHT SPEEDS
Z
I'M YOUR MOTHER
Z
Will Henry

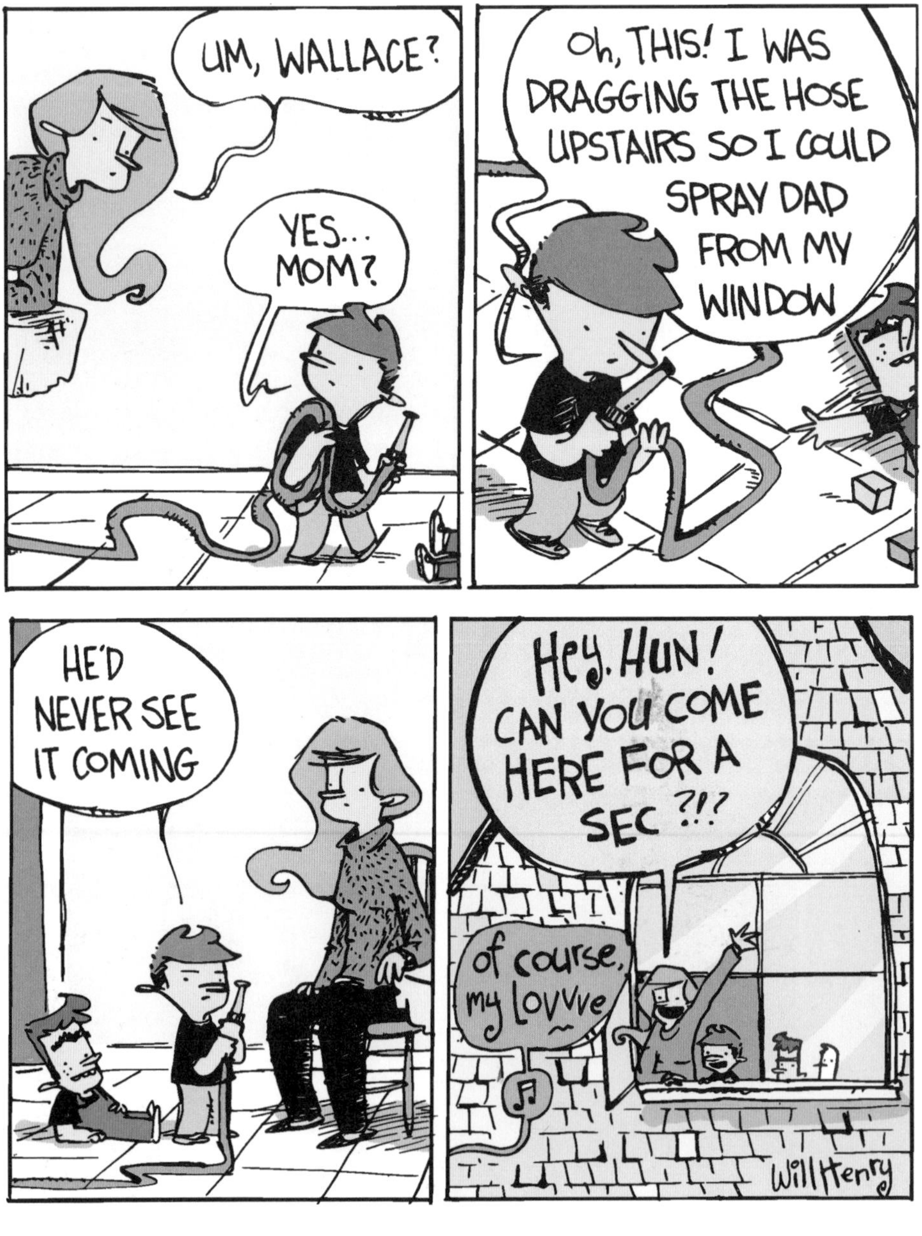
UM, WALLACE?
YES... MOM?
Oh, THIS! I WAS DRAGGING THE HOSE UPSTAIRS SO I COULD SPRAY DAD FROM MY WINDOW
HE'D NEVER SEE IT COMING
Hey, HUN! CAN YOU COME HERE FOR A SEC ?!?
of course, my lovvve ~
Will Henry

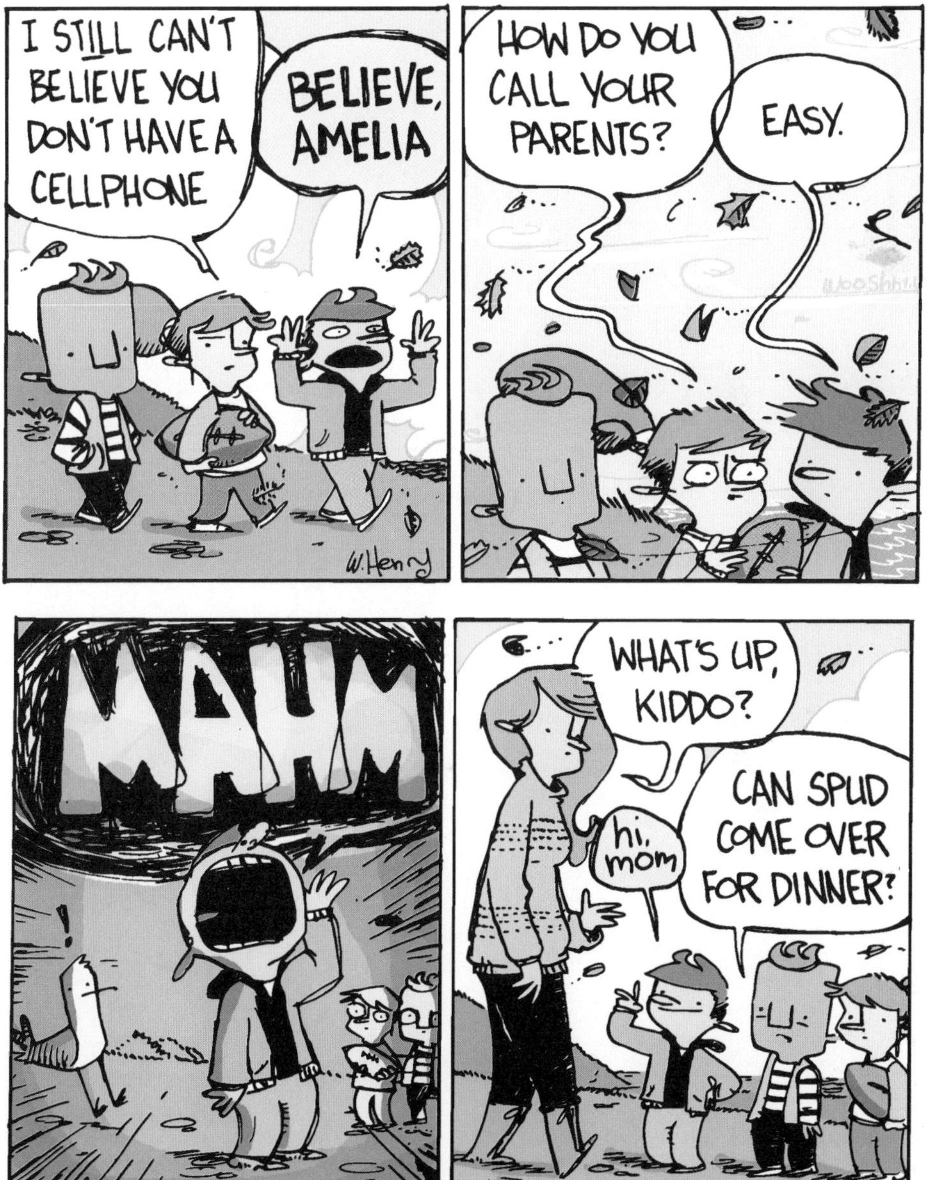
I STILL CAN'T BELIEVE YOU DON'T HAVE A CELLPHONE
BELIEVE, AMELIA
W. Henry
HOW DO YOU CALL YOUR PARENTS?
EASY.
WOOSHH!!
MAHM
WHAT'S UP, KIDDO?
hi, mom
CAN SPUD COME OVER FOR DINNER?

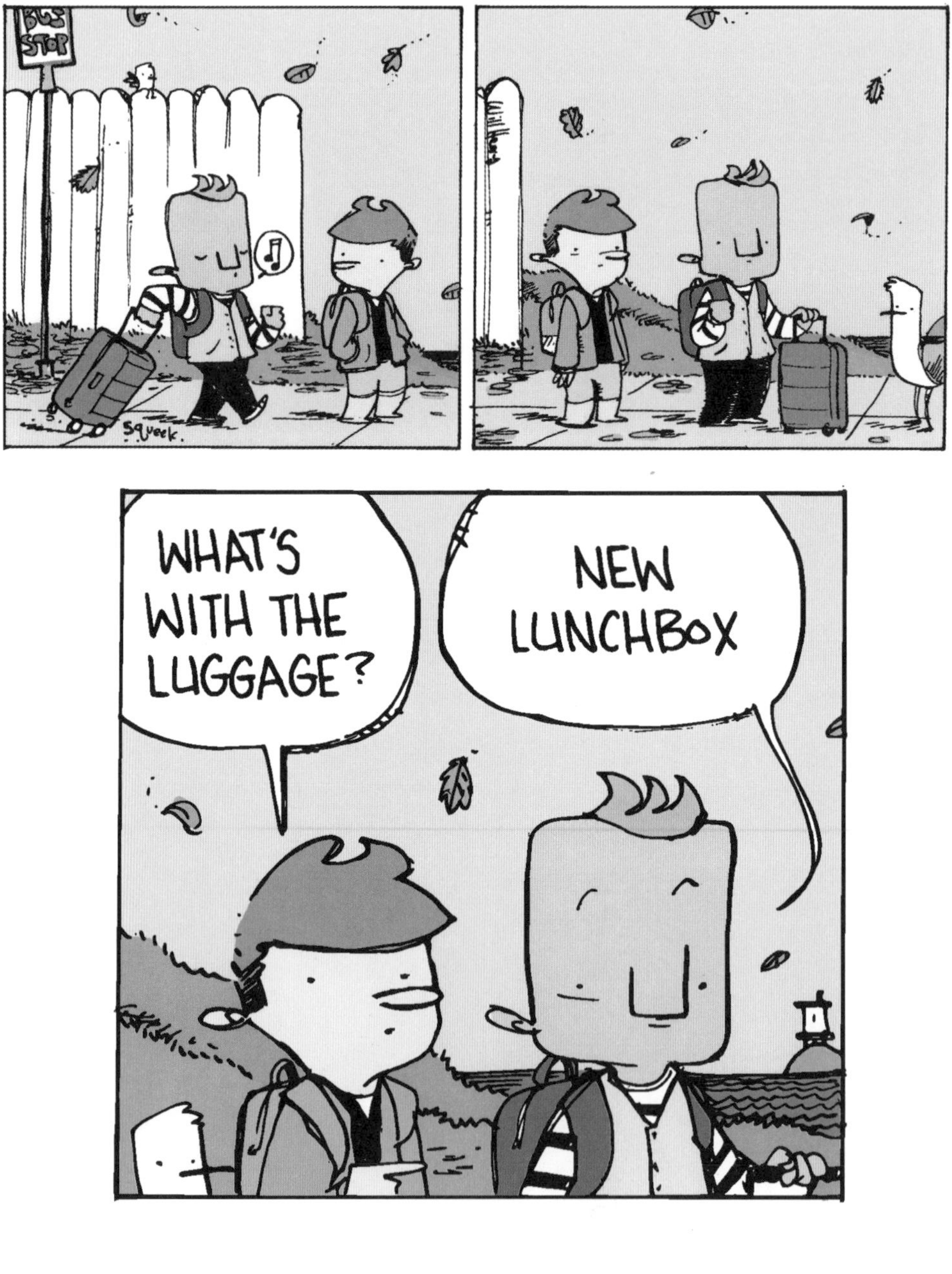
STOP
squeek.
WHAT'S WITH THE LUGGAGE?
NEW LUNCHBOX

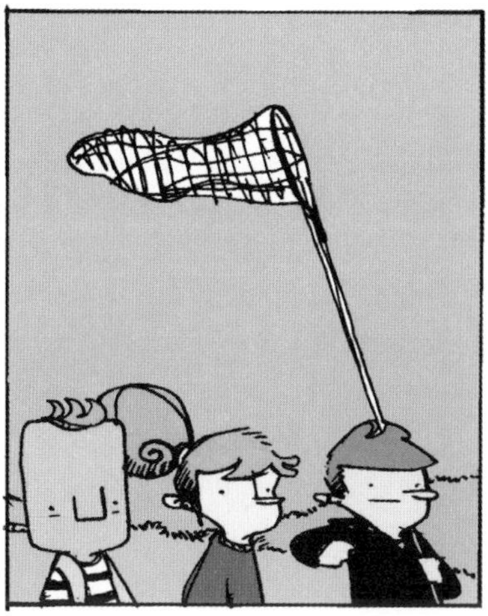

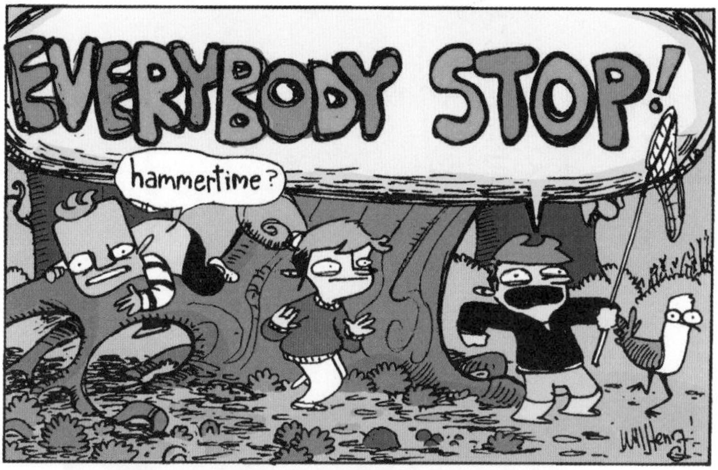
EVERYBODY STOP!
hammertime?

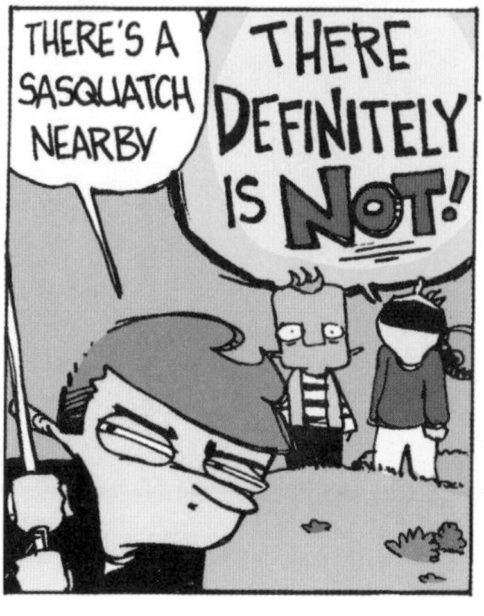
THERE'S A SASQUATCH NEARBY
THERE DEFINITELY IS NOT!

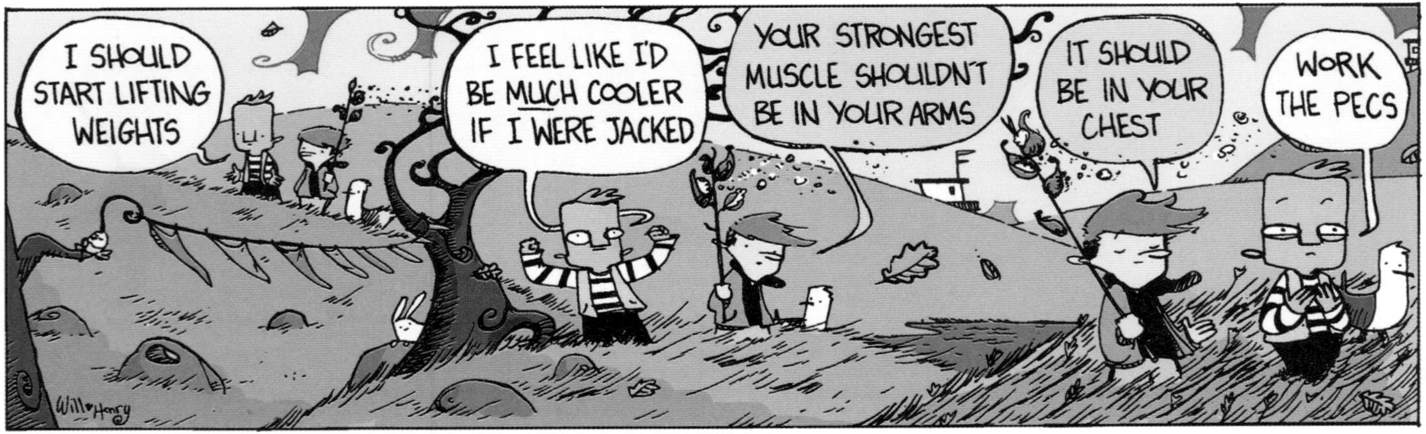
I SHOULD START LIFTING WEIGHTS
I FEEL LIKE I'D BE MUCH COOLER IF I WERE JACKED
YOUR STRONGEST MUSCLE SHOULDN'T BE IN YOUR ARMS
IT SHOULD BE IN YOUR CHEST
WORK THE PECS
Will♥Henry

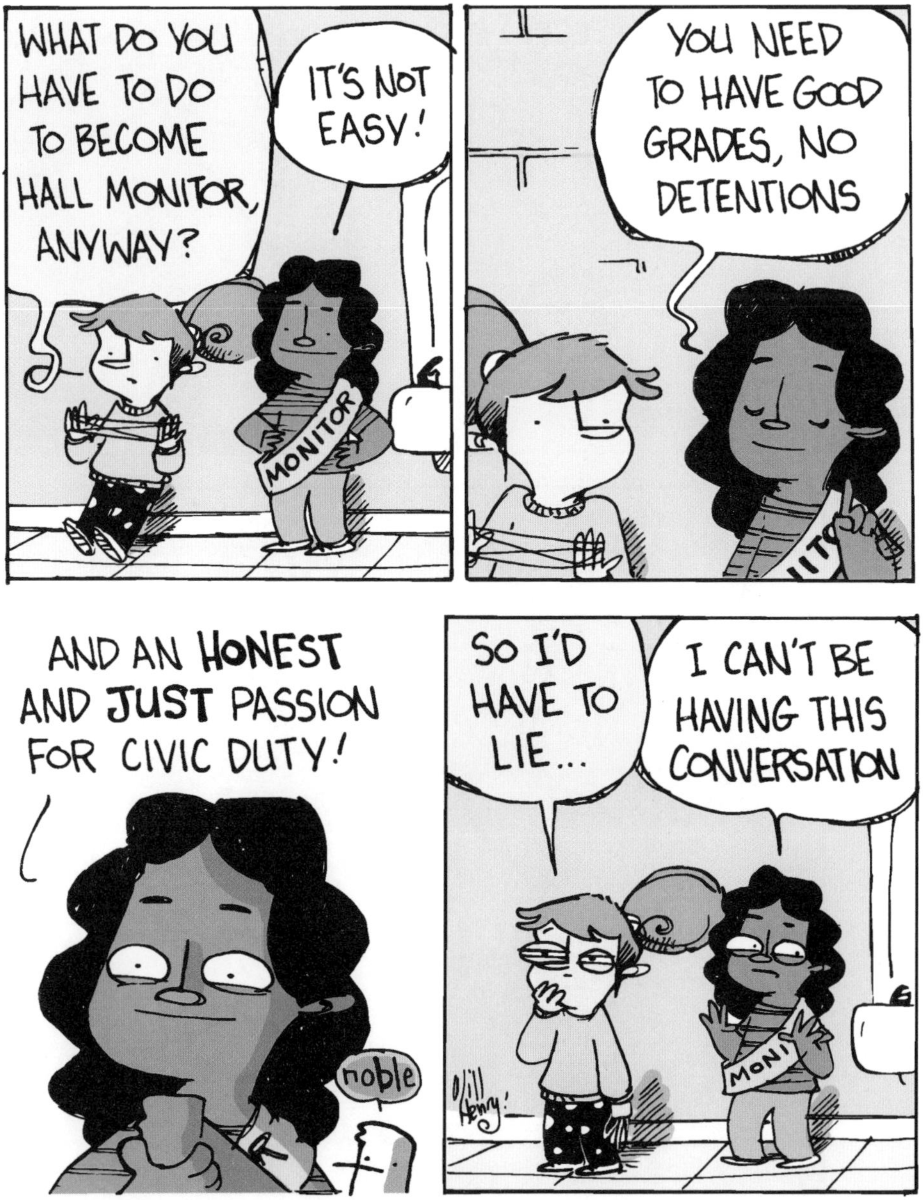

WHAT DO YOU HAVE TO DO TO BECOME HALL MONITOR, ANYWAY?
IT'S NOT EASY!
MONITOR
YOU NEED TO HAVE GOOD GRADES, NO DETENTIONS
AND AN **HONEST** AND **JUST** PASSION FOR CIVIC DUTY!
noble
SO I'D HAVE TO LIE...
I CAN'T BE HAVING THIS CONVERSATION
MONI
©Jill Henry!

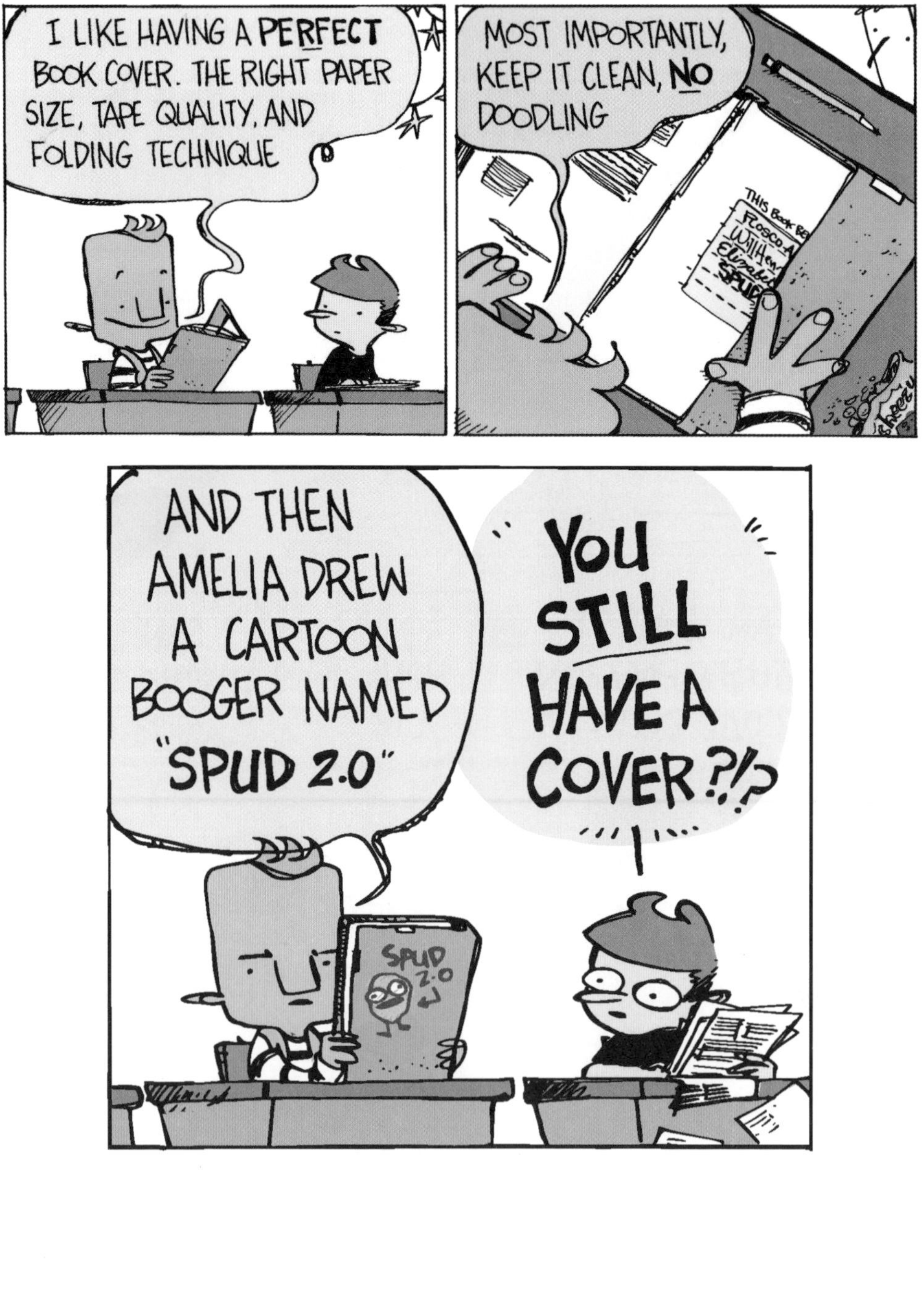
I LIKE HAVING A PERFECT BOOK COVER. THE RIGHT PAPER SIZE, TAPE QUALITY, AND FOLDING TECHNIQUE
MOST IMPORTANTLY, KEEP IT CLEAN, NO DOODLING
AND THEN AMELIA DREW A CARTOON BOOGER NAMED "SPUD 2.0"
YOU STILL HAVE A COVER?!?
SPUD 2.0

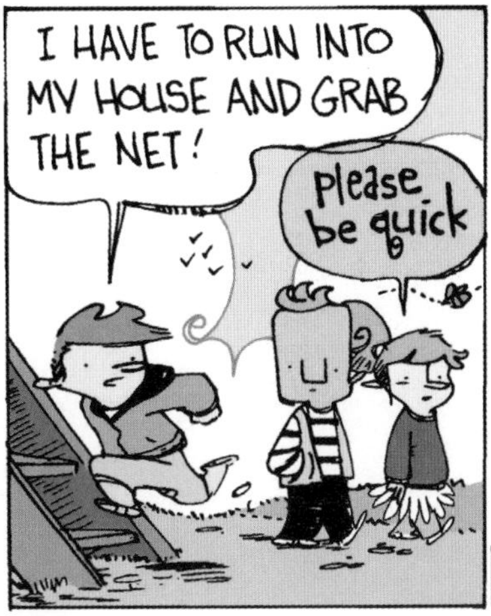
I HAVE TO RUN INTO MY HOUSE AND GRAB THE NET!
Please be quick

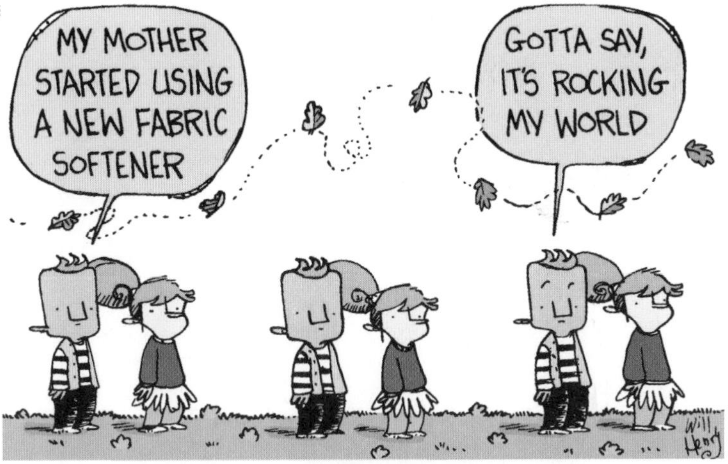
MY MOTHER STARTED USING A NEW FABRIC SOFTENER
GOTTA SAY, IT'S ROCKING MY WORLD

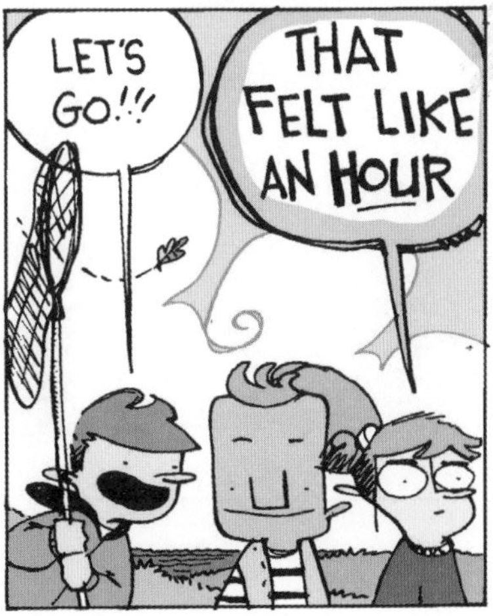
LET'S GO!!!
THAT FELT LIKE AN HOUR

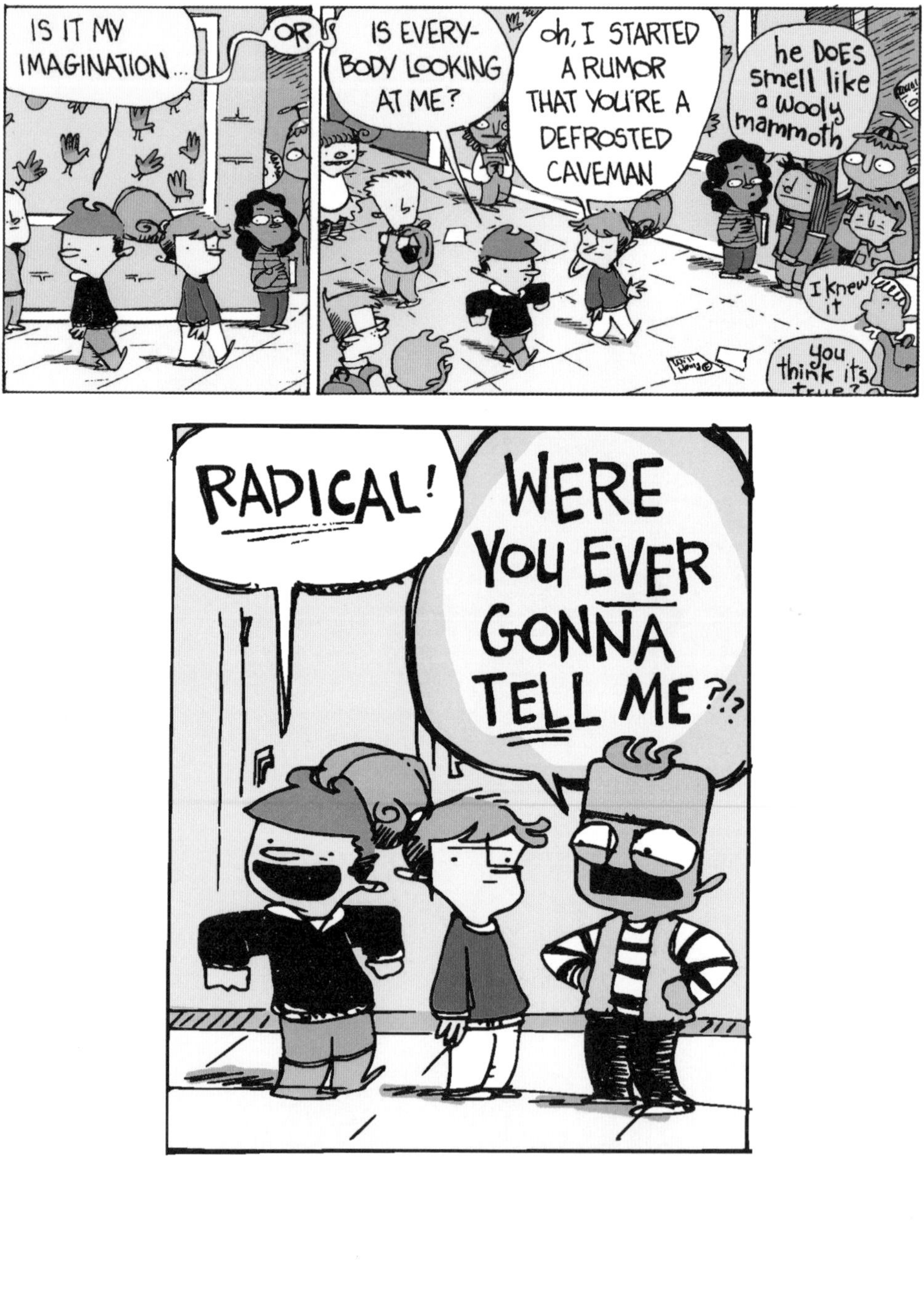
IS IT MY IMAGINATION...
OR
IS EVERY-BODY LOOKING AT ME?
oh, I STARTED A RUMOR THAT YOU'RE A DEFROSTED CAVEMAN
he DOES smell like a wooly mammoth
I knew it
you think it's
RADICAL!
WERE YOU EVER GONNA TELL ME?!?

IF I STARTED GREETING PEOPLE WITH "JELL-O" INSTEAD OF "HELLO"...
WOULD THEY BE MORE INCLINED TO GIVE ME JELL-O?
DO PEOPLE NORMALLY GIVE YOU JELL-O?
ONLY IF I'M PERSISTENT

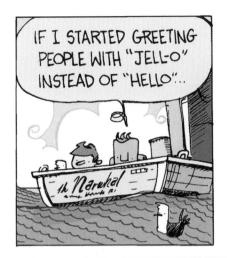

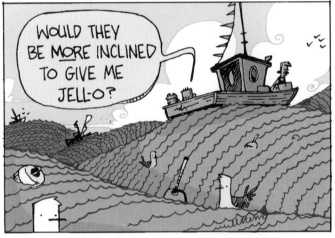

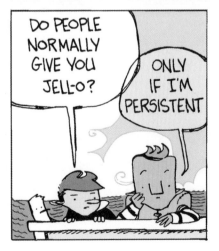

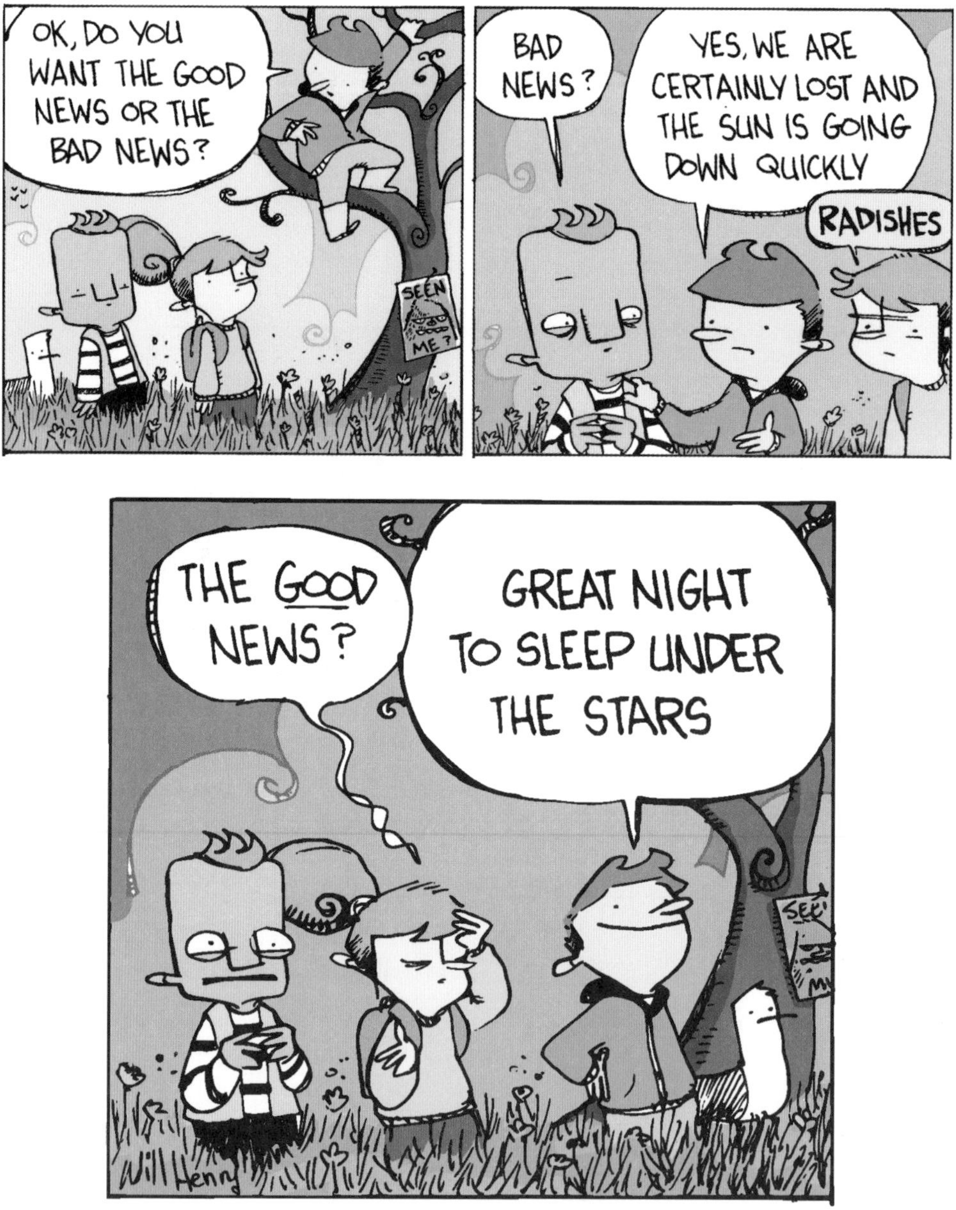
OK, DO YOU WANT THE GOOD NEWS OR THE BAD NEWS?
SEEN ME?
BAD NEWS?
YES, WE ARE CERTAINLY LOST AND THE SUN IS GOING DOWN QUICKLY
RADISHES
THE GOOD NEWS?
GREAT NIGHT TO SLEEP UNDER THE STARS
Will Henry

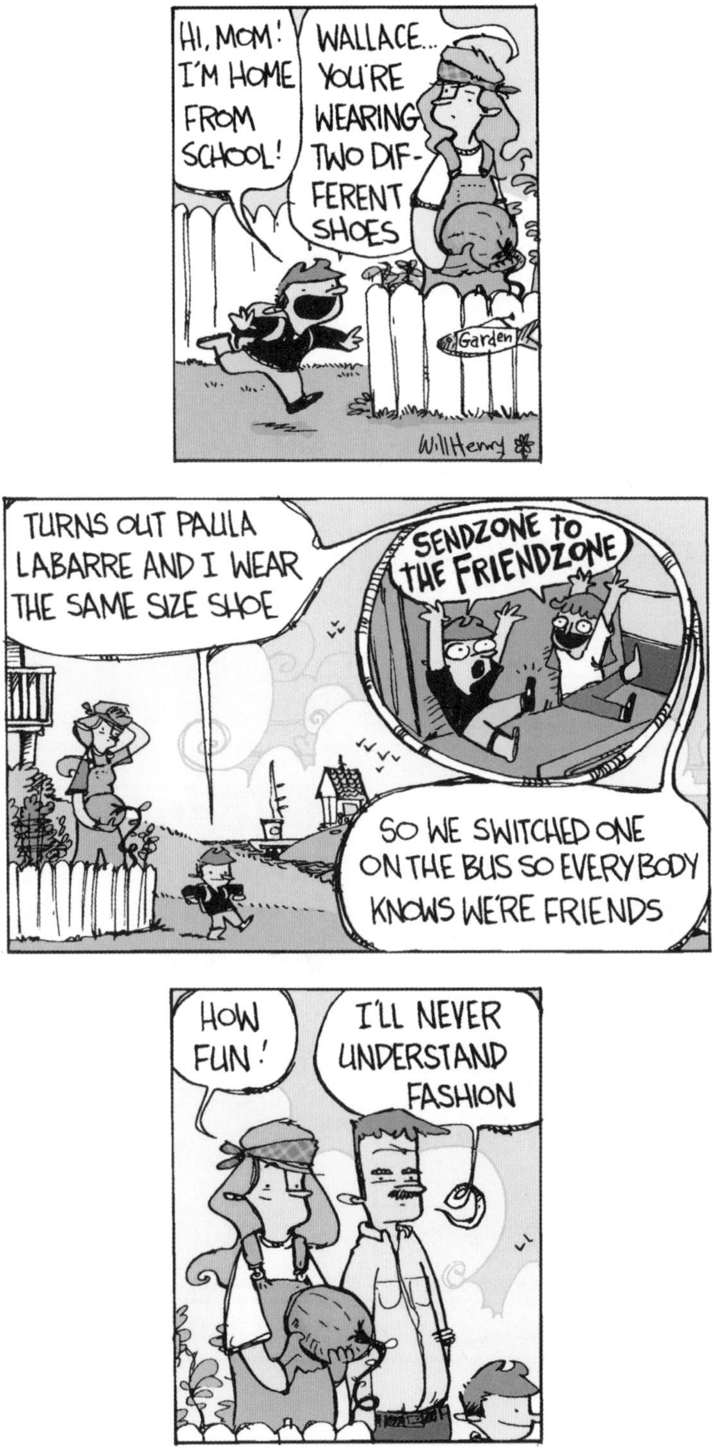
HI, MOM! I'M HOME FROM SCHOOL!
WALLACE... YOU'RE WEARING TWO DIF-FERENT SHOES
Garden
WillHenry
TURNS OUT PAULA LABARRE AND I WEAR THE SAME SIZE SHOE
SENDZONE TO THE FRIENDZONE
SO WE SWITCHED ONE ON THE BUS SO EVERYBODY KNOWS WE'RE FRIENDS
HOW FUN!
I'LL NEVER UNDERSTAND FASHION

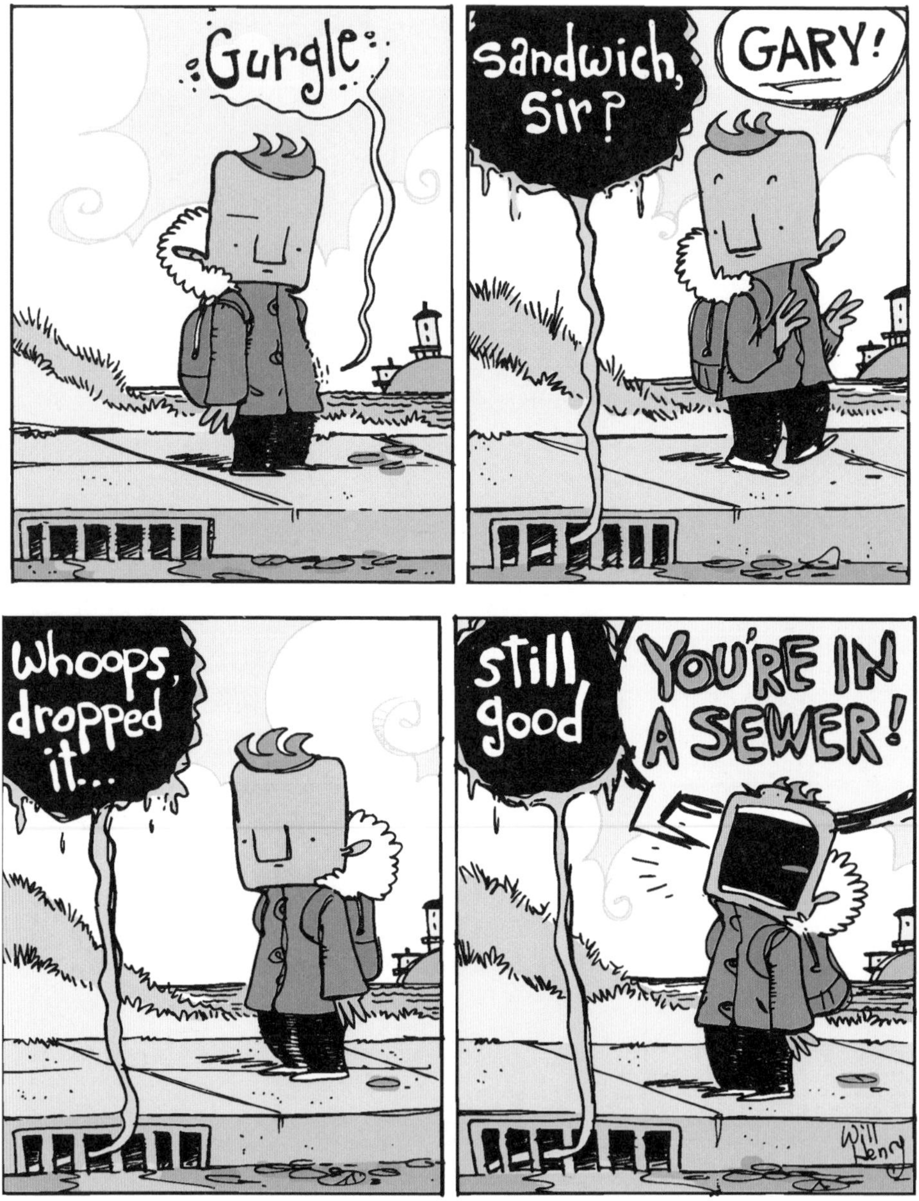
Gurgle
sandwich, sir?
GARY!
whoops, dropped it...
still good
YOU'RE IN A SEWER!
Will Henry

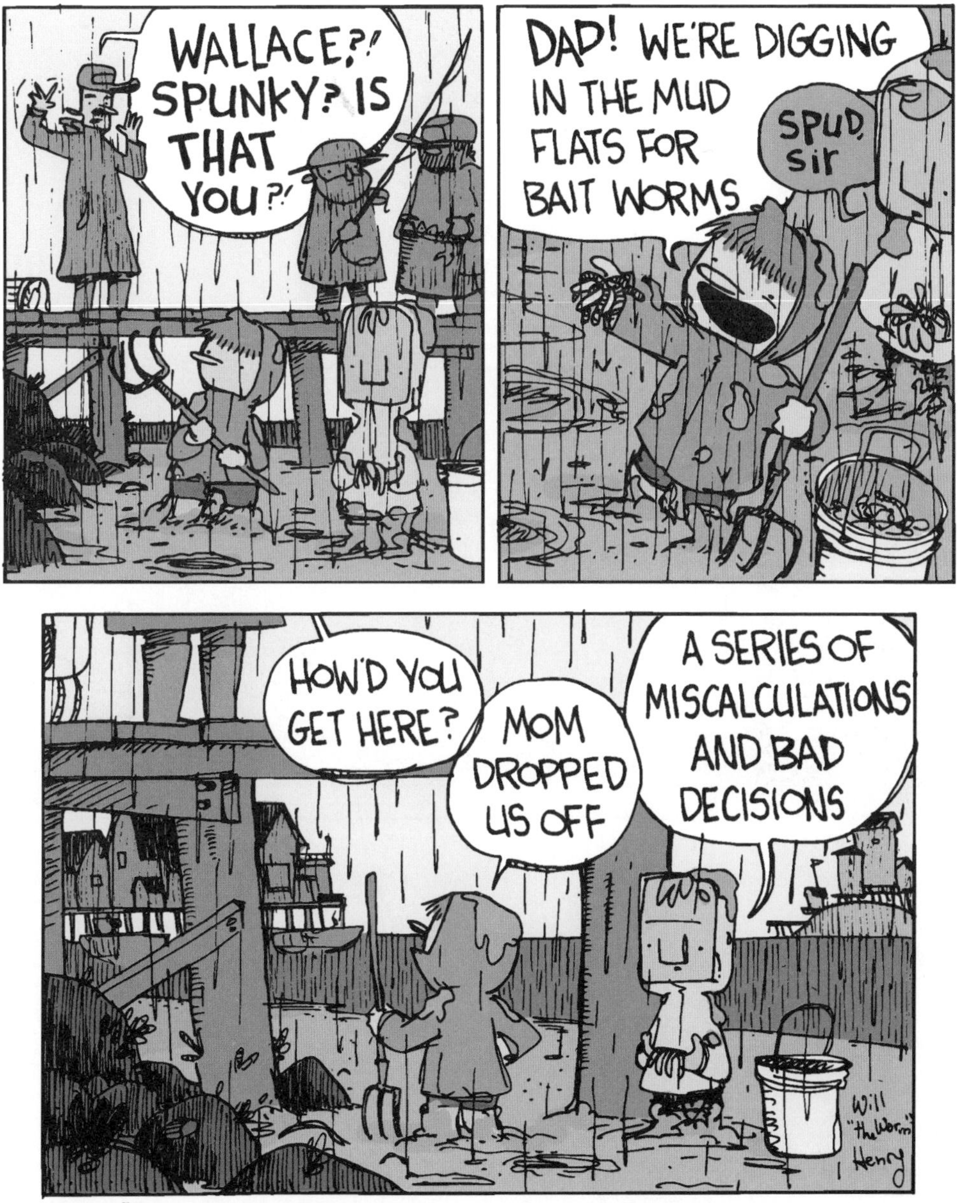
WALLACE?! SPUNKY? IS THAT YOU?!
DAD! WE'RE DIGGING IN THE MUD FLATS FOR BAIT WORMS
SPUD, sir
HOW'D YOU GET HERE?
MOM DROPPED US OFF
A SERIES OF MISCALCULATIONS AND BAD DECISIONS
Will "the Worm" Henry

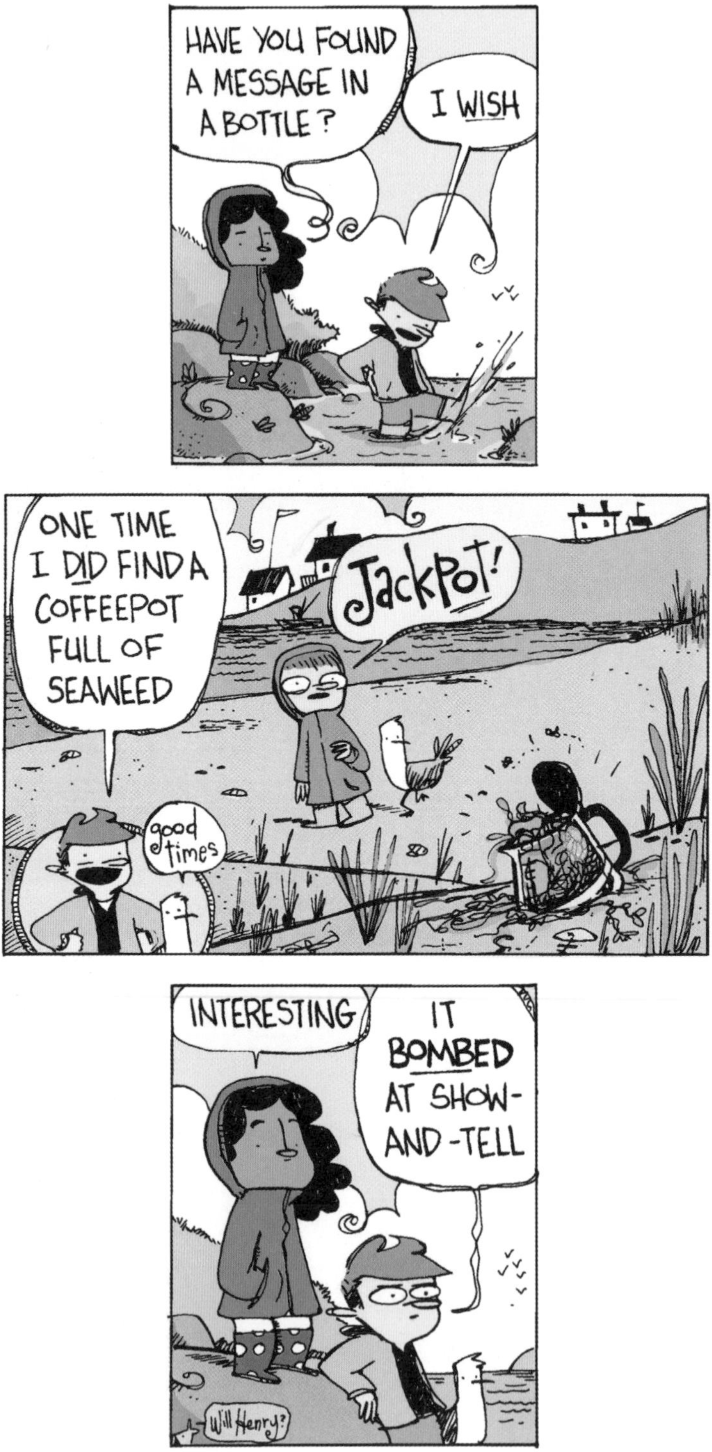
HAVE YOU FOUND A MESSAGE IN A BOTTLE?
I WISH
ONE TIME I DID FIND A COFFEEPOT FULL OF SEAWEED
JACKPOT!
good times
INTERESTING
IT BOMBED AT SHOW-AND-TELL
Will Henry?

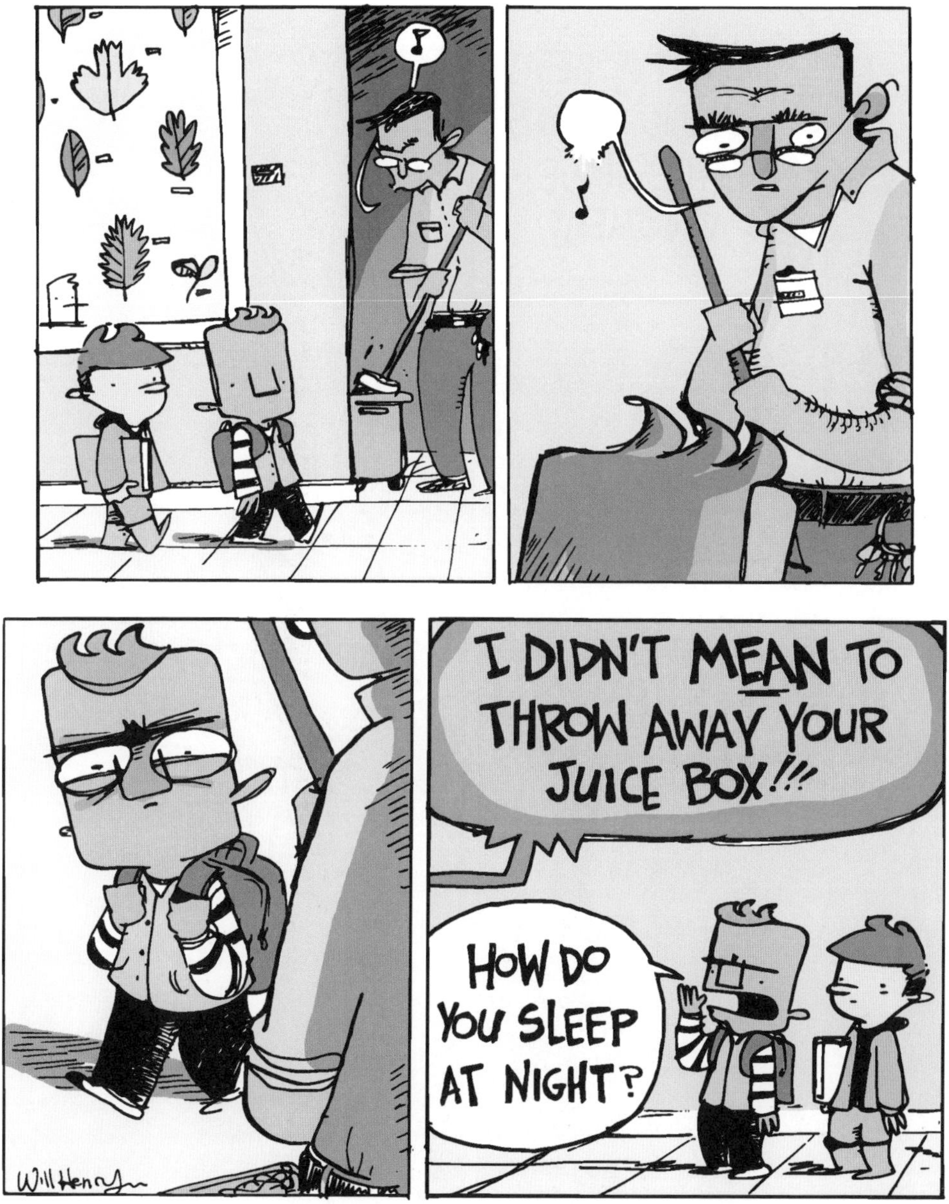
I DIDN'T MEAN TO THROW AWAY YOUR JUICE BOX!!!
HOW DO YOU SLEEP AT NIGHT?

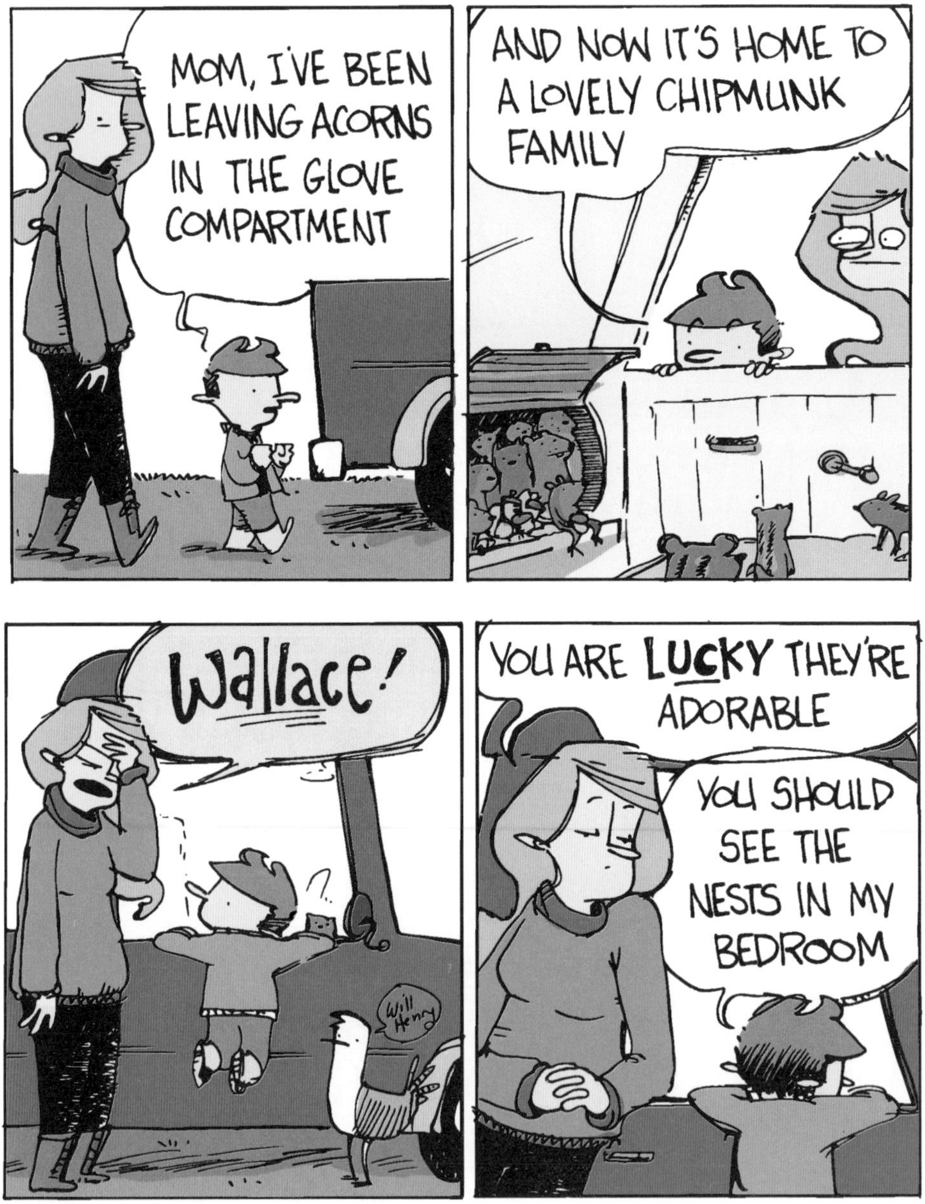
MOM, I'VE BEEN LEAVING ACORNS IN THE GLOVE COMPARTMENT
AND NOW IT'S HOME TO A LOVELY CHIPMUNK FAMILY
Wallace!
Will Henry
YOU ARE LUCKY THEY'RE ADORABLE
YOU SHOULD SEE THE NESTS IN MY BEDROOM

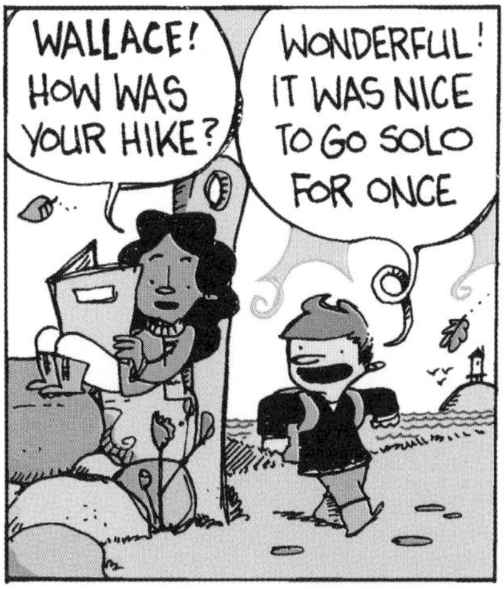
WALLACE! HOW WAS YOUR HIKE?
WONDERFUL! IT WAS NICE TO GO SOLO FOR ONCE

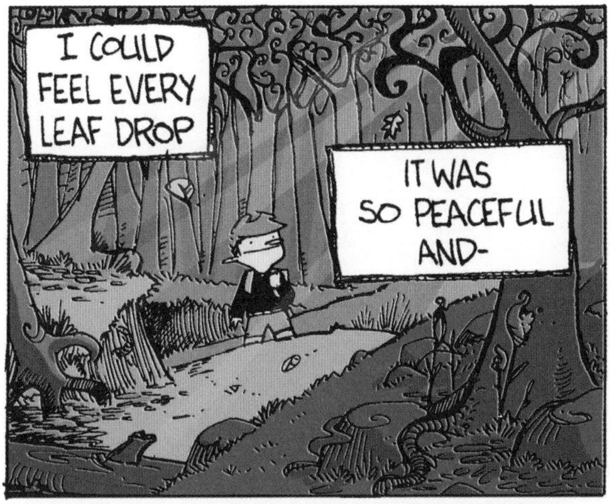
I COULD FEEL EVERY LEAF DROP
IT WAS SO PEACEFUL AND-

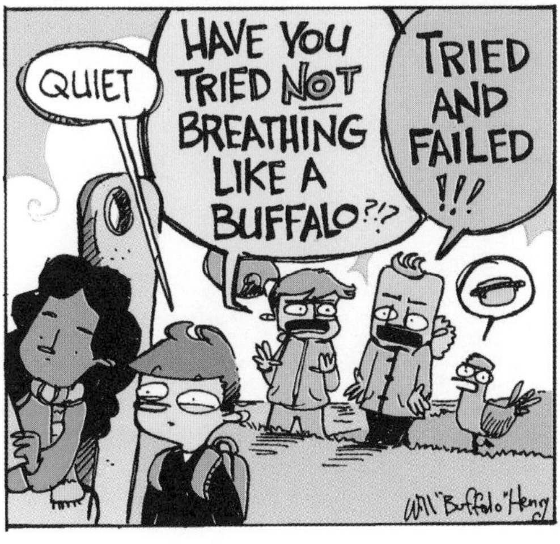
QUIET
HAVE YOU TRIED NOT BREATHING LIKE A BUFFALO?!?
TRIED AND FAILED !!!
Will "Buffalo" Henry

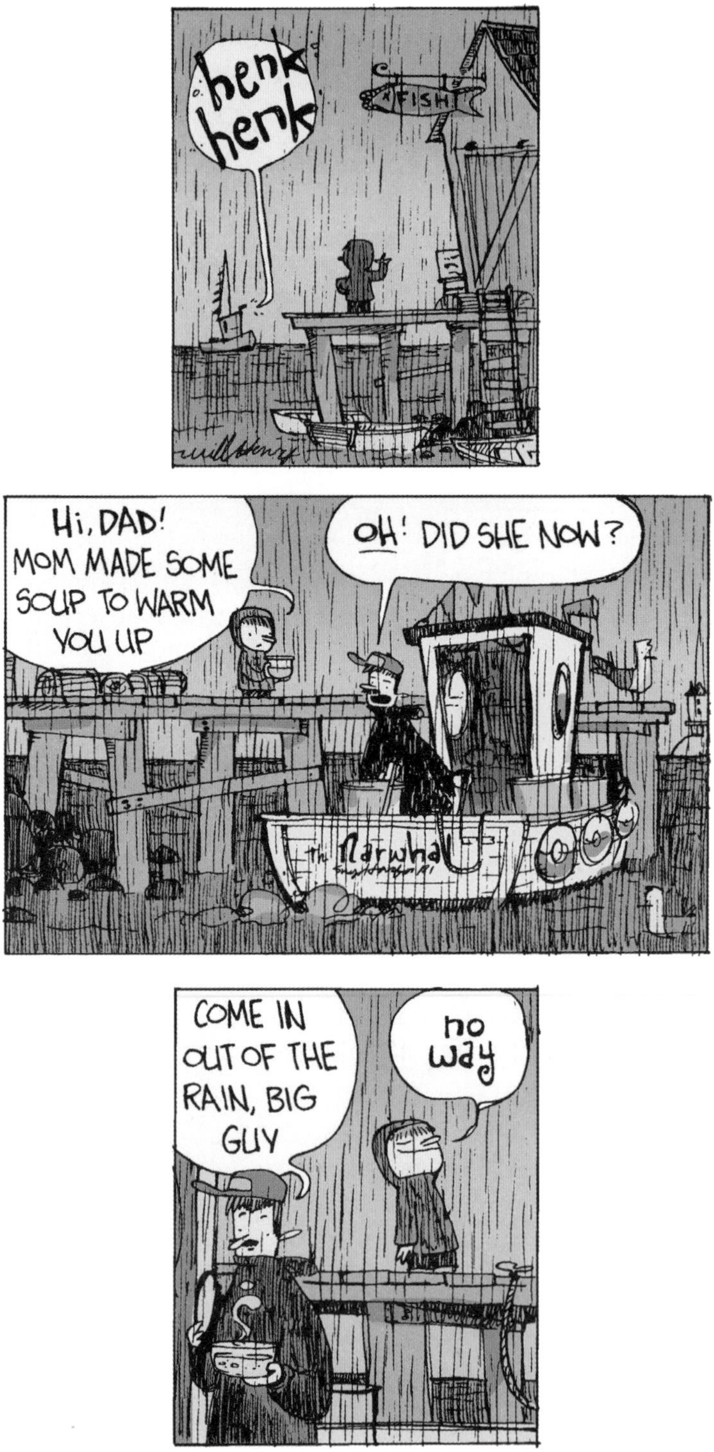
henk henk
FISH
Hi, DAD! MOM MADE SOME SOUP TO WARM YOU UP
OH! DID SHE NOW?
the Narwhal
COME IN OUT OF THE RAIN, BIG GUY
no way

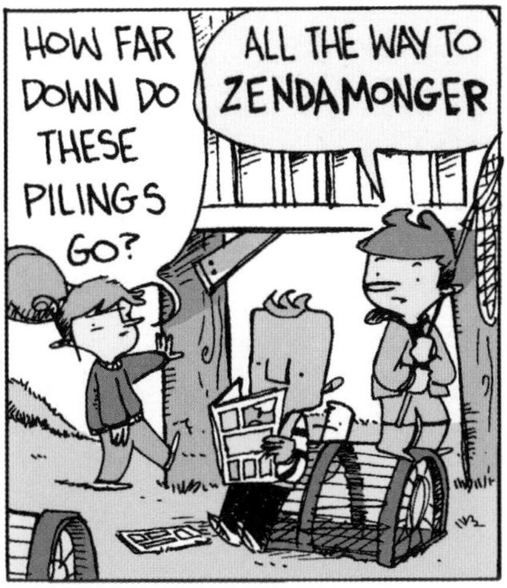
HOW FAR DOWN DO THESE PILINGS GO?
ALL THE WAY TO ZENDAMONGER

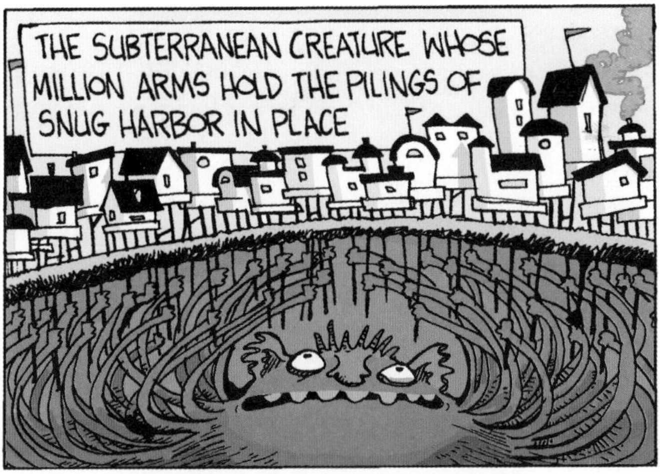
THE SUBTERRANEAN CREATURE WHOSE MILLION ARMS HOLD THE PILINGS OF SNUG HARBOR IN PLACE

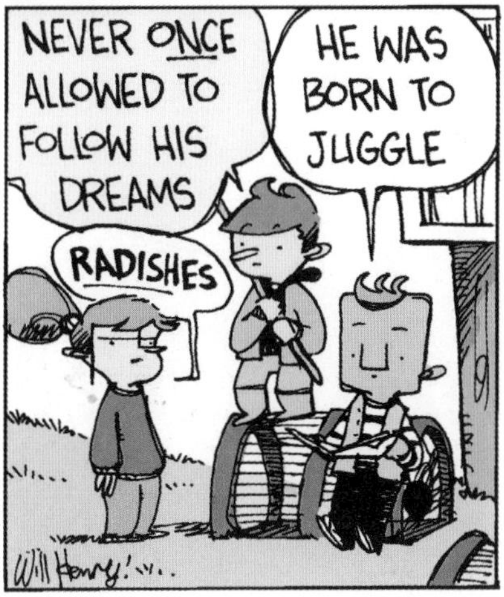
NEVER ONCE ALLOWED TO FOLLOW HIS DREAMS
HE WAS BORN TO JUGGLE
RADISHES
Will Henry!

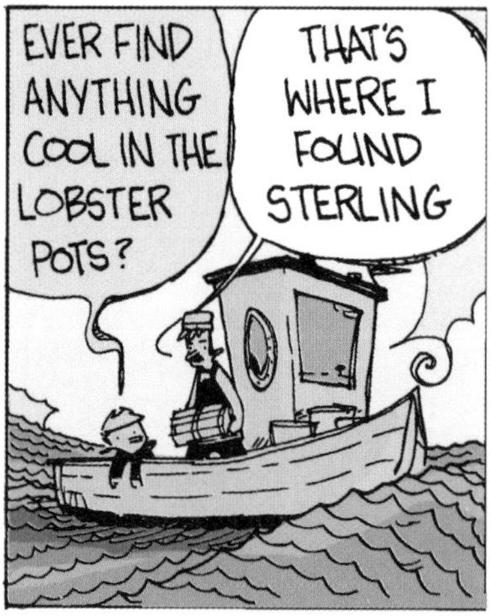
EVER FIND ANYTHING COOL IN THE LOBSTER POTS?
THAT'S WHERE I FOUND STERLING

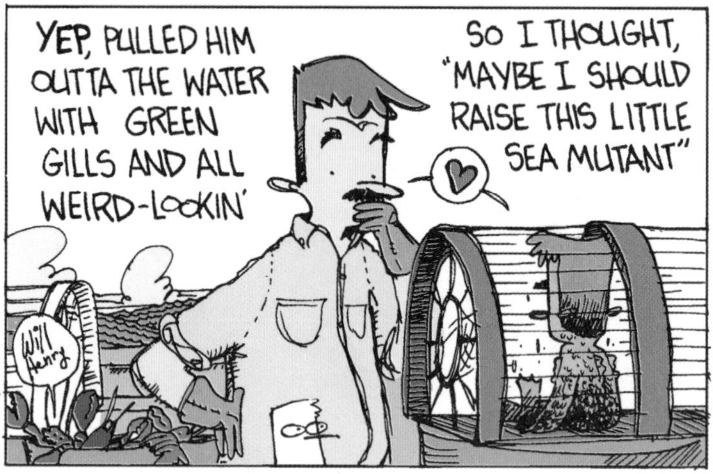
YEP, PULLED HIM OUTTA THE WATER WITH GREEN GILLS AND ALL WEIRD-LOOKIN'
SO I THOUGHT, "MAYBE I SHOULD RAISE THIS LITTLE SEA MUTANT"
Will Henry

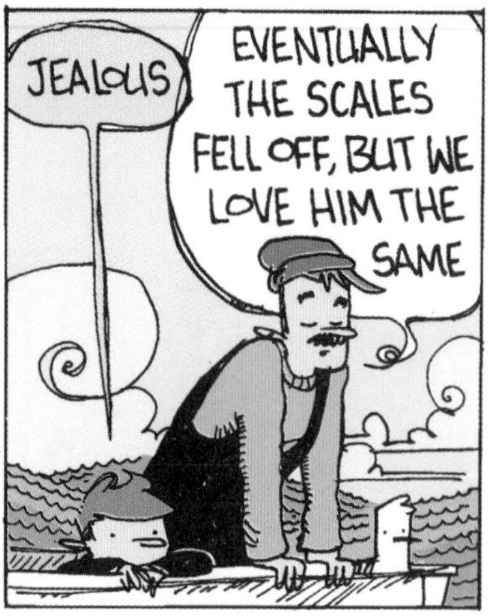
JEALOUS
EVENTUALLY THE SCALES FELL OFF, BUT WE LOVE HIM THE SAME

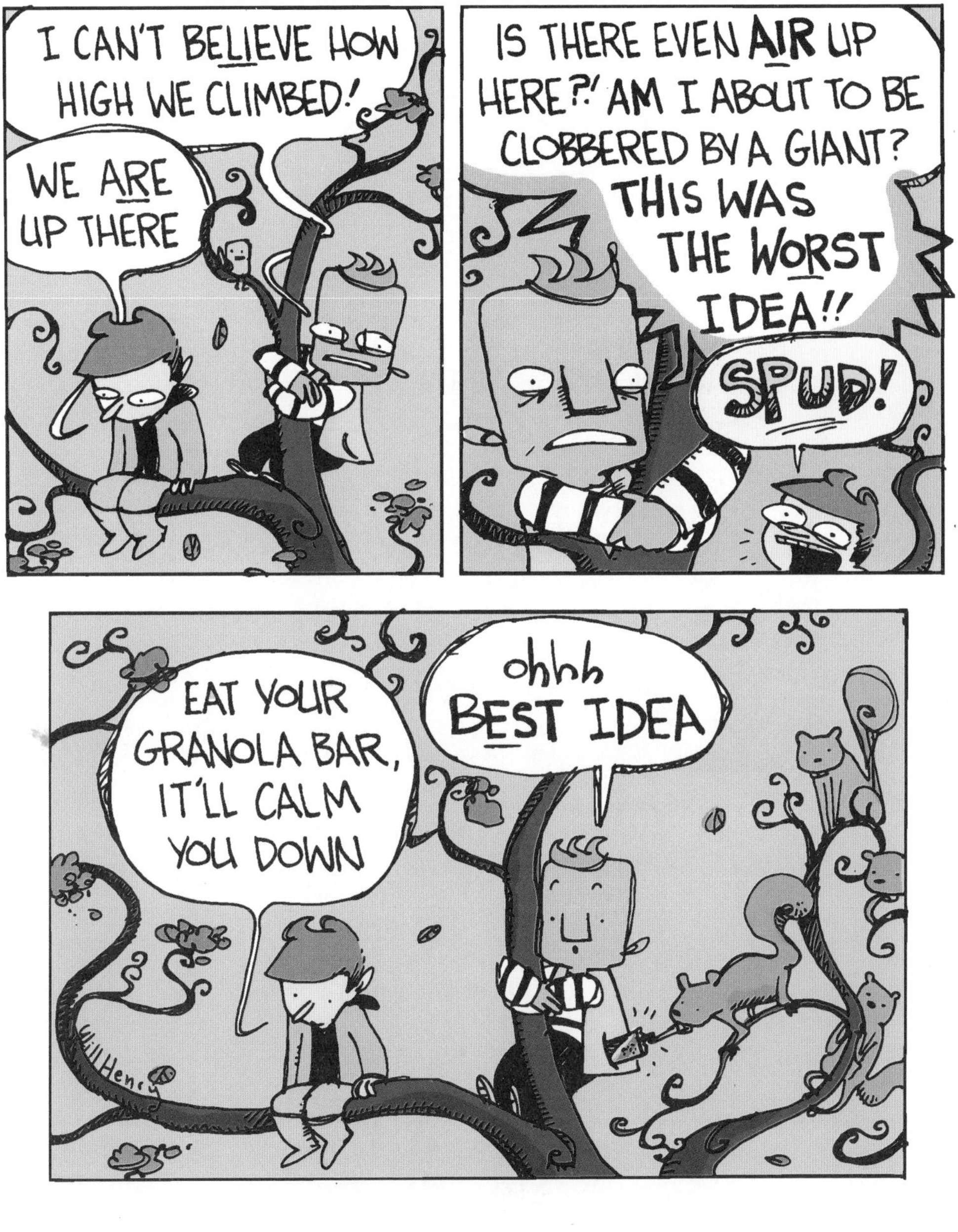
I CAN'T BELIEVE HOW HIGH WE CLIMBED!
WE ARE UP THERE
IS THERE EVEN AIR UP HERE?! AM I ABOUT TO BE CLOBBERED BY A GIANT?
THIS WAS THE WORST IDEA!!
SPUD!
EAT YOUR GRANOLA BAR, IT'LL CALM YOU DOWN
ohhh BEST IDEA
Henry

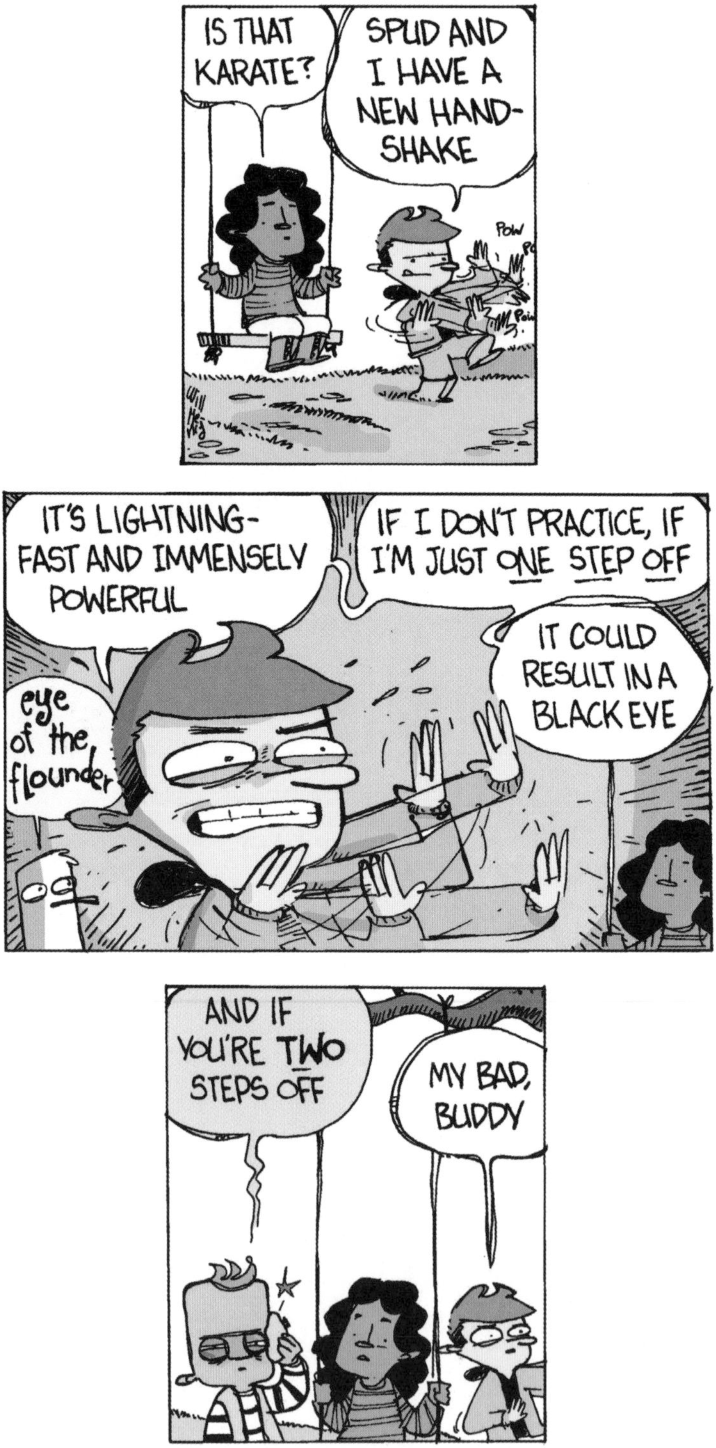
IS THAT KARATE?
SPUD AND I HAVE A NEW HAND-SHAKE
POW
IT'S LIGHTNING-FAST AND IMMENSELY POWERFUL
IF I DON'T PRACTICE, IF I'M JUST ONE STEP OFF
IT COULD RESULT IN A BLACK EYE
eye of the flounder
AND IF YOU'RE TWO STEPS OFF
MY BAD, BUDDY

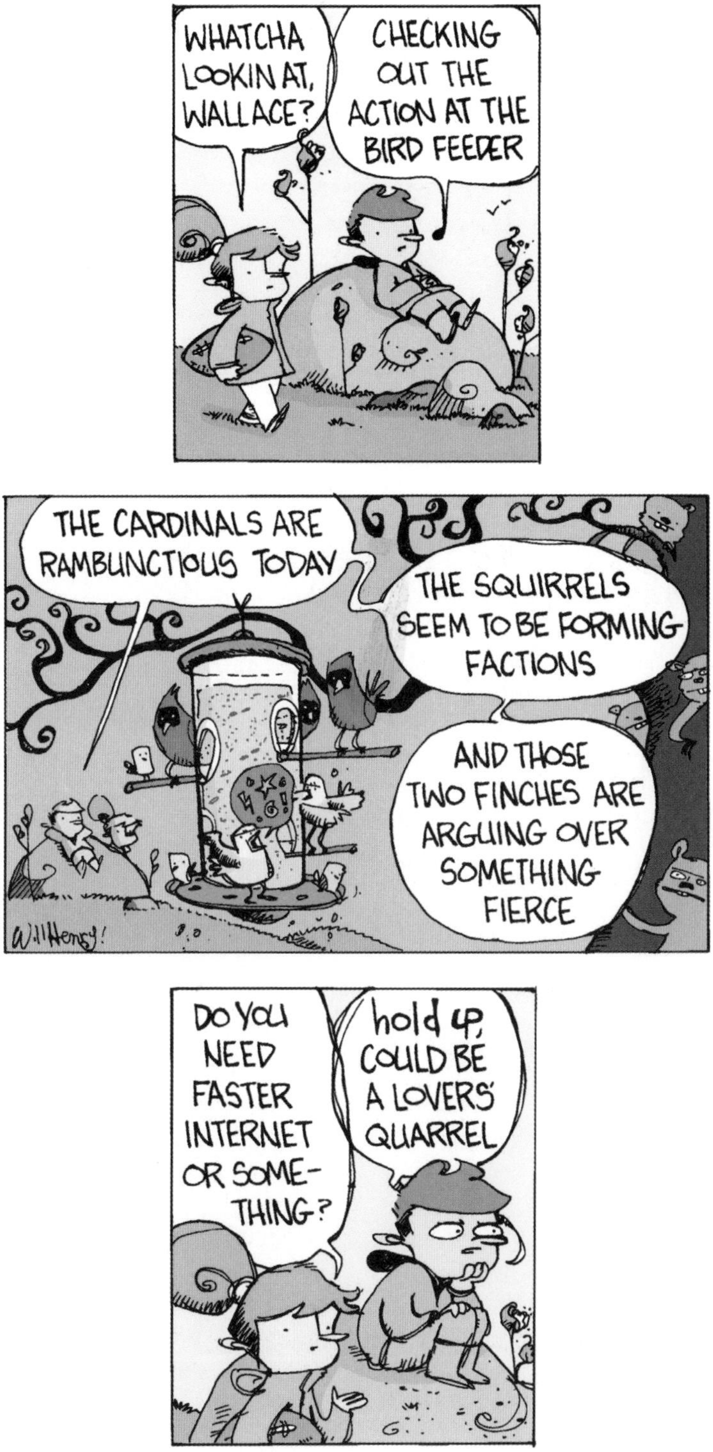
WHATCHA LOOKIN AT, WALLACE?
CHECKING OUT THE ACTION AT THE BIRD FEEDER
THE CARDINALS ARE RAMBUNCTIOUS TODAY
THE SQUIRRELS SEEM TO BE FORMING FACTIONS
AND THOSE TWO FINCHES ARE ARGUING OVER SOMETHING FIERCE
Will Henry!
DO YOU NEED FASTER INTERNET OR SOME-THING?
hold up, COULD BE A LOVERS' QUARREL

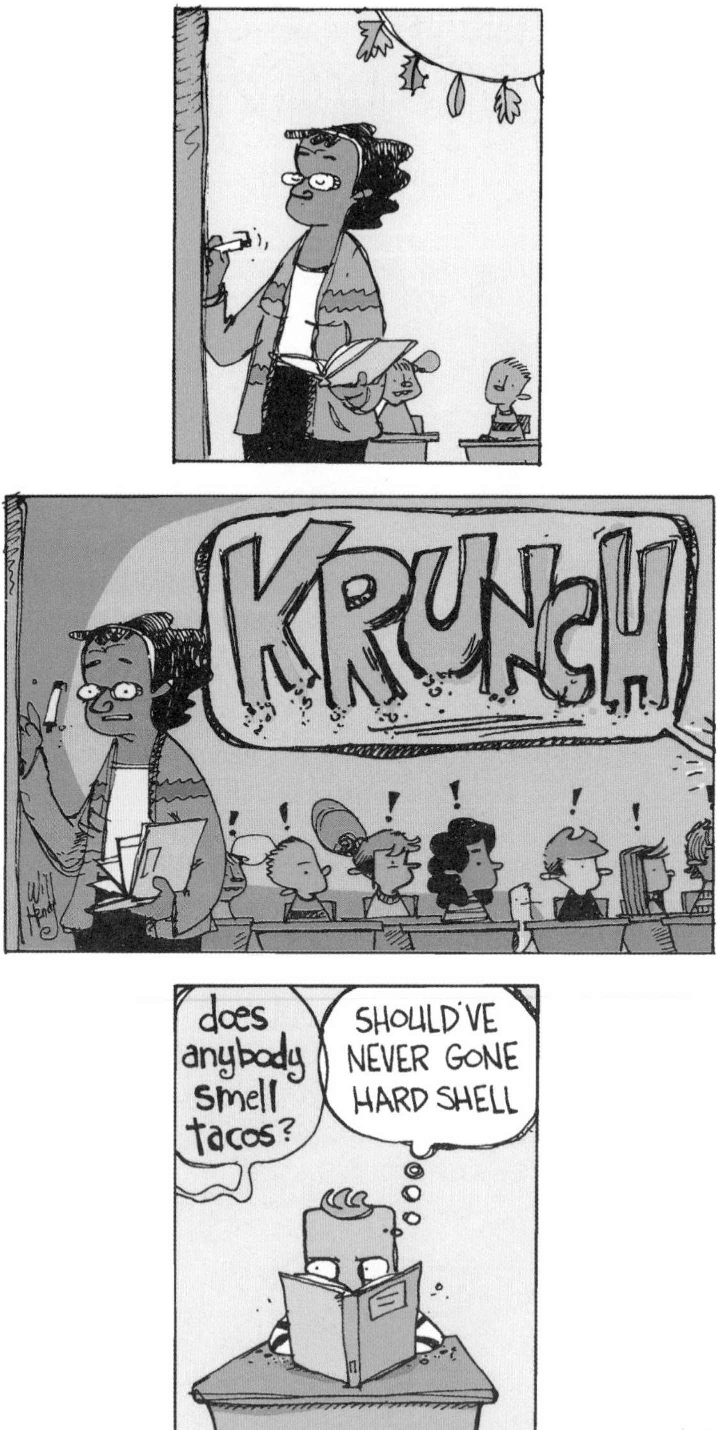
KRUNCH
does anybody smell tacos?
SHOULD'VE NEVER GONE HARD SHELL

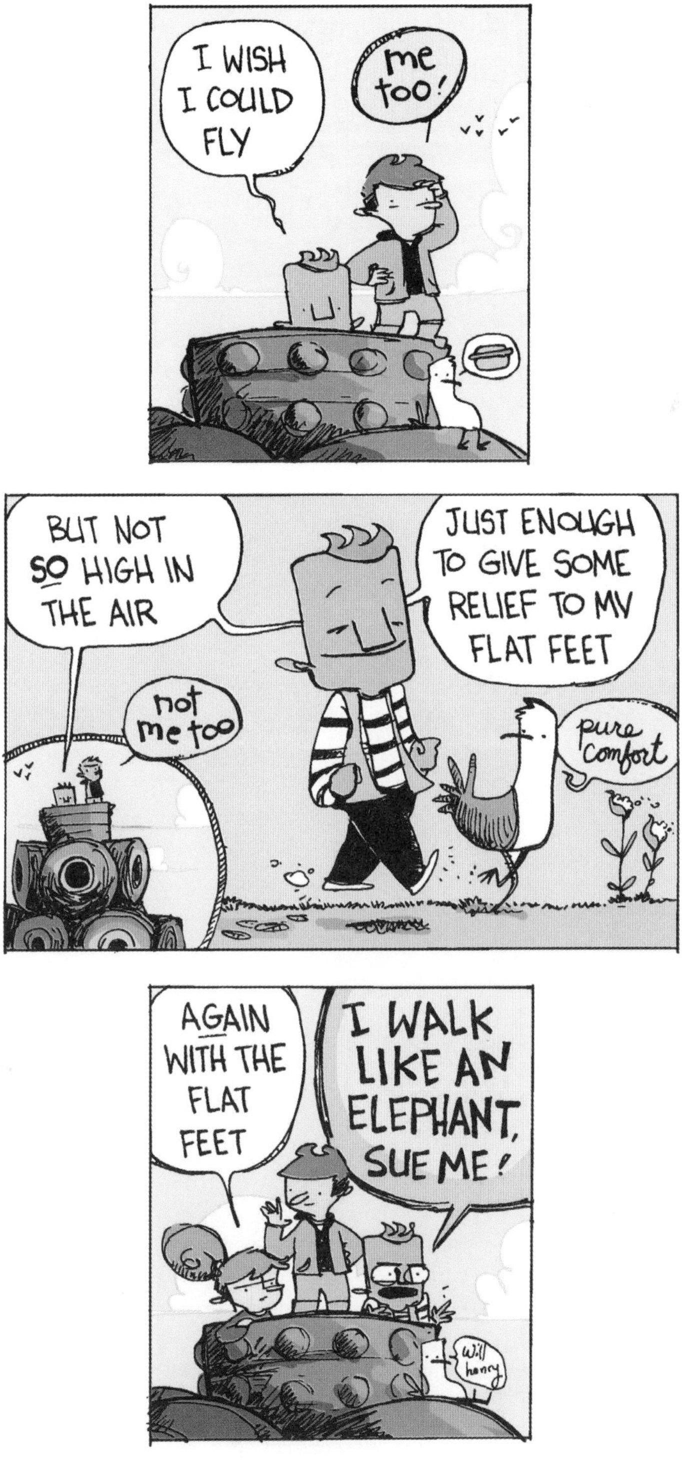
I WISH I COULD FLY
me too!
BUT NOT SO HIGH IN THE AIR
JUST ENOUGH TO GIVE SOME RELIEF TO MY FLAT FEET
not me too
pure comfort
AGAIN WITH THE FLAT FEET
I WALK LIKE AN ELEPHANT, SUE ME!
Will henry

REMEMBER WHEN THAT HYPNOTIST CAME TO THE SCHOOL?
not really
AND HAD SPUD TELL US SOME-THING SPECIAL ABOUT HIMSELF THAT WE MAY NOT KNOW
One time I ate a cheeseburger in the nude
THAT'S WHY I LOVE ASSEMBLIES
THIS ONE IS ABOUT LEAD PAINT
SPOOKY

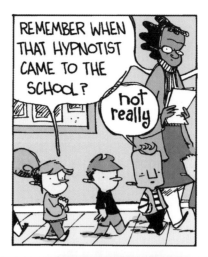

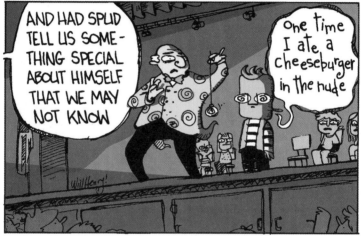

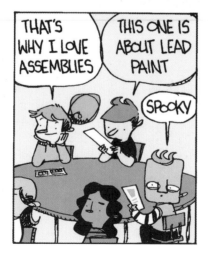

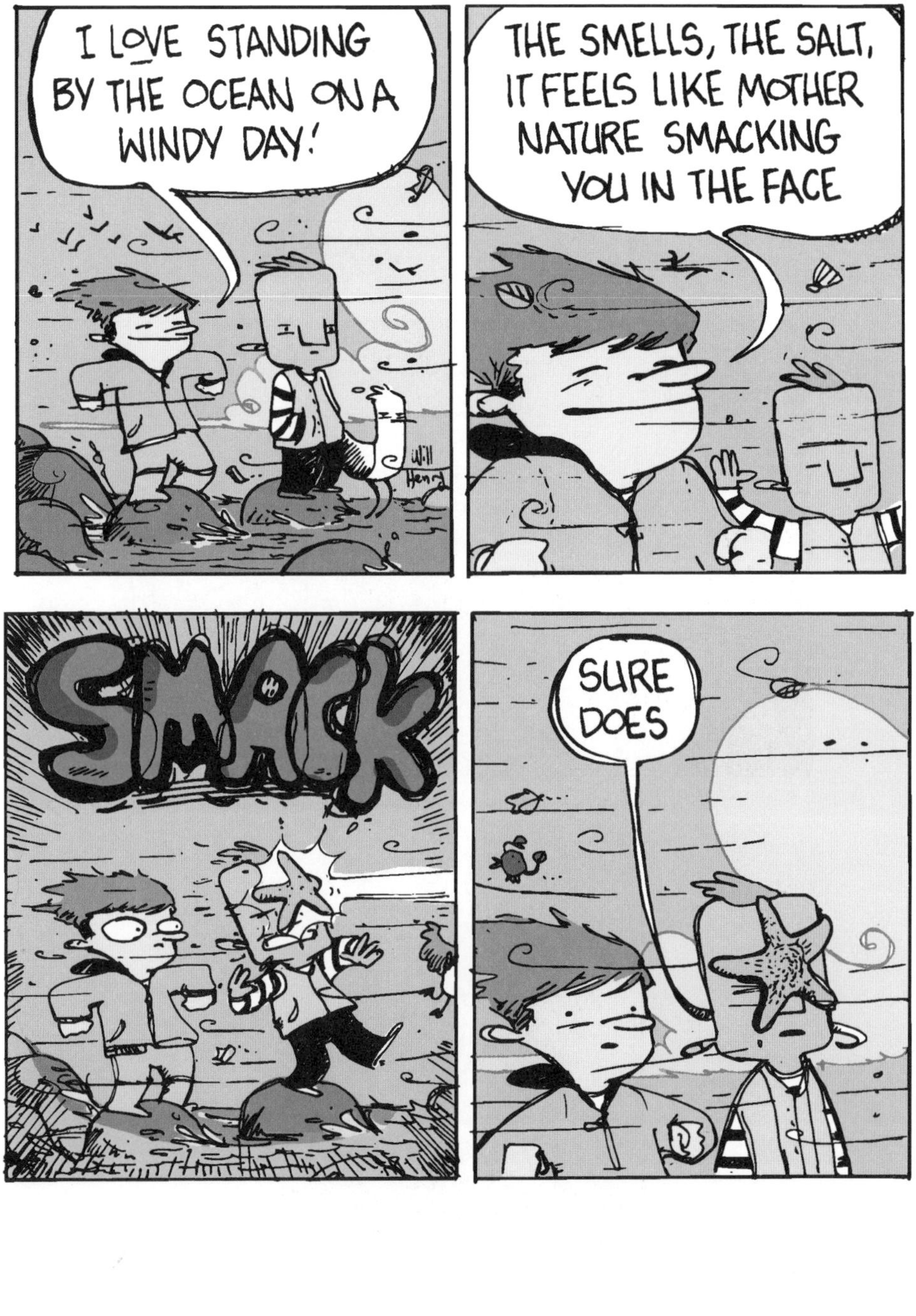
I LOVE STANDING BY THE OCEAN ON A WINDY DAY!
THE SMELLS, THE SALT, IT FEELS LIKE MOTHER NATURE SMACKING YOU IN THE FACE
SMACK
SURE DOES

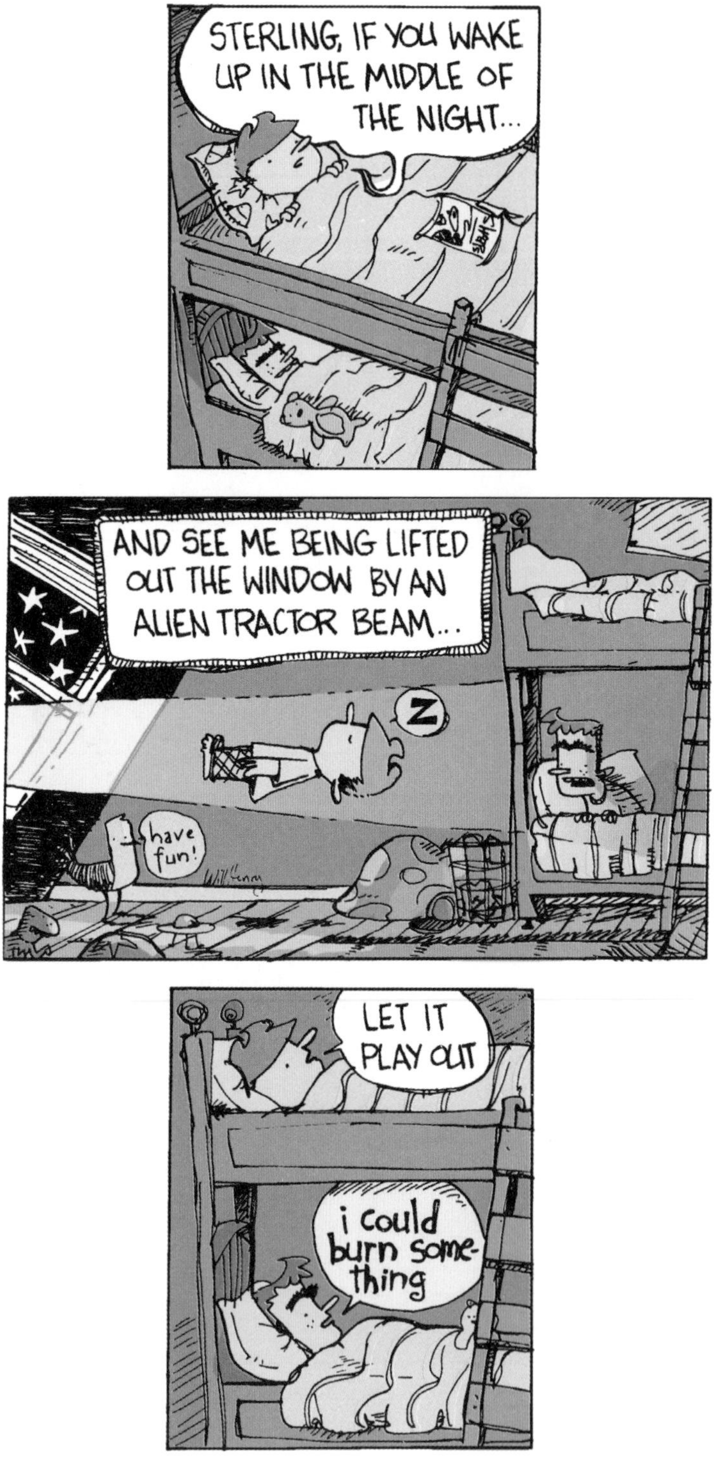
STERLING, IF YOU WAKE UP IN THE MIDDLE OF THE NIGHT...
AND SEE ME BEING LIFTED OUT THE WINDOW BY AN ALIEN TRACTOR BEAM...
Z
have fun!
LET IT PLAY OUT
i could burn some-thing

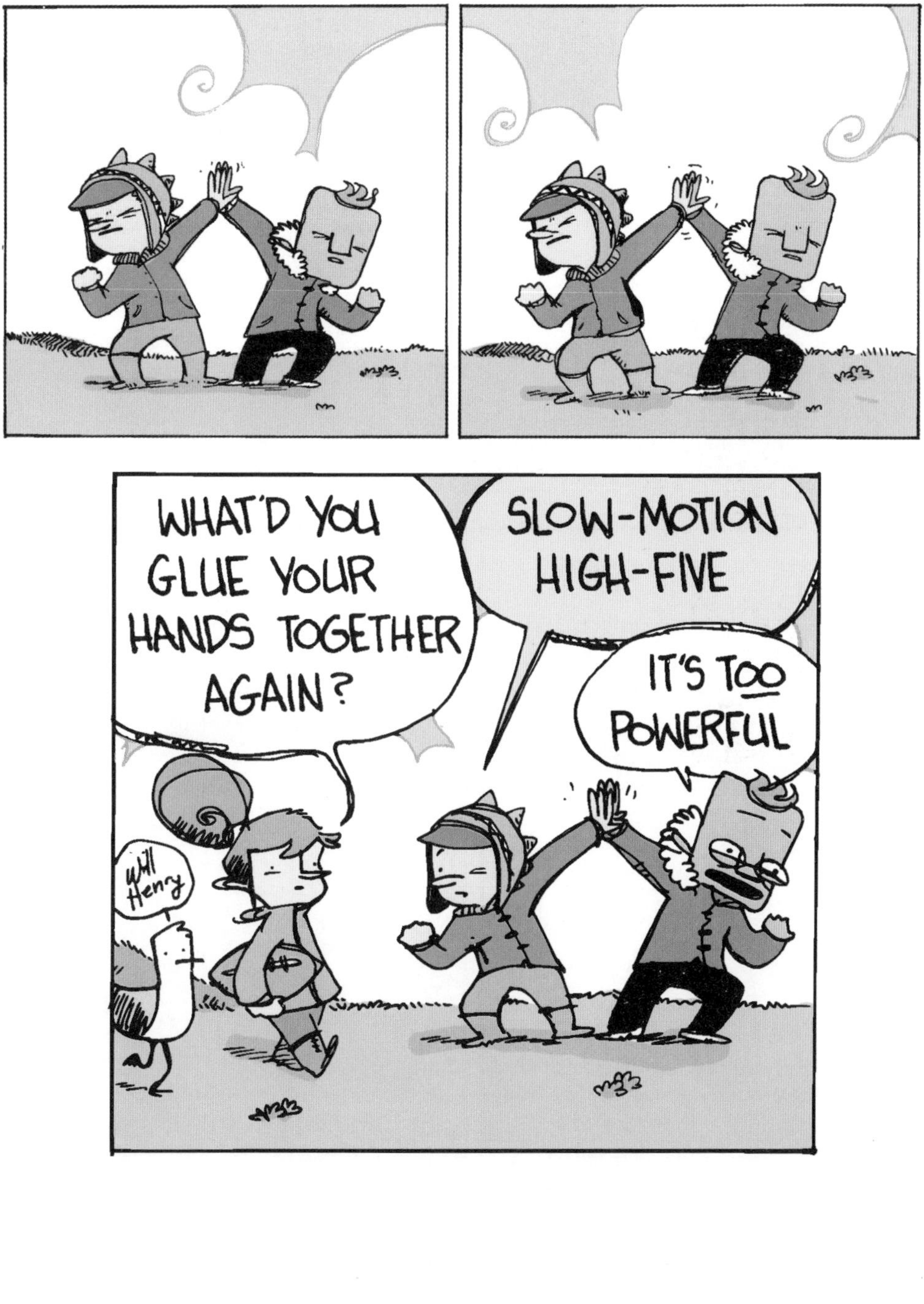
WHAT'D YOU GLUE YOUR HANDS TOGETHER AGAIN?
SLOW-MOTION HIGH-FIVE
IT'S TOO POWERFUL
Will Henry

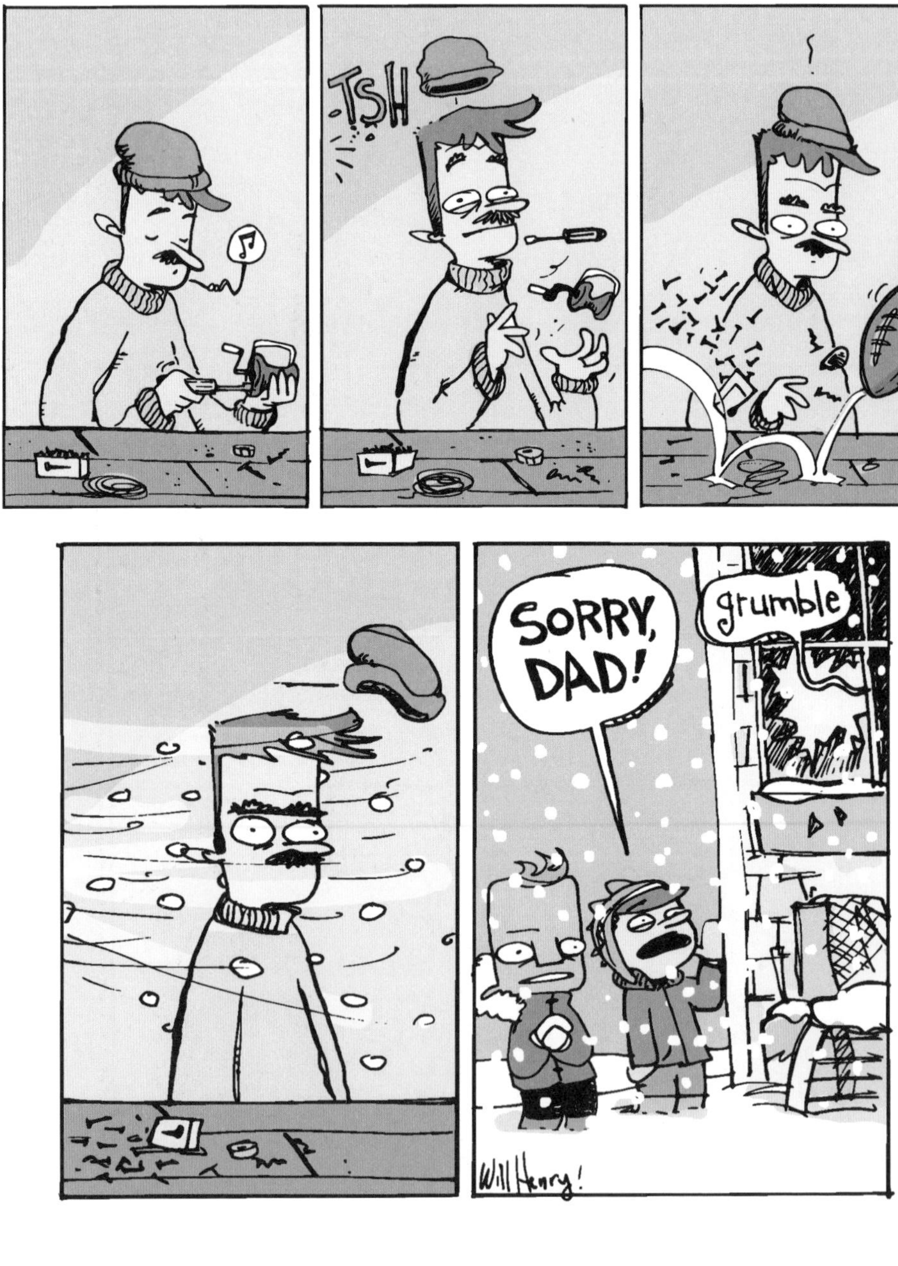
TSH
SORRY, DAD!
grumble
Will Henry!

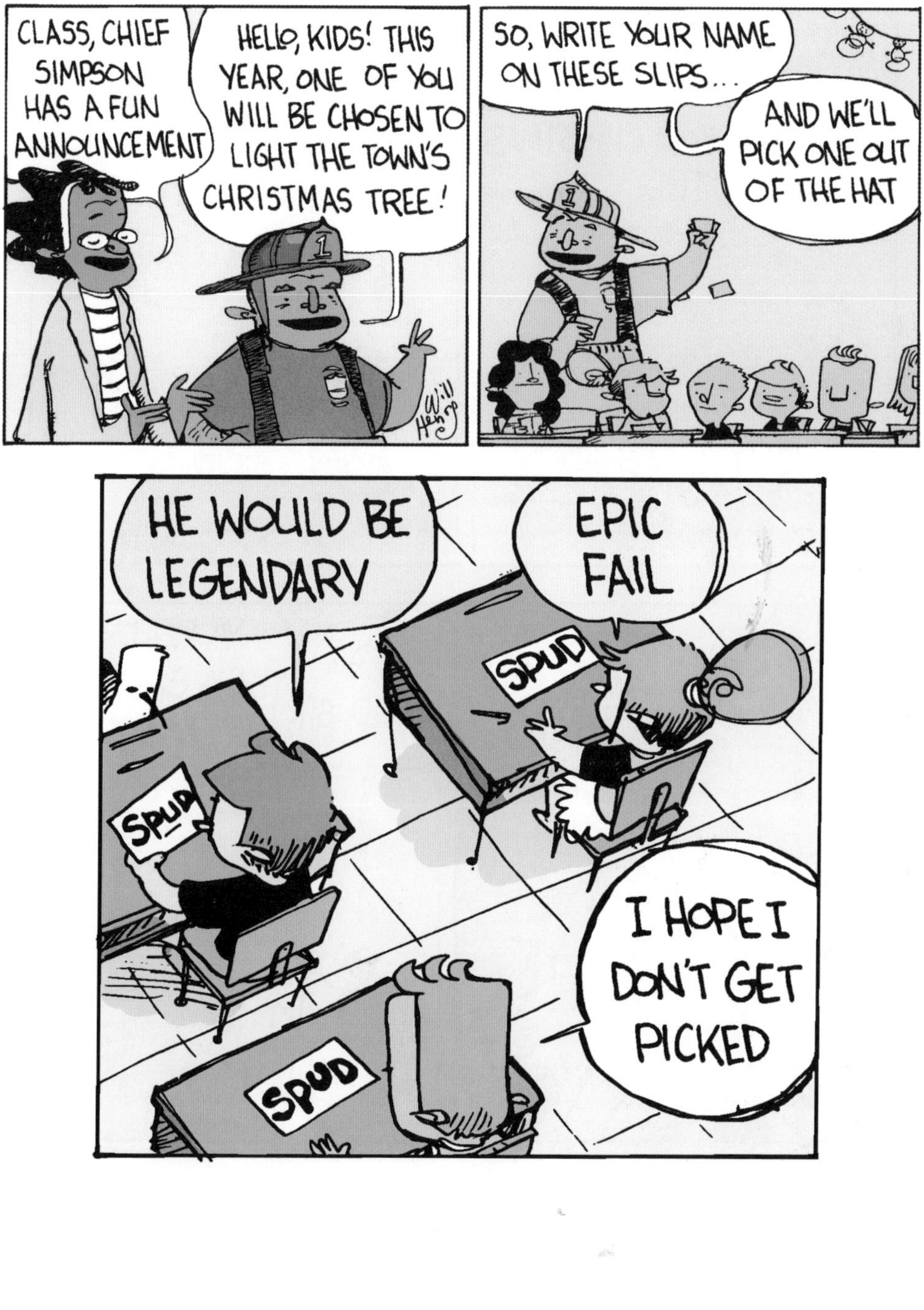
CLASS, CHIEF SIMPSON HAS A FUN ANNOUNCEMENT
HELLO, KIDS! THIS YEAR, ONE OF YOU WILL BE CHOSEN TO LIGHT THE TOWN'S CHRISTMAS TREE!
SO, WRITE YOUR NAME ON THESE SLIPS...
AND WE'LL PICK ONE OUT OF THE HAT
HE WOULD BE LEGENDARY
EPIC FAIL
SPUD
SPUD
I HOPE I DON'T GET PICKED
SPUD

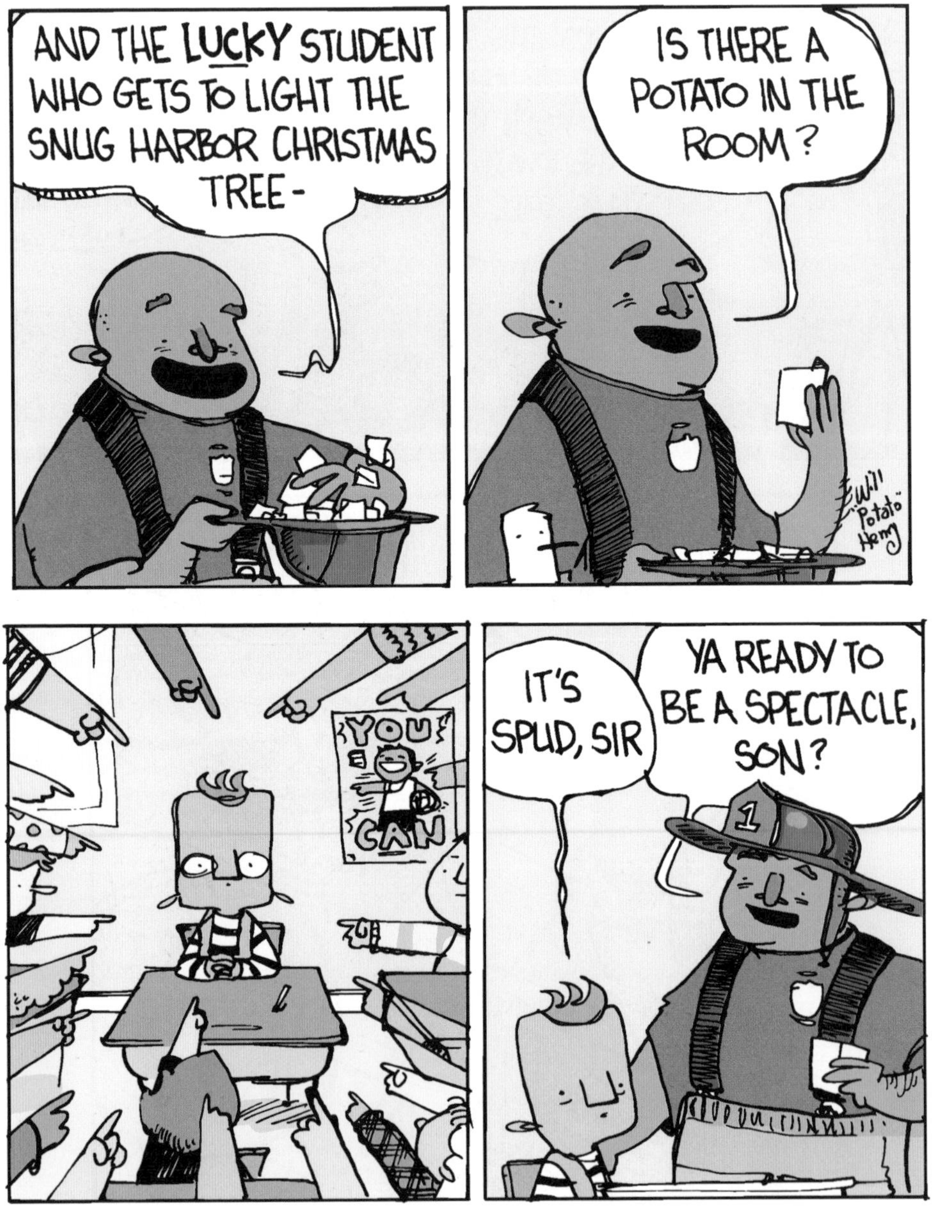
AND THE LUCKY STUDENT WHO GETS TO LIGHT THE SNUG HARBOR CHRISTMAS TREE -
IS THERE A POTATO IN THE ROOM?
Will "Potato" Henry
YOU CAN
IT'S SPUD, SIR
YA READY TO BE A SPECTACLE, SON?
1

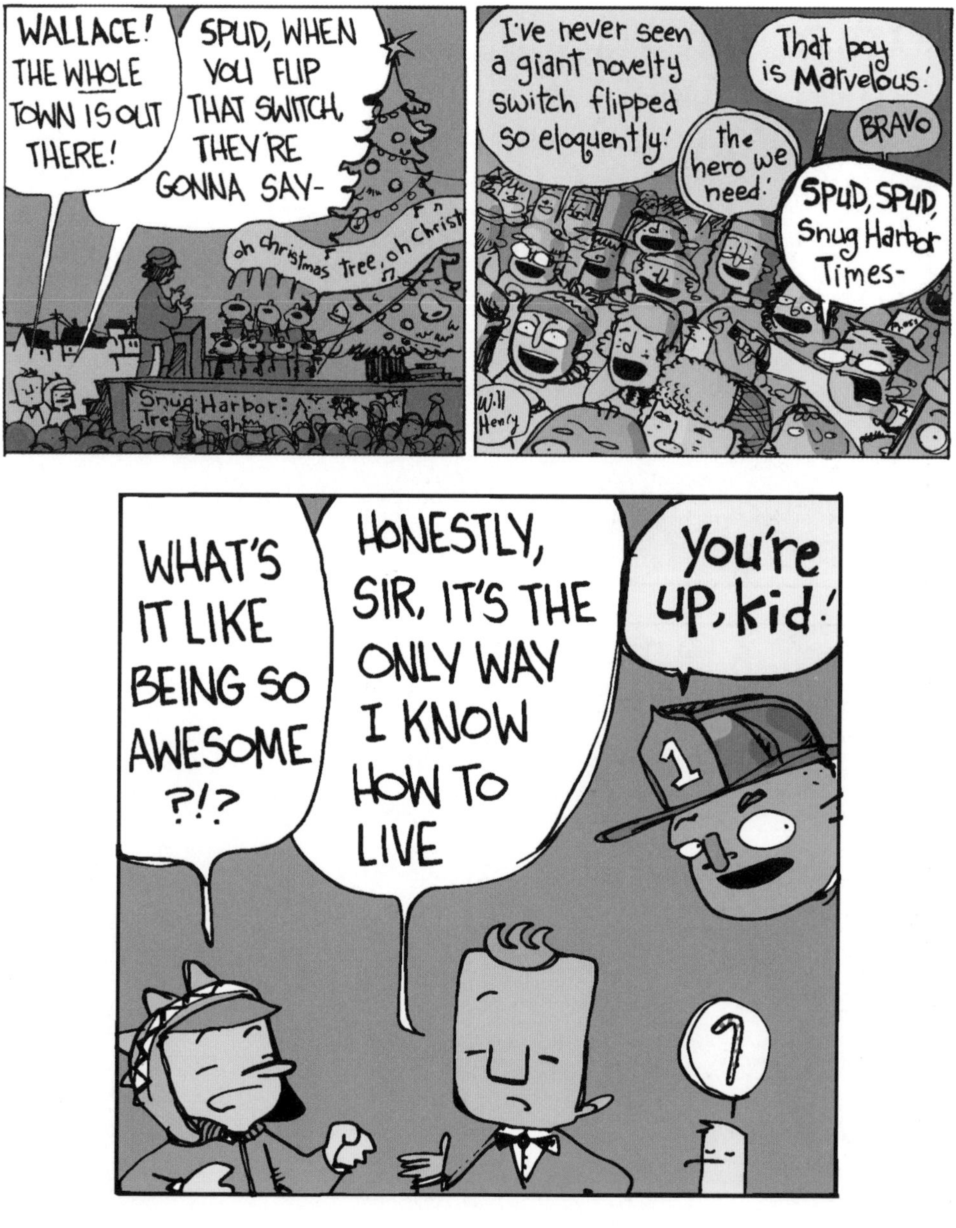
WALLACE! THE WHOLE TOWN IS OUT THERE!
SPUD, WHEN YOU FLIP THAT SWITCH, THEY'RE GONNA SAY-
oh christmas tree, oh christ
Snug Harbor:
Will Henry
I've never seen a giant novelty switch flipped so eloquently!
the hero we need!
That boy is Marvelous!
BRAVO
SPUD, SPUD, Snug Harbor Times-
WHAT'S IT LIKE BEING SO AWESOME ?!?
HONESTLY, SIR, IT'S THE ONLY WAY I KNOW HOW TO LIVE
You're up, kid!

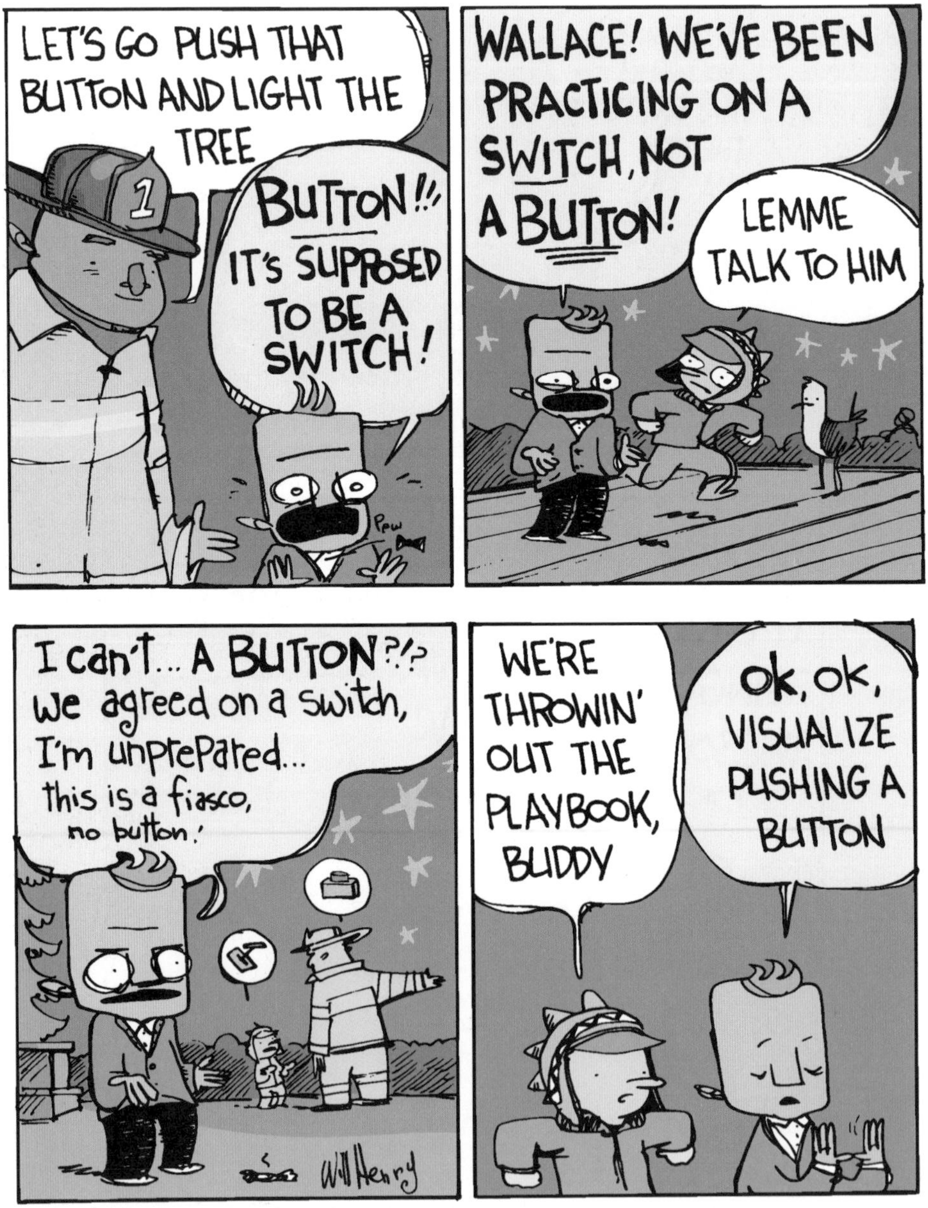
LET'S GO PUSH THAT BUTTON AND LIGHT THE TREE
BUTTON!!! IT'S SUPPOSED TO BE A SWITCH!
Pew
WALLACE! WE'VE BEEN PRACTICING ON A SWITCH, NOT A BUTTON!
LEMME TALK TO HIM
I can't... A BUTTON?!? we agreed on a switch, I'm unprepared... this is a fiasco, no button!
Will Henry
WE'RE THROWIN' OUT THE PLAYBOOK, BUDDY
ok, ok, VISUALIZE PUSHING A BUTTON

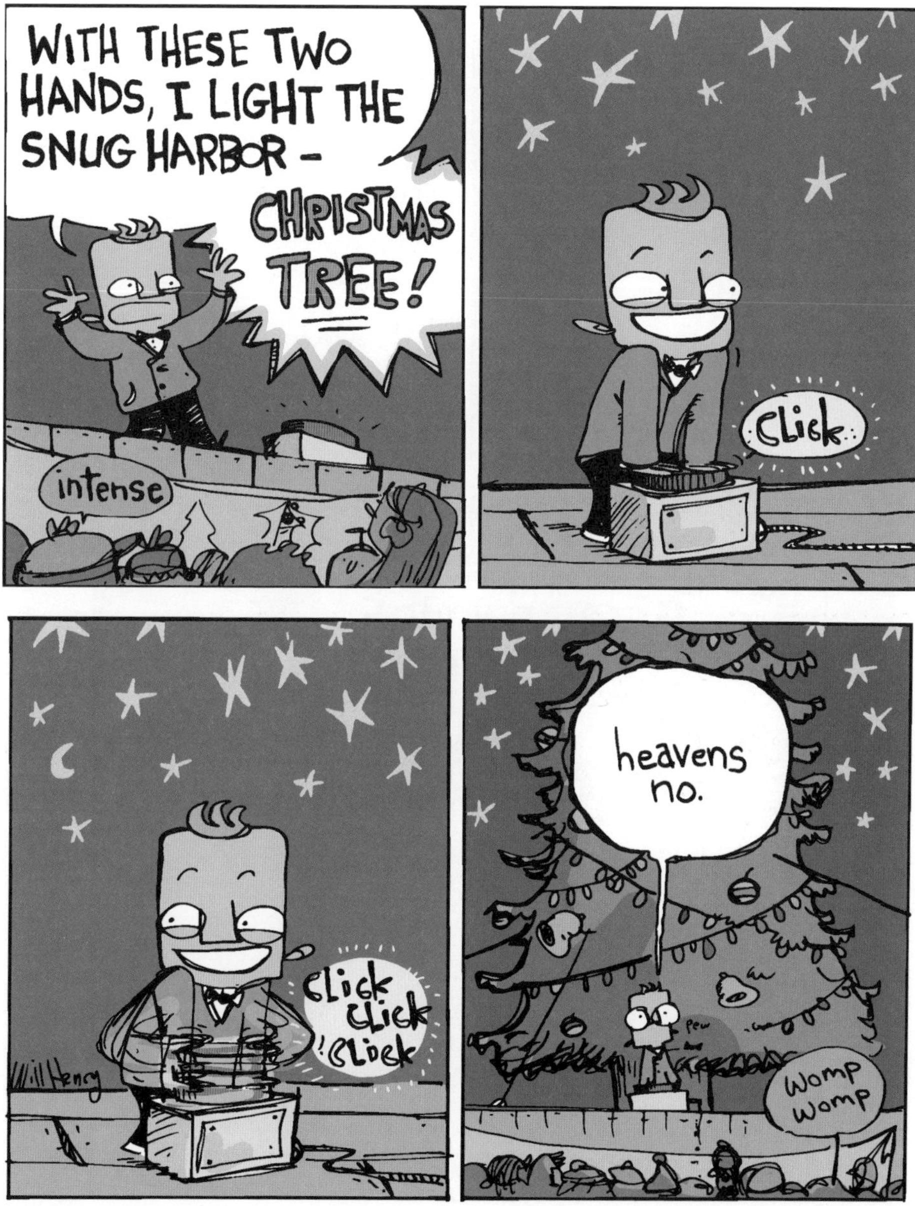
WITH THESE TWO HANDS, I LIGHT THE SNUG HARBOR -
CHRISTMAS TREE!
intense
Click
Click Click Click
Will Henry
heavens no.
Womp Womp

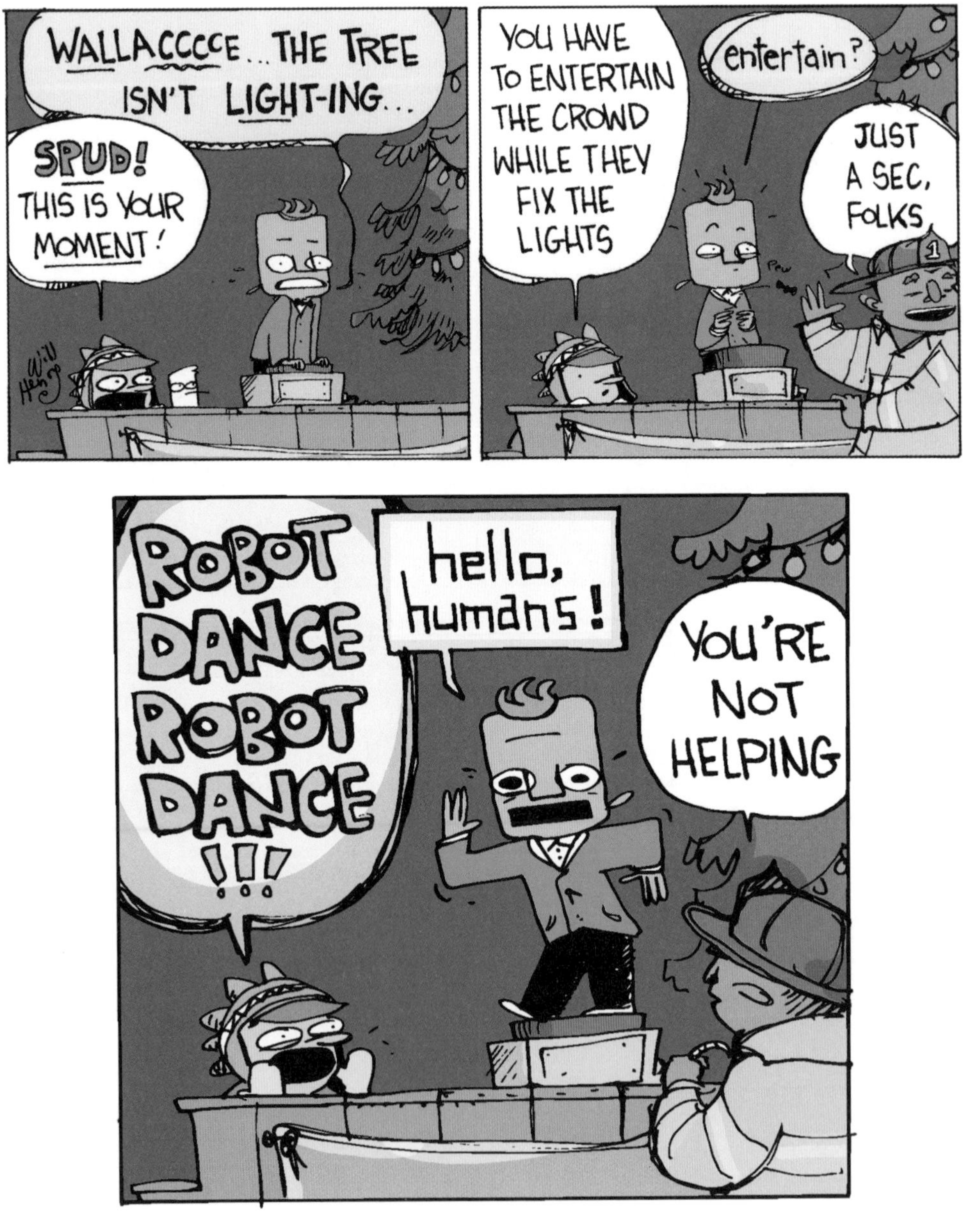
WALLACCCCE... THE TREE ISN'T LIGHT-ING...
SPUD! THIS IS YOUR MOMENT!
YOU HAVE TO ENTERTAIN THE CROWD WHILE THEY FIX THE LIGHTS
entertain?
JUST A SEC, FOLKS
ROBOT DANCE ROBOT DANCE!!!
hello, humans!
YOU'RE NOT HELPING

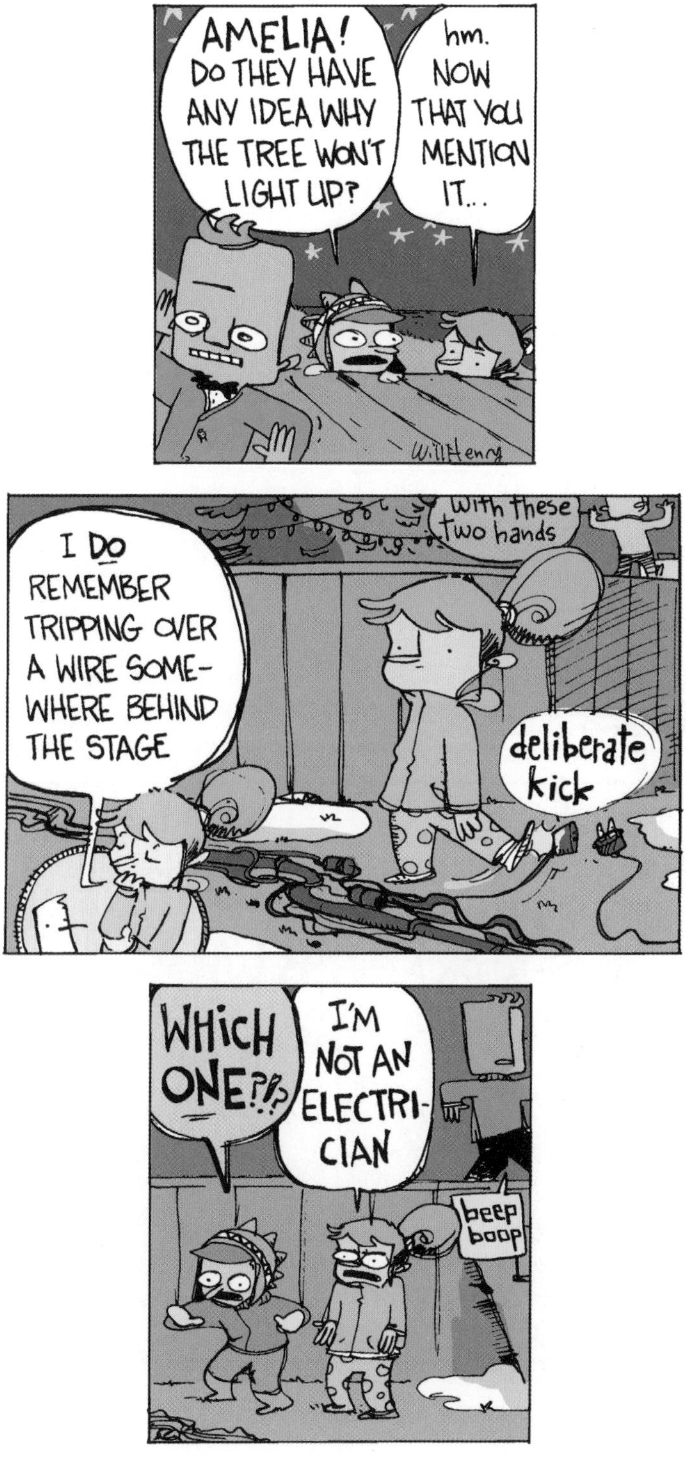
AMELIA! DO THEY HAVE ANY IDEA WHY THE TREE WON'T LIGHT UP?
hm. NOW THAT YOU MENTION IT...
I DO REMEMBER TRIPPING OVER A WIRE SOME-WHERE BEHIND THE STAGE
with these two hands
deliberate kick
WHICH ONE?!?
I'M NOT AN ELECTRI-CIAN
beep boop

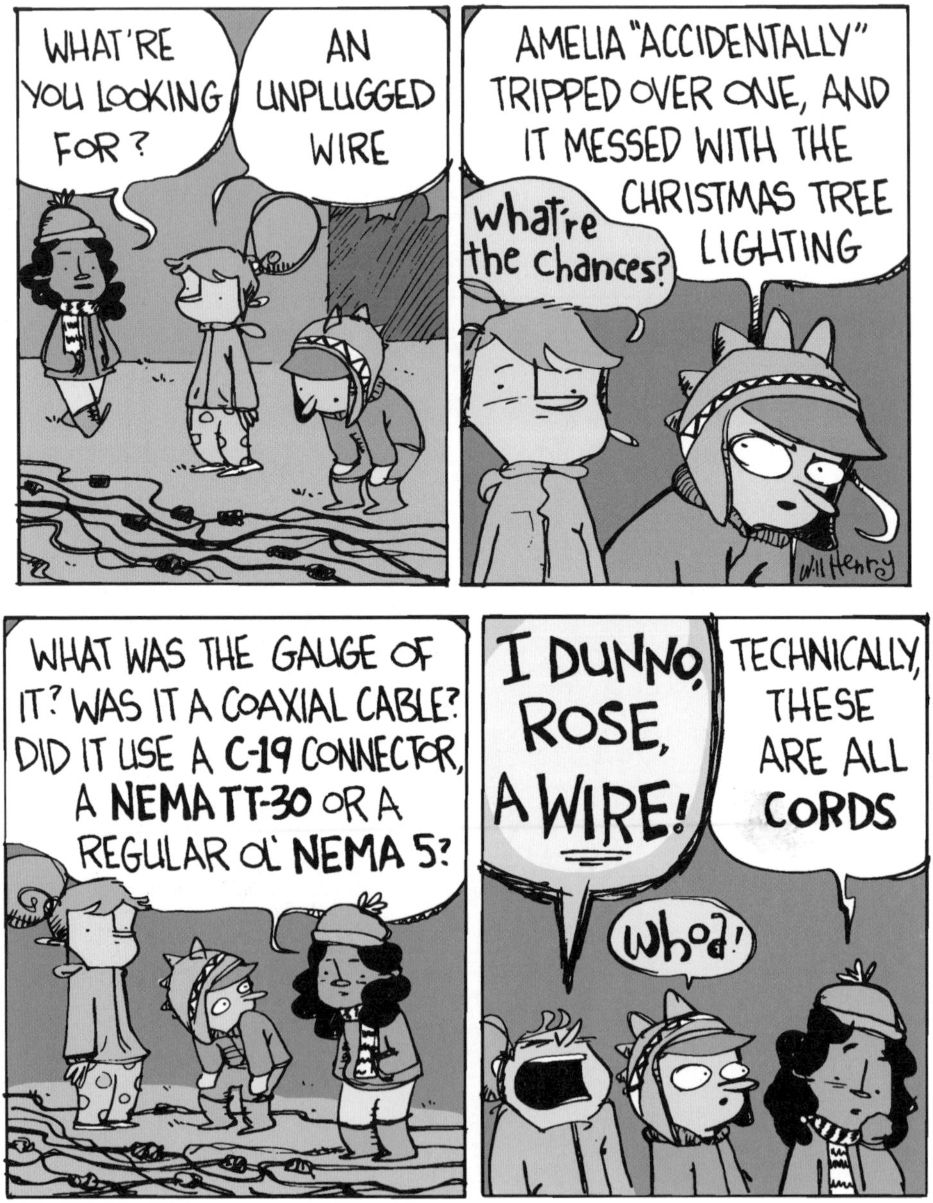
WHAT'RE YOU LOOKING FOR?
AN UNPLUGGED WIRE
AMELIA "ACCIDENTALLY" TRIPPED OVER ONE, AND IT MESSED WITH THE CHRISTMAS TREE LIGHTING
what're the chances?
Will Henry
WHAT WAS THE GAUGE OF IT? WAS IT A COAXIAL CABLE? DID IT USE A C-19 CONNECTOR, A NEMA TT-30 OR A REGULAR OL' NEMA 5?
I DUNNO, ROSE, A WIRE!
TECHNICALLY, THESE ARE ALL CORDS
whoa!

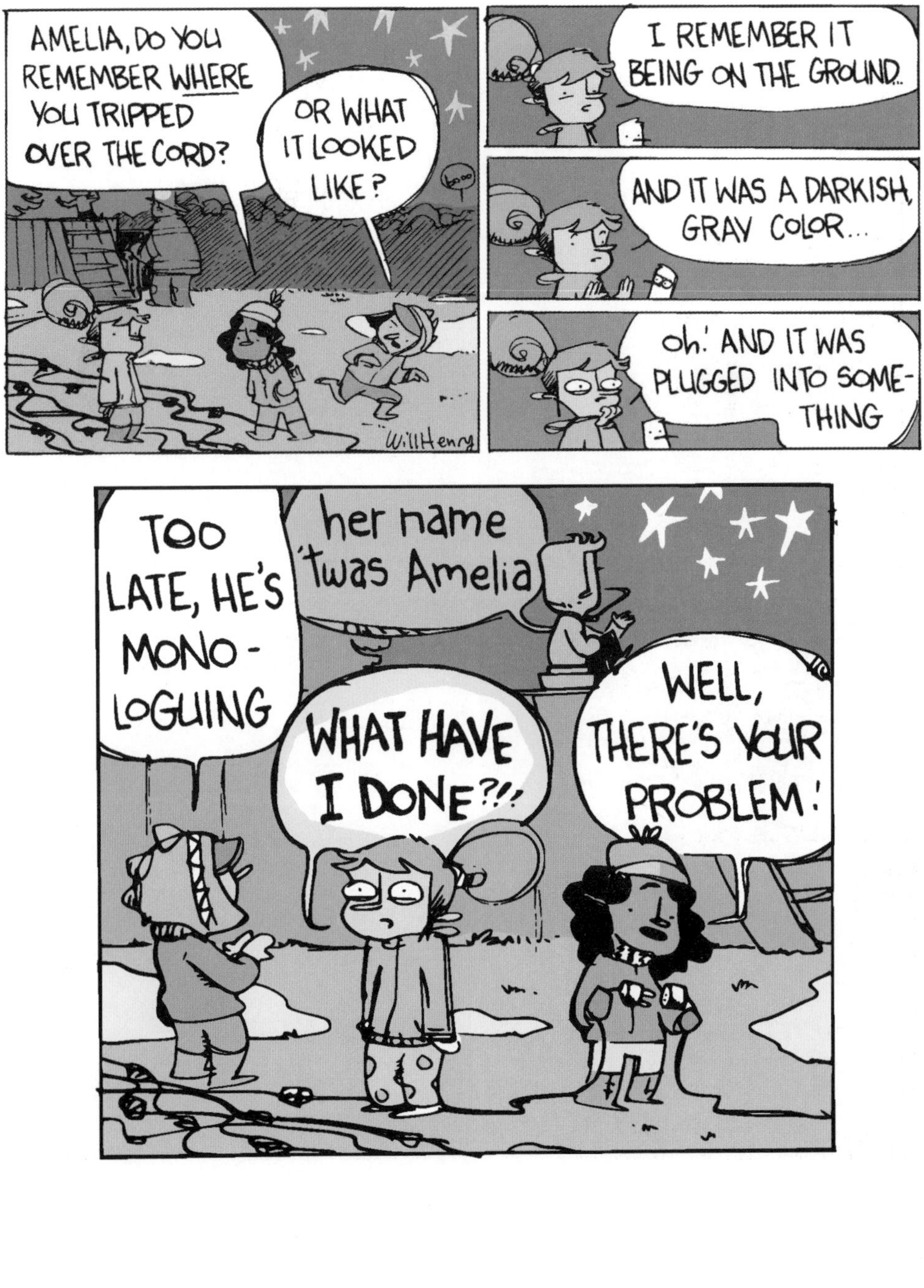
AMELIA, DO YOU REMEMBER WHERE YOU TRIPPED OVER THE CORD?
OR WHAT IT LOOKED LIKE?
WillHenry
I REMEMBER IT BEING ON THE GROUND..
AND IT WAS A DARKISH, GRAY COLOR...
oh! AND IT WAS PLUGGED INTO SOME-THING
TOO LATE, HE'S MONO-LOGUING
her name 'twas Amelia
WHAT HAVE I DONE?!!
WELL, THERE'S YOUR PROBLEM!

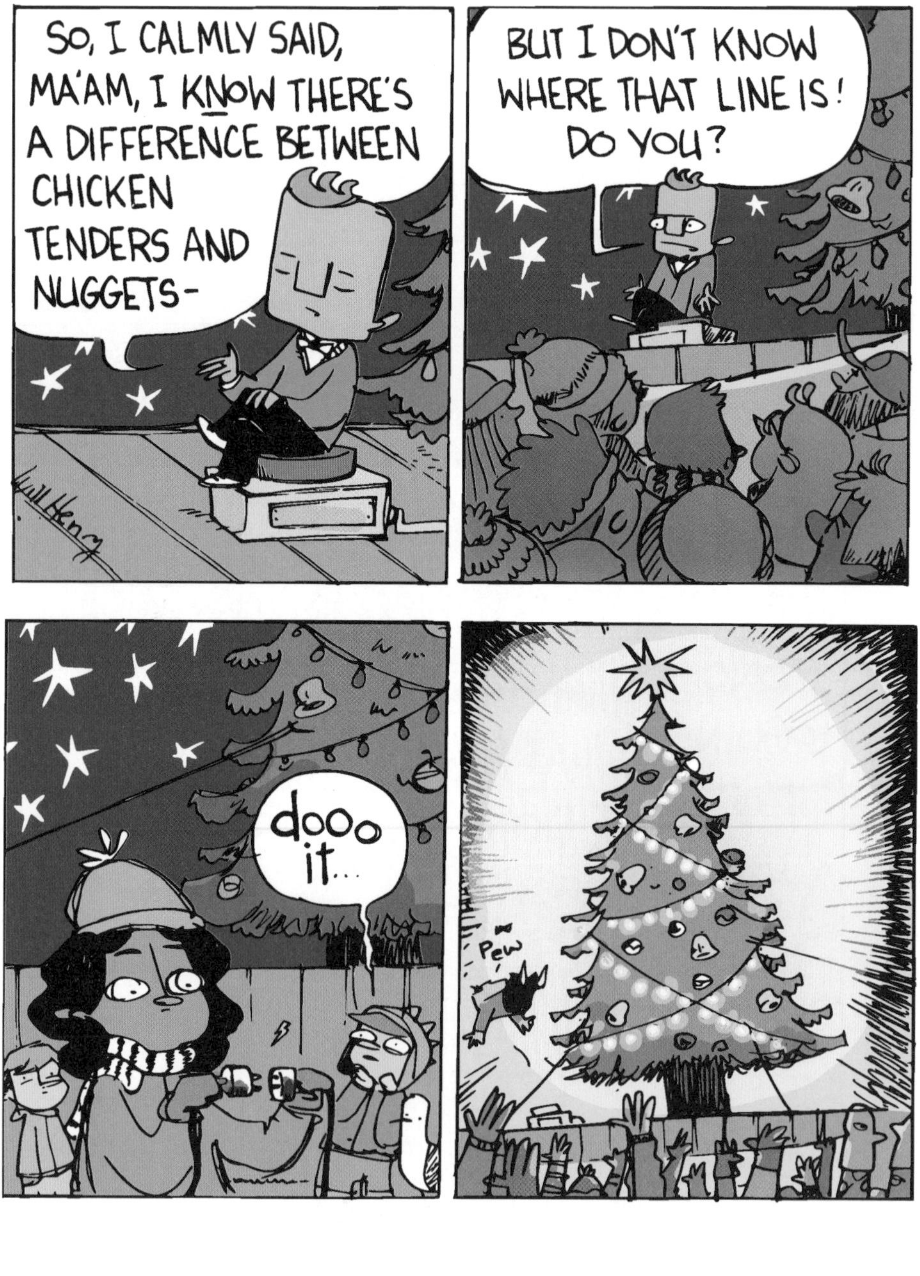
SO, I CALMLY SAID, MA'AM, I KNOW THERE'S A DIFFERENCE BETWEEN CHICKEN TENDERS AND NUGGETS-
Will Henry
BUT I DON'T KNOW WHERE THAT LINE IS! DO YOU?
dooo it...
Pew

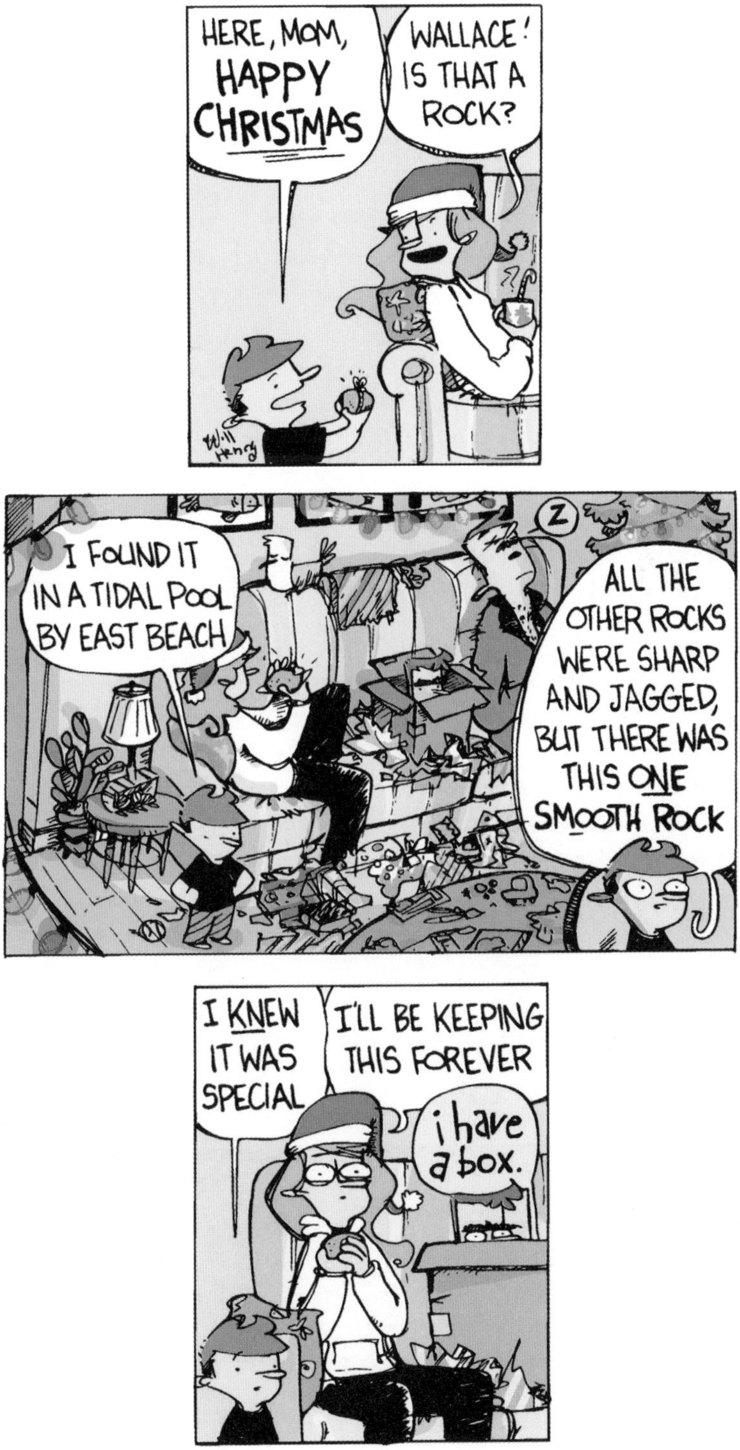
HERE, MOM, HAPPY CHRISTMAS
WALLACE! IS THAT A ROCK?
Will Henry
Z
I FOUND IT IN A TIDAL POOL BY EAST BEACH
ALL THE OTHER ROCKS WERE SHARP AND JAGGED, BUT THERE WAS THIS ONE SMOOTH ROCK
I KNEW IT WAS SPECIAL
I'LL BE KEEPING THIS FOREVER
i have a box.

MORE TO EXPLORE! A special section featuring fun activities!

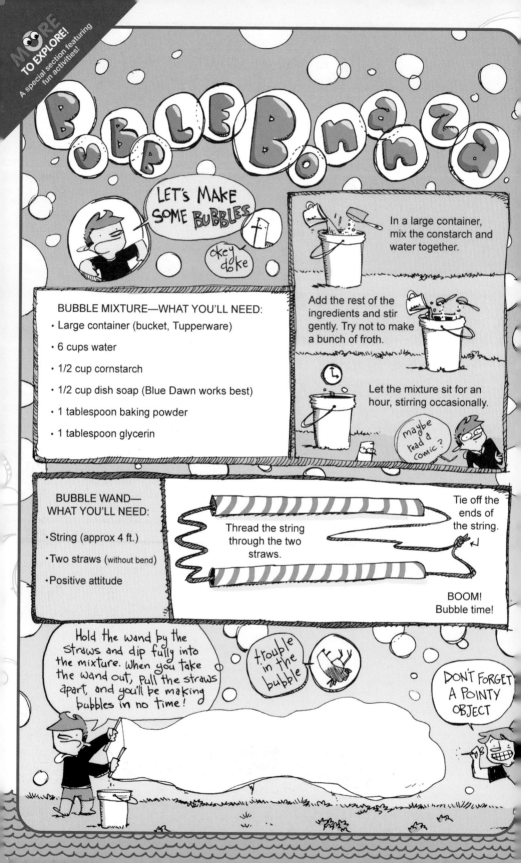

Bubble Bonanza

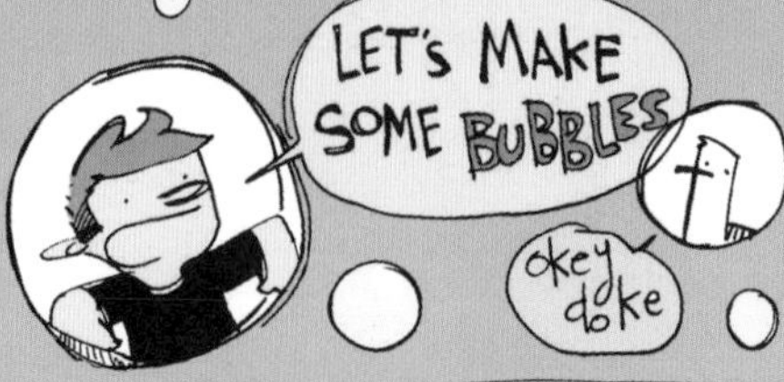
LET'S MAKE SOME BUBBLES
okey doke

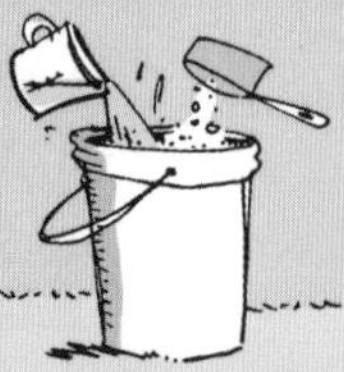

In a large container, mix the constarch and water together.

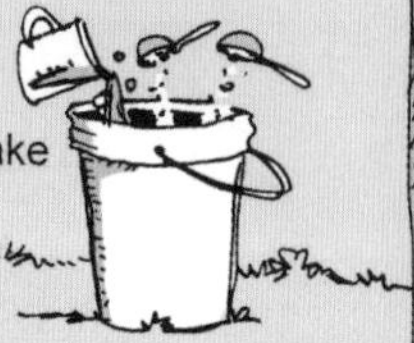

Add the rest of the ingredients and stir gently. Try not to make a bunch of froth.

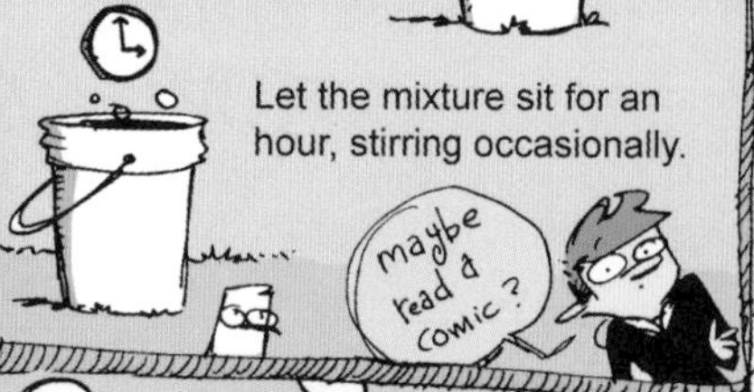
maybe read a comic?

Let the mixture sit for an hour, stirring occasionally.

BUBBLE MIXTURE—WHAT YOU'LL NEED:

- Large container (bucket, Tupperware)
- 6 cups water
- 1/2 cup cornstarch
- 1/2 cup dish soap (Blue Dawn works best)
- 1 tablespoon baking powder
- 1 tablespoon glycerin

BUBBLE WAND—WHAT YOU'LL NEED:

- String (approx 4 ft.)
- Two straws (without bend)
- Positive attitude

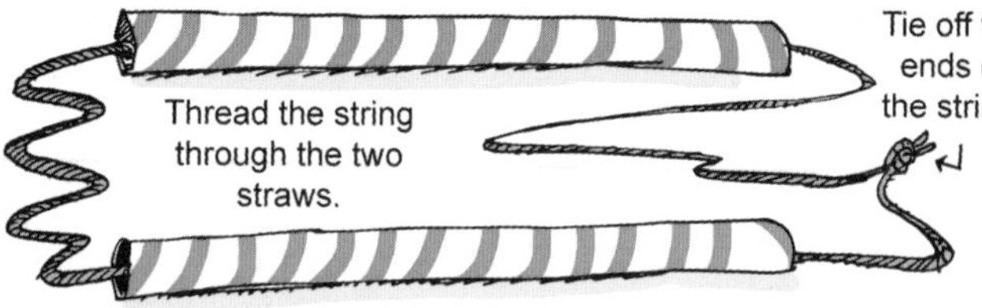
Thread the string through the two straws.
Tie off the ends of the string.

BOOM! Bubble time!

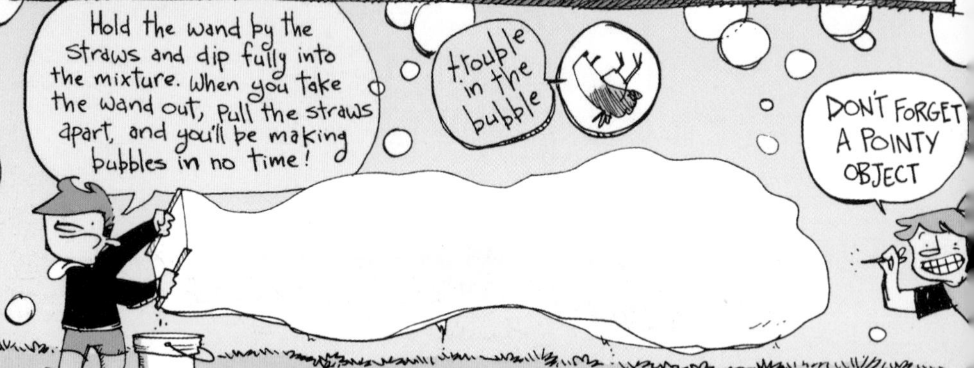
Hold the wand by the straws and dip fully into the mixture. When you take the wand out, pull the straws apart, and you'll be making bubbles in no time!
trouble in the bubble
DON'T FORGET A POINTY OBJECT

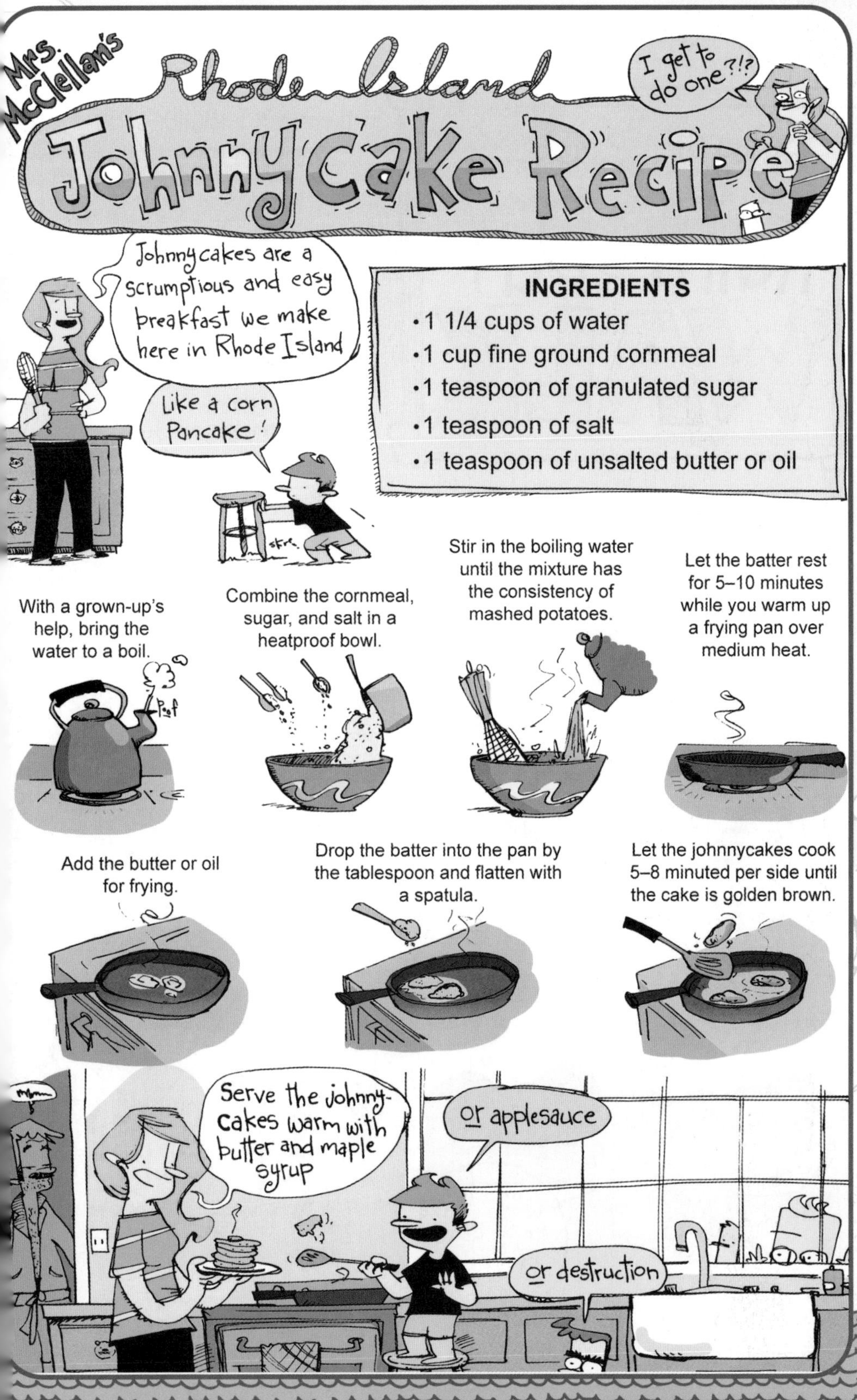

Mrs. McClellan's
Rhode Island
Johnny Cake Recipe
I get to do one?!?
Johnnycakes are a scrumptious and easy breakfast we make here in Rhode Island
Like a corn Pancake!
skre
INGREDIENTS
• 1 1/4 cups of water
• 1 cup fine ground cornmeal
• 1 teaspoon of granulated sugar
• 1 teaspoon of salt
• 1 teaspoon of unsalted butter or oil
With a grown-up's help, bring the water to a boil.
Poof
Combine the cornmeal, sugar, and salt in a heatproof bowl.
Stir in the boiling water until the mixture has the consistency of mashed potatoes.
Let the batter rest for 5–10 minutes while you warm up a frying pan over medium heat.
Add the butter or oil for frying.
Drop the batter into the pan by the tablespoon and flatten with a spatula.
Let the johnnycakes cook 5–8 minuted per side until the cake is golden brown.
Mmm
Serve the johnnycakes warm with butter and maple syrup
or applesauce
or destruction

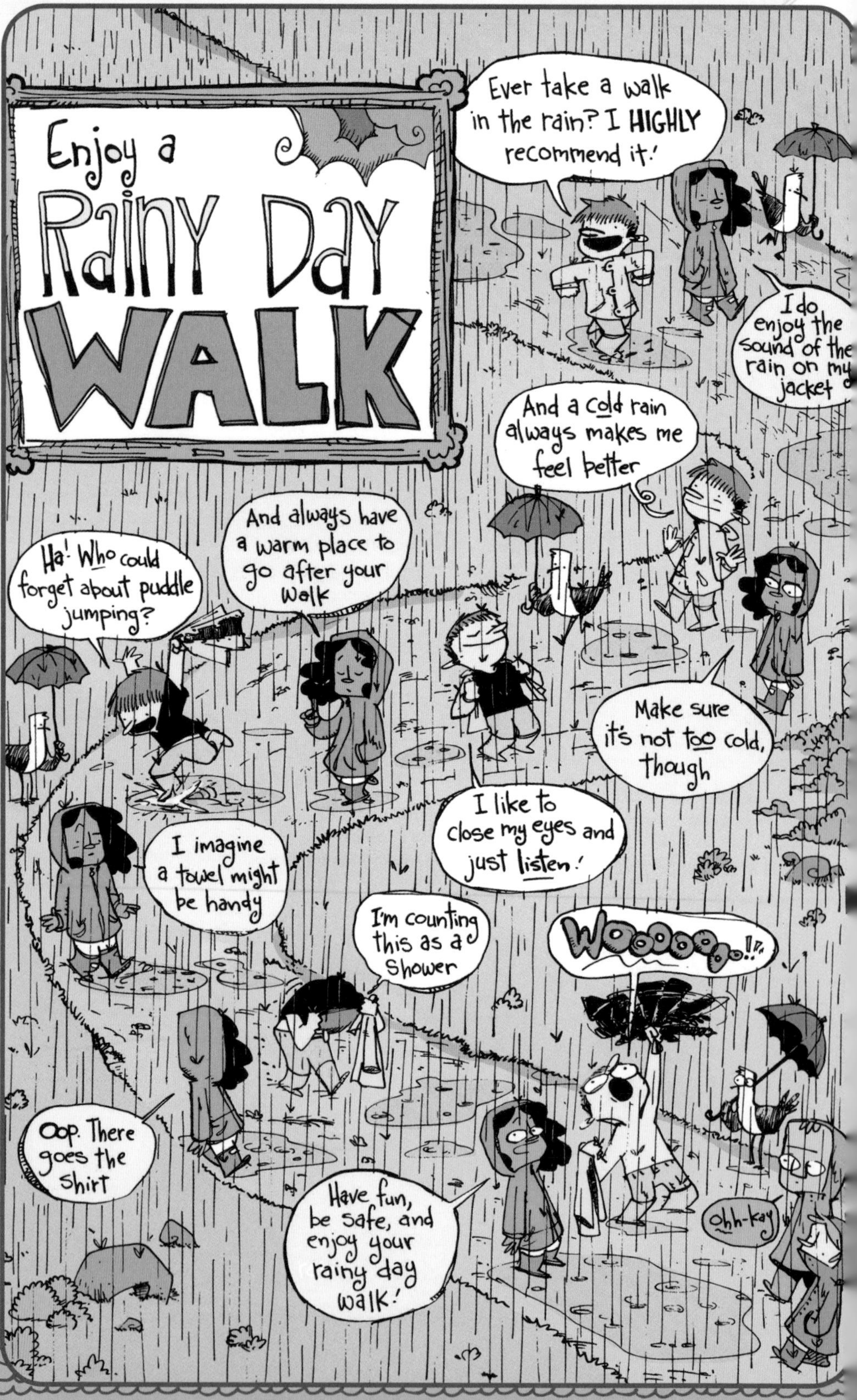
Enjoy a Rainy Day WALK
Ever take a walk in the rain? I HIGHLY recommend it!
I do enjoy the sound of the rain on my jacket
And a cold rain always makes me feel better
Make sure it's not too cold, though
And always have a warm place to go after your walk
Ha! Who could forget about puddle jumping?
I like to close my eyes and just listen!
I imagine a towel might be handy
I'm counting this as a shower
WOOOOOOO!!
Oop. There goes the shirt
Have fun, be safe, and enjoy your rainy day walk!
Ohh-kay

Wallace the Brave is distributed internationally by Andrews McMeel Syndication.

Andrews McMeel Publishing
a division of Andrews McMeel Universal
1130 Walnut Street, Kansas City, Missouri 64106

www.andrewsmcmeel.com

22 23 24 25 26 SDB 10 9 8 7 6 5 4 3 2 1

ISBN: 978-1-5248-7472-8

Library of Congress Control Number: 2021947023

Made by:
King Yip (Dongguan) Printing & Packaging Factory Ltd.
Address and location of manufacturer:
Daning Administrative District, Humen Town
Dongguan Guangdong, China 523930
1st Printing—1/17/22

Look for these books!

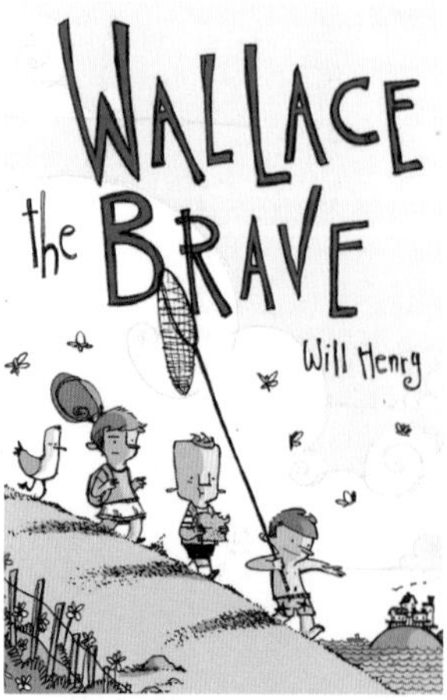
WALLACE the BRAVE
Will Henry

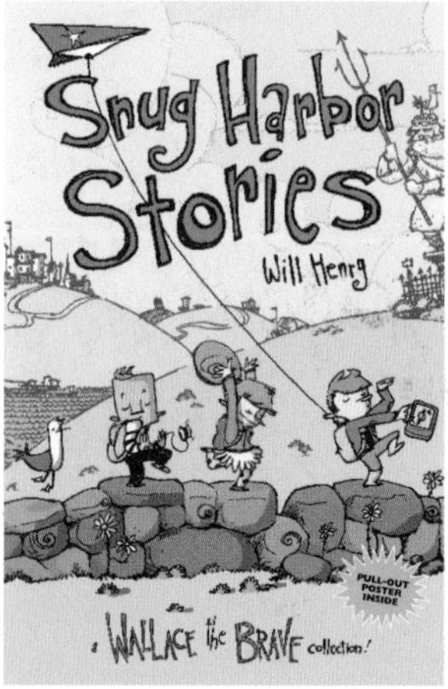
Snug Harbor Stories
Will Henry
PULL-OUT POSTER INSIDE
a WALLACE the BRAVE collection!

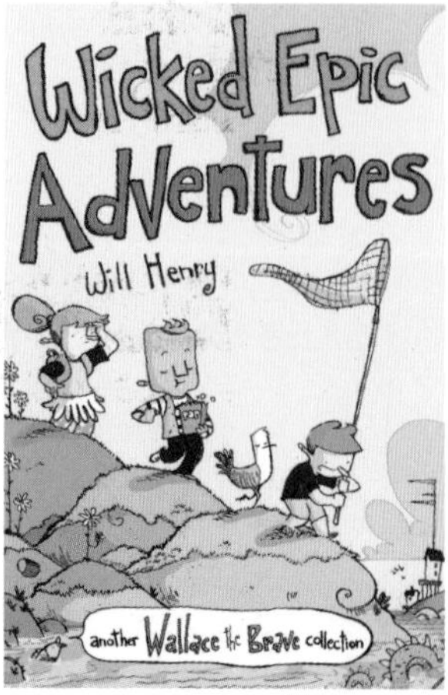
Wicked Epic Adventures
Will Henry
another Wallace the Brave collection

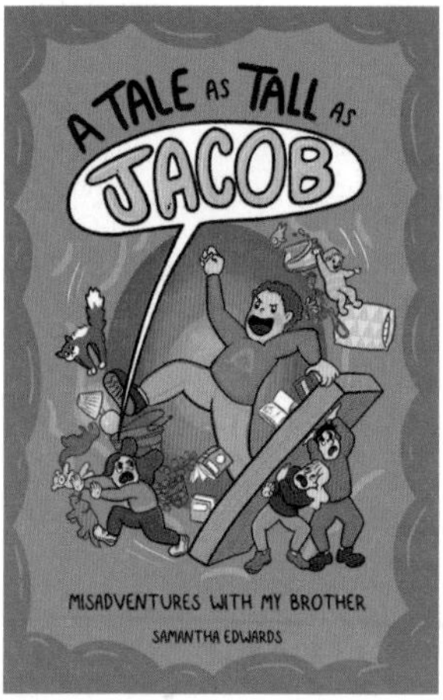
A TALE AS TALL AS JACOB
MISADVENTURES WITH MY BROTHER
SAMANTHA EDWARDS

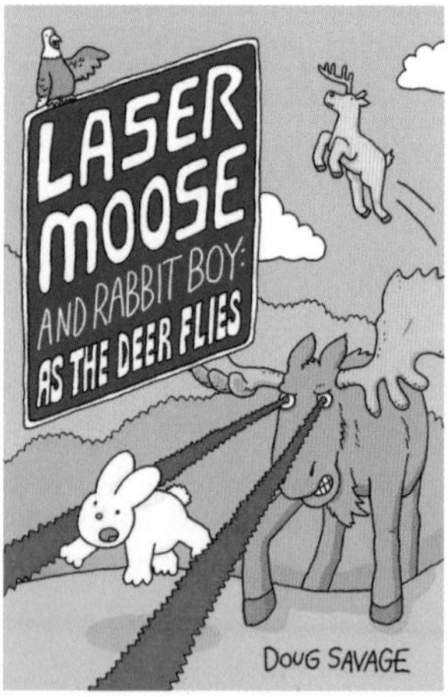
LASER MOOSE AND RABBIT BOY: AS THE DEER FLIES
DOUG SAVAGE

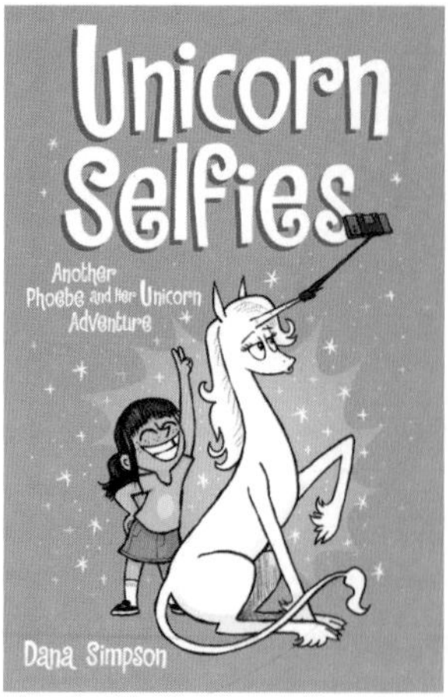
Unicorn Selfies
Another Phoebe and her Unicorn Adventure
Dana Simpson

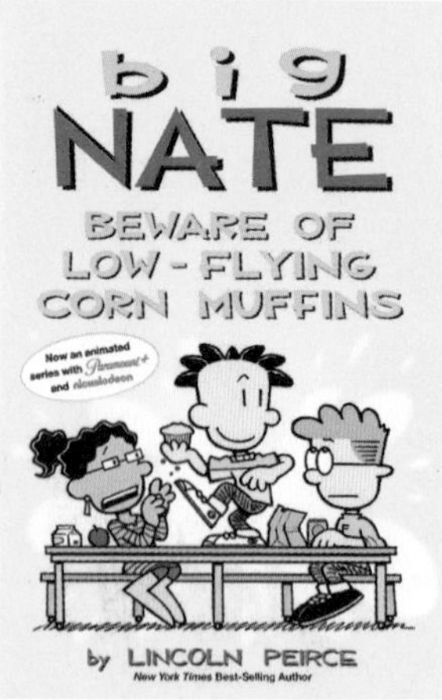
big NATE
BEWARE OF LOW-FLYING CORN MUFFINS
by LINCOLN PEIRCE
New York Times Best-Selling Author

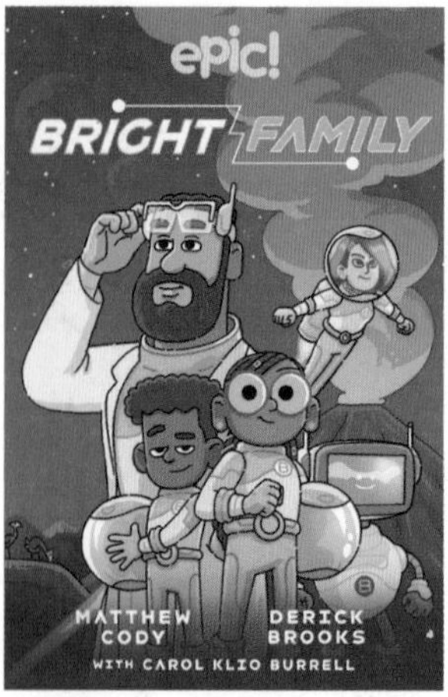
epic!
BRIGHT FAMILY
MATTHEW CODY
DERICK BROOKS
WITH CAROL KLIO BURRELL

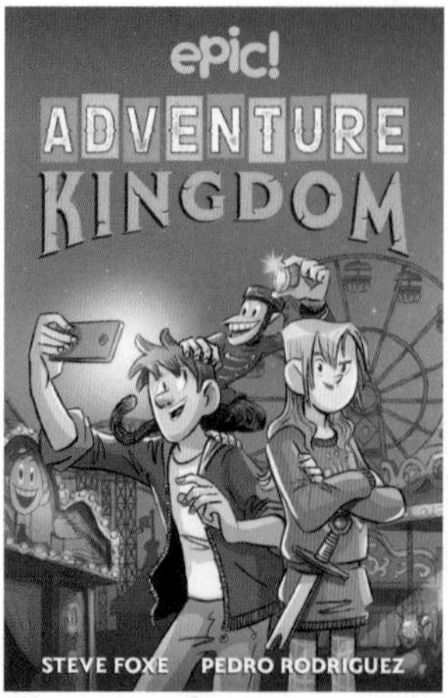
epic!
ADVENTURE KINGDOM
STEVE FOXE
PEDRO RODRIGUEZ